TRAGIC DECISION

The nurse, Leah, handed back the forms. "Your wife has to sign them as well."

"I can't." Her voice was muffled. "It's like signing his death warrant."

"But you know it isn't." Dale knelt by his wife's side. "It's too late for that. Mikey died out there, on the street."

At the diminuitive of the child's name, Sharon lifted her head. "It's easy for you, isn't it? Why is that, Dale? You never did spend much time with him. He was a mouth to feed, a body to clothe and a nuisance when he cried."

Dale pulled Sharon to her feet and began to shake her. "He's dead! Don't you realize that? There's nothing you can do about it, you dumb . . ." He broke and began to sob, a strange dry husking sound that came from somewhere deep inside. . . .

THE PEOPLE BEHIND THE HEADLINES
FROM ZEBRA BOOKS!

PAT NIXON: THE UNTOLD STORY (2300, $4.50)
by Julie Nixon Eisenhower

The phenomenal *New York Times* bestseller about the very private woman who was thrust into the international limelight during the most turbulent era in modern American history. A fascinating and touching portrait of a very special First Lady.

STOCKMAN: THE MAN, THE MYTH,
THE FUTURE (2005, $4.50)
by Owen Ullmann

Brilliant, outspoken, and ambitious, former Management and Budget Director David Stockman was the youngest man to sit at the Cabinet in more than 160 years, becoming the best known member of the Reagan Administration next to the President himself. Here is the first complete, full-scale, no-holds-barred story of Ronald Reagan's most colorful and controversial advisor.

IACOCCA (3018, $4.50)
by David Abodaher

He took a dying Chrysler Corporation and turned it around through sheer will power and determination, becoming a modern-day folk hero in the process. The remarkable and inspiring true story of a legend in his own time: Lee Iacocca.

STRANGER IN TWO WORLDS (2112, $4.50)
by Jean Harris

For the first time, the woman convicted in the shooting death of Scarsdale Diet doctor Herman Tarnower tells her own story. Here is the powerful and compelling *New York Times* bestseller that tells the whole truth about the tragic love affair and its shocking aftermath.

Available wherever paperbacks are sold, or order direct from the Publisher. Send cover price plus 50¢ per copy for mailing and handling to Zebra Books, Dept. 3043, 475 Park Avenue South, New York, N.Y. 10016. Residents of New York, New Jersey and Pennsylvania must include sales tax. DO NOT SEND CASH.

LIFE LINES

Barbara Weiner

**ZEBRA BOOKS
KENSINGTON PUBLISHING CORP.**

ZEBRA BOOKS

are published by

Kensington Publishing Corp.
475 Park Avenue South
New York, NY 10016

Copyright © 1990 by Barbara Weiner

All rights reserved. No part of this book may be reproduced in any form or by any means without the prior written consent of the Publisher, excepting brief quotes used in reviews.

First printing: June, 1990

Printed in the United States of America

Chapter One

It was an ancient respirator, Leah conceded, ancient and noisy, but old or not, it was definitely working. The clamor it made was driving the patient crazy. Each time the bellows rose, there was an eerie screech and when Emma Bond exhaled, the respirator groaned. The machine was as stiff and noisy as Emma's lungs.

Trying to mask her own weariness, Leah bent over the respirator and studied its dials while Emma watched. There was nothing wrong with the machine. It was breathing twelve times a minute, just as it was set. There was the right amount of oxygen blended with air and the red light blinked on and off with every breath pumped into Emma's lungs. It was simply old, that was all and it was doing its best and that was not good enough for Emma. They'd given her this vent because she'd been here the longest and the technicians who serviced the machines were tired of her.

We're all tired of her, Leah thought as she reached across the bed and clicked off the call bell for the tenth time that night. Ever since they'd taken away her modern respirator and replaced it with this relic, Emma had pressed the call bell again and again, frightened and angry. Leah tried to smile at the patient, but she knew it came off badly; it was too late in the night.

The fear in Emma's eyes was unmistakable. With any change in the equipment, she went wild with fright. She could not talk, but she'd learned to communicate with her hands and eyes and as time went by, the nurses had learned the meaning of her every gesture. They knew what a raised eyebrow meant, a toss of the hand. Up signaled compliance. Tossed down was scorn. But worst of all was anger and fear. Then Emma's fingers would fly like a swarm of angry birds, darting and swooping, stabbing the air with pale beaks.

Leah waited as her fingers trembled over the noisy ventilator and then fluttered back to her chest, making clawing gestures.

"You don't think you're breathing? Emma, you are breathing." Otherwise you are a phenomenon, old girl, she added to herself. "I told you before, we have four vented patients tonight, and that's all the hospital owns. That's why they had to put this one to work. It's only for a little while, Emma, while they service yours. It's working just fine. Try to block out the noise, okay?"

But Emma's hand clenched over her chest and the clear plastic tubing that hooked her to the respirator bobbed violently. The gesture meant "Can't breathe." Leah sighed.

"I'll listen to your lungs," she said and Emma's hands instantly stilled.

More to comfort than to assess, Leah leaned over the bed and placed the bell of her stethoscope against Emma's ribs, first one side and then the other. The sounds she heard were unchanged from yesterday, from one week ago, or for that matter, from eight months ago when Emma Bond first came into Liberty Hill Hospital. Air crackled and honked and wheezed as it entered Emma's chest, bouncing over stiff lungs like a racquet ball careening off the walls or the squeal of sneakers against polished wood. The sounds roared over the noise of the ventilator making Leah wince despite her fatigue.

"You are breathing, Emma. I can hear it."

The patient gave an elaborate shrug and closed her eyes. Once she had written "bullshit" on her little erasable blackboard in reply. The shrug said the same thing.

At the nurses' desk, Leah pulled open Emma's chart and scribbled in her notes.

"What does she want now?" Pat Connor looked up from her book.

"New lungs, what else?"

"She needs a man, that's what she needs," Pat replied. "Eight months without sex is enough to drive a person crazy."

"Leave it to you to think of sex before anything else. But she needs lungs worse."

Pat sighed and buried her nose in the book and the two nurses sat in comfortable silence.

"Actually," Leah said as if the conversation had not lapsed, "she needs a new doctor, then lungs, then she'll probably enjoy a sex life. But in that order, not yours. Without the first she'll never get the rest."

"Do you mean that Peters the Great hasn't tried to jump her bones yet?" Pat grinned. "He's tried everyone else's."

Claude Peters, Emma's physician, was the butt of many late-night jokes. Not that he hadn't earned them. It was well known that he would drop his pants at the slightest opportunity and had been seen, by reliable sources, with his pants around his ankles in every department at Liberty Hill, from X-ray to Records.

Leah secretly wondered about Pat and Claude Peters, though she doubted the slim blond would give him the satisfaction of another score.

She stretched and her little chair creaked. "Emma

hasn't given him the chance, she's too busy breathing. In fact, he's stopped going in to see her at all. All he does is stop by the desk, write a few notes, and get paid fifty dollars by the state. I doubt he's seen her, I mean actually examined her, in weeks." She shoved the chart into its slot in the desk. "Do you realize that we'll never get her out of here? He hasn't even tried to wean her off the vent."

"You're a dreamer," Pat said without lifting her eyes from her book. "She's never going to breathe on her own now. Not after all this time."

Just then the call light flicked on. Leah sighed and stood up. "There she goes again." As she walked away from the desk, she muttered to herself, "Just let me get through tonight and I'll start bugging Peters to get her out of here."

The broad, east-facing windows had begun to lighten and as she entered Emma's room, Leah automatically glanced down the hill towards the marina. Nikki was down there. He would be still sleeping, curled on his knees in his pink flannel nightsuit, with his rump high in the air and his chubby fist against his mouth. She smiled to herself and turned to Emma Bond.

Emma lifted a placard with one word printed on it: SUCTION.

"Are you filling up?"

It was an empty question. Both women knew Emma needed suctioning regularly. Unable to cough, Emma's lungs flooded with secretions. Sometimes those fluids were swarming with microbes, in which case, Emma would be given antibiotics. At other times the phlegm was clear. But at all times she needed suctioning. Emma desperately needed every last little lung cell in her chest. She was a chronic lunger. Officially called chronic obstructive pulmonary disease, it was a disease of increasing impairment in breathing. To the staff the patient was simply a lunger.

Leah always asked the question anyway; it gave Emma a little control over her own life and she had so little. There were times when Emma demanded suctioning even though it wasn't necessary. It was at best an unpleasant procedure and no patient liked it. Emma was the only one to ask for it.

At forty-two, she looked like a wizened old woman. Thin to the point of emaciation, Emma's cheekbones jutted like white wings under the glare of the overhead light, giving her face a skull-like appearance. Her false teeth had lain in the bedside table so long that they no longer fit and her lips had caved in over her gums. Hair that was once long, black, and silky, was now dry with silver streaks and sparse against her skull. Though they washed it and brushed it with care, long clumps of it came away in the comb, or floated in the bath water, or tangled on the sheets.

When she saw the suction catheter being readied, her hands clutched the bed railing and her mouth opened like a baby bird awaiting a morsel. It didn't matter that she had a tracheostomy and was no longer suctioned through the mouth. It was habit and Leah gently coaxed her mouth closed with her gloved hand. With a dark, unfathomable glare, Emma lifted her chin and allowed the catheter to slip deep into her throat. Almost instantly, her face contorted. Her hands shook the bed rails. It lasted only for seconds, during which Leah held her own breath, but the effect was immediate. Clear white phlegm floated into the catheter and disappeared into the plastic bottle below Emma's bed. Leah reattached the ventilator hosing and gave her a deep mechanical sigh. Emma's hands released the railing and fell to her sides. She closed her eyes, breathing deeply while tears flowed down her cheeks. Slowly her skin began to turn pink again.

"You really didn't need it, you know." Leah whispered, patting her face with a towel.

Emma replied with an enigmatic shrug, waiting for the respirator to restore oxygen into her lungs. Finally, she fumbled among the bedclothes and pulled out another placard: DRINK. Below it someone had lettered the word *Pepsi*. It was all Emma ever drank. Her eyes glittered in the harsh light and Leah knew she was being challenged.

"You don't want to even try to sleep? Not a little? Okay. I'll get you a Pepsi. Want the TV on? How about your radio?" She picked up Emma's Sony Walkman and thrust it at her, resisting the urge to slam it against the wall. It was manipulation pure and simple and they both knew it.

Behind her, sunlight flooded the room with a clean shaft of light so bright that it tore the two women's attention away from each other. Leah released the breath she'd been holding. Dawn on Liberty Hill, when the sky was clear, was the first place in Boston Harbor to receive light. It sheeted across the ocean, turning itself into a flat stream of brilliance that crept up the hill, and finally bathed the old hospital with a momentary glory.

Nikki would be stirring. His mouth would open and accept the thumb that had pressed beneath his chin all night. His diaper would dampen and soak the pink flannel nightsuit. Soon he'd awaken and stare solemnly through the bars of his crib. Leah wished she were there. She would see the first sleepy wonderment that soon transformed into pure joy when he spied her across the room. She could tell he was always a little surprised that she was there. Only now she was here, and it was Maddy Swift who would be padding into the room to pick up her grandson. Only for a little while, Leah promised herself. Just for a little while longer. She turned back to Emma Bond.

"Gonna be a nice day, Emma."

Emma's mouth turned down and her eyebrow rose. That's right, Leah thought. Not a nice day for you. All the days were the same for her.

"I know you want to get out of here. Would you like to try to breathe on your own? For a minute?"

Almost immediately she regretted her words; the implications were stunning. First of all, she had no right to initiate treatment. That was Claude Peters's domain. If anything went wrong the patient would suffer. First do no harm was the basic precept of medicine. Besides, there was no way to gauge the success of the effort. Without a doctor's sanction she could not order arterial blood gases that defined success or failure. That was the bottom line. Without those, she'd be fumbling in the dark not knowing if oxygen were truly reaching tissue. Oh sure, Emma might breathe easily enough, but if the oxygen wasn't getting through at the cellular level then she'd be suffocating slowly and inexorably, and she would not even know it.

There was also the matter of her nursing license. She could lose it. She could lose her career! Drop it, her inner voice commanded. And she was almost pleased at the look of outrage on Emma's face. It offered her an out.

Still it was a shame that this woman lingered in this strange imprisonment. Otherwise fairly healthy, considering the state of her lungs, Emma was stuck here. She was losing contact with the world, her family, and her husband. Hooked to a breathing machine, Emma was tethered in this small space with no seeming escape available to her. She should be given a chance, that's all. A chance.

Leah stirred uneasily as a change grew over Emma's face. Since she could not talk, her face had become exquisitely expressive, and Leah could see the thought process taking place. From outrage that scored her cheeks in deep lines, from eyes that glittered at her, there was a sudden shift that swept across Emma's face. Gone was the harsh glare as quickly as a light snapped off and in its place came tears that spilled over her tired face. Emma shook her head sadly. Can't do it, the gesture said.

The words came out before she could stop them. "We won't know if we don't try. And that's all it would be—a try."

"I'll die." Emma pointed to the monitor over her bed, the screen reflecting her heartbeat. She clenched her fist.

"I won't let anything happen," Leah said, feeling her own heart accelerate. "In fact, we'll keep the respirator hose here with you. When you get tired I'll put it right back." She waited, half hoping that Emma would shake her head again but instead there was a faint shrug of the shoulders and Emma's eyes closed resignedly.

"Do it," the gesture said.

"You are sure?" Emma nodded. "You must not tell anyone." Emma nodded again, but her eyes flashed opened, staring at her speculatively. It was a little chilling, that stare. Emma's hand came up and disconnected the plastic tubing from her tracheostomy. Air roared through it and Leah reached over to pull it away, saying, "If this doesn't work, then you'll know for sure that you will always need help to breathe. If this does work, then I'll get after Dr. Peters to start regular weaning times. If I have to chase him all over this hospital, I'll get that permission. Do we have a deal?"

But Emma was not listening, she was staring at the clock, her fingers rigid over the respirator tube, holding it near her chest. While she timed herself, Leah studied Emma's breathing effort. There was so little chest muscle left, she thought, that soon Emma would tire trying to lift her own rib cage. She took her pulse. Any acceleration in heart rate would tell her that the breathing was becoming an effort. She found it hard to breathe herself. She watched as a film of sweat broke out on Emma's face. She was beginning to work at it. A little blood vessel in her neck suddenly rose, scored in the harsh light. It pulsed with every heartbeat. Leah began to raise the plastic hose.

"I think that's enough," she said. But Emma's hand tightened over hers. She nodded at the clock. Forty-five seconds had passed.

"Time isn't important," Leah said, pulling Emma's hand away and reattaching the respirator hosing. Instantly, the tension left Emma's body. She shook her head sadly.

"That was very good, Emma," Leah said gently. "You didn't fail, you breathed on your own for the first time in eight months. That was wonderful." Emma's mouth pulled down. "Listen, you haven't used those rib-cage muscles in so long that they've gone slack. It's the same as if you hadn't walked. Your legs would be weak. You have to build them up and that's hard work. But you've begun."

The lines of anger and tension that Emma's face had carried all night were disappearing. She was exhausted but she was listening. The film of sweat had dried leaving her face a little streaked with salt. For the first time in this long night, Leah felt compassion for this woman. Her own fatigue had disappeared and a new energy was flowing, thanks to Emma. This refreshing surge would last until she could get home and spend some time with Nikki—play with him, walk him along the docks to see the boats, listen to his strange baby talk so sternly delivered that she would know his meaning. She moistened a washcloth and wiped Emma's face. The respirator sighed noisily and groaned. The long night was over.

Pat Connor had combed her hair and applied fresh lipstick. Her clumpy straw bag was on the counter beside the cardiac monitor and her jacket draped over the monitor so that half the patients' heart rhythms were obscured. She was bent over her charts scribbling the last of the night's notes.

Leah pulled away the jacket and gave the five heart rhythms a cursory glance. All were normal. She pulled out Emma's chart and sat beside Pat.

"Well," she said, trying to keep a tone of nonchalance in her voice, "I did it. Emma weaned for forty-five seconds."

For a moment, Pat did not respond and then her head jerked up. "Huh? She did what?" Leah nodded. "That's craziness, you could get in big trouble for that. Personally, I don't think Emma's worth it." Though there was a chiding tone to her voice, there was also a little admiration. "What's Peters the Great going to do when he learns about it . . . give you a medal? Like hell he will. He could have you fired."

"Not unless someone rats on me," Leah responded as she wrote in Emma's chart. "Besides, I intend to get the order the minute I see Peters."

"I won't tell," Pat said. "But I wouldn't do it again if I were you. Just forget about it."

Leah shoved the chart at her. "It's already official." Pat read what Leah had written. There in neat order was her note describing the less-than-one-minute episode during which Emma Bond was free of the respirator. She shook her head and looked up at Leah.

"Why tell the world about it? Why didn't you just not mention it?"

"I can't do that. What happened, happened. And it has to be documented. Besides, who reads nursing notes anyway? Doctors? Other nurses?"

"Lawyers, that's who," Pat said crisply. "If you are going to document anything, you'd better do a good job of it. Like how the patient knowingly agreed to it and understood what you told her. And how she tolerated it, and finally how it ended. What were the vent's settings when you put her back on. Every little detail. Maybe Peters won't read it, and just maybe the nurses won't. But you never can tell. You'd better cover your behind with a damn good set of notes. And that's all I'm going to say about it." She shivered and wrapped her arms across her chest. "Ooh, I don't even like to think about it."

Her buoyancy faded with Pat's words and fear crept in. She hadn't thought of lawyers when she took Emma off the vent. She'd thought of Emma's imprisonment here, and of her own vexation and fatigue. She had thought of Claude Peters and the poor management he was giving the patient. But she hadn't given a thought to a lawsuit. Instantly she remembered that her malpractice insurance premium was paid. Still, litigation and possibly loss of job . . . That was the last thing in the world she could afford. Not with Nikki needing her. He was getting bigger. He would need so much!

She bent her head to the chart once more. Pat was right, what was done was done, but she'd better protect herself with scrupulous notes. She lengthened her description of the weaning, detailing Emma's despondance over not completing one full minute of time off the vent. When she finished, she pushed the chart across to Pat and watched her anxiously.

Pat's eyes skimmed the page and then she nodded. "That's better. At least, if someone reads it, they will get the whole picture. I just hope no one does. And if Peters raises holy hell about it, I'll stick up for you. I'll tell him that I agreed with you. In fact, since I'm the charge nurse, I'll tell him that it was my idea." She clapped her hand over her mouth and stared at Leah. "Ooh. Shut my mouth!"

Her dismay was so genuine that it broke the tension. Leah laughed. "And I'll pretend I didn't hear that. But thanks anyway, pal."

During this four-week rotation to the night shift, she'd come to respect and admire Pat Connor. Night nurses were a special breed. Alone, with split-second decisions to be made for their patients, they were resourceful and independant, but sometimes they were viewed with just a little suspicion for preferring this difficult shift.

What did they really do on nights? Sleep on the job? And if not, how *did* they carry on through it? Did they work nights in order to conduct daytime love affairs? In Pat's case, that was a given. She made no bones about her current and past lovers. There were just too many to take seriously. But of her nursing, there was no doubt. She knew when to spend that extra moment with a patient. There was always a pillow plumped just right for support and comfort. A special hot drink in the small hours of the night. And most importantly, the instant reaction in a code situation that gave extra seconds of time in which to save a life. Leah had seen Pat's radiant and buoyant warmth work miracles upon her patients. They adored her, and their praises carried over to the day shift which only aroused curiosity and a little suspicion. After all, if she was so good, why didn't she work days like other normal people? Leah knew why, but it had taken her own rotation through the shift to learn.

It was the night itself. It was unique and it had to do with fear. Fighting sleep was fighting death, a patient had once confided to Leah. Night in the intensive care unit was a time of pain rising unfettered, of terrors that surfaced from dark dreams. That which was not real became frighteningly real at night, and left one trembling over a void, he had said. It was the nurse who made the difference between going mad and accepting the terrifying reality of this place. With Pat Connor, a patient could feel safe for awhile. She was the calm and confident light on a dark side of the world.

As she trudged home to the marina, the implication of

her action with Emma Bond became fully realized and she arrived at the gate with a sick feeling in the pit of her stomach. Even Nikki's adoring face failed to calm her fears. His chatter as she fastened the tiny life jacket around him seemed like a swarm of bees in her ears. She held his hand and allowed him to lead her down the swaying ramp to the floating dock. There he settled himself at the edge and watched as his grandfather set out the spring moorings. Connecting herself to his stocky little body with one hand hooked into the ties of his jacket, Leah lifted her face to the spring sun and Emma Bond into a dark corner of her mind.

She was startled awake when she heard the scrape of oars against the dock. Red Swift sat in his flat-bottomed skiff and regarded her with a little amusement while Nikki strained against her hand. He had crouched as close to the edge of the dock as far as her restraining hand allowed and now looked around at her with a cry of outrage. She let him go a little farther until his legs dangled over the edge.

"It's time that boy of yours went to work with his grandfather. Hand him over. And then you'd better get some sleep."

"How about if his mother helps, too? I haven't forgotten how to handle a pair of oars, you know."

It was only a gesture and they both knew it. Red delighted in being alone with Nikki. With the baby between his knees, he pushed the skiff away and began stroking the water crisply with his oars. He would pretend great effort, he'd groan with imagined strain and Nikki would regard his grandfather with solemn admiration. She watched them for awhile, knowing that Red would parade Nikki around the small cove. There'd be little work done while he amused his grandson. Across the flat calm of the water, she could hear Nikki shriek with pleasure, then she turned and retraced her steps to the ship's store.

Maddy had taken up her position behind the cash register, her books spread before her and work sheets for the men lined up on the counter. She was the business manager of the marina and it was to her that Red's men looked for direction, for their paychecks, and for her sympathy in hard times. It was around her that this little world of yachts revolved. If it hadn't been for Maddy's foresight, Red's machine shop would have serviced a dwindling fleet of trawlers until there was no business left. She had seen the change on the waterfront when he didn't. There was luxury now instead of rotting piers, sleek crafts instead of rumbling trawlers. The events taking place on the Boston side of the harbor had signaled to her. High-rise condominiums and a forest of masts crowded against the waterside and the expansion was headed their way. She prepared their little cove for it. New docks, new services. A ship's store that catered to the wealth of masted yachts. Now Red's little machine shop occupied one small space on the northern side of the cove. The rest was a floating haven for pleasure craft where everything from fuel to teakwood cocktail tables was for sale.

Leah leaned against the counter and reached across to still her mother's hands. "Is there something I can do?"

Maddy snorted. "You already did." She cocked her head towards the small craft in the middle of the cove. "Now he won't get any work done and I'll have to send out one of the men to do the moorings. I swear, since that boy came Red hasn't been worth a tinker's damn around this place."

"He's investing in the future, Mom. Someday Nikki will run this place."

"If I live long enough," Maddy rumbled, but there was a pleased little smile on her face.

They hadn't asked any questions when she returned

from Florida with Nikki in her arms. They'd merely accepted her and enfolded the child in their aging arms. It was as if she'd never left, and yet there was so much she wanted to tell them. That what had begun as a solid marriage with its hopes and dreams had become a nightmare of broken promises. How Tony had left her night after night, soon after Nikki was born, to guide his sailboat through starless nights on island missions that filled his boat with forbidden cargo. There'd been plenty of money when he returned, but he had changed. There were secrets that lined his once-strong face and drew out a nervous energy that frightened her. He no longer told her of his dreams. He had left her behind in the old ones. And so she had come home and taken up her place once again at the marina, and at Liberty Hill. If it hadn't been for Nikki, she often thought, her marriage, the Florida landscape, and the fear for Tony's safety might have been just a bad dream. But there was Nikki, and he had fit himself into the stream of love that had flowed from Red and Maddy Swift, doubling it and swelling their hearts with happiness. She couldn't tell them and they never asked. But something was gone; there was an emptiness where her heart had been. Her days and nights were isolated incidences, one leading to another and she began to wonder if there was a future for her after all.

"You need a new fella," Pat Connor announced one night. "Single life doesn't mean penance for God's sake! Sex doesn't end with divorce. Once you get used to it, you can't live without it." She shuddered at the notion but Leah had only laughed. Someday, maybe, she had replied and dismissed the notion as too far away.

She stirred as Maddy's voice cut into her thoughts. "Don't you think you'd better get some sleep? You have to work again tonight."

Instantly, the scene in Emma Bond's room returned. She'd be faced with the dilemma all over again. Did she have the strength to engage Emma's will once more? And for what? There'd never be a guarantee that Emma would be free of the hospital.

This was another thing she could not talk to Maddy about. Both she and Red shuddered at the notion that she dealt with frightening matters of life and death, of disease and mysterious bodily functions. Though they respected her, they never had understood her need to be a nurse. They'd simply allowed her to choose it. Just don't tell us about the gory details, they'd said, and she was left with the notion that her life on the Hill was nunlike, holy, and mysterious to her parents. It left her just a little more lonely.

When Red carried in Nikki, sleepy and a little sunburned, she bathed and fed him and then put him in his crib. While he slept, she stretched out on the bed overlooking the cove. Come on, she willed herself, get some sleep. Tonight is not far off. But for a long while, sleep did not come and she stared through the window at the bustling harbor outside.

Chapter Two

Liberty Hill Hospital, with the sun at its back, seemed to float on the crest of the hill like a giant gray battleship. At times, it appeared to dip and bob as if a mysterious tide had made its way up the hill to float it above the earth. But that was only when the sun was at its back.

From the harbor at the foot of the hill, the hospital hung over the town like a derelict vessel in permanent dry dock. Its buildings teetered over the narrow streets that ringed the hill, casting shadows that never fled the sun.

Only in spring was there a slightly festive air to the area. Cherry blossoms, lilacs, and rhododendrons circled the building, their delicate shades of pink softening the gray granite walls. A narrow ring of grass that guarded the crest of the hill from the street, turned a violent green in the moist wind that often blew in from the ocean. That same sweet wind bathed the light with dew and gave the hill a surreal glimmer. But it was only a brief time of color and light. As soon as summer came, the grass and bushes and the soft light was defeated. The hill soon seared and burned to brown.

Four roads led to the top of the hill, one at each point of the compass, while three narrow streets spiraled around it like grooves of a well-tooled drill. To the north which lay at the hospital's back, a great swath of earth had been gouged out and the cavity lined with granite and asphalt. It was this side of Liberty Hill Hospital into which life flowed and ebbed. An ambulance ramp was centered in the asphalt hillside. On either side of it, parking lots were tiered into the earth. A discrete ramp wide enough for only one vehicle led to an unmarked door. It was the morgue entrance and few who traveled back and forth across the pavement gave the innocuous door a second glance, for beside it, shaded by a canopy of abstract metal tubing pinned against the granite walls and jutting thirty feet over the drive, was the emergency room entrance. Hidden spotlights threw its shadows against the old stone. Though the actual emergency room was buried deep in the hospital and had changed little over the years, the strange design of the entrance was new and gave the north facade a scaffolded appearance. There were many doors on this side of the hospital: the employee entrance, great loading docks for foods and linen, and others long forgotten and barred from the inside.

In contrast to the north, the hospital's south side, the one that seemed to hover above the earth when the light and air was just right, seemed abandoned. There was only one opening here, a great front entrance made of double oak doors carved by hand and set in granite so cleverly that a gentle push of the hand swung them open.

From the bottom of the hill, the building loomed impossibly tall and South Street, leading from the base of the hill to its crown, was a straight cobbled road. Though it was tiered every hundred feet and three times crossed by encircling streets, its pitch discouraged all but a few who came to Liberty Hill.

Lily Webb climbed South Street three times a week. At the corner of Threadneedle Alley she had to stop. She had run out of breath. She let her green schoolbag drop to the pavement and waited while the roar in her ears settled down. Panting, and with a prickling of sweat running down her back, she peered up at the distant hospital and muttered, "Screw you," to the old building.

It was always a tough climb, but much more so on Mondays. Two days without dialysis and the hill seemed to have risen higher than she remembered. There were one thousand eight hundred and seventy-one steps from here to the door of the dialysis unit, less if she lived on the north side of the hill. She should have let the school bus carry her around to the back but it would have made her late for her machine time. Besides, the raucous noise of her classmates on the bus had made her head begin to ache. She had a monster inside her skull, hammering to get out. But there was always some monster inside her.

There was always her little cast of characters accompanying her on these treks. The headache was green and shapeless. His name was Aragg, a name which if she pronounced aloud would give sound to the pain she felt. There was another she called Amazon. It was the thick rope of skin that jutted from the white flesh of her left arm, the mating of artery and vein to which the dialysis machine was fastened. It was a small piece of herself that she hated the most. It disgusted her, it marred her smooth skin. She kept it always covered with long sleeves. The rest of her veins were simply rivers of poison that tumbled inside her body making her sick.

Her favorite dialysis machine, the one nearest the window, she called Lover Boy. If she was lucky enough to get him, she could watch the sky while she cleansed. Although she hated the process of dialysis, the sneaky thought that she and Lover Boy were engaged in some sort of strange intercourse often came to her as she drowsed away the four hours. After all, he did make her feel better.

She also had special names for the people in her life. Her mother was the Black Queen. She supposed it was because of the artificial tint to Tracy Webb's hair, but mostly it was because of Tracy's annoying habit of intruding on her disease. As a supervisor, Tracy could float through the hospital without question, checking on her, always checking. The lab, the dialysis unit, Dr. Russell's office. There was nothing about her body Lily could keep from the Black Queen.

When she told Dr. Russell what she called him, he had laughed. "A Rook? Why not the king?"

"I'm the king," she said. "You are my guardian, my rook." And he had bowed his head.

She did not think she was truly a king. Not with all the poisons in her veins. She thought of herself as a pigmy mushroom, a fungus whose flesh was filled with acid. That was how she pictured herself after Dr. Russell had explained the kidney failure, the accumulation of poisons that must be drained off. It explained why she was so pale, and worse, why she wasn't growing. At fourteen Lily knew she looked like a tired ten year old. It was those useless bean-shaped organs keeping her locked in childhood. There was no swelling of her breasts. While her friends grew hair on their pubic bones and giggled about tampons, she was still straight as a stick and just as dry.

She picked up the schoolbag and strapped it across her forehead just as she'd seen in pictures of Far East peasants. It might look funny, she knew, but it made the climb just a little easier. Besides, there was never anyone on this side of the hill to see her. She crossed Threadneedle Alley and began counting her steps. By the time she reached the little plaza that circled the hospital, her ears were ringing. She collapsed on a wrought-iron settee and wiped her face. The headache was making her skull feel empty and gourdlike. Even the cries of the gulls in the harbor below tricked her. Were they circling inside her head?

She closed her eyes and lifted her face to the sun. Soon they would call her and she would fly to that hill. Her transplant would be waiting for her. She dreamed of the day when her phone would ring. It seemed that she lived only for that. A simple telephone call. No more Lover Boy, no more days of drowsy death.

She had a store of bad memories that she could summon up at any time. She was six when her father died. She carried with her always the strickened expression on her mother's face which had disappeared over the years leaving only bitterness. There was the memory of her own disease, a blur of crisp white sheets against her hot skin. Of thirst that seemed to swell her tongue. Of cries without tears. Of incomprehension that she could not have water. And of guilt on her mother's face. She supposed it all started then: the Black Queen, the Toadstool, the Amazon River that was her left arm.

Lately, she hadn't kept her creatinine level down. How simple it was to think about but difficult to maintain, and when it was up, how viciously Lover Boy sucked at her blood. The machine pulled water from her body with a vengeance that left her cramped and dizzy. If only someone would die, she would pray. Someone just for me. And then she would feel shame for the thought.

At first, when Dr. Russell talked about a transplant she had been horrified. At fourteen she knew her body was intact and organized and recognizable. How each organ lay symmetrically next to another, how smoothly intact her skin was, covering her nerves and bones. A transplant would change her into someone else. But now she prayed for it, for the death of someone unknown and she thought: this must be how it is to grow up. Her shy poetry began to protest the waiting.

When the headache subsided a little, she got up and

entered the hospital. As she walked down the stairs that took her into the deepest part of the building, she made her usual bargain with God: no steak for a creatinine below eight, okay?

She knew what her chart looked like as well as she knew the contents of her schoolbooks, better perhaps. Especially the graph of her vital signs. Her blood pressure was climbing little by little, no matter how well she stuck to her diet. And the creatinine; it was her watchword. Below the magic number and dialysis was easier.

Somedays, sick of it all, she would rebel and stuff herself with all the forbidden foods. Her mother would watch and shake her head but never say anything. Long ago Lily had taken over the management of her own disease. It was she and Dr. Russell who conspired together. It was she and Lover Boy making watery music together three times a week. When she cheated on her diet, she knew the consequences. On those days she let Tracy drive her up the hill. That was the only symbol of her failure.

Inside, deep within the bowels of the hospital where the air was cool and a little moist, where water dripped off the heating pipes, and strange rustlings were heard just beyond the concrete bend in the wall, she walked slowly to the dialysis unit. It was a shortcut that she had found and though it was a little spooky, it saved a few steps.

The room she was headed for occupied the southeast corner of Liberty Hill where the ground dropped away from the building. Here, there were huge windows set in the granite for the patients to gaze from as they cleansed. The unit was tastefully furnished in quiet colors and paneled walls. There were little television sets with headphones at each bed. A small kitchen was tucked into one corner of the room and it was fully stocked with bland food calculated not to shock a patient with taste or goodness. She never ate any of it; suck food, she called it.

There were six beds in there, technically called beds for the purpose of state regulations. In reality they were leather-covered reclining chairs over which a clean sheet was drawn. Beside each chair was its companion, the artificial kidney. There were coils of tubing within it leading to more tubing draped over the intravenous hooks. Liter-sized bags of fluid hung waiting. It was a place of hushed watery sounds. The door opened easily.

Lily paused and took a deep breath, wanting to hold off the time. A figure was approaching as she waited by the door.

"Hello, Miss Webb. How are you feeling today?"

It was Eddie Shuster. He had a kind and simple face and though she wanted to smile at him, she never did. It did not seem to bother him. She could see the benign gaze of his eyes, the vacant smile that creased his face. She saw him every time she came down here and never knew what he did.

"Wonderful, Eddie. Just wonderful." She turned away and let the door close behind him. The watery sounds filled her ears.

"Only ten minutes late today, Lily," Steve Lambert called out when he saw her. She knew he was about to deliver a stern lecture about dialysis time and how precious it was and how if she were late, the next patient would be delayed, and was that fair?

"Can it, Steve," she said, heading straight for Lover Boy. "Just hook me up and get me started." She rolled up her sleeve, exposing the whitish flesh that corded beneath her skin. She did not glance at it. Ten minutes later, the soft slosh of fluid and Lover Boy's steady drone put her to sleep. Steve Lambert stood back and studied her. She had gained seven pounds over the weekend. One extra day without cleansing. He turned up the dial on the machine, hoping its extra pull would not hurt her too much. *She's too young to go much longer,* he thought, too full of dreams.

He glanced at his watch; it was three-thirty.

That poor little girl, Eddie Shuster thought as he entered Central Supply, she ain't getting any better. It's a damn shame kids have to be sick. The old ones, well they'd had their lives, but children hadn't even begun. It wasn't fair.

Seeing her this afternoon had taken the shine off his day and though he wouldn't admit it to himself, he was a little sorry he had bumped into Lily Webb. It made him feel guilty for being so happy. Here he was feeling so good about his new job title and then she came along, looking so much like a starved cat.

He didn't know what was the matter with Lily, but it seemed to him that she'd been coming to this hospital long enough to start improving. It was lousy to see a kid suffer.

He changed into his hospital greens and began to stack supplies on the big steel trolley. As he worked, he forgot about Lily Webb and began to hum. Although he was alone in the cavernous room, something he disliked, today it did not bother him. For Eddie, the room had lost its impersonality. It was truly his domain now that they had made him supervisor.

It wasn't the raise that thrilled him. After all, his needs were few. He had no wife, no car, and no expenses. Sure, there was extra money now to lavish on his nephews, but they loved him whether or not he had money. It was the new title, the importance of it that was exciting. Now he was as good as anyone in the whole hospital, even as good as the nurses. He couldn't wait to tell them. He loaded his trolley with supplies and began his rounds. His round face was glowing as he entered dialysis.

Steve Lambert glanced up at him as he pulled his cart to the supply room.

"You're grinning like a Cheshire cat, Eddie. What's

going on?"

Instead of answering directly, Eddie puffed out his chest so that the nurse could read his badge. "See?"

Steve read the new badge on Eddie's chest. "Congratulations, Eddie. How did you manage that?"

"Oh, I had it made up at that key shop down on Front Street. They make name tags too."

"No, I mean the title. Since when did you make supervisor?"

"The union did it for me! They got me all lumped in with the other department heads. You know, Sterile Supply, Housekeeping, and all. Each one of us made supervisor that way. It's in our contract now. The union was gonna make me grieve it if the city didn't give in. I'm just glad I didn't hafta do that. I'd a been scared to death to grieve."

"That must mean a hefty raise for you as well, eh?" Steve said.

"Oh yah! Now I'm making as much as you, Mr. Lambert." Eddie fingered his new name badge proudly. He did not see the cloud come over Steve's face. "It ain't the money so much though, it's the feeling of being important. That's the nice part of it." His voice rose as it always did when he was excited.

"Keep it down, Eddie. The patients are trying to rest." Eddie's face flushed; he was always doing something wrong. "Did you bring me those extra basins I asked for?"

"Yessir." Steve sighed at the hangdog look on Eddie's face. He was actually pouting! He did not dislike the little man. If anything, Eddie took great pride in his work, stacking supplies for him with fanatical neatness. And he always was glad to run an errand or two for Steve.

"You'd better get busy," he said. "After all, a supervisor keeps on top of everything, Eddie." Immediately the round face beamed again.

Nodding importantly, Shuster disappeared into the clean supply room. When he finished his work, he pushed the cart into the hallway, calling out, "Let me know if you need anything else, Mr. Lambert." There was no answer. Steve was on the telephone.

At four o'clock the cafeteria began to fill with staff for the early supper shift. Trish Curry grabbed a tray and joined Pat Weeks at the steam table. She sniffed at the meat loaf and, apparently satisfied with its odor, put the plate beside her salad.

"Did you hear the news about Eddie Shuster?" Trish was in charge of Three North and tonight there were just two nurses to cover the twenty-six patients on that floor.

"I couldn't miss it," replied Pat Weeks. "He's been blabbing it all over the hospital since the shift began."

Pat was the covering nurse in the operating room from three to eleven p.m. She worked alone, preparing for the next day's cases and standing ready for any emergency that might come in during her shift. She was feeling a little guilty. The nursing office had tried to get her to help with patient care on Trish's floor and she had refused, claiming duties on her own floor. She hoped Trish hadn't found out.

"Imagine," Trish said, "Eddie Shuster is making the same wage as me! I just spent four years in college . . . four years. And a moron like him makes the same money as I do. It's insulting."

"Yup, there'll be trouble over it." The two nurses pushed their trays along the cafeteria counter.

"What do you mean, trouble?"

"We're in the middle of negotiations and his union gets their contract first? Gimme a break!" She slammed a bowl of jello onto her tray. "That's like rubbing our faces in shit. Our contract is a year overdue as it is."

"I hope something happens soon," Pat said. "I need more money. The loans I have make the federal deficit look puny." The two nurses took seats beside Tracy Webb, the day supervisor.

"Did you hear about Eddie's raise?" Tracy asked.

"The whole hospital has heard about Eddie's fucking raise," replied Pat. Tricia's face reddened. She sneaked a look at the supervisor. "What do you think of it?"

"It's typical of those bastards in City Hall. They're insulting us and laughing up their sleeves about it."

At forty-five, Tracy Webb's face was remarkably smooth, the few lines of age in her face were as crisp as her white uniform and broad-winged cap. She had an affinity for stark colors, dyeing her hair blue-black and daubing lipstick as red as rubies on her wide mouth. Behind her back they called her "the painted lady," a fact of which she was aware but cared little. She intimidated the Liberty Hill employees, and nothing escaped her gaze.

She had never worked anywhere else but Liberty Hill beginning at sixteen as an errand girl. Working summers, she had put herself through nursing school, and then part time through college. Over the years, she had come to know the families of the town of Atwater, child to grandparent, as they streamed into the hospital.

"I've got to go downstairs to dialysis." She said, glancing at her watch.

"Is today Lily's dialysis day?" Pat asked.

"Can't you tell? I wouldn't hang around this place one second longer than I have to, except when she's in." She unpinned her starched white cap and placed it in a case, and fluffed her hair.

"Who knows, maybe this Shuster business will start a nursing strike. Wouldn't that upset the applecart, eh?" She smiled, but her eyes were dark and vicious. "Oh, it gives me shivers to think about it. See you." She swung away and threaded her way through the crowded cafeteria.

"I don't get it," Trish said, watching Tracy hurry

away. "Why would she want a strike just for the sake of one? No one in their right mind wants to strike."

"Tracy does our bargaining with the city. If she can't get a good contract, she'll make it look like it's the hospital's fault. And we're supposed to go out on strike. She'd love that, it's a part of her vendetta against this place."

"But why?" Trish looked puzzled.

Pat shrugged. "She's never forgiven the hospital for her husband's death. The way she figures it, they let him die. And in a way they probably did."

"My God, what happened? And how come I never heard about it?"

"It was long before you came here. Years ago. He was a navy yard worker and got in a terrible accident. They brought him in half-dead and he finished the job out in the corridor. She blames the hospital for bungling his case. It was one of those horror stories that sometimes happens to a patient. They say he lay too long without attention, and then when they finally got around to him it was too late."

"That sounds like a damned good lawsuit to me," Trish said.

"She didn't sue. In those days society wasn't so lawsuit crazy. But she's been making Liberty Hill pay for it ever since. A sort of love-hate relationship. Now, on top of everything else, her kid's going through dialysis and it's keeping her broke. She's a bitter woman but you have to admit that her life hasn't been exactly a bed of roses. She hopes we strike the hell out of the city."

"But why blame the city for her misfortune?"

"Put yourself in her shoes. She's all alone with a sick kid. She sees the same doctors—I won't name names— who looked after her husband and lost him. They're still here making all kinds of money while she's struggling to survive. She sees patients surviving accidents today, better medicine and all, just like the kind that killed Noel Webb and that drives her crazy. Even the nurses. She's tough on us, too. She sees us making mistakes. God knows we're not perfect, but she thinks we're too careless. She can't forget and she'll never forgive. So she's a tyrant." Pat shrugged and added, "and a bit of a troublemaker."

With that, she stood up and pulled her scrub jacket firmly over her ample breasts. "And now I've got six rooms to stock, as well as stand by for emergencies." The last was said to assuage her conscience for only she knew that her job was a leisurely one. She lifted her tray and carried it to the disposal chute. The cafeteria began to empty.

All the while, Eddie Shuster passed among the wards and units, whispering in some, smiling and talking loudly in others, blissfully sending the news of his promotion throughout the hospital, ignorant of the reaction of his friends, the nurses.

On his rounds, he always saved the intensive care unit for last. That place frightened him and he had to summon up his courage to enter it. As always, when he faced the door, Eddie's round face lost its composure. He took a deep breath and waited for his heart to slow.

The patients in here . . . he couldn't talk to them like he did on the other floors. None of them looked real. They were hooked to machines that made them look like they were dead. And the nurses . . . they were always rushing from bed to bed, their faces absorbed in some holy mission. They did mysterious things to the figures on the beds. There was no room for Eddie's kindness in here. It made him feel useless and scared.

He didn't like Mark Berlin, the charge nurse, either. That one had a bad temper, he did. Doing the best he could was never enough for Mr. Berlin. Eddie couldn't help it if he tended to forget things.

He pushed through the door, the light and sounds assaulting his blunted senses as it always did. Keeping his gaze averted from the patients, he pulled the trolley up to the desk.

"Hello, Mr. Berlin." There was no answer but he hadn't expected one. Mark Berlin was bent over a strip of EKG paper, measuring the tracings on it with a pair of calipers. "Guess you haven't heard the good news."

That was better; the lanky nurse straightened up. "Huh? What news is that, Eddie?"

"About my promotion. See?" He held out his badge as he had done so many times this evening. Mark peered at it and then dropped his gaze to the EKG strip.

Disappointed, Eddie persevered. "And I'm making more money, too," he said. "Yep. Almost as much as you make, I'll bet. It's my seniority, y'know. I've got twenty-five years in this place. I'll bet we're equal."

At that, the male nurse slowly straightened and faced the clerk. Eddie's smile faded; he shouldn't have said that. He'd made a mistake and gone too far again. He turned away.

"Wait a minute, Shuster." Mark's voice stopped him. "Do you mean that you're making the same money I do? How come?"

Eddie halted. He would have to be careful about what he said. This man wasn't his friend. Oh, why didn't he just keep his mouth shut in here?

Trying not to stutter, something he always did when his nerves acted up, Eddie explained his new status. The details were not clear to him, and he knew he certainly wasn't making it clear to Mark Berlin. With a sinking feeling, he finished with a grand stutter.

"Th—the—co—contract was si—signed yesterday."

With that, he fled the ward pushing his cart into the utility room, feeling his face burn and his heart race in great thumps. Oh, that man made him nervous! He stacked a pile of bedpans on the shelf, not caring whether they toppled. He'd leave before Mr. Berlin could say another word to him. Just walk away and pretend it never happened. He didn't have to take it, not anymore. He was a supervisor now. Sniffing, Eddie completed his task and then tiptoed by Mark's desk, relieved to see that he was talking on the phone.

Chapter Three

"Take a deep cleansing breath. Good. Now lightly, lightly, begin to puff. Like this." Katherine Weathers pursed her lips and let her breath puff between them. "Puh, puh, puh. Get it?"

Staring up at her, from a sideways position, his head fitting into the narrow shelf of her lap, Ben Weathers mimicked her breathing pattern and crossed his eyes.

"Good," she said, not noticing. She was reading a book that she had propped up on the floor. She let her hand rest upon his bare abdomen and began a slow, circling movement. "This is supposed to create a semi-hypnotizing trance," she said, turning a page.

"It'll do more than that, if you keep it up," he replied, feeling a stir in his groin.

"Come on, Ben, pay attention. Now you are going into transition. This is the hard part. This is where I'm supposed to . . . I mean you are supposed to be on the edge of losing control. Now you must really concentrate on your breathing. Pant, Ben." She looked at him, her gaze compassionate. "I know you're uncomfortable, but it's almost over. The baby will be coming soon. Pant, like a puppy."

Ben gave a low, sorrowful howl and then obediently

began to pant. In disgust, Katherine swiveled her hips away from him and let his head fall to the floor. She rested her hand on her swollen belly and with a huff of exertion stood up, leaving her husband to stare up at her, a grin upon his face.

"Dammit, Ben," she said, "if you'd go with me to prenatal classes, I wouldn't have to do this."

Ben rolled on his side, tying the sash of his pajama bottoms, and then pulled himself to a sitting position. "Cripes, honey, I'm a doctor. I've delivered babies. Why should—"

"Because this is your baby. You are having it as much as I, and I'm going to need your help. I don't need the sanctimonious 'doctor' nonsense. This is going to be your first baby." Katherine stretched, breathing in deeply. "If we don't prepare, it could be a disaster, you know. I don't have a very high pain threshold. I'm afraid I'll end up a screamer. Besides, it's scary."

Ben regarded his wife lovingly. She was not angry at him, he knew. She was too absorbed in her pregnancy to expend energy in anger. Lately, too, she had become distant. If she needed to convey a message, it was done absently. It was not her responsibility to see it understood, that was up to him. In the past month the change in her had become obvious. It amused him.

She let her arms dangle and curved herself over her swollen abdomen. "Ooh, she's matching me, move for move, the little devil." She felt the fluttering movement and let her hand follow the ripple that made her belly seem lopsided. "That's her head, right there." She patted the little mound.

He watched her. Light from the lamp behind her pierced the loose folds of her gown, outlining the length of her legs, the hugeness of her belly, and the fullness of her breasts. He thought to himself that she was more beautiful now, in the last month of her pregnancy, than she ever was, and the notion struck him that he'd never loved her more than right now, as ungainly as she had become. That's my child in there he thought wonderingly and, not for the first time, the notion of it struck him with intensity, holding him frozen for a moment. He saw themselves in the light of this room, as though they were a tableau to be preserved upon the walls of his memories forever.

How was it possible? The venerable old bachelor, a perpetual swinging single, a title he knew he didn't deserve but accepted anyway as part of the price of being single, how had he come to this fierce love for her? He had no answer, only the swelling of his heart each time he studied her. He watched as she sat on the bed and began to brush her hair. When she had cut her hair announcing that now that she was pregnant, she couldn't be bothered with such things as fashion, he had been outraged. But she had been right. Cut short, it curled in a dark cap around her face and highlighted her huge brown eyes. Somehow she looked younger and vulnerable. She peeked at him out of the corner of her eye.

"I bought some ice cream today. Do you want some?"

He didn't but knew it was an excuse for her to have some. He rose from the floor where they had been practicing and slipped into his pajama top. "I'm serving."

She beamed and licked her lips. "Goody. I bought sorbet for me and cream for you. No, maybe I'll have butter pecan. Oh, I don't know which I want. How about a little of each?"

It broke all the rules Ned Price, her obstetrician, had decreed. No fats, one egg a week, low salt. But what the hell, Ben thought. She took such delight in little things lately, and she hadn't taken a day away from her job in months, though that had nothing to do with her diet. Anyway, he would give her more sorbet than ice cream. He padded down to the kitchen. She followed him happily, chattering about new baby sheets and flannels, whatever they were. As they entered the kitchen, the phone rang, a harsh sound that broke the quiet of the night and sent the cat flying off the counter, a forbidden territory that it knew well.

Ben and Katherine eyed each other. "You're off tonight, aren't you?" she whispered as though the caller, whoever it might be, would hear. He nodded, his face clouding. "Then I'll answer it." She waddled toward the phone, grumbling at the intrusion.

It might be trouble in the emergency room, though he doubted it. Ralph Levering was on duty and he never called for help. He could handle any emergency.

"Oh hello, Leah." He heard his wife answer. There was a query in her voice. She eyed Ben and shrugged as she listened. Then she made a scooping motion with her hand. Obediently he opened the freezer and pulled out two cartons, one for him and the other for her.

She tucked the phone under her chin and began to set the table as she listened. She handed him two bowls, never stopping as she moved about the kitchen. Idly he wondered at this call. Katherine was never bothered with hospital business. When she was through for the day, she was through. The ICU hummed along without her.

Katherine sat down, the table ready at last. She gripped the phone with her hand. "Are you saying that the nurses will strike tomorrow? Is that it?" Ben shot her a sharp glance.

"I don't know." Leah's voice came over the wire softly, as though she, too, had considered the possibility. "Mark says they are furious. The whole hospital is in an uproar. I just hope Tracy hasn't heard about it."

Katherine slipped a spoonful of ice cream into her mouth, wincing at the cold. She hadn't thought of Tracy, but Leah was right. As soon as the supervisor heard about the Shuster business, she'd start trouble.

Though this could be a strong bargaining point for the nurses, Tracy might ignore that and call for a strike. She'd been hinting at it for months now. Katherine pictured the turmoil up on the hill. Gossip was always rampant in a hospital. Nothing could be kept secret, not patient confidentiality, not love affairs, and certainly never contract matters. The nurses were tired of waiting. This would be grist for the mill, this Shuster business.

Leah went on. "I guess I just wanted to warn you that there might be some sort of action tomorrow."

Katherine stifled a groan. One more month to go, and she'd be on maternity leave. One short month. Couldn't they have given her that? There were always problems at the hospital. If it wasn't a staffing shortage, it was something else. She had wanted to be out of there before the ominous signs became reality.

She sighed. "Okay, Leah. You warned me, now just don't worry about it. I'll see you tomorrow morning." She caught her breath. "You will be working tonight, won't you?"

Leah giggled. "I'm not a striker, my dear. A poor peon, but not an agitator. Besides, I have a little mouth to feed. And right now he's got his toes in his mouth. Wait till yours comes, Katherine. If it's a girl, I'll fix her up with Nikki." She said good-night and the phone went dead.

Katherine let the phone hang from one hand and stared at a reflection of herself in the darkened window. Was it time to quit? She glanced at Ben. He had become absorbed in a medical journal as he ate. He wanted her to leave now and they certainly didn't need her paycheck, they never did. He made more money than she had ever seen in her lifetime. And Liberty Hill wouldn't close its doors if she left. So why did she persist in going in day after day?

The answer was always the same. Working was as natural to her as breathing and marriage hadn't changed that. They'd simply gone on as they had done before, he as ER physician and she as ICU supervisor. Lately, though, she had been waiting for the baby to arrive with growing impatience, longing for it with an intensity that always surprised her.

She felt the baby move, a slow dreamy roll that brought her hands to her belly. She had become domestically manic. Look at the table she had just set; there was a fanatic precision to the scene. Rose-colored placemats coordinated with the rosebuds on her best china. She'd never cared about such things before! She'd even bought mauve candlesticks because they were the right shade. What had got into her? Touching a match to them, the softness of candlelight pooled over the table. She peeked at the reflection of the scene. It was so pretty.

It had to do with putting her nest in order before the baby came, she knew. The problems of Liberty Hill and lately, the running of her unit, had become less intense to her. Definitely unimportant, if she was honest with herself. At first she had been shocked that the Hill had become less compelling but then she realized that she had become the perfect textbook example of nest building. It was the baby coming, that was all.

She hadn't told Ben about her strange new lethargy. It would shock him. Charged with intensity that she always thought of as electricity harnessed, Ben ran his career in high gear. The frantic pace of emergency-room practice was eminently suited to him, infusing him with even more energy. Or maybe he just set its pace even higher than it should be. Either way he thrived on his career and he would never understand that she was slowing down.

She glanced over at him. If the truth were told, she was still trying to figure him out after one year of marriage. Her pregnancy was speeding up the process. She knew that he hadn't given a thought to parenthood, but hell, neither had she. It had caught them both uprepared. Her hand came up and rested protectively on her belly as the traitorous thought came to her.

She nibbled on a spoonful of raspberry sorbet; it was sinfully good. Mentally she apologized to Ned Price, her obstetrician.

If there was trouble at Liberty Hill, a strike, the ICU might be closed entirely. The thought chilled her. If she couldn't staff the unit, then the state would force its closure. What would happen if someone critically ill was brought to Liberty Hill? They'd have to turn that patient away! How many would die because of a strike?

"What's wrong, honey?" Ben was watching her.

She couldn't tell him. This was nursing, this was not his province. He reached across the table to cover her hand.

"There's trouble up there, isn't that it? Hey, I'm not in some ivory tower, you know. The nurses in the E.R. have been talking, too."

"Just the usual contract business," she murmured. "I hope it'll die down before I leave."

"Ah, you should leave now, while you have the chance. When she comes," his gaze went to her abdomen, "you'll wish you had taken some time for yourself."

He was right. The midnight feedings, the colic that could keep them both up for hours. It was coming. She grinned at him. "I'd like her to go to Harvard, it's just across the river."

He nodded. "Yeah, she could commute. I'll get an application tomorrow." She reached over and slapped his hand with her spoon.

Tracy shifted her bottom on the hard seat and sighed. At the sound, Lily opened her eyes. They had tipped her seat way back so that her head was lower than her feet.

The dial on the artificial kidney was turned up high and it had made her feel faint.

She regarded Tracy. "Go home, Mother. There's no reason you should wait. I can probably hitch a ride home with someone."

Tracy shifted, but there was a flicker of relief in her eyes. "In that case, I think I will run home and get out of these clothes, but I'll be back to pick you up. I know how you'll be feeling."

It was a bad day. Tracy felt her heart break a little as she studied Lily. There were dark blue shadows under her eyes, and a rim of white around her lips. Her fingers trembled lying on the chair arms. Fat fingers, swollen with fluids.

Though they never talked about blood values, or creatinines, or diet, or a hundred other concerns of a dialysis patient, Tracy kept her own record of Lily's progress. But even looking at her was a little like breaking the rules they had set up long ago. Don't study me, Lily had said. Let me handle this by myself. When the dialysis had begun, she seemed to have drifted away. There were things that Lily and Dr. Russell talked about, things she would never know. Maybe they were things *she* should be aware of. Boyfriends, makeup, school. She wondered what Dr. Russell knew about Lily that she didn't. Wearily, Tracy rolled her knitting into an unruly ball and jammed it into her bag.

"Okay. I'll run along." She leaned over and pulled open a flannel blanket, being careful not to disturb Lily's left arm. She kept her eyes averted from it, hating the white cord of flesh that rose along her thin arm. It was hard-used with needle sticks and a constant reminder of Lily's perilous frailty. She watched as Lily pulled the cotton blanket up to her shoulders and closed her eyes once more.

When the heavy doors shut behind her and she felt

safe from curious eyes, Tracy stopped under the street light, fumbling in her bag for a handkerchief. Tears streaked makeup and ran little rivers of black down her cheeks.

The staff crowded around the time clock and when the hands clicked to eleven o'clock, the first of them slid their cards into the slot. The shift was over. Mark Berlin waited his turn at the back of the crowd.

"Hey, Mark! What are we going to do about this Shuster business?" someone called from the middle of the group.

"Yeah, Mark, are we going to let the city get away with it?" another voice called out. "It's an insult giving Shuster a raise and nothing to us!"

No one noticed the miserable figure of Eddie Shuster as he stood in line. What had he done? These were his friends, weren't they? Hurt, he could feel tears fill his eyes. He sniffed loudly, but no one paid any attention to him.

Mark Berlin knew better than to try to answer their angry questions, there were too many of his own. He pushed through the crowd, slid his card into the time clock and punched out. With their angry voices still coming at him, he let the door close behind him. The parking lot was dark and silent.

Emma Bond was better tonight. With her favorite respirator attached to her tracheostomy, the television tuned to Carson, and a can of Pepsi by her side, she seemed content to be by herself. She made no mention of last night's weaning effort. It was as if it had never happened. Even during the routine of suctioning, which she couldn't avoid, she kept her gaze firmly on the television screen. Her routine requests, made with her little placards, for another Pepsi, the bedpan, adjust the pillow, made it clear. Emma was ignoring Leah.

"You'd almost think she enjoys life in here," Leah muttered to Pat. "Now that she's got her favorite vent, she's being the queen of the unit. I feel like a goddamn handmaiden."

"She's no fool," Pat replied. "With a drunk for a husband, and kids in and out of court, why should she want out? She doesn't get beat up in here, she doesn't have to cook or do housework like us poor schnooks. She knows a good thing when she sees it. This unit is heaven for her. So what if she can't breathe? Anything is better than being out in the real world for Emma."

Leah opened Emma's chart and read the day's notes. Dr. Peters had been in. His notes looked like yesterday's and the days before. She sniffed to herself: he doesn't even care what her blood gases are. For all he knows, she could be breathing carbon monoxide.

Emma's day had been routine. Accompanied by her portable respirator and her own respiratory attendant, she had spent the morning in physical therapy. She had walked the wooden treadmill and the stationary bicycle. Nothing wrong with her legs, Leah thought. How much was this costing? How much did vents cost per day, the use of physical therapy? What do her meds cost?

Later, Emma ate her usual hamburger and french fries, requested an enema (which was refused; she was given a laxative instead), and consumed a half-dozen bottles of Pepsi-Cola. Nowhere in the nursing notes was there a mention of weaning Emma Bond from her respirator. No one gives a damn, Leah thought. If Peters doesn't, and Emma doesn't, why should she?

She gazed around the unit. Ten beds of critically ill patients, all of them struggling to stay alive and more importantly, get back to the real world. But not Emma. She'd made this place her home. She was taking up space here and, Leah guessed, not paying one cent for it. Because of her, there was actually one bed less for an emergency. Somewhere out there was a potential disaster, and they would not be able to handle it because of her. It just wasn't right! She slammed the chart closed and Pat Connor jumped.

"Hey, don't get in an uproar. She isn't worth it."

"Oh really? What if your mother needed a bed in here and there weren't any? How would you like it then?" She glared at Pat for a moment and smiled sheepishly. "Sorry, forget I said that."

Pat's face became thoughtful. "You really *are* ticked off, aren't you? Why don't you do something about it?"

"What, go in and force Emma to breathe on her own? She's forgotten last night."

"No, she hasn't. She asked to have you assigned to her again. That must mean something."

Leah thought about that. Could Emma be giving her a signal that she was missing? Did she want to try again?

"Don't do it," Pat said, reading her thoughts. "There's another way. We should demand a staff meeting to develop a plan for Emma. A way of working towards her discharge."

"Oh, sure. Claude Peters would love that. He doesn't want her out of here. He's getting paid for her to stay."

"We don't need him. All we need is a concerted effort from us to get her out. We could present it to the medical committee and they would overrule Peters the Great."

"Yes, and pay for it for the rest of our lives. He could be vindictive, I'll bet."

"And we can be just as nasty, too. He has to live with us." Pat opened her novel and stretched her legs up on the desk. "Now go to work and write a letter to Katherine. Request a staff meeting. I'll sign it, and don't bother me for the rest of the night, okay? This book is the sexiest thing I've ever read. Listen to this: 'His tongue traced the lips of her pubic mouth and she flowered open so that it tickled the hardened little nub.'"

Leah burst out laughing. "Oh God, that's bad."

"Yeah, but just imagine it!" Pat sighed. "Ooh, I'm all a flutter just thinking about it." She wriggled suggestively and uncrossed her legs.

Chapter Four

Two-Gus Ragust leaned over the sink and stared at his reflection. His eyeballs were definitely yellow, and his skin the color of saffron. There were dark red splotches on his chin and chest. He decided he looked like a new species of man: the ultimate evolution. After this, there'd be nothing and perhaps the insects would inherit the world after all.

It was time. He had gone too long now. Trying to ignore the pain in his shoulder he popped the last Percodan into his mouth. He'd better hurry, another chill was coming. He picked up the phone and dialed.

"Dr. Gold's office."

"This is Two-Gus Ragust calling. Is she in?"

"Hi, Two-Gus." The operator brightened as she heard the familiar voice. "No, she's off tonight. Want another doctor?"

"No, give her a message, will you? Tell her I'm admitting myself again . . . over to Liberty Hill Hospital this time. Ask her to drop in to see me in the morning, okay?"

"Sure, Gus." The operator's voice was soft with pity. "Would you like me to call an ambulance for you?"

The chill hit him and his teeth began to chatter. He

pulled a blanket over his shoulders, but the fabric seemed to claw at his skin. "Yes, please. I'm at home." He hung up and hunched over, waiting for the fury of the chill to run its course. He was patient; it would be gone by the time the ambulance arrived.

He stared at the window. Was it getting lighter, or was the pain in his shoulder blazing a false daylight into his eyes?

By the time the ambulance swung silently into the emergency-room ramp, it was morning. The white van circled the drive and with a clunk of gears, backed into the loading dock. Two-Gus winced at the change in direction; they had strapped him too tightly to the stretcher.

The glass doors swung open at a touch of foot to rubber pad. Two-Gus felt the legs of the stretcher drop to the ground and then the cool air of the emergency room hit his face. Another chill was coming. The ceiling tiles, ablaze with lights, hurt his eyes.

"What do we have here?" Ralph Levering said, as he yawned and stood up. The stretcher halted by his desk. He glanced down at the figure and his mouth tightened. "Put him in room four." To the nurse by his side, he muttered, "Call the lab and get them over here stat."

"Stat?" Betty Vernon asked. "You want me to scare everyone this early in the morning with a stat?"

"Stat." Dr. Levering, normally a jovial young man, superb in a crisis and calm at all times, was sober. "Get respiratory over here and call the ICU. Tell them we'll be sending them a patient."

Betty snatched up the phone and began her calls. Her face, sleepy only moments before, was now all business. It had been a boring night and for the past hour, she had dozed at the desk. Now she hurried after Ralph Levering.

In room four, as she helped slide the patient from the stretcher to the examining table, a foul odor hit her nostrils. Automatically she opened her mouth to breathe so she wouldn't gag.

While Levering began a litany of questions to both driver and patient, Betty began to peel off the patient's clothes. Mentally noting their expensive cut, she folded them with unusual care, and placed the soft calfskin loafers in a corner of the cubicle. They were too nice to get lost.

It was then, with the patient fully exposed, except for a draw sheet over his genitals, that his jaundice struck her. His skin was a greenish-bronze color and it was hot to her touch. She slid a paper thermometer into his mouth. Then she turned her attention to the clumsy-looking bandage on his shoulder, the source of the odor.

"Don't touch it," Two-Gus said, the thermometer waggling as he spoke. She withdrew her hand hastily. Betty Vernon had fifteen years of emergency room experience; when a patient warned her, she listened. Instead, she wrapped a blood pressure cuff around Two-Gus's good arm and put her stethoscope into her ears. She bent over him.

"Any history on this patient?" Ralph spoke to the ambulance attendants. Both shook their heads. "Okay, you can go." He turned to the patient.

"What happened, Mr. Ragust?" He held the patient's wrist between his fingers.

"Want a history?" Two-Gus said. "I'll give you a history. It's not a pretty one." His teeth began to chatter again as the chill hit. The thermometer fell from his mouth and Betty snatched it up before it could hit the floor.

"Factor eight hemophilia for a primary disease," he said. "Chronic Type B Hepatitis. And an infected shoulder. That's what brought me in, the damned shoulder. Otherwise I'd have stayed home where I belong."

Instantly, Ralph grasped the implication of Two-Gus's pronouncement. The man was a born bleeder, deficient in one blood component that built life-saving clots. He'd had multiple transfusions over the years and among them, there had been one or more units of blood contaminated with the hepatitis virus. It was a known consequence of hemophilia and it accounted for Two-Gus's jaundice. For a moment, Ralph felt pity for this man, wondering how he had lived so long. He studied him.

Thirty-eight to forty years old, Two-Gus had the hollow eyes of a survivor. Under the fierce light of the cubicle, there were dark raised splotches of skin across his chest. Something clicked in the back of Ralph's mind. He tried to bring it into focus but it hovered just beyond his grasp. He was too tired.

The shoulder wound was obviously septic; Ralph's nostrils told him that. The bandage, crudely applied, was stained pinkish-yellow.

"His temp is one-oh-four," Betty said. "And his pressure is ninety over forty." She smiled at Two-Gus, grateful for his warning. She pulled out some plastic gloves and handed a pair to Ralph.

Ralph nodded, absently dropping the package on the stretcher. The patient was in shock; if the blood pressure went any lower, he'd become unconscious. He laid a hand on Two-Gus's belly and felt the patient tighten in apprehension.

The lab technician, Bill Myers, appeared at the foot of the examining table. His wire basket, filled with test tubes, clinked as he set it down. He pulled on the gloves Betty handed him.

"The usual?" He asked, bored even though his shift was just beginning.

"Yes, and type and cross match him for two units of

blood." To Betty he said, "Start an IV of D and a half-normal saline wide open." He stared at the rash on Two-Gus's chest.

"Who is your attending physician, Mr. Ragust?"

"Milly Gold. She's in hematology at the General." The chill had passed, leaving Two-Gus in exquisite calm. He wanted to sleep. "I've already called her. She'll be in."

"How long has it been since you've seen her?"

"Almost a year," Two-Gus replied. His eyes flashed open. "Why?"

"Just wondering," Ralph replied. It was a relief that this man had a specialist. Hemophilia was a bit beyond his skills. But it was obvious Ragust had neglected himself. He watched as Bill expertly withdrew his needle and tucked a pad into Two-Gus's elbow.

"You must keep pressure on it, otherwise it'll just go on bleeding," Two-Gus said.

Bill looked at Ralph in exasperation. "The nurse'll have to do it; I've got twenty blood sugars to get before breakfast."

"Do a bilirubin and transaminase while you're at it" Ralph said, as if he had not heard the complaint.

"I'll hold it," Two-Gus said. "I always do." His hand, fingers shaking, searched for and found the pad. "Listen, Doc, it's not the hepatitis I'm in for. That I've had for over a year now. It's the shoulder. It's not getting any better. Can you give me something for it? The pills I have don't help at all." He winced as Ralph palpated his belly.

"Let's examine you first, Mr. Ragust."

"Call me Two-Gus."

"How did you get that name?" Ralph studied Ragust's eyegrounds with an opthalmoscope. Their noses almost touched.

"First name's August. The second, Ragust, hence Two-Gus. My mother had a terrific sense of humor."

53

Ralph stared at Two-Gus. There was a wry smile on the patient's lips. "Tell me about your shoulder wound," he said gently.

Emma's call bell rang softly and Leah stood up, yawning. Daylight had crept into the unit without notice. Pat sat wrapped in a hospital blanket, her fist cupping her chin. Her face was pale and tired. She had been watching the cardiac monitors steadily through the long night. Her eyes were reddened. To Leah, she looked like a squaw sitting before a campfire, lost in dreams. She wondered if Pat was sleeping. They had not spoken for an hour.

"I'll get it," she said. Pat did not reply.

The television screen in Emma's room was still lit and cartoon stick characters danced across the screen. The sound was turned off. Emma looked at her and held up the BEDPAN sign, but before Leah could turn away, Emma grasped her arm and thrust her little eraseable blackboard into her hand. It read, CHICKEN OUT? Thought you'd work on me tonite."

As soon as she was sure Leah had read the message, Emma snatched back the board and flipped the plastic sheet up, erasing her words.

Without replying, Leah knelt beneath the corner cabinet and pulled out Emma's bedpan. She held it out to her and waited. Emma glared at her, her hips raised to receive the pan. Finally she grabbed it and placed it beneath her bottom, immediately releasing a roar of gas. She seemed not to notice.

"You don't need a bedpan, you know," Leah said trying to ignore the bowel sounds. "You could have gotten up to the toilet by yourself, Emma, but it seems you like to be waited on."

Sitting on the bedpan, Emma gestured wildly, pointing to the respirator and then to the toilet in the corner.

"Oh yes, it would reach. That hose can stretch to anyplace in the room and you know it. And if you wanted to wean off that vent, you'd raise holy hell to do it." She was dangerously close to losing her temper. It was the end of the shift and it always made her testy.

Emma turned her face away. Leah could see the bottom of her chin quivering. Next would come the tears and for the rest of the day, the staff would suffer Emma's black mood. Nothing would be right. Except to clamor for pain medication, Emma would not eat, would not take her physical therapy, and would not cooperate. What was more, she seemed to sense the worst possible time to call for a nurse and then she would ring the bell over and over, driving the harried staff crazy.

It was no wonder the day shift had little patience with their longest-staying patient. How she managed it, no one knew, but by the end of a bad day, Emma's temperature would be up, her abdomen distended with gas so that indeed she was in true pain, and her sputum would begin to turn green. The next day, she would be back on antibiotics once more. The nurses swore she could manage these declines by sheer will power. For all Leah knew, they were right. Well, she would try to prevent it if she could.

When she had Emma settled once more, she pulled a chair up to the bed. With Emma eyeing her warily, Leah took a deep breath and began to talk.

"What we did last night, Emma, broke all the hospital rules. Dr. Peters is going to have to be told about it, and I plan to have a little talk with him. That is why I didn't offer to wean you again. But I didn't forget it. We'll have to go by another route, that's all."

As she spoke, she could see Emma searching for and finally finding her blackboard. She began to scribble on it before Leah could finish speaking. She held it out and Leah read: "No one gives a damn. I want to go home!

Help me."

The respirator gave a great sigh. Emma's chest rose. She began to erase the blackboard, her expression no longer angry, her eyes dry and flat. It was so simple to her.

The x-ray technician helped Two-Gus to stand against the x-ray frame. She curved his arms around it in an embrace, whispered, "hold it," and quickly left the room. The plate seemed to burn the skin of his chest. He waited for the sound of the machine behind him, imagining that soft buzz as the fraction of a second of light at Hiroshima. His knees trembled from weakness.

Finally it was over and the technician helped him into the wheelchair. While she disappeared into her cubicle of darkness, he waited, his head bent over his chest, dozing. The pain in his shoulder had subsided into a dull throb. He felt tired, resentful; they hadn't given him a thing for the pain. Maybe he should have gone to General.

He tried to conjure up the picture of his chest x-ray. Was there a great dark blob on his lung? Would the technician gasp at the destruction she saw as the film emerged from the developer. He imagined her dashing from her little box of a room and enfolding him in her arms. How he would love some pity. And then cursed himself for the weakness.

With his good hand, he scratched absently at the raised violet patch on his chest. He tested himself. Were the chills gone? The air was cool, but it had not brought on another bout of shaking. He could take anything, but dreaded the chills. For the first time in hours he could close his eyes and rest. They'd forgotten all about him anyway.

* * *

Ben Weathers poured himself a cup of coffee and leaned against the conference table listening to Ralph Levering. The young doctor looked like a wraith, he thought. It's the quiet nights that make you sleepy.

"Except for the hemophiliac, there's nothing holding fire at the moment," Ralph said. He was slouched on the couch, the collar of his shirt open and his tie askew.

"What's his story?"

Ralph began a dry recitation on Two-Gus Ragust while Ben half-listened. He hated himself for quarreling with Katherine. She's stubborn, he thought, beautiful, smart . . . but as stubborn as a mule. They had enough money so that she didn't have to work. Why did she persist? He had seen the swelling of her ankles at night. He knew she slept badly now. Why was she pushing herself? He forced himself to listen to Ralph.

"Mr. Ragust presented with a septic shoulder wound this morning. I suspect that if that hadn't occured he would have gone along without any treatment for his other problems. He's not a compliant patient, I think. Anyway," Ralph yawned, "I called in Terry Sheen to look at the wound. It needs cleaning up."

"Other problems?"

"Chronic hepatitis. Sorry I didn't mention it. Seventy-five percent of factor-eight bleeders have it," Ralph said, "the poor bastards. I looked it up in the library."

He stood and stretched. "He's getting a chest film, the lab work's been done, and I've notified the ICU that they'll be getting him. The only question is . . . shall we keep him here before surgery or there? And that, my friend, I'll leave to you." He snatched up his jacket and headed for the door.

Ben wandered to the nurses' station. Hepatitis, chronic and debilitating. It was more threatening to hemophiliacs than their original disease. And it pushed them into an early grave. He made a mental note to order isolation precautions on the patient's chart as soon as he returned from X-ray. He'd also tell Katherine to keep away from the patient. That's just what she could avoid if she stayed at home, he thought moodily. He sat down and stared at the tight-jeaned buttocks of the nurse's aide as she leaned over the counter.

Ten minutes later he was standing before the x-ray holder absorbed in Two-Gus's chest film. Terence Sheen stood beside him, rolling up his sleeves and tucking his tie into his shirt. Six feet four inches tall, he was a giant of a man, with arms like cord wood and the physique of a lumberjack. His head was shaved clean and the white light of the screen cast deep hollows beneath the shining skin. He could manipulate bones as if they were matchsticks.

"Looks like an infiltrate of the left lung," he murmured. His voice was surprisingly high for such a large man.

"That's my guess," Ben said. "We'll start him on Keflex and get a sputum sample.

They were oblivious to the rush of activity around them. Technicians brushed by with their bottles and flasks. An ambulance stretcher rolled in with a moaning, shrouded figure upon it. A cry came from behind a curtained cubicle and Trish Curry hurried into the room.

Sheen sighed. "I hate septic wounds. They always come last in the day. That screws up my office hours, afternoon rounds, and my supper." Turning to Stacy Price, the head nurse, he said, "Call the operating room and tell them to schedule an I&D of a dirty shoulder."

Ben said, "Let's go take a look at him."

Stacy made a face as she watched the two doctors walk away. "I don't want that patient in my emergency room one minute longer than necessary. We're too busy to babysit him." The ward secretary nodded.

"Call OR," Stacy went on. "If they can't take him

right away then I'm shipping this patient to the unit."

"They'll hate you for it," the secretary warned. "The patient isn't critical and they'll know that you've passed the buck. They'll scream at me."

"Since when do I care what *they* want? Just call them." She dashed away from the desk, leaving the secretary scowling after her.

They had put him back in the same cubicle, but now it was freezing. Two-Gus shivered uncontrollably. This chill was the worst yet. Even the heated blanket the nurse had brought didn't help. It pricked his skin as if it were woven with needles. The intravenous bottle over his head seemed to quiver with little rainbows of light. He knew it was the fever tricking his senses, but he did not think he could take it much longer. He eyed the huge man standing by the stretcher and felt an air of danger around him. He wondered why.

As Terence Sheen peeled the bandage from his shoulder, the stench from the wound floated up into Two-Gus's nostrils. The edges of the laceration looked gnawed, Ben thought, as if by some invisible insect. Between the lips of the wound a pale green exudate oozed. Trish Curry, who had been standing by with a dressing kit in her hands, swallowed convulsively. She remembered to breathe through her mouth, but it was hard to force her jaws open. It was almost like drinking in that smell.

Sheen seemed oblivious to it. He peered at the wound with fascination. Then he stood back and peeled off his rubber gloves. "Gimme another pair," he said without taking his eyes from Two-Gus's shoulder.

"How did you get this, Mr. Ragust?" Ben asked.

"I got hit by a kid on a bicycle, of all things. He knocked me over as if I were a feather." Two-Gus's teeth chattered.

"Well, you don't weigh very much. I can see how it

happened. You should have come in sooner, though. You've got a rip-roaring infection there, as well as what looks like a touch of pneumonia." Ben began to write on the prescription sheet of Two-Gus's chart.

Two-Gus didn't like the turn of conversation. Pretty soon he'd have to say something, tell them. But what would they do? "Has Dr. Gold come in yet?" He heard himself ask. His jaw muscles ached and he was afraid of the look of fascination on the other doctor's face. He knew the shoulder wound wasn't pretty, but this guy looked at it almost hungrily.

"Not yet," Ben replied. "I'll be interested in talking to him."

"Her."

"Huh?"

"Dr. Gold is a female." It was a mistake coming here. He should have gone to Milly's hospital. All he wanted to do was lie down, warm up, and sleep, but these yokels kept pestering him with silly questions.

Now the big one looked at him. "Are you covered by insurance?"

Two-Gus closed his eyes wearily. He did not see the look of indignation that Trish threw at Sheen. "Yes, don't worry," he said.

Sheen turned away and began to scrub his hands at the little sink in the corner of the cubicle. Trish laid a sterile gauze dressing over the wound.

"Don't rip your glove," Two-Gus whispered. "Hepatitis, you know." He looked up at her and saw a smile as sweet and gentle as he'd ever seen in his life. It pierced his heart and brought tears to his eyes. He should say it now.

"Don't worry," she whispered. She layered the dressing with paper tape.

Suddenly, Ben glanced up from the chart. "How long have you had that rash?"

"I don't know. Months, I guess." Two-Gus felt his heart accelerate. He watched as Ben whirled away and hurried from the room. He knows, Two-Gus said to himself and turned his eyes towards Terence Sheen.

The big man had finished wiping his hands. Now he lobbed the paper towel into a bin in the corner and, satisfied that it was a neat basket, turned to Two-Gus. Leaning back against the sink, he folded his arms across his chest.

"We are going to have to operate on that shoulder of yours. I'm sure you realize that." He waited for a response and when there was none, went on. "And when we're finished cleaning it out, we will leave a continuous drain in there to make sure all the infection washes away. Do you understand?"

This time he waited until Two-Gus finally nodded. Satisfied, he rubbed his hands together and cracked his knuckles with a rich arching of his fingers.

"How about my bleeding?"

"We'll have to work around it. And we'll have a blood supply on hand in case you run low. Don't worry about it."

Two-Gus bit his lips together to prevent a harsh bark of laughter. "I won't."

"Good, then I'll see you later today." Sheen left the cubicle and the little room suddenly seemed larger, cleaner.

He hadn't realized when the chill left him. Probably when he felt the big ball of fright settling in his stomach, he thought. Scared the shit out of it. He pulled up the cotton blanket and managed to cover his shoulder with it. The pain was less now. He closed his eyes feeling abandoned once again.

At quarter to seven Emma Bond put on her light once

again. With a pointed fingernail grown long and sharp just for the purpose of using it as a pencil, she wrote what was for her a lengthy note on her plastic blackboard. Then she pressed the call bell.

When Leah entered the room, Emma held out the board. As usual, her note was simple and direct: "If I use the toilet instead of bedpan will you wean me tonight? Deal? I have to know if I can breathe for one minute off this f---ing machine."

Leah suppressed a grin. Emma's use of profanity was confined only to silent mouthings of the word.

"Do you mean that there's to be no more bedpan?"

Emma nodded.

"Ever?"

Emma wrote: "Throw it away."

"Alright then. But the deal is that I'm in charge of the weaning. If I think it's time to quit, I'll put you back on. No heroics, understand?"

Emma wrote: "You think I can do it, huh?"

"I'm sure you can."

Emma held out her hand and Leah grasped it. They looked at each other. Despite the misgiving she felt over her commitment, there was a little excitement deep in her heart. Leah thought of Dr. Claude Peters. He would have to accept weaning her. He'd be forced to if she have to drag him in for a demonstration. She shook Emma's fragile hand.

"Deal. Now to prove it, tell the nurses on the day shift that you'll be using the toilet from now on. I want it written in the chart for Dr. Peters to see and to prove to me that you're keeping your side of the deal."

Emma shrugged and nodded as if to say, "Of course." Then her lips opened up and she mouthed the words, "Have a nice day." It was a sneer in perfect parody of an inane television ad, that coming from Emma looked obscene. The funny part was that she knew it. Her hair was standing up in gray wild wisps and the caved-in toothless smile on her lips made her look like a haggard witch. Leah knew she knew it. She burst out laughing.

Katherine Weathers looked up at the sound coming from Emma's room. As Leah sat down beside her, she lifted an eyebrow questioningly.

"I thought you were going home."

Leah shook her head. "I thought so too, before I went in to Emma. Now I have to wait to talk to Claude Peters. He and I have some dealing to do."

"Care to tell me about it? I mean, as head nurse, don't you think I . . . ?"

"Can it, Katherine. I was just going to talk to you. Don't get yourself in an uproar. Mothers-to-be have to learn patience y'know."

"Can it yourself, my dear. Just because you've already accomplished motherhood doesn't give you an edge on perfection."

They smiled at each other. Leah's gaze slid to Katherine's belly.

"You should be home knitting booties. Why don't you?"

"You should be home tending your baby. Go."

"Emma wants to get the hell out of here," Leah said abruptly. "I'm going to twist Claude's arm about it. Will you check with the switchboard and see if he's checked in?"

Katherine sighed. "Sometimes I hate primary nursing. It tends to make autocrats of us. In the good old days, nurses never did this. They gave backrubs, made beds, and stood in the presence of physicians." She picked up the telephone.

"If it makes you feel better, I'll go down on my hands and knees before Dr. Peters."

"He'd love that," Katherine said, rolling her eyes. "He'd unzip his pants in a flash." She spoke into the phone and then hung up. "He's on Four West. Want me to page him?" When Leah shook her head, Katherine took a deep breath.

"Listen, Leah. Don't think we all wouldn't like to see Emma get better. She's stuck here, it's as simple as that. When she first came in, we tried everything to get her to breathe, you know that. But she fails everytime. If it isn't pneumonia, it's her belly, or her nerves, or it's simply her personality. Whatever it is, she fails to wean. Chronic lungers have something other than poor lungs. They have character defects, I think. It makes them play breathing games with themselves and later with us. Maybe they are at war with the world, I don't know. I hate to see them coming, because they are a pain to get rid of. Emma's the worst of 'em."

"Yes, that's true. But I think we've given up on her and that's not right, either. It must a living hell in here for her. I've got to try and if we all work at it, maybe she'll get out of here. I'm not saying that she'll walk out of here and into the sunset, but even to get her into a bed on the floors would be an accomplishment, don't you think?"

"I'll go along with anything you can work up. Just don't be disappointed if you fail." The telephone buzzed at Katherine's side and she picked it up. It was Ben. She could hear the background noises of the emergency room behind his soft voice. She waved Leah away.

"I just wanted to tell you that I'm sorry," he said.

Katherine's eyes widened. Coming from Ben an apology was a major concession. They had quarreled on the way to work. Not seriously, nor too angrily, either. Simply what she had come to term, 'the same old issue': he wanted her to leave nursing and settle down into domesticity. She drove the car as he slouched against the passenger door, arms crossed and dark face staring through the window.

She tried to explain again, for what seemed the

hundredth time, that if she left her job now to await the baby's arrival, she'd have less time after it arrived. It made sense to save up her maternity leave.

But he had remained unconvinced. She dropped him at the emergency room door. Before leaving, he had leaned into the car window and said, "Dammit, Katherine, how long can you carry on this female macho crap? Look at yourself, you're as big as a house. I'll bet you can't get out of your own way in an emergency."

That stung. She pressed the window button, forcing him to withdraw hastily. She backed up the car with tires screeching and by the time she reached the employees's parking lot, tears were running down her cheeks.

"Please," Ben said now, his voice strained. "Let's forget this morning. I don't know why I'm so damned stubborn with you. I . . . ," he coughed. "I love you, babe. Can we forget the whole thing?"

Out of the corner of her eye, she could see that Leah had gathered up her coat and was preparing to leave the unit. Sandy Pearson, her hands filled with intravenous lines, had stopped her and was talking excitedly.

"Look, Ben," she said quickly. "I accept your apology, but only because I don't have much choice from here. If I were there, I might take a poke at you for what you said." She could hear him laugh. "Will you meet me for lunch?"

"Yes, but there's another reason for this call. I've got a troublesome case down here and you'll be getting it."

She searched for the telephone message she had gotten from the emergency room. "I have it. Mr. August Ragust, septic shoulder, right?"

"Among other problems. The shoulder is the least of it. He's going to be on wound precautions and, Katherine, I want you to stay away from him. Do you understand?"

"No, but I will. I don't have time to go around

touching patients, not with this phone always ringing, and prima donna physicians calling me to apologize for their little temper tantrums. Will you meet me for lunch?"

"Yep. Twelve o'clock on the nose." He hung up.

When she replaced the phone, she eyed Sandy until the other nurse caught the gaze. Sandy was, as usual aglitter with excitement. She flushed as she noticed Katherine's gaze.

"I was telling Leah about the Shuster creep's raise. If it's true," she rattled on, "then I'll resign my job. There are other hospitals that would grab me up."

Sandy's rush of words seemed to assault Katherine. There was little that escaped Sandy Pearson's attention. She was always ready for trouble; she thrived on it. Though it made her an inveterate gossip, and a minor troublemaker, that very quality made her a good emergency nurse. The problem was that she knew she was good and if she left Liberty Hill it would be a true loss to the hospital.

"I already know about it, Sandy," Leah said. "And I'd wait to hear the truth before I submit my resignation if I were you. Let's give the city the benefit of the doubt. Maybe they're planning a bigger raise for us than we know."

"Dreamer! We'll see. Tracy's calling a meeting to discuss it. Are you going? Everyone will be there."

Leah opened the door to the corridor. "I wouldn't miss it for the world." She winked at Katherine before letting the door close.

Sandy turned to Katherine. "Well, I've got two I.V.'s to change, three suctionings, and, if Emma lets me, a complete bed bath for her. Will she or won't she? Only Emma knows."

"Let her bathe herself. She isn't a cripple." By the tone of her voice, Katherine let Sandy know there was not to be an argument.

"That's okay with me, it's less work, but you know she won't wash. . . ." Her argument died away at the steely look Katherine gave her. With a toss of her head, she disappeared into Emma's room to deliver the news.

In the emergency room, a steady stream of patients flowed in. One by one, Ben attended to their problems. A laceration to be sutured, an asthmatic that needed a breathing treatment, an eighty-year-old man with mild heart failure. A dose of Lasix and later a urinal filled to almost overflowing relieved the breathing. Protesting that he could now return home, the old man was wheeled away to be deposited in a bed on the third floor. In less than an hour, the cubicles were empty and the flow of patients had diminished. Ben entered Two-Gus's room.

"I thought I'd been abandoned," Two-Gus said. "Is Milly Gold here yet?"

Ben shook his head as he dragged a tall stool to the edge of Two-Gus's stretcher. "Not yet. But I suspect she's on her way. Right now, you and I have to have a little talk, Mr. Ragust."

Instantly, a wary look came over Two-Gus's face. "Alright. I'm listening."

Bluntly, Ben said, "I believe you haven't told us your complete story. If I am right, then you simply must. It might be tough to do, but there still remains patient confidentiality between us. I can't order any treatment for you until I know about the total patient. Is there something more?"

"That's why I'm waiting for Milly," Two-Gus replied.

"Dammit, man, do you have AIDS? I have to know!"

Two-Gus struggled to sit up and automatically Ben reached over to help. Finally, with his legs dangling over the edge of the stretcher and his shoulder cupped by his left hand, Two-Gus darted a level look at Ben.

"I never liked being flat on my back when I'm threatened. Now you understand something, Dr. Weathers. I have hepatitis. It's documented in that record of yours," he cocked his head at the chart in Ben's lap. "It requires isolation precautions that involve bodily secretions. That's all this place has to know."

"How can I help you if you won't level with me?"

"What are you going to do, cure me?"

There was a deadly silence in the little room and a sad smile came over Two-Gus's face. "Gets 'em everytime, that phrase."

Both men glanced at the doorway as a thick gutteral voice said, "Are you bullying the good doctor, Two-Gus? Now stop it this instant!"

Milly Gold teetered into the examining room on the highest heels Ben had ever seen. Even with the extra four inches it gave her, Milly's head was no higher than the highest bar on Two-Gus's stretcher. Ben stared at her. Though her hair was a white with little tufts that stood up around her face, her eyes were dark and humorous, with a fringe of heavily mascaraed eyelashes. Instantly, Ben was reminded of a certain pygmy lemur he'd seen at the Bronx Zoo. He was unaware that his mouth had fallen open, until Milly reached up and gently forced it closed. Then he blushed.

"Milly Gold," she said, "and I am not Dr. Ruth though I admit to a resemblance." She held out her hand and Ben took it. "If you like, I'll take him off your hands and back to Boston where he belongs." When she smiled Ben could see a row of sharp ferretlike teeth.

"How do you do?" He felt like a schoolboy. "I'm Ben Weathers. And if he is your patient, am I ever glad to see you." He wasn't aware he had risen until he realized that now Milly came up to only his belt buckle, forcing her to tip her head back at a sharp angle. He didn't know whether to sit again or not. She didn't give him the chance. She pulled herself up onto the stool and turned to face Two-Gus. Covertly, Ben looked her over.

He guessed her age as sixty, give or take a few years. That she had had a face-lift was obvious to his practiced eye. The skin of her face was taut as a sheet, pulling at the corners of her mouth so that she had a perpetual grin. Bad plastic work, he thought automatically. Up close, he could see that her hair had been sprayed with something that forced the tufts of hair to stand up by themselves. Around her eyes, and even drawn on the inside of her inner lid, she had penciled a black line. The mascaraed lashes were fake. Her shocking pink suit rode up over fleshy knees as she sat on the stool. There was a run in one of her stockings. Ben swallowed back the smile he felt coming over his face. He had to remind himself that this startling-looking creature was a bona fide physician.

Milly leaned close to Two-Gus, and Ben could see an almost sheepish expression come over the patient's face.

"Answer me, young man. Have you been fooling around with this good doctor?"

"Oh Christ, Milly, I came here to avoid all that crap. I just wanted to get something for this shoulder and be on my way. Now it seems they want me to stay, or they want me to go. I don't know."

"You're a damn fool if you think you can run away from the truth." She pronounced it "troot." "How long did you think you could get away with it?" She swiveled on the stool to face Ben.

"Last year, we picked up the HIV virus in his blood. He must have been transfused with contaminated blood at some time and up to now has carried the virus without symptoms." As though Two-Gus was merely a specimen, she pulled down his johnny and studied the spotted chest. "Now obviously, he's demonstrating a manifestation of disease."

Angrily, she went on, "Dammit, Two-Gus. Why haven't you been in to see me?"

"I'll ask the same queation I've just asked the doctor here. What are you going to do, cure me?"

"Of course not, you fool. Don't be dramatic. But we must keep track of you for the record. And there are new treatments available—"

Two-Gus held up his hand to stop her. "Spare me. All I want is to clean up this shoulder and go home."

"That's what we want also," Ben reminded him.

"No, you want to indict me and leave me to the mercy of a frightened bunch of nurses."

"Oh, for God's sakes," Milly exclaimed. She turned to Ben. "He knows there's isolation with hepatitis, he's afraid of solitary confinement. It's the same routine, Two-Gus. No more, no less. You know the protocol for hepatitis. It's the same for AIDS."

"Tell that to the nurses," Two-Gus said, suddenly weary. He tried to lie back on the stretcher. Milly reached over and supported his shoulder while Ben lifted his legs.

"Now that I know, I will," Ben said. It sounded simple, but he knew there'd be some problems on the floors. Liberty Hill now had its first AIDS patient. How would this place handle it? He tucked a blanket around the patient and pulled up the safety rails. Then he turned and saw the hand held out to him.

"Help me down, big boy, will you?" Milly batted her eyelashes at him with a wide helpless stare. Together, they left the examining room. Two-Gus watched them until they were out of sight.

This time he was wide awake staring at the tiled ceiling and listening to the thud of his heart. It occured to him that he hadn't had a chill in over an hour. The antibiotic must be taking hold, he reasoned. How simple that was. As for the other . . . He couldn't even say the word. He had tried to put it from his mind, these past months.

Careful, oh yes, he'd been careful. Even to the point of carrying his own utensils into restaurants, staying locked in his apartment at the slightest sign of a cold or cough, avoiding crowds and finding only quiet streets to walk. He'd even stopped visiting his sister. The children, after all, were only tots. The lifelong loneliness of a bleeder was nothing compared to his self-imposed isolation of these past months, watching himself carefully for some sign of this new disease. It had been lonely, yes, but at least he'd been free. Now he was trapped and scared shitless.

It wasn't the disease; its outcome was certain and years ago he'd faced up to his own mortality. After all, his body had never been a safe haven, it was always devising some nasty little trick that left him flat on his face. It was that uncertain look on Milly's face and in Dr. Weathers's eyes that terrified him. They didn't know what to do with him!

He could hear Milly's high voice bark staccato laughter outside the door. If it weren't for this damned shoulder, and the fact that he needed the intravenous, he'd gather up his clothes and leave. An inner voice agreed.

Chapter Five

"Nikki's fine, dear. He's getting ready to help me open up the store." Maddy's voice came over the line, clear and happy. She went on to describe Nikki's breakfast, diaper change, and Red's clumsy efforts to help. With the phone clamped to her ear, Leah eyed the doctor sitting in the cafeteria. "Have your breakfast there and come home when you can," Maddy went on.

"Thanks, Mom. I shouldn't be too much longer." She hung up and walked quickly through the cafeteria line, keeping an eye on Claude Peters. He was alone at a table and she wanted him to stay that way until she could get there. She loaded her tray with milk and cereal and coffee, and fumbled for change at the cash register. He was through. She could see him folding up the newspaper and gathering up his dishes. Balancing her tray and jacket, she hurried through the cigarette haze of the smokers' section, holding her breath. She did not see Tracy Webb's curious gaze.

"Dr. Peters? Hello. Will you wait a moment?"

He glanced around to see who was calling him and when he saw her, an eyebrow rose and a little smile crept over his face. Instantly she felt stripped and naked. He always did that to her.

"I wanted to talk with you about a patient," she said, placing her tray on the table. "Have you got a minute?"

"For you, all the time in the world." He was trying to read her name badge, for although he saw her every day, to Claude Peters she was just another luscious body.

She became suddenly aware of the little stir of interest she had created in the cafeteria. Oh, lord, she thought, now I'm going to be his next conquest. It'll be all over the Hill by noon today. Even Julian Plumhouse, the administrator, had glanced up at her call. She flushed at the mild interest he gave her.

"I'm Leah Swift. I work in the ICU, remember? Well, probably you don't, but I wanted to talk with you about a patient up there, Emma Bond." She sat down in the chair he held out for her.

"Emma Bond? Emma Bond..." Then his face cleared. "Oh yeah, our chronic lunger. What's the matter with her? Pneumonia again? I'll order a chest x-ray, okay? How's that for service? Now, what *else* can I do for you?" His gaze was fixed on her chest making her feel slimy.

"I want to try weaning her again."

He was, despite all the nasty gossip he generated, a handsome man with straight blond hair worn fashionably cut across his forehead. It was perfect. He probably worked on it, she thought. His mouth was full and wide under a brush of blond moustache and his teeth were perfect. Five thousand dollars perfect, they said. Claude Peters was forty years old, enormously rich, if one could judge by the twin Mercedes he and his wife drove, and an uncomplicated Don Juan.

Whatever she had said, he found amusing, for he threw his head back and gave a hearty bray of laughter designed to capture an audience. She wanted to spill her Rice Krispies down the front of his dark silk suit. Instead she managed a sweet smile. He gave Julian Plumhouse a little wave and the administrator nodded at him.

Peters leaned over and covered her hand with his own. "Emma Bond is my patient, dear, not yours." From afar she knew the gesture probably looked like a lovers' tête à tête. She managed not to move.

"Then why don't you treat her like one?" She batted her eyelashes at him.

"I'd rather treat you. Forget Emma."

"I can't, she's stuck there. We have to look at her every day, which is more than I can say for you. Have you seen her lately? I mean *really* seen her?" His hand tightened over hers.

"Don't fuck around with me, honey. I'd hate to see a pretty thing like you get hurt. Do you know what you need? You need a good—"

"I know what Emma needs. Emma needs some attention," she broke in quickly. She felt a tremor go through the hand holding hers. "As a matter of fact, she's my patient, too, and she's getting damned good nursing care. I wish I could say the same for her medical treatment. She should be working on getting out of here, for God's sake." She bared her teeth and held the smile until her cheeks ached.

Claude Peters pulled his hand away and sat back in the chair, studying her. The covetous look was gone. Now there was only cold curiosity in his blue eyes.

"Why do you care about her?" He said. "A patient is a patient. They either get better or they don't. Emma's not a good one. She has lungs like rocks and without a ventilator she'll croak. You've been here long enough to know that."

"She still deserves a little effort from us. Look, all I want is your permission and the blood gas orders to wean Emma Bond. We'll take it from there and if we fail, we fail. If, however, she improves it'll look good for all of us."

"Apparently you think I've not tried with this patient. Read her chart, it might open your eyes. And it might keep your mouth from running overtime. You bleeding heart nurses operate on emotion, not scientific data. Cool it, Miss Swift. Stick to your bedpans and backrubs and I'll handle the medical aspects of my patients. And thanks for the vote of confidence."

He stood up, shot his cuffs into place and buttoned his silk jacket. By the time she could muster an outraged reply, he was threading his way through the cafeteria and she was left sputtering to herself. And then cursing her own lack of diplomacy. Swell behavior, old girl, she said to herself. The first encounter with Peters and already he hates me. Her hand was shaking as she picked up the cup and sipped the cold coffee.

"That was quite a little exhibition. Good for you, Leah. He made a move and you turned him right around. That'll make him think a little. Maybe for five minutes." A voice came from behind her. It was Tracy Webb, standing with her head cocked to one side, her dark eyes inquisitive. She slapped her hand against her mouth. "Mind your own business, Tracy Webb." Her great white cap was quivering. "There I said it for you."

She was being playful this morning and Leah wondered why. It was not Tracy's style. In fact, the supervisor's eyes were dancing with excitement. "I can only stay for a minute before rounds. I wanted to ask you a favor. Since I never get a chance to see the night nurses, I wondered if you could pass the word on that I'm calling a meeting tonight at seven o'clock. They'll want to come, I'm sure."

"What's it about?" She knew already, thanks to the hospital's night-time grapevine, but she could see that Tracy was anxious to pass the word on herself.

"The possibility of some sort of action to protest our contract stalling. I suppose you've heard that Local 207 got theirs and a damned good one, too. Everyone is furious over Shuster's raise. You'll come, won't you?"

"What sort of action, Tracy?"

"That depends on the nurses' mood. I'm just their representative. Whatever they want, I'll give them."

"Not a strike. I'd never go along with a strike."

"I doubt it'll come to that, but it's time we woke up those city attorneys. They've stalled us long enough to justify some sort of action. Will you call them?"

Without waiting for a reply, she gathered up her report books and clasped them to her chest as if they were government documents, which in a way, they were. The books contained information on all two hundred and fifty patients at Liberty Hill. With them, Tracy could keep track of the condition and change on each one.

Abruptly, her manner changed. "I know it's none of my business, but did that little altercation with Peters happen to concern a patient?" There it was.

She knew Tracy wanted the details, but she'd be damned if she'd tell her. What she had done was a sin in Tracy's eyes. Nurses and physicians did not collaborate, because doctors couldn't be trusted, Tracy maintained. If "push comes to shove," as her favorite saying went, the nurse would always be the loser.

Though they were on different sides of the fence, Tracy and Claude Peters were a lot alike. If he knew Leah had started the weaning process without his permission, he would report her to Tracy and Tracy would be only too happy to record it on her personnel file. It was the ultimate threat hanging over any nurse's head.

She shook her head and Tracy sighed with relief. "Then I'm off. See you tonight."

The cafeteria had emptied and now Leah was alone, except for Julian Plumhouse. He was outlined against the plate-glass window and sunlight threw his form into darkness. She picked up the *Boston Globe* that Peters had left behind, and skimmed through it rapidly. On the back page of the living section, a short article caught her eye, the announcement of a new drug treatment for hemophiliacs with AIDS. She hadn't thought of hemophiliacs when she thought of the epidemic. She read then that sixty-two percent of all hemophiliacs are exposed to the AIDS virus. She put the paper down, feeling her scalp crawl. There had been hemophiliacs in the unit. Carefully she tore out the article and folded it up. It would go on the bulletin board in the ICU for all to see. Then she creased the newspaper into a semblance of its original form so that if Peters came back for it, he would not see the mutilation right away.

Julian Plumhouse followed Leah through the corridor until she pushed through the oak doors. For a moment he hesitated, torn between the endless paperwork that awaited him in his office and the vista of sunlight and blue sky outside. Then he pushed through the doors and stepped outside. Instantly the glare of light blinded him and the salt air from the harbor floated into his nostrils. It was as if he'd taken a whiff of nasal spray. He inhaled deeply, always a little shocked at the smell. There was nothing like this in Minnesota. He looked around for the girl.

She was seated on the granite bench that ringed the front of the hospital, her head thrown back and her eyes closed to the sun. She had unpinned the long blond braid and it was dangling over the back of the bench. Her lips were scrubbed of color and her cheekbones were porcelain white wings over hollowed cheeks. She had pushed off her shoes, and now with legs stretched before her she looked like a Nordic princess asleep on a hill beside a fjord. Too romantic as usual, he chided himself. She was just damned tired after a long night.

He had tried to avoid watching her fend off Claude Peters, but knowing what the physician was up to, it had been hard to ignore. In another moment he would have gotten up and walked over to intervene. Instead, he had watched as she neatly sent him on his way without any help from him at all. Mentally he gave her a private cheer. That damned fool Peters was going to lose his job if he didn't keep his sex life out of Liberty Hill. As soon as he could find the time he was going to give the playboy physician a strong lecture.

His shadow crossed before her, darkening the brilliance behind her closed eyelids. She opened her eyes and squinted at him. When she saw who it was, she straightened up, feeling a blush rise along her neck. Fumbling with her toes until they found her shoes, she thrust her feet into them and began to rise.

"No, please don't leave," he said, his voice gentle. "I'm sorry if I disturbed you." On impulse, he sat down beside her and lifted his face to the sun. She stared at him.

"I almost dozed off completely," she said. "It's so warm and peaceful here." She turned to gather up her jacket and glanced at her watch. It was eight-fifteen.

"I'm Julian Plumhouse," he said, not opening his eyes. "What's your name?"

She laughed. "I know you. Everybody knows the new administrator. I'm Leah Swift from the ICU."

He reached over and shook her hand. "It's rare that I get a chance to sit with a member of the staff. Maybe I ought to schedule something like this for every sunny morning. Front porch diplomacy, I'd call it."

"It would get you a lot of friends," she laughed. She found herself perched on the edge of the bench waiting for him to say something. Instead he stretched his legs out and closed his eyes. The light seemed to take out the deep crease between his eyes.

Over his shoulder, the Boston skyline loomed through the cables of the Tobin Bridge, a city of glass and steel.

From the harbor below, a faint cry of gulls lifted to the top of the hill. She could see them milling at the stern of a fishing trawler that was making its way to the pier.

The marina was tucked out of sight, but she knew Red was down there setting out moorings, probably with Nikki clamped between his knees helping his grandfather with the oars. It took several days to place the red floats in the water, but soon the cove would be dotted with them as if some child had let his box of marbles fall loose upon a sheet of blue. And later, there'd be a forest of masts filling the harbor. The frantic pace of a busy yachtyard in summer would begin.

It was this time of year she loved the best, when the water slapped lazily against the empty docks, when the marina shop was a quiet place of dusty light and oil smells and coils of line. She thought of the cove as her harbor of refuge. Later when the yachts came and nudged against the docks and the wind made a noisy concert of flapping sails, she would feel a little stir of resentment at the sight of the sleek boats. They would crowd her cove. It would make her restless and edgy.

This year it would be even worse: she'd have Nikki to worry about. She would have to keep an especially careful eye on him when the marina got busy. A careless door left open and he would be down on the dock in a flash. When the store filled with customers and Maddy was busy waiting on them he'd be vulnerable to either the water or some overly friendly stranger. The thought made her stand up abruptly. Plumhouse looked up at her startled.

"I'm sorry, but I can't stay. I have a little boy waiting for me."

"Let me give you a ride home. It wouldn't be any trouble. In fact, I would enjoy the break."

She shook her head, conscious of the warning signs inside. The look in his eyes was not impersonal, it was warm and curious and it had been so long since she felt an answering stir that she did not recognize it. She only knew that it had nothing to do with his being the head of Liberty Hill or her being an employee. It made her a little weak in the knees.

"It's only down the hill. I walk it every day." A feeble set of words if she ever heard them. She could tell he thought so, too.

He stood up. "Hills can be torture to tired legs. I insist. Besides you can talk to me about hospital problems. It'll be a good chance to air your feelings and I'm a good listener. We'll call it a professional conference. That way I won't feel guilty about leaving this place and you won't have to walk home alone."

He held out his arm so that automatically she had to take it. Together, they descended the stairs to the next level. At the curb he guided her towards the parking lot. Oddly, she had the feeling that he was rescuing her, but from what she did not know.

He settled her into his car, taking care to help her with her seatbelt. She had thought it would be a conservative car, but she hadn't expected a dark blue Cadillac. It had honey-colored leather seats that smelled new and deliciously rich. With the engine purring, he pushed a button and the sunroof slid open. Instantly the car filled with the sweet scent of spring. Somewhere nearby a lilac bush was in full bloom. The Boston skyline dipped behind the Hill and as he drove down the spiraling street, she covertly studied him.

She knew he had been brought to Atwater in a last ditch effort to save the hospital from bankruptcy. Choked by its own proximity to Boston and hopelessly outclassed by its great hospitals, Liberty Hill was fast becoming a liability to the city of Atwater. How could it survive with that giant across the river? It was old, its physical plant was hopelessly outdated, and the city council could only patch and repatch to keep it going.

In a last desperate effort, before closing its doors forever, they'd charged Plumhouse with the job of bringing new life into the old hospital. It was a desperate gamble for they sensed that without Liberty Hill, Atwater would become a failed city, absorbed into the sprawling giant across the river. There was already a tired air to the town: the navy yard had closed its doors and unemployment lines seemed permanent. There had to be a way to keep the old place going if only to give jobs to its workers.

Somewhere out in the Midwest, she'd forgotten where, Julian Plumhouse had saved a hospital under similar circumstances. She had read about it in the newspaper when his appointment was made. He'd even been pictured on the cover of *Hospital Times* for it. They'd called him the Great White Hope of Hospitals.

In one furious year of hard work, he had done it. He had turned it around so that Liberty Hill was becoming a source of pride in the city. "He had a simple solution," Red Swift had commented, "too simple for those politicians at City Hall to think of. Leave it to an outsider to solve their problems for them."

Julian Plumhouse had been clever enough to recognize the value of patriotism. He went directly to the people, begging, cajoling, and instilling a sense of pride among the townsfolk. Soon, what was a trickle of promises, almost laughingly given, became a torrent of pledges and the town began to unite to protect and defend their old hospital. Even Julian had been astounded at the response he'd generated. Like a terrier after a rat, he charged across the river and into the capitol building. Soon state coffers began to tilt his way. From there to federal funding was almost easy. Once again his picture went on the covers of papers and magazines and there were rumors of a senate seat that was his for the taking.

How he'd done it, Leah did not know, but she sensed it

had been a herculean effort. All she knew was that since she'd come back to Atwater, there was pride once again in the city. The Hill had come alive. Even the four streets leading to the summit had become part of the excitement. Row houses were spruced up and young executives flocked into them. Trees were planted along the cobbled streets and gas lamps restored. Finally the harbor at the foot of the hill began to stir. Though the navy yard was not to reopen, great designs for the waterfront were drawn.

He drove skillfully, weaving the heavy car through the narrow streets, his hands resting lightly on the wheel. He was a handsome man. He had a strong nose over full lips, and with the light flashing through the sun roof, she could see flecks of silver in his tightly curled hair. It was kinky and soft and she suspected that he kept it cut short because it would otherwise halo in a wild fringe around his head in a style that was no longer fashionable. She guessed he was in his forties and decided that he would age beautifully. He caught her study of him and smiled.

"Do you think they'll stage a walk out?"

His voice startled her. "Who?" she said.

"The nurses . . . The meeting tonight. Are they going on strike?"

Naturally, he'd know about the discontent. After all, he was part of the bargaining committee. Still, she wondered how he'd learned of tonight's meeting.

"They're very angry and I don't know what they will do. If they walk out, I don't think I'd blame them. They've been insulted."

"I know," he said, tapping his blunt fingers against the leather steering wheel. "And I don't blame them either. Those damned fools at City Hall have thrown a wrench in the cog. And they don't know it, either. It threatens all the work I've done this past year. To think we've come this far only to have those idiots jeopardize the hospital.

They just don't know what a strike will do to them."

"What will it do?"

"It will close the hospital," he said simply. Almost to himself he added, "This is a good example of why a city should not be in the health care business. They don't know hospitals.... They haven't the first notion about running one.

"Don't spread this around, Miss Swift, but my next goal is to establish a hospital authority. And when that happens..." Leah was amused that to him it was only a matter of time to accomplish it, "then the nurses will have an easier time bargaining. They'll be dealing with professionals like yourself."

The heavy car dipped onto Front Street. He looked at her.

"Which way?"

"Straight across," she replied.

For a moment he looked puzzled. "But there's nothing there, just a boatyard."

"It may be a boat yard, but it's home to me." She began to laugh at the discomfiture that came over his features. "Don't apologize. It *is* strange, I know. It's like living in a glass bowl, but I'm used to it. I grew up here."

She could see his interest. His eyebrows rose and he cocked an eye at her. "I knew there was more to you than meets the eye. How intriguing! And how lucky you are to live right on the water."

The Cadillac eased across the street and pulled into the parking lot. Julian shut off the engine and leaned across the steering wheel with his arms crossed over it. He studied the cove with undisguised interest.

"I'll bet you have a boat, too."

"Just a day sailor," she said. "But I haven't put it in the water this year. Nikki's too young to take out."

"Is there a husband around, also?" He let the question slip out a little too casually.

"No. There is an ex-husband somewhere in Florida." For a moment she felt a tug of disloyalty towards Tony and then dismissed it. That was over.

"I have one of those, too. Only she's back in Minnesota. No kids, thank God. I don't think I could leave a kid behind."

She fumbled with the door handle. "I really must go. I'm late as it is." She felt his hand on her arm.

"It's Leah, isn't it?" She nodded. "Well, Leah, I won't keep you, but I want to come back. May I? I mean, to have you show me around? I'm a landsman and this is a whole new world to me." He lifted his hand and let it sweep over the cove.

"Any time," she said. "As soon as I'm off nights, that is."

Quickly he asked, "When is that?"

"In two days."

"That makes it Sunday. Perfect, I'll bring sandwiches."

She laughed, but quickly sobered at the look in his eyes. It was dark and promising and once again she felt an answering stir inside. She slid from the car, pulling her coat and bag behind.

"But you didn't say yes," he called after her.

"Yes!" The word spilled over her shoulder as she fled through the chain-link gate.

She walked slowly down the gangplank, listening for the sound of his car driving away. Somehow, she hoped he would follow her down this deeply swaying walk. It was crazy but she wanted to show him the marina now, not Sunday. She wanted him to see Nikki and see what the two of them made of each other. Why that mattered, she could not say. She heard the heavy-throated purr of the Cadillac and the soft crunch of his tires on the gravel.

* * *

When Milly's high voice faded from the corridor outside, Two-Gus began to get angry. All the haste to get here was wasted. The speed with which the ambulance attendants had bundled him onto the stretcher, the low growl of siren at each intersection as the ambulance sped through the sleeping streets, the way they'd pounced on him the minute he'd entered the hospital was, in retrospect, ridiculous. All he'd done since then was wait.

He should have known better. All a patient does is wait. Wait for the next test, the operation, the treatment. Whatever it was, it was always coming and never over till the day of discharge. Still, it seemed that the least they could do was put him in a room of his own while he waited. Somehow, if they would do that he could accept the next chill that was coming or endure the pain in his shoulder. Narrow it down to just a bed of his own and he could create a nest of it. Its homey comfort would help. He stared morosely at the ceiling.

There was a flurry of activity in the cubicle next to his. He could hear the low rumble of voices. Something struck his curtain and sent it billowing around his stretcher. When it settled into place he could see a set of wheels being pulled into the space next to his. He knew it was another patient brought in haste and condemned to wait.

There was no sound from behind the curtain, no gasp of pain, no protest. Only silence. He listened idly to the quiet voice of Dr. Weathers.

"Standard blood work, EKG, and an intravenous of . . ." Two-Gus knew Ben was weighing his options. "One quarter dextrose. We don't know what we've got with this woman. Why the hell is she unconscious? Is there anyone who came in with her?"

"A boy." Trish replied. "Maybe a son, I think. Want me to get him?"

"Yes. Maybe he can tell us something. No wait a

minute. Doesn't she smell sweet?" There was silence for a second. "Get a Foley catheter in her and test her urine."

Two-Gus looked through the glass panel at the foot of his cubicle. There, pressed against the glass, was a boy stretching his neck and trying to peer through the curtain. His eyes slid over Two-Gus's face unseeing. Fright filled his face. It boiled up in red pimples across his forehead. The rest of his face was blanched. A sweep of blond hair curled over his ears and his lips were full and trembling. Two-Gus thought he saw the sheen of tears in the boy's eyes.

Then he heard Trish call out softly. "Mrs. Fellows? Dorothy! We're going to put a tube in your bladder to help empty it. Can you hear me?"

There was no answer. Two-Gus glanced back at the youngster, but he had turned away and now leaned against the glass, his head bowed. Ben Weathers came into view and placed his hand on the boy's shoulders. The child seemed to cave into the curve of Ben's arm and Two-Gus felt a lump form in his throat. He watched as they walked away from the glass wall and disappeared. Some good doc, he thought.

Stacy Price was watching also. She saw Ben take the boy into their lounge. "They're not supposed to do that. That's *our* room," she sniffed. "At least Dr. Weathers is out of sight finally. I thought he'd never leave. Let's get that hepatitis patient out of here right now, before he gets back."

The secretary stared at Stacy. "He's supposed to wait here until the OR takes him."

"The hell with that. I'm moving him. Did you call Katherine?"

The secretary nodded. "Yes. You told me to, and I did."

Without another word, Stacy rose and headed for

Two-Gus's cubicle. When Two-Gus felt the stretcher move, he opened his eyes and gazed up at Stacy. "The operating room?"

"No. Your own room. Intensive Care."

As his stretcher passed the curtain, Two-Gus peered in and saw the still form of the woman beside him. The bedside rails were up around her and the overhead light had been turned off. Hanging beneath the stretcher a urine bag drooped. It was nearly full. The woman snorted suddenly and a little plastic airway which had been placed in her mouth popped out. As Stacy passed by, she reached over and pushed it back in without a missing a step.

The arctic air of the ICU sent him into another spasm of shaking. He gathered the blanket under his chin and waited for the cold to consume him.

Stacy pushed him alongside Katherine's desk. "Here's your patient," she said sweetly. The stretcher rattled slightly under the assault of Two-Gus's chill and Katherine looked up. Before he closed his eyes, she was struck by the yellow whites of his eyes. This was the patient Ben told her about. He wasn't supposed to be here until later. She looked at Stacy as she rose to her feet.

"Ahead of schedule, I see. Does Ben know about this?"

"Dr. Weathers doesn't run my unit," Stacy replied. She thrust out the blue binder. "Here's his chart. There's a ton of orders in it for you. Now where do you want him?"

Katherine ignored her. "We'll put you right to bed, Mr. Ragust, and get you warmed up. I know the air is cold in here." To Stacy, she muttered through clenched lips, "Room three. Sandy Pearson will take him."

"That woman is going to drive me up a wall someday," she said to Barbara Haines as Stacy disappeared into the room. "I should report her for this but I won't. It's just what she's looking for, a good fight. Some day though..."

"She's probably in love with your husband, don't you think?" Barbara asked.

"I don't blame her," Katherine said, opening Two-Gus's chart. As she looked at the two full pages of orders Ben had written, she moaned. The first was underlined in red: *bodily secretions precautions*. It was nothing new to the ICU, they'd had many isolation cases before, from simple respiratory precaution to the full reverse-isolation procedures. Gowning up before entering the room was a nuisance to the staff because it slowed the pace of work, but it was all a part of critical care and grudgingly accepted.

Quarantine was a matter of degree, but with hepatitis it was the most stringent of them all. Not only did the nurses protect themselves from accidental innoculation, but every piece of linen, towel, and gown was double bagged and red-labeled for the safety of the laundry workers. Food utensils were made of paper or plastic and disposed of within the room the same as soiled clothing. Contaminated needles, tubings, and soiled bandages were sealed in rigid plastic and taped shut with "hazard" strips across the seams. These would be handled by collectors under strict environmental guidelines. Even after the patient was discharged, the isolation of the room continued until the housekeeping department had thoroughly disinfected it.

It was tiresome to have a quarantined patient in the unit. The long-term stay would become disheartening. Katherine could hear Sandy Pearson grumble to herself as she pulled on a paper gown and mask. It had started already.

She closed the chart and looked at Barbara. "I am not going to listen to that right now. I am going to lunch." Then she grinned. "That's not my stomach grumbling, that's the babe inside telling me to leave while I have the chance."

"Go for it," Barbara replied.

"Will you paste up the red signs while I'm gone?"

Barbara slid the "isolation" warnings from under her hand and waved them at Katherine. "One look at the yellow skin on that patient was all I needed."

"Ah, you should have been a nurse."

Barbara feigned a shudder. "No, thank you very much."

She stopped at Two-Gus's room and watched as Stacy and Sandy helped the frail man slide over onto his bed. No wonder Ben had warned her to stay away from this patient. His skin was the color of a old copper penny. A roaring case of hepatitis if she ever saw one.

To Stacy she said, "You can give report to Sandy, I'm going to lunch."

One of Stacy's eyebrows rose. "Don't be gone long, I'm sending you another patient."

Just as sweetly as she could muster herself, Katherine replied, "Not until I have an empty bed." Then she turned away.

As she passed Emma Bond's room, she glanced in. Emma was sitting upright in her bed, signaling Katherine in the only way she had, by rapping continuously on the metal rail of her bed with long ragged fingernails. It made Katherine's skin crawl.

"What do you want, Emma?"

The long hand beckoned to her and Katherine sighed. For some reason, she did not like this woman. Partly it was because of the way Emma manipulated her staff, but also it had to do with Emma's disease itself. It wasn't just this patient, it was all chronic lungers. They were strange.

She saw that Emma had written a message on her little plastic board. She tilted her head to read it.

Where's that damn doctor? I want him. (He'd love that, Katherine thought.) If he don't come, tell him I wrote the welfare people. He is cheating them and me too.

"Dr. Peters is making rounds, Emma. He just hasn't reached here yet."

The board slammed into Emma's lap and her lips worked furiously over pink gums. It wasn't easy but Katherine could make out what Emma was saying.

"He don't come in when he comes in. I want him here." Emma's long fingernail stabbed the bedside. "Right here. Not out there."

"Okay, Emma. You've made your point. I'll send him in to you."

The respirator gave a loud honk startling them both. Emma reached up and disconnected herself. Taking a tissue, she held it at the hole in her throat and silently coughed. Then expertly she rehooked herself to the machine and flicked off the alarm button. There was a loud sigh and Emma's chest rose with it. Through the whole procedure she glared steadily at Katherine.

Weird lady, Katherine thought as she left the room. At the elevator she stood by herself as the first group of nurses began to gather for lunch. Trish Curry beckoned to her.

"Are you alone?"

"I'm meeting Ben but you can join us. Is he down there yet?"

"Not yet. I'll sit with you if you don't mind."

She liked this new nurse. On steady rotation through the different services at Liberty Hill, Trish was soon to enter the ICU as a full-time nurse, and Katherine was glad to be getting her. She was going to make a fine critical-care nurse. There was an unflappable serenity about her, despite her inexperience, and eager curiosity. Just the qualities needed in a high-stress place.

Trish's gaze flicked over Katherine's abdomen. "Not

too much longer, eh? I'll bet you'll be glad to be out of here."

They entered the elevator together. "It can't be too soon," Katherine replied. And suddenly, the empty phrase took meaning. She hadn't realized how stiff and achy she'd become. What before was simply a few hours grind of paperwork had become a source now of backache and breathlessness. Ben's complaint had more meaning than he knew, but she'd be damned if she would tell him.

The first stirring of trouble came in the line to the food counter. Instead of the usual chatter about the lousy food, the shortness of their lunch hour, or numerous other gripes that marked a normal day in the hospital, there were excited voices all around her. The meeting tonight. What would be said? Decided? Katherine counted the number of times she heard the word *strike*.

She kept silent, listening, but not joining in. She had forgotten all about the Shuster business, but not this group of nurses. Her spirits plummeted. It seemed as if a rogue wave was building upon itself here in the cafeteria. She felt it gathering strength as she and Trish carried their trays to an empty table. She saw it in Trish's face as she settled opposite her. There was both excitement and anger in her blue eyes. She drew into herself and ate without tasting. For some reason, she had a notion of danger for the baby.

When she saw Ben appear with a loaded tray in his hands, searching for her, she swallowed a lump of relief. He was followed by Claude Peters.

"We're not sitting with Peters, are we?" Trish groaned. "I've already turned him down once today."

"Ignore him," Katherine replied, waving to attract Ben's attention.

"How can I with him playing feelie under the table?"

Trish edged closer to Katherine so that her knees were pressing against her. "Self-defense," she grinned apologetically.

Katherine watched as Ben's face lit up when he saw her. He threaded his way through the crowd, oblivious to the angry glances coming his way. She gave him a dazzling smile and leaned over to receive his kiss on her cheek. Behind her someone sniffed, and then there was a sudden silence all around.

The two doctors ate rapidly, unaware of the whispers around them, but Katherine heard them. She felt the little ache in the small of her back grow larger.

"What're they doing here, of all days?" someone whispered. "Why don't they eat in their own dining room?" The voice came from behind her.

"They're probably spying on us. After all, Weathers runs a tight ship in his emergency room. Do you think he's going let the nurses down there go out without a fight? Bullshit, he is."

Ben did not seem to hear it, either that or he chose not to listen. Katherine knew her own antennae were more sensitive to the nurses than his. Still, she trembled inside.

Claude Peters was another matter. With characteristic disdain for those around him, he began a loud tirade against the nurses.

"The girls are spreading ugly rumors around here," he said. "Are they rumors, or what?" he forked a carrot and a chunk of potato into his mouth.

"Oh Lord, Claude, don't call them 'girls.' They are nurses. Some of them are men, in case you haven't noticed," Ben said mildly.

"You know what I mean." Peters said, stabbing the air with his fork in Katherine's direction. "Let's hear it from the horse's mouth. Is it true, Kay?"

How she hated the diminution of her name, especially

from him. It was as though it gave him a special intimacy with her. She gritted her teeth and smiled.

"I'm hearing the same rumors too, Dr. Peters. But it's nothing new. This has been coming for a long time, you know."

"Goddamned unions. See what I mean?" This time he pointed the fork at Ben, his voice rising. "This is just what I was talking about the other night. Nurses are not professionals, they are union punks, no better than common agitators." There was a gasp somewhere behind him. "Where is their devotion to the patients? Their dedication? What are they going to do, abandon the sick? Some professionalism that is."

Katherine felt her face redden.

It was Trish, young Trish, who broke the silence. "Come off it, Doctor. They've heard you. Now clam up. They are in an ugly mood and you are just stirring them up."

Ben joined in. "Yes, Claude, take it easy. They have a legitimate gripe and I, for one, support them. I may not agree with their methods, but I believe they're entitled to a contract."

Peters ignored him. He pounced on Trish as though he'd sprung a trap and Katherine knew it was more than just a political diatribe. Peters was getting his revenge on the young nurse.

He leaned towards her, his fork now pointing directly at her breasts. He began to stab the air with it. "You people think you can control this hospital with your damned union but all you've done is diminish yourselves by it. You nickel and dime yourselves to death, with your grievances, senorities, your paid holidays and paid shit days, but you'll never be professionals, not in my book.

"I'm warning you, strike this hospital, abandon the patients, and I'll work my butt off to see you all lose your licenses."

There was a stunned silence at his outburst, with Trish's face a mixture of outrage and embarrassment. As she gathered herself to leave, a voice roared behind them ragged with fury.

"Who the hell do you think you are, Doctor? You, who drive the biggest car in the world, whose wife puts on a different mink coat every day of the week, never knowing the real reason she gets them? What the hell do you know about us?" It was Tracy Webb. She had risen to her feet and her face was white with anger. The other nurses at her table began to stand up.

Another voice cut in from a different table. "Yeah, Dr. Peters, we know where you're coming from. From about one hundred thousand dollars a year after taxes! You can afford to mouth off." She pushed back her chair and, as one, her group stood with her.

"Come on," Tracy said, "I'm not listening to that garbage." She left her meal untouched on the table and circling the room like a grand dame, she beckoned to the rest of the nurses sitting there. Table by table, the cafeteria emptied until only Ben, Katherine, and Trish remained. There was a tumult of angry voices in the corridor.

"Well," Trish said finally, "now the camel's back is broken."

There was a slightly astonished look on Peters's face. "What happened?"

"If that didn't start a strike, maybe nothing will. But you've certainly mucked up." Ben said.

Trish rose, gathering her dishes together with shaky fingers. "Swell lunch, wasn't it?" Her smile at Katherine was sickly.

Ben shook his head. "Damn you, Peters. You've just antagonized the whole nursing staff, including my wife, and that insults me. You'd better prepare a public apology to all of us." He threw down his spoon in disgust and it bounced on the floor.

While he was speaking, Katherine struggled to get up, but her chair was stuck in a crack in the floor. The more she pushed, the more firmly it remained wedged.

Finally, she cried out, "Damn it, Ben! Help me up." Her husband saw her difficulty and immediately pulled the table away from her belly. The table jolted sending a paper cup of water onto Claude Peters's lap. He sprang to his feet dabbing at the stain that darkened his lap. His face had become a picture of outrage and self-pity.

Before she walked away, Katherine knocked on the table to get Claude's attention away from his crotch. When he finally looked at her she said, "I'm glad I heard this, Dr. Peters. It explains a lot about you, like why you go on making passes at the nurses even when they don't like it. It's contempt, isn't it? The few macho conquests you make confirm it for you, don't they? It's loud and clear to me now.

"It must be awful to have to work with those you hate. How sad for you." She leaned both hands on the table and faced him directly. "Well, what do you think I am, chopped liver? I am a nurse. One of them," she nodded towards the door where the nurses had gathered. "If you ever want Ben and me as your friends, you'd better remember it." She looked at her husband for confirmation and Ben winked at her, a slow grin coming over his face.

Chapter Six

By the time Katherine returned from lunch, her insides quivering and lumpy with half-digested food, the new patient Stacy Price had promised was in room one. She said nothing but marched past the door where Sandy and Carol Rafferty were maneuvering the stretcher by the bed.

Not bothering to sit down, she reached over the counter and snatched up the blue chart that lay on her desk. The new patient's name was Dorothy Fellows, a forty-three-year-old white female admitted with a diagnosis of diabetic coma. In disgust, she closed the chart for a moment. The problem was, of course, why was this patient admitted here? She could have gone onto the floors and if she worsened, then she'd come to the unit. She'd be a true ICU patient under that circumstance. Not this. She looked up and caught Barbara Haines's amused expression.

"What's so funny?"

"I know exactly what's going on in your mind. Why is this patient in the unit, right? Well, it has to do with staffing out on the floors and nothing to do with Mrs. Fellows. We got her because they can't handle her today. Shortage of nurses, remember?"

"So that's the way it's going to be. Pretty soon, we'll be a regular ward instead of an ICU. What's the scoop on this lady?"

Barbara's nose turned up just a bit. "I'm just a secretary, not a nurse, remember? You'll have to get a report from Sandy or Carol. Carol's going to take her."

"Alright, alright, now that you've gotten that out of the way, what's the scoop on this patient?"

"She's in a coma. Blood sugar's twelve hundred."

Katherine whistled softly.

"Not only that, but x-ray just called. This lady's got foreign bodies in her lungs. They don't know what, but there's more than one." She paused for a moment and then said. "You're shaking like a leaf. What's the matter? Was lunch that bad? Just when I'm starved, too."

"I had a little run-in with Peters the Great. And I'm expecting him to barge in at any moment to take it up with me again."

"Oh." Barbara's lips curled. "Is he after pregnant ladies now?"

Katherine reached over and pretended to throttle her secretary. "Go to lunch. And I hope you get ptomaine poisoning."

In room one, Sandy and Carol slid the unconscious patient onto the bed. The intravenous bag swayed over their heads. Then they began the first of many steps, all to assess and evaluate and preserve Dorothy Fellows's life. They stripped her clothing off, neither speaking until she lay nude before them.

"She can't weigh more than eighty pounds," Sandy whispered. "My God, what did she do, starve herself? With diabetes? Who's her doctor?"

Half-listening, Carol replied, "From the looks of her, no one." She fastened the monitor leads on Dorothy's flat chest. The oscilloscope brightened and Dorothy's heart rate and rhythm were revealed. Mentally Carol noted that she was in sinus tachycardia. With a rate of one hundred and twenty-five, the patient's brain was trying to fight off the high metabolic acids that had accumulated. Her rapid and faint respirations, sounding like wheezes of a bellows were another sign. She was trying to blow off the acids. For some reason, Dorothy had consumed a diet high in sugar.

Carol wrapped a blood pressure cuff on Dorothy's arm, then she bent to pump it up and listened as the cuff eased pressure on Dorothy's artery. The manometer dipped to ninety before she could hear a faint thumping begin. At forty, the sound drifted off. She wrote down the numbers. For a while, it would be figures and graphs that Carol would be concerned with, not the patient herself. It was going to be the insulin requirement, the fluids and the medications that were going to help this patient. Especially the fluids.

Dorothy had not stirred at the squeeze of the cuff. Except for her panting breath, faintly sweet to smell, she looked dead. It was evident that she'd lost a great deal of weight, for her gray, dry skin was crumpled like an empty paper bag over her bones. Her hair had simply given up the fight. Lank and streaked with gray it haloed around her head like a worn steel brush. Carol bent closer to peer at her. There was something caught in her hair, a sticky clump that pulled hairs out as she tried to peel it away. Then she looked more closely at Dorothy's face and her mouth. There was another mass, this one purplish in color, sticking against dried tissue. Taking a gauze pad, Carol pried it off and a little welling of blood oozed up and instantly dried to a clot. There was another glob, this one pink, tucked far back against her cheek. And another tangled in her hair behind her ear. It was a perfectly formed jelly bean, shining pink and intact. It was then she began to find them everywhere: in the tangled sheet beneath Dorothy's form, under her tongue, stuck to her teeth. With an irrational giggle Carol lined them up on the gauze pad by Dorothy's head. There were thirteen globs of candy when she had finished. Sandy said nothing, watching with eyes wide.

"Jelly beans," she said finally.

"Thirteen of 'em," agreed Carol. "How many do you suppose are in her stomach?"

"Probably hundreds," Sandy replied, her voice soft with awe.

"What if she aspirated some? Would a jelly bean show up on x-ray?"

"In living color? Can you see the radiologist? He probably is tearing his hair out to figure out what he's seeing." The two nurses began to laugh as they pulled a johnny over Dorothy's body.

"Oh, look at that ulcer," exclaimed Carol.

On the outside of Dorothy's left ankle, a cratered wound was weeping pale fluid. It was the cardinal sign of unmanaged diabetes.

"You're right," Sandy said. "No doctor."

"Guess what, ladies?" Katherine Weathers poked her head in the door. "This patient has something queer in her lungs. The radiologist thinks she must have aspirated—"

"Jelly beans," the two nurses sang out. Again they burst into laughter.

There was a moment of silence and then Katherine said, "I see." She stared fixedly at the patient and then turned on her heel and marched back to her desk. She grabbed the chart and looked at the patient's admitting sheet. There were two names listed as next of kin. Two sons. But they were nowhere to be seen.

On her way to the visitor's room Claude Peters brushed by Katherine with a sheepish smile. She stopped him with a gentle hand on his arm.

"Be sure you stop in and see Emma. She's been waiting

all day for you." Somehow it did not make her feel any better to say that.

At the waiting room she could see that there were two boys slouching by the window. They were dressed in leather jackets with winged creatures in peeling paint drawn on the backs and their kidney belts were cinched so that their waists had feminine curves. There were reddened boils sprouting through a patchy growth of beard on the older boy's face and his hair stood up in bristles above slicked-back sides. There was an air of electricity gone wild and the smell of hot grease in the room. The younger boy looked scared to death. She could see that by the sickly smile on his face when he saw her, his cheekbones bleaching under the fluorescent light. These were Dorothy Fellows's next of kin, her children.

When she beckoned to them, the older boy dropped a cigarette to the floor and crushed it out with his boot. It left a black streak across the shiny tile. In the unit he gazed around the nurses' desk and then placed his helmet directly over Dorothy's blue chart. Leaning on both hands he studied the bank of cardiac monitors. Over his shoulder, he said to Katherine, "Hey man, you'd better get them TV's fixed—you're missing "General Hospital." There was a gap in his teeth as he grinned at her.

She forced a smile onto her face. "Very funny, fella. Come on, I'll take you to see your mother."

His eyes slid over her belly and he nudged his brother.

This time the younger boy spoke up. "How is she? Is she awake yet?"

"I'm afraid not," Katherine replied. "Your mother is still unconscious."

"That's nothing new for good old Dotsy Fellows," the older boy snorted.

"Just shut up, Frankie." his brother said. "Shut up, huh? She's really sick this time."

"Tell me about it. She's got sugar so she takes a little

medicine and thinks she's going to get better." In the doorway he looked around the room, his eyes barely flickering over the figure on the bed. He hooked his thumbs in his belt and leaned against the wall. "Let's make this fast," he said to his brother.

To avoid the argument she could see was building, Katherine interrupted. "This is Carol Rafferty. She's your mother's nurse. She'll explain everything to you."

Carol nodded at the boys. "I'd like to know about the jelly beans," she said. She nodded towards the lump of colored candy on the bedside table. "How come she's been eating this?"

Both boys grew solemn and to Katherine they looked like grimy little guerrillas.

"We did like the doctor told us," the older boy replied. "He said if she got sick we was to get some candy into her real quick. So we did." He looked down at his boots and his voice grew resentful. "We only did what he told us to do."

Billy's gaze was fastened on his mother and his adam's apple bobbed as he swallowed back tears. "We did the wrong thing, didn't we, miss? We should have brought her in yesterday when she got sick."

"At least she's here now," Katherine said, "but I think it may be quite awhile until she's better. Do you have a regular doctor?"

Frankie shook his head. "Nah. We go to the clinic on Hancock Point. But we ain't been there in awhile."

"I told you we should have gotten her there last week. but no, you wouldn't." Billy punched his brother on the shoulder.

"Hey. How could I know she was gettin' worse?"

"If you'd stay home once in a while . . ." Billy stopped suddenly and sighed. "Then you come in like a big deal and start shovin' candy in her mouth and you don't even know what's the matter."

Katherine's heart swelled with pity when she heard the despair in the boy's voice. She had an instant grasp of this family's predicament as soon as she heard the name Hancock Point. It was the town's poorest section, a barren piece of water-bound land that stretched just beneath Logan Airport's busiest runway. She wondered if they had any money between them.

"I'm going to call the cafeteria," she said, "and tell them you are coming down for lunch. It's a free service that we give to families of our patients. You go ahead down there and then you can come back up. We'll have your mother all settled in by that time."

Carol stared at her bald-faced lie. She gave Carol a level gaze over her shoulder as she ushered the two boys from the room.

Arguing in low voices, Billy and Frankie passed by Two-Gus's room. The younger boy met the hemophiliac's gaze. Two-Gus gave him a little wave of his hand. He swore there were tears in the kid's eyes.

In the cafeteria, Billy Fellows eyed his brother nervously. Something was coming and he didn't think he wanted to hear it. The look on Frankie's face was all too familiar. It was his "getting disgusted and ready to run" look. It was a wonder he was still here at all, but it all happened too fast for him to escape. It stunk that Frankie was leaving. He watched his brother wolf down a double cheeseburger. It made him feel a little sick to his stomach.

Frankie cleaned the last french fry from his plate. "Listen, kid, you know I was heading out. I mean before all this happened. It was all settled long ago. *She* knew it too. Now this job down in New Bedford ain't going to wait for me. Either I show up or somebody else will get it. The money's too good to pass up. She agreed to it, remember?" His voice was growing whiney, Billy thought.

He wondered why it was always "she" or "her" when Frankie talked about their mother, as if there were something to be mad about. Frankie leaned back in his chair and belched, sending two elderly women a helpless grin. Then he began to pick at the pimple on his chin. His mother always said he was born with a chip on his shoulder.

"I'll send money on a regular basis," Frankie said, "so she won't have to go right back to work." His gaze slid past Billy's face and fastened on the ample buttocks of a girl dressed in blue.

"So you are leaving. And what am I supposed to do? I mean, why don't you stick around until she's on her feet at least."

Frankie leaned forward. There was an excited look in his eyes. "You know me and sickness. It turns me right off. Besides she'll be better off without me. I'd only fuck up probably." He pushed his chair back. "Come on. Be a brave little man."

"Ah, cut the crap." Billy rose and picked up their trays. "You want to bail out, then do it. But if you are feeling guilty about it, that's tough shit." It was useless to argue with him. When he got that look in his eyes it was like talking to a wall. "Come on, I'll walk you to the door. Someday I'll probably throw you out of one."

Frankie grinned at him, picking at the boil until a little drop of blood welled up.

On the terrace facing the harbor, Frankie turned away from the harsh glare of the sun and held out his hand. Billy took it and the two brothers looked at each other.

"I'll see you in September, kid." Frankie said.

"Take it easy, Frank, and call home once in awhile, huh?"

Billy watched as Frankie rounded the hospital corner, then he heard him cry out, "Don't be sore at me, little brother."

Typical, he thought. Frankie's words always came from another room, another corner, so that no one could talk back to him. He wandered to the ledge of granite that ringed the top of the hill. The smell of salt in his nose made his eyes water. Hoisting himself to the ledge, he sat there letting his legs dangle over the edge. Except for a girl poised on the wall a few feet away with a book on her lap, he was alone.

It wasn't as if he was afraid to be alone. He was used to that. It was being left with her sick. There, now he was calling Dorothy "her," too. But she never got sick. She was always the strong one, the one constant in his life, like a brick wall that warmed in the sun and threw off its heat at night. It was being left here without the comfort of her perfume in his nostrils or her fleshy hip to lean against. He was scared. It was the damned diabetes. It had taken their lives and turned them upside down. It asked Frankie to be something he could never be, not in a million years. It changed her into a scared silly girl, and it was making him decide things she always decided. For a moment he fought the urge to run after Frankie, to keep the tears from burning the back of his eyes.

Somewhere across the harbor a tug hooted three times and an answering bellow came from a tanker, so low on the horizon that he couldn't see it at first. It was a low throaty sound that bounced against the building behind him. He heard a thud and glanced over at the girl. Her book had dropped to the pavement. She looked up at him and smiled.

"Pick it up for me, will you? If I get down I won't be able to get back up."

He slithered down and walked over to her. The spine of the book had cracked and a page fluttered away in the wind.

"Oh shit, catch it!"

The page danced away, darting left and right just as his

fingers reached for it. He heard her laugh and felt his face flush.

"Get it yourself, if you think it's so funny." But he caught it anyway.

She held out her hand and grinned. He pretended not to notice, thumbing through the destroyed book and placing the errant page in its place. It was poetry. The phrases upon the page caught him.

"Hand it over."

"Not until you thank me," he said, holding the book behind his back.

"Help me down, then." She held out her hand.

It was then that he saw the pain in her face. Instantly, he reached up with both hands and circled her waist. She was as light as the breeze that tossed the page. He could feel her hipbones, sharp and frail. She stood before him, her head reaching only to his chin. She was sick and his heart fell. Probably another damned diabetic, he thought.

"My name is Lily Webb," she said, holding out her hand. "And I thank you for helping out."

In that fraction of time, Billy lost his heart to her. "William B. Fellows," he replied. How could he say Billy when it rhymed with Lily and she might think he was a wise-ass? "What do you do besides read this stuff?" He handed her the book.

She tucked it into her schoolbag. "Nothing," she said. "I wait. Just wait."

It was an opening and they both knew it. He leaned against the granite wall. "I'll bite," he said. "What are you waiting for?"

It wasn't strange that she would tell him everything. When she finally stopped talking, he found himself opening up to her, telling her about Dorothy and how Frankie had deserted them. She nodded. There was a tough smile on her face. A wise smile. He couldn't imagine that deep inside this girl was a "river of poison." That's what she'd called her veins. It was the first time he'd ever heard anyone speak so coolly about her body, as if it belonged to someone else. She even showed him the thing she called a fistula, her "rope." He had to admit it was ugly and that had made her laugh aloud.

"Come back in a year," she said with an arch smile, "and you'll see the metamorphosis." He did not know that word, but said nothing. "I'll be fully developed then, after my transplant." She ran a hand over her hip in a gesture that he knew was supposed to be seductive. "You won't know me then."

"I ain't . . . I'm not going anywhere." He remembered the feel of her waist in his hands. It made a heat that spread over his face. She glanced at her watch.

"It's time to go in. I hate it when the air's so soft and I have to go in. It's not so bad in the winter."

He carried her books to the door of Dialysis.

"I hope your mother is better," she said.

"When do you finish here?"

"At seven."

"I'll be here then."

In the ICU, they gave him a chair by Dorothy's bed and he waited through the afternoon. She did not awaken, but she looked better already. They'd given her a bath and combed her hair. Her face was unlined and peaceful as she slept. Even the heart line on the monitor over her bed was comforting. It was as if he had a direct access to the center of his mother's being, and as long as that line spiked across the tiny screen, she was alright. He dozed, awakening once in a while to glance up at the green screen above Dorothy's head.

When the unit doors flew open, Katherine did not bother to raise her head; she knew that only Tracy Webb would swoop like a hawk into the unit. She pulled her Kardex open and prepared for the process of giving report to the supervisor. Tracy sat down beside her, her eyes flying over the unit, not missing a thing. She barely glanced at Katherine.

"How many new patients?" She flipped open her book and scanned it. "One?"

"No, two, thanks to Stacy. We weren't ready for the hepatitis patient when, lo and behold, she delivered him to our door unannounced."

"Oh that woman, she does push us too far, doesn't she?"

Katherine knew Tracy did not care about patient distribution to the unit. It was her unconcealed protection of the regular floors that rankled. She suspected it was because the ICU patients were sometimes beyond the supervisor's comprehension. It showed in her critiques of the nurses' notes from here, from the speed with which she issued incident reports to the head office about lapses that mattered not a whit except that they were done in here. And it showed in Tracy's disdain for the procedure of a code 99, those critical last moments of a patient's life when all the life-supporting measures are called into action. When it's their time, it's God's time, Tracy always said. We shouldn't interfere. As far as Katherine was concerned it was a bit of nonsense that only diminished Tracy's power and she suspected the supervisor knew it. Still, she wished it were easier to get her to transfer a unit patient.

Tracy's starched uniform rustled. "Lord, I've done nothing but stave off rumors all day. To strike or not to strike, that is the question." She had a pleased little smile on her lips. "That's why I'm so late on rounds today. Are you going to the meeting?" She did not wait for Katherine's reply. "I think we'll have a record turnout."

"I wouldn't miss it for the world," Katherine replied. She flipped open the Kardex with a great show of deliberation, hoping it would get Tracy's attention. "I need some beds."

"You always do," Tracy said. "What else is new?"

"Mr. Crantson's CT scan came back positive. He's had a left-sided stroke and is still bleeding. I don't think he'll last much longer. Anyway, we can't do a thing for him. He's transferred."

Tracy clicked her tongue. "I don't know why the nurses out on the floors have to be burdened with him. He came to you first. They're too short handed out there."

It was an unveiled attack on the staffing differences between the floors and the ICU.

"You know our policy. We don't care for stroke victims; there's nothing we can do for them." Katherine knew it was a mistake to remind Tracy about policy. The supervisor wrote the book. She watched her, mentally giving odds on Tracy's next move. She'll open her notebook, sigh, and shake her head. In that order.

With a great show of reluctance, and to Katherine's glee, in the proper sequence of resignation, Tracy opened her notebook. "I have a room on Three North," she said, as though it were a prize that Katherine surely did not deserve.

Katherine suppressed a grin. "Is that the room Mrs. Avery came from last night? If so, she's ready to go back to it. Dr. Hardy wrote her transfer order too."

Outraged, Tracy cried, "Now just a minute. You said one bed, now you're telling me two? I can't send two patients to one floor at the same time, they'll have a fit up there."

"I have two patients to go. Besides I wasn't supposed to get Mr. Ragust until later today. I got him, didn't I?"

"You should have notified me at the time. That is policy, too, as I recall."

The look on Tracy's face, triumph or aggression, whatever it was, caused something to snap inside.

"Listen, Tracy, if you've got a hair across your behind this morning, take it up with someone else. I don't have the time for games this morning. We've been dumped on enough for one day." Immediately she knew she'd said the wrong thing. Tracy's face froze.

Barbara Haines turned away discreetly. There was a combination of pity and amusement on her face. She had never heard her boss explode like that. She found herself smiling directly at Two-Gus who stared rather tiredly back.

"You forget yourself, Katherine, but I'll put it down to your advanced condition and forget it." Tracy's mascaraed eyelashes fluttered as she picked up the telephone. There were two high spots of color above her rouge.

The comment left Katherine speechless with rage and she watched as Tracy dialed first Three North and then Two South, and in the space of five minutes arranged for both ICU patients to be moved. When she replaced the phone, she turned towards Katherine and with a coolness designed to put Katherine in her place, said, "Finish up with report. I'm late, very late, this morning."

Katherine was reminded of the March Hare but said nothing. She turned to Two-Gus's Kardex. Out of the corner of her eye she could see Tracy's fingers drumming impatiently on the desk and then she leaned back to peer into the room.

"There's more to the eye than that awful jaundice I see. Gossip has it that there's a cover-up with this man," she murmured.

"What does that mean?" Katherine looked at her.

"You'll find out."

Another game, she thought, opening her mouth to protest, but then the double doors crashed open and distracted her. It was Ben and from the look on his face there was more trouble coming. Behind him she could see a tiny woman hurrying after him and teetering on the highest heels Katherine had ever seen. They were at least four inches, she thought to herself. Then she felt Tracy stir beside her.

"Is there something wrong, Doctor?" There was an artificial concern in Tracy's voice and Katherine wanted to clap her hand over the supervisor's mouth to stop what was coming. But there was a look of delicious anticipation on Tracy's face and it came to her that this was what she wanted: a good battle. She leaned back in her chair and folded her arms across her chest watching Tracy's face for the change she knew was coming.

Ben leaned over the counter barely acknowledging his wife. "You bet your ass, Mrs. Webb." Tracy sucked in her breath. "Your emergency-room supervisor sent a patient up here directly against my orders. He was to be held there for surgery. I want her on report, Mrs. Webb, on report."

There was a distinct rustle of white uniform as Tracy gathered herself. "I already know about it, Dr. Weathers. You needn't shout at me as if I were a common—"

"Stacy Price goes on report, Mrs. Webb. She's been asking for it lately. She's forgotten who's boss down there."

"I'm sure no one could forget that, Doctor."

Ben stared at her and Katherine could see he was trying to contain himself. "That is all. You may go," he said, his voice deadly.

"And before I do, Doctor, let me remind you that there is a time and place for everything. I suggest that this is neither." She nodded towards Milly Gold who was leaning against the counter with a look of suppressed glee on her face. "Our visitor must think we're awfully—"

"Oh, don't pay any attention to me," Milly chirped. "I'm just here to see my patient." She tottered away towards Two-Gus's room. "There you are. All settled?"

she cried out.

"Who is that?" Tracy murmured.

Katherine looked at Ben, the question in her eyes.

"That is the hemotologist, Dr. Mildred Gold, our patient's attending."

"You understand, that this...er...doctor cannot write orders here. Not until she's been granted privileges at Liberty Hill." Tracy gathered up her papers and stood up, preparing to depart with that final shot.

"Within the hour, Mrs. Webb. Within the hour, she'll have privileges faster than you can bat an eyelash or two." Katherine smothered a giggle.

Tracy stared at Ben. "In that case I have nothing to worry about, do I?"

Katherine knew she would keep a close check on Dr. Gold's presence at the hospital. It was clear that no orders were to be written or obeyed until her credentials had been approved.

Tracy walked around the counter. "Tell me, Doctor, why was this patient admitted here?"

"Why not, Mrs. Webb? Are we restricted here?" Ben's tone of voice made it clear that the conversation was at an end. Tracy swept away from the counter and pushed through the unit doors, like a cold north wind.

Two-Gus had heard it all, and so had Trish. Her young face was flushed with embarrassment. So they hadn't expected him up here. That was one more strike against him and all because of the stupid emergency-room supervisor. Still he liked the way the doctor had exploded at the over-painted nurse with the starched white cap. Anyone dressed that way, these days, was surely trouble. And he liked this little nurse, too. She had helped him slide into his bed and fussed over him making sure that he was comfortable. She was trying at least. He looked up at Milly Gold.

"So, how long, Milly?"

"A week or two, I would think. Then you can go home." There was a mixture of pity and exasperation in her face. "Why did you wait so long, Two-Gus?" She plunked herself down in a chair and pushed off her shoes.

At the desk, Ben pulled his wife up and walked her away. "Come on," he said, "let's go talk somewhere privately."

Mystified, she allowed him to lead her to the treatment room. With the door closed behind them, Ben leaned against an empty gurney. His face was troubled. "This new patient," he said, "he may present some problems for us. I thought I'd better prepare you."

"What is it?"

"First of all, he's a hemophiliac and he has chronic hepatitis."

"I didn't think that was a Florida tan."

"Come on, babe, don't make this tougher than it is. This guy has AIDS."

She almost knew the word was coming before he said it. "Are you sure?"

"Yeah. He tested positive for the virus almost a year ago. Now he's showing symptoms. Pneumonia. Probably Kaposi sarcoma. He knew it, too. He's been avoiding medical care ever since, living like a hermit and trying not to have an outbreak of bleeding. If it weren't for some kid knocking him over with a bicycle, he'd have still been hiding out, at least until he began to show signs of dying. He's no fool; he knew that he was at risk for the disease. All those blood transfusions."

She stared at him. "We've never had an AIDS case here. How do we treat him? What do we do?"

He reached out and pulled her to him, stroking her hair. "First of all, you stay out of the room, darling. There are no studies about pregnant nurses and AIDS."

She nodded, her cheek against his, her belly making him lean over her. She felt the baby roll against him and she grinned at the look of surprise on his face.

"She's a flirt already, isn't she?"

"She loves her dad, that's all. She'd rather be with me downstairs where it's safe, than here putting up with the likes of Spider Webb."

"Tracy's not so bad. We've learned to put up with each other. Now, what kind of precautions do we take?"

"Strict hepatitis routine."

"Masks, too?"

"No, though that might come later if he's intubated or coughing up secretions."

She looked thoughtful. "I think I'm going to have my hands full with the staff coming to grips with this. Some of them might not want to care for him. And when he goes out on the floors, it could be even worse."

"By that time, we'll get plenty of information to them. Inservice will have some classes on AIDS. Once they know how to deal with the disease, they won't be uncomfortable. If they take precautions, that is."

"That isn't what I mean, Ben. In the mood they're in, I can't say they won't use this as ammunition for their complaints. They could use this as an excuse to strike."

She felt him stiffen. The little muscle at the corner of his mouth twitched. "They'd better not; they're nurses."

Katherine paled suddenly. "I forgot poor Trish," she exclaimed. "She's been in there with him forever! I've got to get her relieved."

"Now that's just what I meant," he said. "For chrissakes, Katherine, I didn't think that you'd be like that."

"I only meant exactly what I said, Dr. Weathers. She's supposed to be on duty in the ER, not here. And besides, how do you know if she's pregnant or not? I certainly don't."

It stopped him cold. It was a perplexing thought. If pregnant nurses are exempt from caring for AIDS patients, was it the hospital's responsibility to test each one assigned to that patient? And if not pregnant on one day, what about the next? And what if she didn't know she was pregnant?

There were going to be some thorny questions for Liberty Hill to address with its first AIDS patient. Things like liability, disability, and lawsuits. He made a mental note to tell Julian Plumhouse about the potential problems. Let the matter go right to the top, he thought.

He shook his head. "I can't worry about it. I simply take care of the sick, no matter what the sickness is."

It was one of the reasons she had fallen in love with him. She pulled his head down and kissed him deeply on one corner of his mouth and again just under his ear. She could feel his hands tighten against her back.

"Let's jump on the gurney and see if it holds the two of us," she whispered. "Er . . . the three of us."

"Have you no decency? You're an animal," he said, grinning.

Arm in arm they returned to the center of the ICU. When she saw Claude Peters seated at her desk, in her chair, she sighed. "Trouble. I'll see you later tonight. Prenatal classes, remember?" He groaned.

Milly Gold was waiting for him. "He's all settled but not a very happy camper," she said. "I've lectured him, in fact I've been reading him the riot act, but I can't promise he'll behave. An expert in harassment is our patient. I expect it is purely defensive."

At that moment a stretcher was wheeled into the unit and turned towards Two-Gus's room.

"That's the operating-room porter," Ben said. "They must have finished up early." The porter was garbed in an operating room gown. His mask hung over one shoulder.

In the room, Two-Gus eyed the man with distrust. Sure enough, the mask was placed over his face and from his pocket, the attendant pulled out a pair of gloves.

"There's no need for that," Two-Gus said.

The man did not answer and the Two-Gus felt the first stirring of danger. He watched as he tossed a mask at him. "As far as I'm concerned, there is, buddy. Put it on." His voice was cool and his flat eyes seemed to rake Two-Gus with ice.

It would be funny if it weren't so damned incriminating, Two-Gus thought. Already it was apparent that rumors were sweeping the hospital, if the swaddling of the man were any indication.

"No mask," he said.

"Then we don't travel," the man replied, leaning against the wall.

"Take off that mask right now!" Ben roared from the doorway.

At once, the attendant removed the offensive piece of cloth, but his eyes glinted nastily.

In the room next door, Billy Fellows stirred from his drowsy state. He flashed an anxious glance at his mother. Something had awakened him. She was still there, though, and the green line spiked across the screen with reassuring regularity. He arose, stretched, and waited for the thudding of his heart to slow. Then he walked to the door. The noise must have come from the next room. He peered around the frame and saw the same patient he'd seen in the emergency room. The man glanced up as he slid onto the stretcher they'd placed alongside his bed. Billy smiled at him. There was an infinite kindness and more than a little sadness in the man's return nod.

"Good luck," Billy said as the stretcher rolled by him.

"Thanks, kid. See you later."

The attendant pushed the stretcher from the unit with unnecessary speed, the intravenous bottle clattering against its steel holder. Once outside, the man muttered something that Two-Gus could not hear. He glanced up and saw the mask once more pulled over the attendant's face.

Billy looked at the wall clock and disbelieved what he saw. Only one hour had passed. He wandered to the window on the far side of Dorothy's bed and pressed his forehead to the glass. Behind him, his mother tossed her arm over her head and sighed.

At her desk, Katherine had pulled up another chair and sat beside Claude Peters. He began a litany of complaints about Emma and she felt the first throbbing of a headache begin. It was obvious that Peters was not paying attention. Not to Emma, not to her, and never to Leah.

"For chrissakes," Peters said, "all she did was blubber! I couldn't understand her. Do you know what it's like to read the lips of a crying woman? What's the matter with her?"

"I think the technical term for it, Doctor, is depression," Katherine said dryly. "Emma is very sad and I don't blame her. She's not stupid. She knows all too well that she's stuck here."

"I'll order Elavil for her. Anything else?" Peters seemed cheered by such a simple solution. He leaned over Katherine's shoulder and wrote the prescription for the drug.

"How about weaning her?"

"Not a chance. That lady's never going to breathe on her own." Peters hesitated and then he looked at Katherine thoughtfully. "We'll get a set of ABG's while she's on the vent just to see what her status is. Will that make it up to you? For the little misunderstanding at lunch?"

Katherine rolled her eyes. That should have been done ages ago, she thought. "Why not give the poor woman a chance, Claude. Try weaning."

Claude's face closed. "Call the office with the results and leave the numbers with my girl."

"And what does *your girl* do with them? File them in the circular file?" Katherine gritted her teeth. "And will *she* give me my orders? Or is it, 'Don't call me, I'll call you.'"

"Exactly. Look, Katherine, I apologize for my outburst, okay? But don't think you can twist my arm about my patient. That's forbidden territory. I'd like nothing better than to have Emma Bond out of my hair forever. But unless she's up for a lung transplant, it's unlikely that she's going to walk out of here. Nevertheless," he began to walk to the door so that she could not reply, "I'll look over her gases and we'll go from there." As the door closed behind him, he called over his shoulder, "Take a look at my orders."

She glanced through the prescription page of Emma's chart. There, underlined in red, Claude Peters had written: Do Not Attempt To Wean. The nerve of him! Oh, that infuriating man! She cursed him thoroughly in her mind. He should know that no nurse would attempt a weaning without the doctor's consent. That was a medical decision not nursing. But to imply, by the order, that nurses would step over the line was positively insulting. Why would he have written that at all? Unless . . .

With a sinking heart, she turned to the nurses' notes and began to skim through them. Routine day notes. And nowhere in them was a notation on weaning. One or two mentioned Emma's desire to try, but that was all. Until she began to read the night notes and the words leapt out of her. Her pulse began to throb and she could feel it flashing through her head. Oh Leah, she thought, how could you? There in Leah's neat handwriting was written, "Weaned for sixty seconds without distress. Eager to continue."

It was grounds for a reprimand if not something more serious. Could she be fired for this? If only she hadn't written the words. No, that wasn't right. At least Leah had done the honest thing and reported it. But why? Why had she taken on this responsibility? Surely she must have known she would be reprimanded for it.

The answer was simple when she thought about it. It was Leah's way of gently reminding nurses of their profession. She did what she should have done and that was to fight for her patient's recovery. All of them, Katherine included, had given up on Emma. Peters didn't care. He was paid for his time whether or not she improved. No one cared. Emma had become a fixture to them, as constant as the respirator she was hooked to. It was Leah who took the risk to shock them into action. Only it backfired. Claude's order was his way of slapping her on the hand. And that's all it was, a slap on the hand. He hadn't even been indignant when he read her notes. Come to think of it, why hadn't she checked the nursing pages? There was just too much to do and not enough time to do it all. No excuses, she said to herself. It was part of her job to see that her staff was doing its job correctly. Still . . . it was also her job to help patients. that came first. And nothing had changed for poor Emma. Damn the man!

She hadn't wanted to transcribe the offending order to the Kardex for all the different shifts to read. Why insult them? She had thought it was merely an egocentric act of Peters. Now, though, it was a different matter.

She picked up a heavy red marker and, writing in large letters, she transcribed the order to the bottom of Emma's Kardex. She'd be damned, though, if she was going to report Leah for this. They would have a quiet little talk and it would go no further. As for that miserable little Peters, she was going to pester the daylights out of him. Now the gloves come off. If poor Emma was miserable, and Leah was willing to risk her job for her, then Claude Peters was going to feel the results of his own negligence. She closed the Kardex cover. As usual, though, she felt frustrated.

Chapter Seven

Julian Plumhouse was having trouble keeping his mind on his work. He kept seeing the way Leah ran so lightly over the gangplank, her hair sweeping her waist, and the way the sunlight sheeted it with silver. He did not think he'd ever seen a woman of such grace.

He sat at his desk, the stack of correspondence that Betsy Conte had placed before him unseen and untouched. Leah Swift. The name and the figure silhouetted against the deep blue of the harbor. For the first time since he'd come to New England, Julian felt better about the move. They were difficult to get to know, these New Englanders. They were not unfriendly, but simply involved with their own lives and unwilling to intrude on someone else's. He'd been lonely these past months and never knew it. The long hours, the dark worries about the hospital's survival. He'd mistaken all that for normal career concerns. But he hadn't anyone to talk to, no one to tell his fears to, or for that matter, his triumph once the hospital began to show improvement. He'd been a fool to plod along in isolation. Leah . . .

He shook his head. Like a schoolboy, he was. He was grabbing at the thought of her as if he were a drowning man and she the last pure draught of sweet air. She probably hadn't given him another thought. He shook his head and tried to concentrate on the paper heaped before him. It was no good. He found himself gazing at the sky from his window.

The phone buzzed softly and almost reluctantly he dragged his thoughts away from the girl. Rubbing the spot between his eyes, he picked up the telephone.

"Yes?"

"Oh, Julian." The breathless voice of Evelyn Holden sent a tingle of warning down his spine. The director of nurses rarely called him. "My phone is ringing off the hook." He swore he could hear her gulp. "There's something going on out on the floors," she said. "I'm not sure what it is, but I'm going to walk around and take a look. I want you to come with me."

"Give me a hint, Evelyn," he said. "So I'll know which hat to wear. Hard or soft."

She ignored his attempt at humor. "I'm fielding calls from head nurses all over the hospital. Lunch trays have been delivered to the floors, but the nurses are refusing to serve them. They are saying that it is nonnursing work. What are we going to do?" she almost wailed.

Without hesitation he said, "We are going to feed the patients, Evelyn, that's what we are going to do. I'll be right there as soon as I make another call." He disconnected and immediately dialed the kitchen. The phone rang and rang. For a moment he thought they had deserted too, but a bored voice came on the line.

"This is Mr. Plumhouse," he said swiftly. "How many workers do you have down there right now?"

The dietician hesitated and he knew she was mentally tallying her help. "Twelve, sir. Why?"

"They are to go out on the floors and distribute trays to the patients."

He heard her gasp. "But they are on their lunch hour. They'll refuse. Besides, it's not in their contract."

"If they are not out on the floors in five minutes, they are fired. Round them up and send them out. You pitch in, too." He hung up before the woman could reply.

When he opened the door to his office, Betsy Conte looked up. "Don't run off," she said. "Drs. Tremont and Hardy just called. They sound mad as hornets. Their patients are hungry and they want to know why. They are coming down here. I told them you were busy, but they wouldn't be put off."

"I'll see them tomorrow. If that won't do, you take care of it."

"What, and get my head bitten off? No thank you." But her smile faded when she saw that her boss meant what he said.

Evelyn Holden was waiting for him in the corridor outside her own office. She was pacing back and forth, her normally smooth face worried. She began to chatter nervously. "I've never had this happen before. I can't imagine what is getting into them. This is grounds for dismissal. Why would they risk that?"

"It's a job action, Evelyn. Very simply, they are making themselves heard. You and I are going to see to it that the patients get fed, if we have to serve them ourselves. Let's start at the top."

"That's Bev Britain's floor. She was the first one to call. She says her RN's are up in arms. And if I know her, it's due to her own goading. She sounded positively smug."

In the elevator, there was a sullen group of white-clad kitchen workers. They had food stains on their clothing and the air in the elevator was sharp with the odor of sour milk. At each floor, two workers stepped off. On the fourth floor, Julian watched as they began pulling trays from the food cart, grumbling to themselves.

When he was certain that the trays were going out correctly, he turned to the nursing station. Bev Britain sat there, a smile flickering at the corners of her mouth. She reached up in a self-conscious gesture and traced the folds of her starched white cap with a finger.

Evelyn Holden spoke first. "Where are they?"

"Do you mean my nurses?"

My: the cold possessive with which a head nurse too often fed her ego. "My nurses," "my staff," "my girls." Julian sighed in disgust.

"Why, I believe they are at their patients' bedsides, doing their jobs." She slid a smile at Julian.

Evelyn bit back her annoyance. "Why aren't they passing trays?"

"One mentioned something about doing care plans. One said she had a dressing change and my other one is passing her twelves." She referred to noon-time medication distribution. "And when I mentioned trays, they simply disappeared. See for yourself."

Julian spoke up, his tone soft and deadly. "That leaves you, Mrs. Britain. Let's go." With that he turned to the serving cart and began to pull trays. "One for you, one for Evelyn, and one for me. Let's move it, we have two more floors to cover."

Bev's eyes flew open in shock. "Let me remind you, Mr. Plumhouse, that I am head nurse here. It is not my responsibility to feed patients."

"You've made yourself clear, Mrs. Britain, now get up and make yourself useful. Our patients deserve better care than they are getting at the moment." He read the little card on his tray and began to walk down the corridor, looking for the correct room. A kitchen worker followed him. Over her shoulder, Evelyn saw Bev reach into the food cart.

It was the same on every floor. No nurse was found idle or absent, but not one had lifted a tray either. They were at the bedsides and the patients were receiving an extraordinary amount of nursing care, but no food.

By the time Julian and Evelyn had finished, one hundred and nine patients had been served, some with difficulty. (One little old lady threw her tray at Julian, barely missing him and setting off gales of laughter among the patients and staff.) The kitchen workers had fallen in with enthusiasm and now stood by, ready to collect the empty trays. In the end, the job action was defused, the patients fed, and with a sense of satisfaction, Plumhouse and Holden returned to their offices.

It had made Julian feel good. For the first time since he'd come to Liberty Hill, he'd been able to roll up his sleeves and pitch in. He'd forgotten what patient contact had once meant to him, it had been so long. The satisfying smell of his own sweat, and the little twinge of muscles unaccustomed to lugging anything heavier than his briefcase was a good feeling. He suspected that even Evelyn Holden enjoyed the hour. He sailed passed Betsy Conte's desk.

"Get me the biggest local temporary agency on the phone. Tell them that we want twenty-five registered nurses on standby."

Betsy's mouth dropped. "The nurses are going to strike?"

"The handwriting's on the wall. We'll have to plan something, Betsy."

He disappeared into his office. In a moment the red light on her intercom flashed on. "And while I think of it, call Dr. Sheen. Tell him I want to cancel all elective surgery until further notice starting tomorrow."

A look of dismay came over Betsy's face. She sat there and looked at the telephone as if it were a poisonous snake. As head of surgery, Terence Sheen was responsible for the smooth running of that department. By the sheer force of his abrasive personality, the operating rooms ran full tilt five days a week, two full shifts each day. It was not a popular job, but then Terence Sheen was not a friendly surgeon. This order would make him howl in outrage and Betsy knew she would get the brunt of it. She picked up the phone.

When the three o'clock shift of nurses gathered around her desk for report, Katherine stood up, postponing the process. Annoyed at the delay, the oncoming nurses gazed suspiciously at the little woman seated at the desk. The fact that the day-shift nurses were still there, also gathered around, meant that something unusual was taking place.

Milly sat there, tapping her fingers on the counter, her face bright and curious. She scanned the little crowd of faces.

"My name is Dr. Gold," she said. "I know I'm fouling up report, but I must. Today we have admitted Liberty Hill's first AIDS case. I am from Mass General where we've had quite a few of these patients. I will try to explain things to you so that you can deliver the same excellent standard of care we do."

It was a challenge and a few of the nurses were disdainful. "Big deal," Nancy Musen muttered. "If they are so good, why isn't the patient over there?"

Milly went on. "First let me ask a question. Have you ever cared for a hemophiliac?"

"Of course we have," Nancy said. "We're not quite in the dark over here."

"Pardon me," Milly said with a smile. "I should have known better. Then I'm sure you all know that ninety percent of all hemophiliacs are positive for chronic hepatitis. And I am also sure that you have taken the proper precautions against that disease, true?" A few heads nodded. "I review anyway, for you. Gowns and gloves for all bodily secretions." Her voice began to take on a singsong quality. "Masks when there is a ventilator-dependant patient. Proper disposal of wastes. Double-bagging of linens and scrubbing equipment with hypochlorite. True?"

Someone whispered, "Hypo what?"

"Bleach, dummy," came the whispered answer.

Milly waited for the buzz of voices to end. "The care of an AIDS patient is exactly the same as for hepatitis. No different, understand?"

Nancy Musen raised her hand. "The outcome is certainly different, isn't it?"

Katherine sighed. Here it comes, she thought.

"I mean, how do we protect ourselves from this disease? And what about those who are afraid?"

Unperturbed, Milly went on as if Nancy had not spoken at all. "What is important is the manner in which we treat our patient. He is entitled to our best efforts, regardless of outcome."

Ah. There's her response, Katherine thought.

"He has a disease that may be socially stigmatizing, and I would argue that point, but it has no bearing on the care we give him. Absolutely none, is that clear?"

"I think you are being a little judgmental of us, Doctor." Katherine broke in smoothly. "What we are concerned with is the technical and physical aspects of this disease."

"Don't be too sure of that, Mrs. Weathers." Milly said. "There may be some here who don't have experience with the disease and are therefore frightened by it. The more they know, the stronger they will feel." She glanced around the group. "I simply want to explore what might be a problem here. Is there one?"

"We don't have a policy on it here." Nancy spoke up. "It's only fair that we do, isn't it? Is the hospital going to cover us for accidental innoculation?"

"I can't speak for Liberty Hill," replied Milly, "but it is an issue they know they'll have to deal with. In the meantime, however, the patient is here and we must care for him. Let me tell you what I can. First of all, Mr. Ragust will be returning with an irrigating shoulder wound. That means there will be a constant flow of fluid into and from his incision. That fluid will be treated as contaminated with both hepatitis and AIDS, and we will wear gowns and gloves. If there is a danger of splashing yourselves while disposing of waste then you may want to wear masks, too. I leave that up to you." She fell silent, watching them.

Katherine watched them also. How would they react? Was there a troublemaker among them, one who would seize on this problem and use it to advantage? She was sure that at tonight's meeting, news of the hospital's first AIDS patient would be flashing through the gathering.

After Milly Gold left the unit, Katherine fell to giving report with unusual speed, wanting nothing more than to go home. The thought of wrapping herself in Ben's huge velour robe and then dozing away the afternoon was tantalizing. When she finished, she looked up at the five faces around her desk. Usually friendly, today there was a mixture of fear and hostility written on their features. No one said good night to her as she gathered up her jacket.

While Red Swift tossed a giant salad, Maddy and Leah opened up the deck chairs and table, and Nikki toddled behind with a fistful of spoons. Soon they had the deck above the marina transformed into outdoor dining room. They debated whether to drop the awning over the deck but then decided against it. Even though it was still daylight, the sky was dusky with streaks of rose-tipped clouds and the candles flickering on the redwood table were growing stronger in the fading light.

Far out on the horizon an airplane aimed for the

runway on the outer shore, looking like a giant mosquito hovering against the deepening sky and the whine of its jets reached them only after it had landed.

Maddy handed Nikki a toasted garlic round. He mouthed it solemnly and then his face wrinkled in a grimace as the herb filled his mouth.

The older woman turned to Leah. "Don't eat so fast, you'll get a belly ache."

"I have to get to the Hill by seven," Leah replied. "The nurses have called a meeting."

Maddy and Red exchanged uneasy glances. "I hear there's talk of a strike up there," he said, pouring the last of the wine into their glasses. There was a troubled look on his face and Leah knew he was trying to conceal it.

"I'm not going to strike, Dad. It's illegal, first of all, and second, it's against my principles." She began to stack the dishes but Maddy placed a restraining hand on her arm.

"Listen to your father for a minute," she said.

Leah shrugged and settled back. Just then, Nikki threw his piece of toast. It bounced against the railing and hung in the air for a moment, only to be scooped up by a diving sea gull. His eyes rounded into saucers. It broke the tension and the three adults grinned at each other. It gave Red the courage to speak up to her. He never interfered in her life and she could tell it was troubling him even now.

"Some of the men have been hanging around the union hall," he said. "What they are hearing is that the men still out of work are urging their wives and sisters to go on strike. It doesn't make sense. You'd think they would be grateful to get those paychecks right now, but it's working the opposite way. They want their wives to get paychecks equal to what they were getting before the heavy yard closed."

"That's because nurses have always been underpaid

and now their unpaid husbands are finally realizing it. It's funny how the men never cared before, as long as they were bringing home big paychecks themselves." Leah shook her head. "Male chauvinist—"

"I just don't want you caught in a crossfire, honey," Red said. "If they decide to go out, get out of there. You can always get a job in Boston. Or you can work right here. God knows Maddy could use another pair of hands in the store."

"Don't speak for me, Red Swift," Maddy sniffed. "The day I can't pull my own weight, I'll let you know." She turned to Leah. "The trouble is, those damned men don't realize that they bargained themselves right out of work. The navy yard close up because of their union. And just like stubborn, pig-headed, unthinking boors that they are, they want their wives to do the same thing. I just hope the women know better."

Her outburst startled Nikki. His eyes filled with unshed tears and his lower lip fattened into a quiver. He looked from Maddy to Leah as if waiting to decide whether or not to cry. Leah reached over and gathered him into her lap. From the shelter of her arms, Nikki regarded his grandmother a little warily.

Later, with Nikki tucked into bed and Maddy engrossed in a book, Red walked with Leah to the marina gate. Her arm was entwined in his and she could feel the cord-hard strength of him against her side. He would never grow old, she decided, and crossed her fingers.

"I'll keep the light on," he said.

"Don't worry, Dad. I won't get into trouble," she whispered.

She closed the chain-link gate and settled into a steady jog, knowing he was watching her until the block of houses on the hill would put her out of sight. Halfway up, a pair of headlights caught her and a horn honked softly. She stopped, panting, and peered into the car.

It was Katherine.

"Want a lift? You'll be late if you don't." Katherine pulled up the parking brake and waited for Leah to settle in beside her. They grinned at each other.

"Did you get Ben to go with you to prenatal classes?" At Katherine's contented nod, Leah burst out laughing. "Tell me, how does a doctor handle being told what to do in childbirth?"

"He kept his mouth shut, like a little lamb," Katherine replied smugly as she strained a foot to the gas pedal. She had put the seat so far back to accomodate her stomach that her arms were as straight as sticks. "In fact, I think he was a little overwhelmed by the whole thing, or else he was a damned good actor. All I know is that he was pretty quiet on the way home."

Leah eyed Katherine. "So are you feeling alright? Any signs of you-know-what?" They had agreed not to mention the impending delivery.

"Oh, the signs are there," Katherine replied. "I have Braxton-Hicks contractions all the time now. The little she-devil is practicing for her debut." She swung the car around the circular drive and pulled into the physician's parking lot. "This is one of the good things about being a doctor's wife. An incentive, you might call it." She reached over and placed a hand on Leah's arm. "Don't get out for a minute. I want to talk to you."

"Sure, Katherine. What's up?"

"I . . . er . . . don't know how to begin."

"Let me guess, then. You want me to run the unit while you're out on maternity leave, huh?" At Katherine's surprised look, Leah giggled. "No, huh? Okay, try this. You want me to partner you through childbirth and leave Ben out of it altogether."

Katherine began to grin. "I guess I'd better come right out with it before you say something wild. It's about Emma Bond."

Leah's face sobered instantly. "What about her?"

"I read your notes, honey. And so did Claude Peters. He didn't appreciate them."

"Well, it's nice to know that all the writing we do doesn't go to waste. I've often wondered if anyone reads nursing notes."

"Lawyers make a speciality out of it."

"I wasn't thinking about them."

"Perhaps you should have," Katherine said gently. She took a deep breath. "I'm not going to let this go any farther. What's done is done. But you are on notice. Don't try to wean her."

"But why, goddamn it!" Leah burst out.

"Because you are not her doctor, that's why. You've crossed the line, Leah, and it could get you into big trouble. I happen to agree with you that Emma should be given a chance to wean. I argued that point with Peters myself and all I got was a figurative black eye for all the good it did. I was told to mind my own business, which means running the unit and putting a restraint on your treatment of Emma. It's that simple . . . Now I've done my job, let's go." She opened the door and stepped out into the night.

They walked together in silence towards the great oak doors of the hospital's front entrance. Neither of them noticed the teenage couple huddled together on the granite walk, she leaning heavily on his supporting arm.

Promptly at seven Billy had been at the door of the dialysis unit waiting for it to open. What if she had already left? Maybe she had forgotten him. He was a fool—he should be upstairs with Dorothy. He glanced at the clock. Three minutes after seven. He would wait until five after. He leaned against the wall, his eyes on the black-and-white tiled floor. He almost missed the door opening, his thoughts as dark as the darkest square beneath his feet.

"Hi."

He glanced up at Lily Webb, his heart thumping heavily in his chest. She was here. Then his thoughts tumbled in confusion. Was this Lily? She was different. Ashen and wasted somehow. The same but changed and utterly consumed by what happened inside that room. What did they do to her?

As if she read his mind, Lily whispered. "I'm okay. It takes a lot out of me at first. But this will pass, it always does." But he didn't believe her. How could they do this to her and then let her simply walk out the door? She could die! He wished he'd never met her. And then promptly cursed himself.

"You look half—"

"Thanks. I knew you'd say that." She let the door close behind her and shakily began to make her way down the corridor.

"Hey, I didn't mean anything. You just looked changed, you know."

"Well I am, stupid. Four hours of cleaning does that, you know."

"You could've told me. Warned me about it. How am I supposed to know?" He followed her down the hall, not yet willing to catch up to her, to see what they had done to her. She wobbled a little and held a hand against the wall to steady herself. He heard her mumble, "Shit," to herself.

"Hey." He found himself hurrying to her side and putting his arm around her waist. "Don't fall down, for God's sakes." She melted into the curve of his arm and her head drooped on his chest. He held the weight of her in his arms and together they walked through the silent hallways.

Outside in the dark, he heard her take a deep breath of air. He did it himself and smelled the damp, salty night.

"There's a cab supposed to be waiting, but I don't see

it," she said. He heard the catch in her voice.

"Can you call a relative?"

"There's only my mother and she's already here at some big meeting."

"So I'll go in and get her. Jeez, she should be here with you." Women, he thought in disgust.

"Don't tell that to Tracy Webb. She'd eat you alive for those words," smiled Lily.

She was looking better, he decided. Either that or it was the night and it covered up the ashen sheen of her skin. He half-carried her to the granite seat that edged the sidewalk. From there he could see the yellow glow of a taxi light at the bottom of the hill, swinging up and then down as it crossed the rings of streets. Thank God, he thought. He looked down at her and saw that she had leaned back against the bench and stretched out her legs. Her eyes were closed. He'd put her in a cab and that was that. He didn't have to ever think about her again. He walked to the edge of the sidewalk and swung up and down on his toes, waiting. Tapping his toes against the curb. Hands in pocket.

She could hear the jingle of coins in his pants pocket. He wasn't handling this at all well. She should have known better. Now he'll never see me again, Lily thought dismally. Well, that's tough, isn't it, Lily Webb? What did you think? Did you think you could cover up? I mean, like, never let him know that you had something wrong with you? If he can't handle it, that's his problem. She swallowed away the lump in her throat.

"It's here," she heard him say.

She opened her eyes and saw the cab rolling across the empty plaza and swinging in front of the curb. She pulled herself up while he waited, holding the door open for her.

She looked at him. "Thanks a lot, fella. I mean, you've been great about all this. I don't know how I've gotten along before you came into my life. Now bug off." She collapsed onto the seat and told the driver her address.

"I don't think you were very nice to him, miss. He was only helping out, wasn't he?"

"Mind your own business."

He was glad it was dark and no one was out here. "You fool! You asshole." He kicked the stairway with each word. His eyes burned. What a fucking day. He turned the oak handles and the door swung silently open before him. He'd never see her again. In the ICU, they had turned his mother onto her side and she smelled of baby powder. He stood over her breathing hard.

In the crowded auditorium, Leah and Katherine found seats against the back wall. There was a low roar of voices all around them.

"My lord, this might be Tracy's night of triumph," Katherine whispered. She looked around at the crowd of nurses. Many of them were in uniform, excused from duty for the meeting. They would carry information back to those still on the floors. Others were in street clothes. Some carried babies. There were angry faces in this crowd, Katherine thought.

She saw Tracy Webb sit up straight, a high flush staining her cheeks. "She doesn't need all that makeup tonight," whispered Leah.

"Alright everyone," Tracy called out. "Settle down, please." Instantly the low rumble of voices ceased. "As you all know, this is not our regular monthly meeting—"

"You bet it isn't. We want to know when we get the same breaks Eddie Shuster gets. Where's our contract?" a voice cried out.

"Never mind that," a male voice boomed, "when do we strike?"

Tracy held up her hand. "Let me finish, please." There was a little smile on her broad lips. "Eddie Shuster's contract is none of our business. But since we know about it, it will be leverage for our own bargaining, you can be assured of that. As for a strike, you all know that as city employees, we are prevented from striking."

A chorus of voices rose in protest and Tracy waited for it to die down. A baby wailed from the back of the hall; its cry went unheeded.

"They've stalled us too long," someone yelled. "It's a slap in the face to us, that Shuster gets a big raise and we get nothing." It was Bev Britain. She laughed, a short derisive laugh. "As usual, nurses are ignored."

"Still," Tracy went on. "We've been bargaining in good faith. Bargaining for months now. And if you think sitting in the same room with George Tratten, the city attorney, isn't hard work, believe me, you are wrong. However, as long as bargaining goes on, our hands are tied. When it fails, when it breaks down, then we can take other steps."

"Such as?"

"Arbitration, of course."

"And that can go on for months," the voice cried in disgust.

Tracy shrugged. "Listen, people. I've been here for sixteen years. For the past five years I've been on the bargaining committee." She spat the words out as if they were obscenities. "It's the politicians at City Hall who are the villains, not the Eddie Shusters. They are trying their damndest to keep us in poverty."

"Right on," a voice cried out.

"They forget that for years this hospital paid its own way. We kept it self-supporting, not them. And they never put a dime back into it. They let it run downhill until it was ready to close. Well, it's finally turned the corner. They are paying Mr. Plumhouse a fat salary to put Liberty Hill back on its feet and we've waited. And waited."

Now the crowd had grown silent. What Tracy was telling them was all true. She had them in the palm of her hand.

"Liberty Hill has finally entered the twentieth century with Mr. Plumhouse at the wheel. And let me remind you that he's being paid out of taxpayers' pockets. That's you and me, folks. Our pockets. So not only have we paid for the hospital's improvements, but as employees, we've been lost along the way. We've been screwed in more ways than one, by my reckoning." She held up her hand to quell an angry response.

"If this were an election year, you can be sure that we'd be listened to. But it isn't and they are telling us that it isn't our turn. Why do you think that two-oh-three's contract was never made public in *The Courier*? Because they didn't want to let you or your families know about it, that's why. Thank God, Eddie Shuster's got a big mouth, otherwise we'd have never found out.

Bev Britain raised her hand and Tracy nodded at her. Bev stood up, a stocky figure in too-tight blue jeans. She jammed her hands in her pockets.

"Our pay scale is way below Boston's scale and that's because supposedly our cost of living is lower. But it ain't true. Has anyone taken a good look at Atwater lately? Have you seen the changes going on? We've become a bedroom community for Boston. Our rents and taxes have gone sky high, affordable housing for people like us has become scarce. And I was born here. This is my town!" Her voice broke.

"I am also the head of my household," Bev continued. "My rent is now five hundred and fifty dollars a month. I have two mouths to feed as well as bodies to clothe. I can't make it on my salary. And do you know why? Because of this very building itself! It's because Liberty Hill Hospital has suddenly become attractive and the Hill is luring all kinds of yuppies here." Someone laughed and

Bev glared in the direction of the sound. "Laugh all you want, but it's true. They love those darling little gas lamps on Circle Street and the adorable cobblestone drives. It's quaint here. Quaint and cute and too damned expensive for poor folks like me. It's not a question of living and working here anymore, it's a question of survival."

The auditorium broke into a thunderous applause and Bev sat down as if someone had pushed her. There was a bewildered look on her face. Tears began to fall from her eyes.

Tracy waited for the noise to quiet, then she nodded to a nurse standing in the front row of seats. The girl was young and her hair had been sprayed so that it spiked straight up. The area of hair above her right ear had been spray with pink glitter.

"I just graduated from nursing school last year," she said.

"Do they let her work here with that hair?" someone asked.

The girl flushed. "What I do at night is nobody's business. What I want to say is that I have college loans that I can't pay back, because I have to pay rent to my parents. My father's out of work and he needs that money. So I'm stuck. Stuck living like a kid at home, and holding a fistful of bills I thought I'd be able to pay once I was a registered nurse. Being an RN is like being told your dinner is a quiche but when you take a taste you feel like you've just put a lot of crap in your mouth. I can make more money selling dog houses." She sat down and put a wad of gum back in her mouth. Strangely, she did not look upset at her predicament.

Another voice called out, this time from the ICU group seated at the back of the hall. It was Sarah Purdy. "My husband is one of those laid off from the navy yard. Thirty years there and now he can't find work. We need every penny I can get. So get it!"

Leah heard Katherine sigh and begin to stir. When she saw Katherine pushing herself up, she wanted to grab her and hold her down. "No, don't," she whispered but Katherine shrugged off her hand.

Tracy's eyes widened when she saw who was waiting to be acknowledged. She gave Katherine a bare nod.

"I have something to say." Katherine pulled down her maternity smock and then held on to the hem of it with shaking fingers. "What we're doing now is discussing social issues, not the contract we're bargaining for. As far as I can see, as long as the city bargains with us, there's nothing we can do. Tracy's told us that already. We must stop this whining and feeling sorry for ourselves; it doesn't do any good. As Tracy has said, we now have more leverage. Let her use it. Encourage her to fight for us and I'm sure she will succeed."

Leah's heart sank when she saw Bev Britain come to her feet. She stood with her arms crossed over her chest, a wry smile on her face.

"We all know Mrs. Weathers, she *used* to be one of us," she said, a gasp going up across the room, "but now she's a doctor's wife. Her point of view has changed to say the least. No, the thing we should consider is another job action like we had at lunch today. That makes this place sit up and take notice. Enough sitting around and wringing our hands. Let's use our power. We may not be able to strike, but we sure can demonstrate the hell out of this place."

"What do you have in mind, Bev?" Tracy said, ignoring the still-standing Katherine.

"We can't help it if we all get sick at the same time, can we?"

An excited roar went over the crowd.

Leah reached up pulled Katherine into her seat. "I think we'd better get out of here."

139

"Maybe we ought to stay and learn what they plan to do."

"We can picket," someone called out. "Every day. First here in front of the hospital, then in front of city Hall. Anywhere we can get attention. We can keep *The Courier* informed every day about our progress."

At that Tracy shook her head. "Not about bargaining, that's illegal. But we can make damned sure the paper follows our little actions. They'll eat it up."

"Let's refuse to serve lunch trays every day," the pink-haired nurse called out. "That's culinary work, not nursing."

"I agree wholeheartedly," Tracy replied. "Today's little action was spontaneous and easy to accomplish. I'm sure the hospital knows that we mean business. Don't say you will refuse, though. You can be fired. Simply say, if anyone asks, that you are doing nursing care and cannot serve trays at that time, and be damned sure I'll be checking on you. You'd better be at the patient's bedside, not in the lounge when trays are delivered."

Katherine grinned at Leah. "Good old Tracy. How she manages two hats at the same time I'll never know. You know, she's going by the book on this. She could have urged a walk-out, legal or illegal, and she'd have gotten it. But she didn't. There's still hope."

"And she's right about that lunchtime business," Leah replied. "How did the hospital react?"

"Our Mr. Plumhouse and Evelyn Holden got right into the thick of it and served trays with their own little hands. Not in the unit, of course—it doesn't affect us—but from what I heard they covered all the floors. If the nurses do that every day, I'd say there'll be an impact. And I bet it won't take long."

"If they go on this route, I'm going to help out. But if they decide to strike, I'll leave," Leah said more to herself than to Katherine.

"I can't do a damned thing." Katherine smoothed the folds of cloth over her belly. "Not with punchkin about to make her debut. But, by God, if I weren't blimped out like this, I'd picket. right in front of the emergency room. Just to make Dr. Weathers sit up and take notice."

"Why is there trouble in the Weathers house?"

"Oh, just the usual. He's after me to quit now and laze about the house like a queen. We sort of argue about it every day." She yawned. "Wouldn't it kill him to see me carrying a picket sign?"

They missed the motion made from the floor ... something about committees. Several nurses were gathered in corners at the back of the auditorium while Tracy sat alone on the stage, the spotlight sending jagged streaks of white across her face. Leah thought she looked a little like Queen Nefertiti, alone and powerful on her throne.

Later, when the auditorium began to empty, Leah and Katherine walked through the darkened hallways together, Leah's blue shoulder bag making little thumps against her hip.

"You've got a couple of hours before you have to go to work. Want to come back to the house for a cup of tea?" Katherine asked.

"Thanks, but I'll stick around here," Leah replied. "There's the lovely isolation of the cafeteria at night that somehow lures me. I can read, I can put quarters in the vending machines and see what I get. You punch tomato juice and sometimes you get coffee. Push the sandwich button and get a bowl of soup. It's a challenge, that place."

They parted at the door and Leah made her way to the darkened cafeteria. She could hear the excited voices of the nurses as they headed for the doors. Smiling to herself, she thought: if there is one thing nurses love, it's committees. Tonight they had organized so many that they had decided they needed one just to keep track of the others. There was a picketing committee, an informational committee, publicity, telephone squad, and finally, a reporting committee to liason between Tracy's bargaining unit and their own. She shook her head thinking of her own vote to help on the picket lines. Maddy will have a fit, she thought. Her daughter picketing. But Nikki is going to love it. Maybe that's why she chose it, to get him out in his blue stroller, to see the excitement.

Lights from the vending machines marked a pathway for her. She stared at the array of beverages, unseeing. Finally, she dropped a quarter in, punched a button, and hoped for a carton of milk. She got it. She sat in the semidarkness and tried to sort her thoughts. How had she fallen in with such enthusiasm when an hour before the meeting she had regarded the nurses with trepidation?

It was, partly, a way of breaking the ice between the ICU and the regular floors. The unit nurses had isolated themselves from others. Maybe they regarded themselves as just a little sharper in their nursing care than the medical nurses. She was sure there was a bit of snobbery involved. The medical nurses, in defense, of course, indeed cried "snob" and avoided them altogether. Night nursing was another barrier. No one knew the swing shift nurses or cared about them. A breed apart, they were left to their own devices. Tonight, however, the barrier had been crossed, and her loneliness had disappeared. She was one of them.

But the true reason she had found herself on the picketing committee, was that they were right. Right to care about their lives, their paychecks, their work conditions, and going about it in a legal and sensible fashion. They were not wildcatters. They simply were tired of being shoved to one side while others climbed the financial ladders. It wasn't the out-of-work husbands on the waterfront. It wasn't even the demeaning chores nurses were forced to perform only because there was no one else to do them. It was simply a matter of economics. And if it weren't for Red and Maddy, she knew she would be feeling the same pinch most of the others felt. She sipped her milk feeling a little guilty about that snug haven on the waterfront.

She reached in her bag and pulled out her book. An hour later she looked up at the clock and gasped. She was late! And not dressed, either. She took a quick look around, but the area was dark and deserted. Pulling off her jeans and sweatshirt, she stood in the light of the vending machine and unfolded the blue scrub suit. She did not see the foolish grin of the kitchen worker behind the swinging doors. He hung on to his mop and hummed, "Oh yeah, babe, give it to me," picturing her spread-eagled beneath him.

At report, the news was gloomy. Emma Bond had spiked a four o'clock temp of one hundred and two. It was not enough to notify Dr. Peters yet, but she also was refusing to be suctioned and that guaranteed a higher temperature as time went on.

Jane Carlson looked tired as she flipped the Kardex to Emma's page. "The day shift said she cried all day. Refused her physical therapy, didn't eat, etcetera, etcetera. The usual crap Emma comes up with. And I predict by morning, she'll have a pneumonia. What kind she develops, we won't know, but all those nasty little creatures will be down there. And Emma knows it. Emma doesn't care." She began to sing to the tune of "Row, Row, Row Your Boat": "Emma's out to lunch today and getting in my hair." She bit off the laughter that threatened her.

It was evident that no mention of Leah's efforts to wean Emma had been made throughout the different shifts. She glanced over at Pat Connor and gave her a slow wink. Nurses don't read nursing notes, she thought to herself, only vindicative doctors do. And just because I wouldn't let him feel me up.

Pat made a motion that indicated Leah was to take care of Emma Bond once again and Leah nodded.

"And now onto our most interesting case. Our newest and most exciting event of the day . . . the thing we've all been waiting for, ladies and gentlemen . . . AIDS." Jane made herself sound remarkably like the six o'clock arts and entertainment commentator on WBZ. She even had the same dopey smile.

Pat giggled. "How is he doing?"

Jane struggled to contain herself. When she was tired she had a tendancy to get silly. Three to eleven had been outrageously busy and all because Mr. Ragust had come back from the operating room just as the supper hour had begun. Alone, she had to run down into the bowels of the hospital to drag the man in charge of supplies back from his meal. There were hundreds of items she needed and no one else to get them for her—bottles of irrigant, bottles of bleach, red-marked needle disposers, special tags for soiled laundry bags. Loading her supplies onto a shopping cart and trundling it onto the elevators, she had banged her shin against the cart. That had started it all. She began to laugh instead of cry, and knowing she had missed her dinner seemed the funniest of all.

"He's still dopey, but aren't we all?" She rubbed her hand over her face and sniffed. "Let me start again, okay? He's had an incision and drainage of the shoulder wound and now has a continuous irrigant. Dr. Sheen says that will stay in for the night. I've gotten enough fluid to last you. Mr. Ragust is awake and alert. His vitals are stable and he's taking fluids. One thing, though, he hasn't voided since surgery, so I'd check that out. He may need catheterizing. Everything is in his room for disposal. And the red sign is on the door. He hadn't had visitors, except for the kid whose mother is next door and I've told him to keep his distance. He's lonely, so I've let him and Mr. Ragust keep each other company."

She ran her finger down Two-Gus's Kardex sheet. "I think that I've covered everything."

"How's his mental status?" Pat asked.

"Oh, I knew you'd find something," Jane sighed. "As far as I can tell, he's holding on pretty well. He's quiet. But that might just be anesthesia. You'll be able to tell better than me. I only recovered him."

They were talking about him. He could tell. They kept glancing towards his room as they held conference. The lights had been dimmed, signaling the coming of night. He dreaded it.

Sleep was permitted, but he knew it would hover just beyond his grasp. And the sloshing sound of the fluid in his shoulder was holding him pinned there. At times he dozed dreaming of the sea and wind, but when he moved to balance himself upon a wave, pain jolted him awake. How could he sleep in this place? Red blinking lights became the eyes of feral cats. Green heartlines spiking across the monitor held him mesmerized. If there should be a break in that line, he was dead. He wished they'd placed the damned machine out of sight. Then he laughed at himself. It was out of sight, he'd been craning his neck to watch it.

He wanted to sleep, but his distorted dreams frightened him. He decided that these post-operative hours were worse than the weeks he'd endured before. Nothing came together to make sense, dreams and reality blended with a cacaphony of noise, confusing and rousing him to startled awakeness. And then the pain would hit. Nothing in the weeks since that kid knocked him over could compare with this.

The fluid in the bottle over his head looked so cool and clear as if it had come from a natural mountain spring. It felt, though, as if hot oil were pouring into his flesh.

He wanted to move but couldn't. His back and bottom seemed stuck to the mattress. He was sure he was lying in a pool of blood. He tried to bend his knees but they weren't connected to him. He hadn't realized he'd been staring at the group of nurses at the desk until one of them arose and stood by the door.

"How are you feeling?" She began to robe herself.

"Pretty good, if you don't mind pain." His lips were stuck to his gums. "And thirsty. I've got a flannel mouth."

She walked into the room. And he swore to himself that he wasn't dreaming of a Nordic princess. She really did have a braid of silver hair that touched her waist. And her skin was creamy gold. She had bright blue eyes that regarded him with, what? Pity? No, she was simply measuring everything she saw. The fluids, the bottles, the heartline over his head, and the monstrously soggy dressing that pinned him to the bed.

Finally she smiled at him. "I'm Leah Swift, and I'll be taking care of you tonight. Before I get you some pain medication, I'm going to give you the urinal."

"But I don't have to..."

"Yes, you do." She handed him the goose-necked urinal. "You just don't know it. I'll run the water in the sink and you think about it. It will come." She held the covers up and helped him guide the bottle to his penis. There was nothing strange or embarrassing in her gesture.

"Ordinarily I'd give you some privacy," she said, "But you need a cycle change."

His eyes followed hers to the irrigating bottle. It was almost empty. Then he saw the damned gloves and mask come on and disappointment welled up. She was like all the others. To her he was a leper. She disappeared at the side of his bed and he heard the clinking of glass. It was only when she lifted the nearly full drainage bottle into sight that he forgave her the insult. That was no spring water in the bottle. It was cloudy and shot with clots of dark red blood. He heard her give a little grunt as she carried the heavy container to the toilet. Soon the fresh tang of bleach filled the room as she swabbed the toilet with the cleaner.

Without realizing it, his bladder began to empty and only when the bottle was half-full did he feel the tiny muscles in his belly begin to work. There was exquisite relief that made him shudder.

He handed her the bottle and she smiled at him mockingly. "Works every time, almost." There was another dose of chlorine as she emptied and cleaned the bottle.

Later, he lay in wondrous comfort. She had cushioned pillows against his back and between his legs so that he felt suspended in a nest of feathers. His shoulder was dry and immobilized with folds of soft towels. She had rubbed warm oil on his skin, easing the cramps that knotted his back.

He was sure it wasn't the shot she had given him. It was the way she had arranged his body, so that it seemed to float above all corners or edges. It was the dry dressing she had fluffed upon his shoulder. And finally it was the hot, sweet bit of tea that she held for him to sip.

He lay facing the door, away from the sight of that ominous heartline. She had told him that he didn't need monitoring at all but it was a rule in here. She didn't realize how anxious that screen had made him feel. He could love her. He did love her, and for the next few hours, each time that he awoke, he watched for her with something close to reverence.

When Leah entered Emma's room, she saw that the room was in darkness, save for the ghostly glare of the TV set. There was a closed-in smell, an air of neglect about the room. Empty bottles from the respirator stood on the windowsill uncapped, as if the technician had serviced her machine and then scurried away. The wastebasket was filled to overflowing and the bedside table littered with crumpled papers. It was after eleven and Emma's untouched supper tray stood amid the mess. It was obvious that she had forbidden entry to the housekeeping department. Even the cardiac monitor looked feeble, its glow competing with the light of the television.

Leah read the digital figures. Emma's heart was up to one hundred and ten. Surely her temperature was climbing and Emma was helping it along by not moving and not coughing. She knew just how to do it. The staff called it, "Emma's shutdown."

Leah reached over the bed and turned off the television. Instantly Emma snatched back the controls and flicked it on.

"I knew you weren't asleep," Leah said. She switched on the soft back light against the wall. Emma shook her head violently.

"Oh yes, my dear. I want to talk to you."

She picked up the pile of clean laundry from the chair. It was obvious that Emma's bed had gone unchanged this morning, accounting for the sour odor in the room. She said nothing, simply placed the linens on the window sill and sat down facing Emma. From the set lines in her face and the closed eyes, talking was the last thing Emma wanted.

"I almost lost my job because of you," Leah said. Unfair, she thought to herself, using guilt to pry her out of her state. "Dr. Peters found out what we were doing and he raised holy hell about it." Emma opened her eyes. "I've been warned by my head nurse to mind my manners or else. So, here we are."

Emma rolled onto her back and pressed the electric button. The head of her bed began to rise. She reached into the hidden drawer beneath her tray and pulled out a piece of hospital stationery. Without looking at Leah, she handed it to her.

"What's this?" Leah asked. "A piece of hate mail? That's okay, join the crowd."

The ventilator gave a heave that set off a wave of coughing. The tubing blew off the globs of sputum dribbled onto Emma's gown. Swallowing hard, Leah handed her a clean towel.

"I'll get you bathed and cleaned up later." She held the ventilator tubing ready for Emma's hand. And when the spasm ended, she flicked on the bedside light and began to read Emma's letter.

As she read, a mixture of rage and pity flooded her. Emma's handwriting was spidery and looped downward as if she could not see over the tracheostomy tubing.

"My sister was in today. She takes care of my kids. Arlene is 14 and they say she is a slow learner. I know she is retarded. My sister says she stopped her periods. Only she don't know it. She don't talk much. My old man moved back in the house when I got sick. He isn't supposed to be there, the court says. But he is. I got to get home. I want to wean."

Leah's hand shook a little as she refolded the note and pushed it into her pocket. She felt Emma's hand tapping on her arm and looked at her.

Reading her lips was easy tonight. Her mouthings were slow and thoughtful as though hoarding strength. "If they don't wean me, I will try to die. I know how to do it."

"You've got a temperature."

Emma nodded, as if to say, "See?"

"In order to wean, your lungs must be clear."

"That's what I mean," the lips moved. "I can make them fill up if I want. I don't want to, but I will."

"This is blackmail."

"Yup."

"I can't start you until I suction you clear and then make sure you have the strength." Leah nodded to the supper tray. "You haven't eaten. Emma, you will have to take the first step and stop making trouble for yourself. I will work with you as soon as you pull yourself together, I promise."

Emma pulled out her plastic blackboard and wrote on it with her sharpened fingernail, "That's not enough anymore. You are going onto days. And I don't have the time to break in another night nurse. My weaning has to come from the asshole Peters. You get him to do it. Until then I'll let myself go. This ain't for me, it's for Arlene."

She pulled up the plastic sheet and the words disappeared. Then she snapped the board against her hand, indicating that the interview was over. She picked up the remote control device and aimed it, like a gun, at the television screen. Leah had never felt so helpless.

Pat Connor glanced up at her as she walked to the desk. Seeing the stricken look on Leah's face, she sighed.

"For God's sake, don't take it so personally. You'd think you're the only nurse Emma takes to. Well, honey, you aren't. Emma's pulling her big stunt on you for the first time. She did it to me weeks ago and to someone else before me."

"She's going to get so damned sick, though."

"She knows that. And she also knows that we aren't about to let her die. So she goes through hell for nothing."

"Do you know that she thinks her fourteen-year-old daughter is pregnant by her father?"

Pat looked at her in astonishment and then exploded with laughter, clapping a hand to her mouth and doubling down behind the counter so that her laughter would not fill the unit. Leah watched her, uncomprehending at first.

Finally she said, "Emma doesn't have a fourteen-year-old daughter, does she?"

But Pat was unable to answer. She took a tissue and wiped her streaming eyes. Every few seconds, a giggle erupted all over again and soon her eyes grew apologetic.

Fortunately, a light came on over her patient's room and she could escape the look on Leah's face. With a tissue bunched in her fist and an occasional burst of laughter escaping from her lips, she scurried away. Leah sat down and stared at the cardiac monitors without seeing the lines of QRS spikes that flashed across the screens.

She manipulated me! Leah thought to herself. Just as if I were a green schoolgirl. And I bought it lock, stock, and barrel. I pictured a poor retarded girl with a big belly. I even saw the baby. Deformed and doomed at birth. I was ready to fight the world for Emma. Oh, how she must be laughing behind her plastic blackboard.

Unaware, Leah's hands had curled into fists as she thought about it. For the rest of the night, she avoided Emma's room.

Chapter Eight

He was there the next morning looking for Lily but knowing she would not be here. The terrace before the hospital was deserted. He made his way to the ICU trying not to think about her.

As soon as he saw his mother, he could tell she was getting better. The nurse said she was getting lighter, whatever that meant, and now he could see it for himself as the morning wore on. Dorothy was moving her arms and mumbling to herself. He tried to understand what she whispered, but some of the words did not even sound like English to him. But it was okay, at least she was coming out of that deathlike sleep.

He watched, fascinated, as her arm came up and stayed suspended over her face as though hung by invisible threads. Then the other hand rose up to meet it and she began to pick at the needle in her arm. Alarmed, he rushed to the desk and dragged a nurse back with him. She quickly wrapped Dorothy's arm in multiple layers of cotton and fastened a soft mitten to her free hand.

Why didn't they simply tie her arms to the bed, he asked, and the nurse told him that tying Dorothy down would only make her more restless. He liked her for that, for treating him as an adult, but more importantly, for knowing the right thing to do when he didn't.

When it came for them to bathe his mother, he wandered out of the room. It was then that he remembered the man, Two-Gus, in the room next door and shyly he peeked around the door at him.

He looked dreadful. Exhausted and drained, he seemed as though he'd fought some battle in the hours of darkness while he had been sleeping. There was a blankness in his eyes that made Billy think he was looking into pools of utter hopelessness.

The room was filled with huge bottles, some of them empty and some of them filled. Towels littered the floor beneath a large bottle, as big as a commercial mayonnaise jar. It was slowly filling with pink fluid that he knew was draining from Two-Gus. Heaps of laundry bags leaned against the wall. They were tied with red warning tags marked "Caution" just like the sign on Two-Gus's door. He looked at it. There were instructions to check in at the nurse's station printed over it. He hadn't seen that last night. It was a little scary, he thought, and certainly he wasn't going to risk going in. Besides, the nurses were busier now than last night. They didn't talk to him, just rushed by with anxious apologetic smiles.

Billy gave Two-Gus a timid wave but there was no kind smile in return. The man's face look chewed and tight. Dark lines circled his clenched lips and dragged at the bottoms of his eyes. Billy fled the unit.

For awhile, he wandered through the corridors of the hospital. Give us a half-hour, the nurse said, then you can come back. Somehow, he didn't know how, he found himself standing at the door to the dialysis room. She wouldn't be in there now, he knew, but at least he could find it if he wanted. From there he followed the hallway until he came to the basement door of the hospital, and when he stepped out into the sunlight, he was almost blinded. The crisp gray of the granite terrace was bleached white in the sun. It had rained in the night, and dampness steamed up out of the stone as if it had lain there for centuries and was at last released. It formed a mist around his feet.

The night nurse, Leah, had given him some pamphlets on diabetes. They were still in his jacket pocket. He pulled them out and leaned against the wall reading.

His spirits began to plummet. It was clear that he should have learned all this before Dorothy got sick. The first line he read was marked in red: *Manage this disease by yourself!* That was a joke. She would never do that. It was going to be up to him. Another laugh. She'd say, "No fourteen-year-old kid is going to tell Dot Fellows what to do."

She wasn't like Lily Webb. She didn't care about lab values, or diet, or the daily insulin shots (she'd been skipping those). That was too boring, she had said, but he knew that needles scared her to death.

One day, he watched her take out the hypodermic and her hands trembled like leaves in the wind. How she hated those needles. She fought back tears until she cried out that she couldn't even see to measure up the damned medicine. With a sob she threw the syringe, still stuck into the vial, into the kitchen sink. The bottle shattered as she stormed from the room. An hour later, when she calmed down, she sent him to the drugstore for another vial. He didn't stick around to see if she took it. He fled.

There'll be no more running, he thought to himself a little sadly. When he finished the booklet, he jammed it into his pocket and began to walk around the terrace, following the ring of stone.

Yesterday when he had met Lily Webb, something had begun; he was changing. How astonished he had been at the cool way she looked at herself, for knowing all about some disease he'd never heard of before. The way she took control of herself, even though she had so little control over the sickness. Or maybe it was the long hours he'd spent in the ICU waiting for his mother to wake up, watching the nurses in there. Their vigilance astounded him. The smooth way they had taken control of his mother, a fearless way. That was it. A matter of control. When he began to understand, he felt as if he'd awakened into a new world of sharp, crisp edges, that made his eyes burn with clarity.

He began to pace the wall around the hospital, and shortly it came to him that the old building resembled a fortress. From any vantage point in the perimeter of this walk, he could peer down the hill or scan the horizon. It *was* a fortress. On all four points of the compass, he realized, there was a clear view of the town below. No one could mount an assault upon this place. For a long moment, he had a glimpse of history in his mind's eye. He could see the ragged line of colonials leaning against this very wall. He ran his hand over it. He could see their muskets pointed down the hill, their homely brown hats shading tired eyes. Could they see the flash of British weaponry and red-coated figures in the narrow streets below? He leaned far over the wall to see what they must have seen. He caught sight of Lily.

She had found a niche in a little pool of sunlight between the other wall and the strip of grass it circled. From the shape of her shoulders, Billy could tell that she was crying. For a second he wanted to shout with joy at seeing her. Instead he ran for the narrow set of stairs he'd seen on the north side of the hospital. They were covered with silvery gray moss, and barred at the bottom by a wrought-iron gate. He vaulted it easily and sprinted around the corner, feeling the air swelling his lungs. She was still there.

"Hey!" He skidded to a halt waiting for her to collect herself.

She hurriedly wiped her eyes before turning in his direction.

"Hey yourself," she replied.

"What are you doing here today? I thought you came every other."

She did not reply. Instead, she began to collect her books. Standing up, she brushed her skirt and picked up her jacket. He wanted to put his hand on her arm, to stop her, to explain how he'd been a coward last night, but he wasn't any more. She tossed her schoolbag over her shoulder.

"Where're you going?"

"Home, I guess. It doesn't matter."

"So I'll walk you. That's alright, ain't . . . isn't it? I myself was just going down the hill, too." She did not answer, but instead began to descend the stairs. He followed behind and for awhile they walked in silence, pausing at each street corner and then crossing thick cobblestone lanes. Finally she turned to him.

"Why are you following me?"

His heart sank. "I'm not. I'm walking with you because I was such a jerk last night and don't know how to explain why." She shrugged. "You scared me. I thought, jeez, you might die on me and they'd think maybe I killed you."

She burst out laughing. "It's alright," she said when she caught her breath. "See? I'm not dead. I'm better, in fact."

He could see that. Whatever dialysis did to her, it did not last. Except for the puffy and reddened eyes, she looked fine. Pretty. Her hair was shining.

"You were crying up there," he said. "What happened?"

She cocked her head towards him. "Come on, the light doesn't stay red forever." He followed her across the street. "And stop following me. Keep up, will you?"

Happily, he reached for her schoolbag and tossed it over his shoulder. "The only way I'm going to get a kidney," she said so softly that he had to bend near her, "is to go off my diet. I have to skip treatment and get really sick. Then, I might get a transplant."

"That's crazy," he said. "Who told you that?"

"I just came from Dr. Russell. He's my doctor. I've been bugging him lately. I mean like how long do I have to wait? I've been on dialysis a year now. I know it doesn't take that long. someone *has* to die, right? Where are those kidneys going?

"He must have gotten sick of listening to me today because he finally let the cat out of the bag. He said that since I've been such a good patient, they keep moving others up ahead of me. Others who aren't so good. Do you believe it? I mean, if I were some dummy and couldn't handle the diet or the dialysis, they'd have transplanted me ages ago."

That couldn't be true, he thought. She must be exaggerating. There is a list of candidates, she had told him yesterday. One for each section of the country. They wouldn't screw around with that, moving a name up, moving hers down. That would ruin the whole purpose. It would mean that someone could sort of buy themselves a kidney if they wanted to. She looked at him narrowly and he tried to arrange his face so that she would not see his doubt.

"There was a kid from Puerto Rico here last year. She moved up here to live with an aunt or someone. She didn't know she had anything wrong with her when she left the island. She was just sort of sick and getting to look like a blimp. Her aunt took her to a doctor and he started her on dialysis. She used to come in on the same day as me. I tried to be friendly with her because she couldn't speak English and she cried every time they put her on the machine. She lasted two weeks and then I never saw her again. She got a transplant. I even wished her luck. That kidney could have been mine." Her voice was bitter.

"I've been dumb. Here I was, trying so hard to be a good patient. Thinking I was going to get rewarded." She wiped viciously at her eyes. Billy watched. "The diet sucks, you know. It's the worst way to live there is." She pushed up her sleeve. "This damned thing that looks like a snake. They stick it with needles three times a week and it never has a chance to heal up. I hate it. Do you know that? I despise it. It makes me ugly!" She took a corner of her jacket and wiped the tears from her face.

"It is sort of gross," he agreed, looking at the thick cord of flesh on her arm. "But you ain't . . . are not ugly. I think you are nice looking. Even beautiful, maybe." Jesus, he was babbling, making it worse.

"I don't even know why I'm telling you all this, I don't even know you. It was just Russell saying, 'Keep up the good work,' and then dismissing me, like I was some kid. He's really screwed me, the bastard."

"Don't you have someone who could donate a kidney? What about your mother?"

Lily shook her head. "She's working on only one, herself. I don't have anyone else."

"You can have one of mine," he said, adding, "I mean it," when he saw the look on her face. "No big deal. Go back and tell the doctor you found yourself a kidney."

They faced each other in the deep shadows of the narrow old street. They were alone. She reached up and pulled his head down and then kissed him on the lips.

Instantly he had trouble breathing. Her lips were sweet and faintly salty and he could feel his own trembling against her. He hoped she wouldn't notice. Then he remembered that he was supposed to close his eyes, but he could not stop staring at the wet clumps of her eyelashes sweeping her cheek. And then it was over, she pulled away. His breath exploded in his ear and the green schoolbag swung between them, thumping him in the crotch. He knew his ears were burning red.

"What did you say your name was?" She whispered, smiling up at him.

"William B. Fellows," he said, feeling stupid.

"Thank you for offering, William B. Fellows. No one ever did that before." There were two bright spots on her cheeks and he could see a pulse pounding in her throat.

"I was not kidding," he said. "Let's turn right around and go back up there."

She shook her head. "I can't. Besides, it is my good day. I don't want to spend it up there if I don't have to. Dr. Russell would want you to think about it and I would too. There's no great rush. This is major surgery you're talking about."

He hadn't thought that far ahead, like it wasn't really real to him. What if he couldn't afford it? He wished he'd thought of that before offering. As if she could read his mind, Lily reached over and took his arm, squeezing it in comfort. They emerged at the bottom of the hill into bright sunlight.

"I didn't even ask how your mother was," she said as they crossed the street. "Is she waking up?"

He'd forgotten all about Dorothy! What if she were awake and wanted him? "She is beginning to come to, they say, but she hasn't opened her eyes. She doesn't answer me."

"It's almost as bad as my disease, diabetes. At least there's a cure for mine. I wouldn't change places with her for one minute. You never know if you have too much sugar in your blood or not enough. Or too little insulin or too much. And the diet and needles . . ." She shuddered.

"How do you know so much about it?"

She laughed. "My mother is a nurse up there. I read her books and we talk about nursing. It keeps us friendly.

I mean, she doesn't know much about kids, or music, or what's the latest in designer jeans or hair. For that matter I don't either, but she thinks I do. I let her think I'm a horrid teenager." Her finger began to trace the outline of his hand. He did not dare move.

"It's strange, when you're sick you want to know why, so you study it. Then you want to know more. After awhile you forget about things like hairstyles. I'll probably be a nurse. After my transplant, that is. But I don't tell my mother, she'd smother me if she knew."

He didn't know about things like that—relationships. All he could remember was clinging to his own mother when he was little, with a knot of fear tied tight in his belly. She was good-natured, but a little flighty, his grandmother always said. Give Dot a drink and she'll give you the shirt off her back. He often felt like a discarded shirt of Dot's. She used to forget he was around when he was little.

"I have to get back," he said and cursed his mother.

"Okay. I'll be on the wall at two o'clock tomorrow. That'll give us an hour together." She took his hand and shook it gravely. "And thanks for the offer, but I couldn't let you donate a kidney. I don't think anyone else would, either."

"There's no harm in finding out," he said. "Who knows, maybe we would fit together just right." Her smile was so pure and sad that he thought he might drown in it.

He watched as she crossed the street and opened a gate to the waterfront. Above her, a red sign announced Red's marina. He wondered why she was going there. Then he turned around and began to jog up the hill, imagining to himself that she would someday race with him to the top.

Nikki was dressed and waiting in his stroller when Lily appeared. With a crow of impatience, he held out his arms to her.

"He's in love," Leah called out to Lily. "He knew you were coming and he's been impossible all morning." She watched as Lily knelt and nuzzled the baby's cheek. He giggled and pushed away. Then Lily straightened. There was a bloom in her face, Leah could see. A good day, she'd say.

"Well, I'm here now," Lily said. "And we're off to see Old Ironsides."

It was only a short ride and they had made it many times together, but it was the longest Lily could manage. Besides, Nikki wouldn't care. As long as he could view the world from his stroller, he was happy. Leah tucked a brown paper bag in the deep pocket of his stroller.

"Juice, cookies, and an extra diaper. And there's a little something for you, too. It's no-fat, no-protein, no-potassium lemon cake. Maddy made it just for you."

Lily smiled at her. "Is it food?"

"Almost, I think. If you don't like it, give it to the sea gulls." Leah watched as Lily pushed the stroller down the dock. Nikki never turned back.

When they were gone, she settled into a deck chair, put her feet up on a dock barrel, and pulled out her writing pad. At the top of the sheet of paper, she wrote in pencil, "PRSO." She had forgotten what the letters stood for . . . well she'd ask Katherine. All she knew was that it was a committee made up of physicians and its job was to insure patient management. Peer Review, that was it. Self-policing, it kept a strict watch over the cases at Liberty Hill. Supposedly, it was merciless when it came to an errant physician though she, as a staff member, never learned of its disciplinary actions. It was strictly between physician and physician. To her, PRSO had to be the logical place to voice her complaints about Emma's doctor, Claude Peters.

She began to write, and then to erase, and finally she tore off the sheet of paper and began again. How could she point out what was wrong with Emma's care when there was nothing left undone for her? Her every need was answered. She was being serviced by not only the nursing staff, but respiratory as well. She was fed, kept warm, and even entertained. Physical therapy was, for her, a diversion to cure boredom. Even social services had intervened in disputes with her husband or the business office. It was more than anyone could expect.

She stared out over the cove, watching the way the boats swung quietly towards the wind. Who would believe her?

As long as Claude Peters was paid for his services and there was no gross mismanagement of her case, no one would believe that there was a patient at Liberty Hill being neglected. Then the germ of an idea began to grow. What if Peters stopped getting payments from welfare?

She crossed out the few sentences she had written and began to make a list instead. Monday: call welfare. Question: policy on long-term coverage for patients. How long would they support Emma? And how was the determination of need made? Whose report carried the most weight with them: Peters or Liberty Hill?

She wrote fiercely, trying to keep up with the questions that arose one after the other. The more she scribbled down, the more she thought of, as if her brain had awakened suddenly to the challenge. Finally she realized that she knew absolutely nothing about her state's welfare department. Where to begin?

The soft honk of a car horn roused her. She shaded her eyes and saw a sleek navy blue Cadillac nosing against the chain-link fence. When the car door swung open and she saw who it was, she gulped. It was Julian Plumhouse. It wasn't just idle chatter the other night, he had meant what he said. He was here. And she saw him reach into the back seat and pull out a large wicker basket.

She looked down at herself with dismay. Her cut-off

jeans were paint spattered and the old gray sweatshirt of Red's was just as bad. "Oh, damn. I didn't think he meant it."

She glanced around looking for a place to hide. She could jump in the water and duck under the dock. She could take the dinghy and row out to the center of the cove. She could—

She waved at him and began walking towards his car. By the time, she climbed the ramp, he had a little pile of items resting on the blacktop parking lot. "Give me a hand," he said. "These picnics involve a lot of equipment, you know. It's got to be done right." when he turned to her, she felt herself drowning in his smile. It was a smile of pure delight. His eyes stared at her, seemed to cover her with warmth and she knew he never saw the grimy shorts or sweatshirt. She grinned back at him.

For a moment everything disappeared. The harbor, the sun, even the gulls that shrilled at them from the water's edge. She began to feel a little dizzy. Finally, his eyes deepened and she could see a redness staining his cheeks. He was blushing.

"What is all this?" she asked, looking at the little pile between them. She knelt and began to pick through it, grasping a silver cannister, capped against the sun. She could hear ice cubes rattling inside as she lifted it. She spotted a blanket folded inside a zippered leather case, then studied the basket. Curious, she unhooked the wooden clasps and stared at the contents. There were tiny jars of caviar banked in iced thermoses. And fruit— gleaming apples and grapes so perfect and slightly moist that the beads of water on them shone like tiny diamonds. Delicate sandwiches with their crusts trimmed off were individually wrapped and tied with red ribbons. They rested on an iced tray. She gasped and looked up at him.

"Where did you get this?" But she did not wait for his answer. She rummaged through the basket, running her fingers over the cunning compartments. The lid of the basket was festooned with small china dishes held in place by red velvet bands. Wine glasses, new with tiny labels still stuck on their sides. Silverware wrapped in red plaid napkins and bound with bone rings. Tucked into a roll of tablecloth, there were foil-wrapped towelettes. She could smell them, lemon and glycerine. Mouth swabs gone fancy, she thought, grinning to herself.

"It's pretentious, I know," he said, "but I didn't have time to go shopping. This place is in Faneuil Hall. Picnic Palace, it's called. I just telephoned and it was ready when I got there. I thought I'd get the usual bologna sandwiches and soggy bread. Hard cheese . . ." His voice drained away. "It's a bit more than that, I'm afraid."

"It must have cost a fortune," she breathed, not seeing the look of dismay come over his face. She refastened the hasps. "And what's this?" She lifted a black leather box.

"Music to eat by," he said. "Mostly Mozart."

It was a compact disk player and a half-dozen records nestled beside the tiny speaker.

She settled back on her heels and looked out over the water while he turned away and busied himself with locking the car doors. Then he waited while she gathered herself. Finally she stood up and looked him square in the face.

"No one has ever done something for me with such care and thought. I . . . I don't know how to thank you."

His shoulders slumped with relief and joy came into his voice. "You don't have to thank me, just find me a shady place by the water and let's eat. I'm starved." He took her arms and settled them into a little shelf. "Here, make yourself useful." He began by laying the blanket and compact disk set across her arms. Over one shoulder, he hung the thermos of what she suspected now was champagne. "Lead the way," he said, lifting the basket.

There was a perfect spot, she knew, but it meant

165

climbing over the skeletal remains of the boat cradles in the back yard and romantic that wasn't. Once by it, however, the secret spot lay in perfect isolation. "Follow me," she said and set off behind the marina store.

It was an old abandoned pier that jutted into the one crazy-quilt corner of the cove. At the farthest end of it Red had long ago nailed a cable spool he'd found floating by the dock one day. Though he maintained it had been carelessly dumped by navy yard workers, she knew better. At seven she knew it belonged to the wife of a giant and it was she who had tossed the empty spool of thread into the sea. Half-round benches were fastened around it for her to play at tea when she was little. It hadn't changed. The wooden spool was bleached to a weathered gray and the benches were a bit splintery. But the magic of the place was still there. It was a world of ancient and weathered boards, of pilings hung thick with bearded mussels, and salt water turned to silver when the sun was just right.

It was a place she'd never shared before and as she walked the length of the old pier she felt suddenly shy. It was her world. When she came to the end of the pier, she turned and looked behind. He had stopped and was now gazing around with a look of wonder. He would be the one, she thought, to see her silver kingdom.

Later, when the last of the delicate smoked ham and turkey sandwiches were nothing but crumbs and the last of the champagne was drunk, they sat in contented silence while Mozart filled the air around them.

Whether it was the champagne or the heat of the sun that was making her sleepy, she did not know. She also could not remember when she'd felt such a delicious languor creeping through her bones. She found herself confiding in him of her marriage and the fears that had grown out of it, then coming back from Florida—the shock of stepping from the lazy pace of palm trees in a blue sky where life to her had seemed so easy that she forgot it really wasn't, to the hard, earnest driving force of New England.

When the conversation switched to her frustration over Emma Bond, it seemed an easy step. She hadn't noticed the wary look which crossed Julian's face; it seemed so natural for her to tell him. Who else was there?

"There's no winner here," she said. "Not the hospital which surely will be paying the cost of supporting this patient. Not the unit, which should have that bed available for emergencies, and not her doctor. Oh sure, he's getting paid to see her, but he's losing our respect and he knows it. But the most important figure in all this is Emma.

"She's not a likable person, but I doubt that she was before this happened to her. Now she's becoming a basket case. She's difficult to care for, she's manipulative—" She caught herself. She was not going to tell him about the phantom daughter, Arlene. That was her own private embarrassment.

She began to place the fragile china plates back into the basket as she talked. He'd become silent, a small bunch of grapes in one hand and the fluted champagne glass in the other.

"But most of all, there doesn't seem to be any way out for her."

"I can't believe that," he said softly. "There are other resources besides Liberty Hill. Isn't she on the list of rehabilitation hospitals?"

"Oh, sure. But the waiting list is over two years long. In the meantime, the longer she goes on a ventilator, the more improbable it is that she can get off it."

"Can't you begin the process while you wait?"

She sighed. "We have many times and each time we fail. For the past three months, we haven't done a thing.

Dr. Peters is adamant. He says she will never get off the damned vent."

"And you don't believe him," he said.

"I don't know what to believe. I just think we can't give up." She rolled her napkins into the bone rings and tucked them into one corner of the basket. "I'll launder these for you," she murmured.

He shot back the sleeve of his sweater and glanced at the heavy gold watch on his wrist. "Not for me," he said. "The basket is yours. For the next time. Much as I'd like to stay here forever, I must be going. Why is it," he said, reaching over and taking her hand in his, "that time sometimes goes into fast forward and hours become like seconds and you can't hold them back? I hate to leave."

He leaned over and placed his lips on hers. His face had darkened in the sun and when she reached up to lay her hand against his cheek, she could feel the heat of his skin. Her own hand felt cool. His lips parted and she could feel the tip of his tongue tracing the inner folds of her mouth. His breath became thunder in her ears. She leaned against him.

"Don't go," she whispered. "Stay with us."

"Us?"

She laughed and straightened away from him, her hands resting on his shoulders. "I'm an 'us' now. There's Nikki."

"Of course. Where is he, by the way?"

"Being escorted to see Old Ironsides. Over there." Her hand waved in the direction of the navy yard.

"Old Ironsides? It's here? Where? I don't see it." She turned and using her hand as a guide for him to sight along, she said, "Right there. See the masts sticking up over the building?"

His breath was warm against her cheek. "Oh damn," he said, "I've never seen Old Ironsides. Imagine, history sitting right in your backyard."

"Nikki would be delighted to show it to you next time," she said.

"He's a man after my heart. Yes, next week we'll do just that."

Together, they gathered the remains of their meal and placed it in the elegant basket. Sleepy and somewhat drugged by the sun, they made their way through the abandoned yard. At his car, Julian took her hand.

"It's been a wonderful afternoon, the best I've had since coming to New England." His eyes were soft and dark. "I don't know what I can do about this patient of yours, but the first thing I'm going to do is to review her records."

Alarmed, Leah burst out, "Oh no, I didn't mean for you to do anything about Emma. You were the friendly shoulder I needed, that's all. Please, don't get involved."

"It's my job," he replied. "Besides, I haven't tangled with a physician in ages, it'll do me good. Let me see what the finances on this case are and then we'll go from there. In the meantime you just go on doing what you do best, nursing. I'll do the rest."

She watched him turn the Cadillac around in a tight circle on the dusty parking lot and then saw him wave at her. She lifted her hand in return, sure she had made an awful mistake.

Chapter Nine

Leah sat with Two-Gus's chart open on her lap. So much had happened over the weekend and while the day staff flew about the unit, she sat in isolation, trying to read his progress notes.

He'd become deeply depressed. (Her own night notes reflected that.) It was the long hours of trying to tolerate the constant irrigation to his shoulder that had worn him out. On Saturday, Milly had called for a psychiatric evaluation and it was this solemn note that Leah wanted to read. She found it tucked behind the laboratory values. As usual, no one knew where to place it in the chart. Was it a progress note? Or did it simply reflect some chemical imbalance like Two-Gus's blood? It certainly read like a piece of data from a dusty lab. Dr. Malcolm's terse report filled only two paragraphs.

> This thirty-eight-year-old male hemophiliac with a recent diagnosis of Human Immune Deficiency Virus was admitted on Friday with an infected shoulder wound. An incision and drainage was established that day. Since then the patient has become increasingly withdrawn.
>
> This obviously sick white male responds only in

monosyllables and has poor eye contact. He seems, as yet, untouched by dementia (a frequent sequela to AIDS). Due to his poor prognosis, of which he is aware, it is well within our expectations that this patient will succumb to periods of depression. How he handles it, what his strengths and support system are, is unknown at this time. Recommendations: suicide precautions, Elavil, 100 mg. per day in divided doses, and ongoing psychiatric evaluation. Thank you for allowing me to see this most interesting patient. Harvey Malcolm, M.D.

Except for a pill, there was nothing new or helpful in Malcolm's note. How about finding what those so-called support systems are? Is there a family, any friends? She shook her head in disgust. So much for psychiatrists, she thought, staring in the direction of Two-Gus's room.

He'd been absolutely uncommunicative all morning, and nothing she did for him loosened the stony set of his face. His shoulder wound was closing nicely. The antibiotics were clearing his lungs. Even the jaundice seemed to have decreased. If it weren't for the precautions he was on, she'd never know he was an AIDS patient. He looked too well to be so sick. And now he was under a suicide watch. That meant open doors at all times when he was unattended and a room that was within constant view.

She helped him from the bed and tucked him into the bedside chair while she tidied his room. When she was finished, he looked better, the room was spotless, and even the sunshine cooperated, flooding across his blanketed knees. The silence was heavy, though, and soon she fled, at a loss for words.

She watched as the boy next door tied a mask over his face and tapped at Two-Gus's door. Good luck, my young friend, she said to herself as Billy went into the room. She closed Two-Gus's chart and put it away. It was time to face Emma. She'd put it off too long.

Two-Gus watched Billy tie on his mask. There was no need to cover his face, but for some reason Two-Gus had insisted upon it and now he did it routinely.

"Here," Billy said, holding out a can of soda. "I thought you might like it. I didn't know what else to bring."

"You didn't have to bring anything, boy. Just a visit now and then. How is your mother?" Secretly, he was pleased with the gift.

"She is getting funny acting, but they say it's part of the waking-up process. I don't know. She still doesn't know I'm here."

Two-Gus took a long draught of the soda. It was cold and sweet, catching in his throat and making him cough. He sputtered, groping for the box of tissue Leah had left on his bedside table. Billy reached over and handed it to him. Nodding his thanks, he collected himself.

"She'll be fine," he managed to say when the spasm ended. "Once they begin to wake up, it's all uphill from there. And she'll be on her feet in no time."

"I know that. The nurses tell me that they'll be moving her to a regular room as soon as the intravenous is over."

For some reason, Two-Gus felt a pang of sorrow at Billy's words. He'd gotten used to the kid hanging around. Without him, the weekend would have been unbearable. Even Milly had not shown up yesterday. Instead the kid had found a deck of cards and while he waited for his mother to improve, they had played endless games of gin rummy. And the questions the kid had! Once he warmed up, it was like an ice dam melting. Soon they had become like two old cronies hunkered down beside an old fashioned woodstove, solving the world's problems. The difference in their ages evaporated.

"Do you remember I was telling you about this girl, Lily?" Billy sat down upon the footstool. "The one down in dialysis?"

"Yes. What about her?"

"She's getting ready to do something to force them to transplant her. This ain't for publication. You wouldn't tell . . ." Billy pinched the mask over his nose to hold it in place. His voice was muffled.

"Ready to do what?"

"Like skip her treatments and go off the diet. That'll make her sick. They told her that she's been so good on the treatment that they've been skipping over her on the transplant list. She's so damned mad, she's gonna do something about it."

"I don't blame her. If she doesn't stick up for herself, no one else will." He really didn't want to talk about some girl he'd never met. It was far removed from his own problems and it brought the outside world too close to this room.

But Billy's face had become glum.

"Look at me," Two-Gus said wearily. "What I am saying is that part of growing up is making difficult decisions with no clear or satisfying conclusions. Sometimes, no matter what you do, you lose. It's how you handle it that matters."

"I don't want her to get hurt."

"It isn't up to you."

"I can give her my kidney."

Two-Gus's mouth fell open.

"They can't stop me, can they?"

"Hell, boy, I don't know." Jesus, what a kid. "What if your mother won't let you?"

Billy gave him a disgusted glare. "She's lying in a

friggin' daze and I'm supposed to ask her permission? She couldn't give me permission to take a leak, for God's sakes." He stood up in disgust. Two-Gus's heart sank.

"Wait a minute," he said. "Please."

Something in his voice made Billy's face go soft. It wasn't pity, he could see that. This kid has the sensitivity of a saint, he thought.

"Give her a chance. Your mother, I mean. She'll be coming out of this soon and when she's thinking straight you can talk to her about it. The girl, what's her name?"

"Lily," Billy said.

The name alone could evoke love, he thought. He saw it in Billy's face. He'd better be gentle. "Lily's waited this long," he said. "If she knows you are working on it, won't she wait a little longer?" Billy shrugged, but Two-Gus could see that his mind was working on it.

"I don't know your mother, Billy, but I do know that mothers have an unlimited capacity to help their kids, even for crazy things like this." He saw his mistake. "I mean for wild things, okay? Who knows, she might surprise you and agree simply because you are her child and she knows you better than anyone else. But remember, you must be a compatible donor. That's the bottom line. If you aren't, then the whole matter is academic. Go talk to her doctor."

Billy's face brightened. "Yeah," he breathed. "I will."

Two-Gus was a little relieved when the intercom switched on and announced the end of the visiting hour. He hadn't realized how tired he'd become. His voice had grown hoarse and his throat felt scratchy. Billy pulled off the mask and headed for the door. He looked even younger than fourteen.

"Will you come back?" Two-Gus called out.

"Don't I always?" he shot back.

With Emma propped in her chair watching her closely, Leah began to set the room to rights. She could feel those hooded eyes following her about the room. Without words, she knew Emma was wary of her this morning, knowing Leah was still smarting over the nonexistent daughter. The nurse could tell by the subtle increase in her respiratory rate and the ten-beat heart increase on the monitor.

There was, however, a decided change in Emma. Somehow, she had managed to pull herself out of the impending pneumonia of last Friday. She knew, Leah thought, just how to bring it on and how to end it. The weekend nursing notes charted Emma's improved temperature, her cooperation in suctioning, and her sudden interest in nourishing foods, not just the ever-present soda. She had passed the weekend safely. Now she was sitting there waiting for Leah to make the first move. The nurse lifted the mattress and made the last neat tuck in Emma's blanket. Then she turned and faced her.

"Okay, you win," she said. "You did a nice job getting better this time. What came over you?"

There was the hint of a smile on Emma's lips. "I'm sorry," she mouthed, the overly elaborate lip movements making comprehension easier. "About Friday. I thought if it worked, I'd start to wean faster. Now I know it was wrong. But I want your help just the same."

Leah stared at her, torn—she had promised Emma, but she had been forbidden by Peters.

"Give me five minutes to wean." Emma held up her hand, fingers spread like claws.

"Five minutes? Do you know how long five minutes are?"

"I did four last night."

"What do you mean?"

Emma did not reply. She merely nodded and again shoved Leah four fingers, stabbing the air with them for emphasis.

"You managed to wean yourself for four minutes and didn't tell anyone?"

"I'm telling you," Emma mouthed. She picked up her blackboard, a look of pride on her face, and began scribbling. When done, she beckoned Leah closer. It read, "I have a plan. I will wean myself at night when no one can see me and you get blood gases every morning at seven o'clock to see how I did. Will you do it?"

Leah exploded. "Wait a minute. Back up a little. How did you do it? What about the alarms on the vent? Didn't anyone check on you?"

Emma flipped a hand scornfully at the vent then she poked one finger delicately at the alarm button. It shut off. She gave Leah a look as though to say, "Watch me." Then she touched the sigh button and the ventilator heaved. Emma's chest rose with it. She waited until it settled down again, then she flicked her fingers over the dials. She knew the correct pressure setting and the volume amounts that her lungs required. Finally, she pressed the alarm light and it flashed on again. She settled back in her chair and folded her hands in her lap.

There was a derisive look on her face as she wrote, "I know every button on that machine. I could shut it off, but the quiet would bring someone running in here. I wait for the nurse to finish her rounds, then I shut off the alarms. I've been doing it on days, too, but not as much. There's too much activity in here. But I need to know if I'm getting enough oxygen. Without blood gases, I can't tell."

Leah nodded. "Of course. Naturally. And you'll adjust the vent for any discrepancy, right?" She sat on the bed and faced Emma. "Now you want to practice medicine."

Emma shook her head. "Only on myself. I don't have a doctor."

"How do you think I can order gases without Dr. Peters finding out?"

"I can't think of everything, you know. You figure that out."

Leah burst out laughing and Emma sat back, a pleased look on her face. Finally she tapped on Leah's arm to show her the blackboard.

"I am keeping a record. When I get up to thirty minutes out of every hour, I'm going to show it to that asshole Peters, and I want those blood gas reports right in there beside my notes."

"That's when I lose my job," Leah said, but somehow the notion did not bother her. She was too intrigued with the notion that all her beliefs about chronic lungers were wrong. Being continually deprived of oxygen, Emma wasn't supposed to have enough imagination to conceive such an idea. She was supposed to be concerned only with the next breath she drew. Yet she had worked it all out, even to the log book that she would keep. It would be incontrovertible proof of her success, if she succeeded. Emma was supposed to be a dullard but she wasn't. She never had been, if the story of the phantom daughter was any indication. I don't like her, Leah thought, but she surely did not fit the picture of a chronic lunger.

"There are a lot of unanswered questions here," she said finally. "What if you get tired out? You have to sleep sometime. What if you get another pneumonia?"

Emma shrugged. "What if I die tomorrow? I'm not going to sit and wait anymore. I must try, at least. I'm the only one with something to gain for trying, right?"

Leah thought for a moment. "I'll get those gases for you. But if you wean yourself during the day, do it out of my sight, okay?"

"Deal." Emma held out her hand and Leah grasped it. Emma then made a motion for Leah to leave the room. She mouthed, "I'm tired now. I will sleep awhile."

Leah watched her and saw that soon the respirator slowed to long deep breaths and the cardiac monitor responded by recording Emma's slowing heart rate. It settled at eighty beats a minute. Emma was asleep.

She gathered up the soiled sheets and walked thoughtfully from the room. While she scrubbed her hands with antiseptic soap, she began to review her options. Who in the respiratory therapy department would help? Certainly not the director, he was never there. It had to be one of the regular technicians who serviced Emma's vent. Mentally, she ran down the list of therapists who most often worked in the unit. It couldn't be Shirley, the one who had the vacant smile and artificial concern for patient welfare. She couldn't care less about Emma. And she'd never break a rule. It had to be someone who grumbled along with the nurses, who knew as well as they that Emma had been shortchanged, and who wasn't afraid to admit being as sick and tired of the case. Her thoughts settled on Danny Thomson. Danny might do it. He was not a new technician. He had been at Liberty Hill the longest of any of the respiratory workers and he was becoming disillusioned with his job. He was leaving soon for college. Business college, she thought he'd told her. Maybe he'd be willing. He was here every morning drawing all the gases on the intubated patients. Why not simply add Emma to his list? He could hand her the report and no one would be the wiser. Would he do it?

She wiped her hands on the paper towels and then looked at her reddened fingers. They were, as usual, raw from scrubbing throughout the day. Automatically, she thought of the gloves she wore in Two-Gus's room. Then she thought of him. There had to be something to get him out of his depression.

An hour later, she entered Two-Gus's room with an armload of magazines. He looked at her, a dark question in his eyes.

"I could get killed for this," she said, "but I think it is

important. Here, take a look."

She plunked the stack of magazines down on his bedside table. Without looking at him, she spread them out before him.

"This one is from the Department of Public Health. Here's the latest FDA drug bulletin, and this one is the *Journal of Surgery*. All of them have information on AIDS." It was the first time she mentioned the word aloud and it seemed to sit between them like a wet sponge. She met his eyes. "It's not much, but when you're finished with these, I'll try to find more."

He did not reply, nor did he reach for the pamphlets she laid before him. Finally, she planted both fists on his armchair and leaned over him.

"You might as well know what you're dealing with. It's what you did when you learned about hemophilia and now you know more than most doctors about that disease."

This time he cocked his head at her. "That was a little different, wouldn't you say? At least then I had a fighting chance."

She shrugged. "I don't know about chance, but I think I know a little about you. You've managed a tricky disease for many years. I can't imagine that you wouldn't want to try on this one. When the cure comes, and I think it will, you will be ready and armed with information and first in line. Others will keep their heads in the sand, but I don't think you're that kind."

She saw a flicker of amusement in his eyes. She straightened up, keeping a stern expression. "I suggest you read the surgical article first. It's not as cut and dried as the public health sheet and it deals solely with the disease, not the social issues. Start there." She glanced at her watch. "I promised the librarian I'd return these before going off duty, so you'd better get going." She pushed the bedside table so that it straddled his chair, lowered it so that he would not have to reach with his bad arm and finally switched on his reading light. "Ring the bell when you're finished," she said and left the room.

He straightened up, his fatigue suddenly gone. Keeping his left arm steady so that the intravenous catheter would not be dislodged, he managed to pull the first magazine so that it tilted half off the table. He steadied it with his right hand. And then the thought struck him: what he was doing was a simple act of survival. An hour ago, he wouldn't have cared if the fever killed him. He almost wished it would rather than face what was coming later. Now here he was grasping at these books as if their words contained the ultimate truths, and that they were all he needed to begin the process of building hope. Information.

The glossy cover of the surgical journal was stiff. Probably never read, he thought. The first article dealt with cancer of the colon. It recommended the screening, by proctosigmoidoscope, of everyone over the age of forty. He smiled a little at the thought of aging yuppies lined up with their pants down.

The next article was a spirited debate over the ethics of artificial heart transplant. Fascinated, he read it through to the end, forgetting completely what he was supposed to be looking for. It wasn't just the surgery, a matter of hooking tubes to their plastic mates; the mechanics of pumps and electricity; pressures, blood clots, and rhythms; or even patient position in bed which could influence the artificial heart. It was the medical ethics that physicians were facing. Thorny issues of the continuation of life as it was meant to be lived. Family considerations, mental stability, and finally, the specter of lifelong commitment for both the patient and his doctor. Medical ethics, since the advent of the artificial heart, was facing thorny issues. What was more important, he realized, was that the profession was dealing with these problems while he had hidden himself away like a coward.

When he turned the page and the word *AIDS* leapt out at him, he felt an almost physical blow to the pit of his stomach. With his heart thumping, he began to read. Twenty minutes later, when he finished the article, he turned the pages back and reread.

One infant cell, he thought, called T. Too young to begin functioning, it was the cell the AIDS virus attacked. He laid the magazine down and began to think. It was always his blood. First a missing link in the clot-manufacturing mechanism, a defect his mother had carried. Now a deadly piece of protein was attacking another part of his bloodstream. He thought of the hundreds of transfusions he'd had over the years. They were not just red cells or plasma he'd been given, but a special component of blood that came from hundreds of donors. It was these Factor Eight transfusions that held the lurking virus. He remembered how blithely he had presented himself for those few hours. There had been no concern over reaction, which happened with whole blood. It had been as simple as taking a pill. So simple.

He picked up the public health notice. This dealt with the latest treatment of AIDS. AZT was the latest. But he had already known about the drug from television and newspapers. He almost missed the last article: a paragraph that some editor had tacked onto the piece as almost an afterthought. It was a new treatment for hemophiliacs. The hair on the back of his neck rose and the paper trembled in his hand. While he had hidden himself away, someone had begun to work on his case. It was called Monoclate and it was a substitute for Factor Eight. It seemed to strengthen and increase those baby cells that the virus attacked. Carefully, he tore out the article and hid it away in the drawer of his bedside table. Then he refolded the bulletin so that no one would see the torn paper. He glanced up at the clock. An hour had passed. He rang the bell.

When Leah appeared, he held out the magazines and said simply, "Get me some more." She nodded without smiling. "And see when Dr. Gold is coming. I want to talk to her." Again she nodded.

Outside the room, away from his gaze, she grinned and hugged the bundle of papers to her chest. It was a small victory but at least the despair in his eyes was gone.

Julian walked quietly by Betsy Conte's desk, but she looked up from her desk and shook her head. "Oh no, you don't," she said. "I'm still waiting for you to handle this little matter."

"What's that?" he said innocently. He could feel his stomach rumbling with hunger.

"You know damned well what it is. It's from Medicaid. They are putting us on notice and I can't stall them any longer."

He looked at his secretary. If it hadn't been for her, he'd have sunk under the pressure of this job. For twenty years she had managed the details of Liberty Hill's myriad problems and when he arrived, she simply carried on. She knew every nook and cranny of the old building and furthermore, knew which system was due to fail. The boiler, the stand-by generator, the union contract that wasn't working. Name it and Betsy could rattle off the facts. "Bubble-gum management," she called it.

"You give up? I don't believe it."

"Believe it," she said. "Here, take this letter with you and try to enjoy your lunch. I am going out and I won't be back for thirty minutes." She rose and tossed a sweater over her shoulder, the same dull gray as her hair. She looked at him over the rim of her glasses.

"Welfare," she announced gravely, "is going to kill

me someday. We send in their forms and they ignore them. When I scream for money, they blithely accuse me of cheating the government and I do it, believe it or not, by forgetting to dot an i, or cross a t. According to them, that's a sin worth the electric chair. Well, I've managed all these years, but this takes the cake."

She marched through the door. "Have a nice lunch, sucker."

He tucked the letter in his jacket pocket. If Leah wasn't in the dining room, he'd find a quiet corner by himself and read the offending letter. The bulk of it weighed down his jacket and that did not bode well for its message. He tried to ignore it.

The line to the cafeteria stretched from the doorway to the bowels of the food line. He bypassed it, and walked directly to the center of the room, scanning the line as he passed it. A few nurses tossed him curious glances and he could feel his face flush. Somehow he had hoped she would be waiting for him, but, of course, he knew she was subject to the dictates of the ICU. Sometimes, he knew, the nurses never got to eat, not if an emergency was in progress. But he'd have heard the emergency call, code 99, over the intercom. No, he concluded, she must have eaten in the first shift of nurses. Damn.

He walked into the kitchen, a bustling damp place of food smells and noises. The dietician looked up at him.

"Can I fix you a special tray, Mr. Plumhouse?" The woman heaved herself to her feet. Though she had a sweet face and an anxious smile, he tried to avoid looking at her. The woman was massive. From her shoes, over which her ankles rolled, to her cheeks there were endless rolls of fat. When he looked at her, the picture of an Angus steer came to his mind. Short legs on a huge body that was bred purely to deliver flank steaks and fat-streaked roasts to the grocery store. She was not able to cross her arms over her chest; they were too short.

Instead, she had developed a habit of grasping great hunks of her own fleshy waist and kneading it, as though estimating her readiness for market. It was an almost sensual gesture. He tried not to smile as her fingers began probing her hips.

"Whatever is the biggest seller today, Mrs. Fitzgerald."

"That would be the macaroni and cheese." She waddled away.

While he waited, Julian leaned against the wall and pulled out the letter that Betsy had given him. Reluctantly, he unfolded the sheets of paper and began to read. The noises of the kitchen faded away.

Attached to a copy of the hospital's request for payment, was a terse note: "This patient has used up all welfare benefits and is no longer eligible for further consideration. Recommendation: Immediate discharge."

Nothing unusual in that. It was the formality used to procure further documentation of need. He wondered why Betsy was so angry. He flipped through the rest of the letters. Then his eye caught the date of the first submission. November! The hospital had been billing welfare for eight months on one patient and for six of those months payments were made. They were late but that was nothing new. That was the "cross the t's" and "dot the i's" nonsense that Betsy mentioned. Suddenly the payments stopped.

"Bureaucrats," he muttered to himself.

"Pardon me?" Selma Fitzgerald stood before him holding a tray.

Julian straightened and tucked the papers back into his pocket. He took the tray from the dietician. "Thanks, Mrs. Fitzgerald. It looks delicious, as usual." And enough to feed an elephant, he said to himself. "By the way, I like the way you've dressed up the workers when they deliver trays. It's a nice touch."

The woman blushed. Since the first lunchtime job action of the registered nurses, her kitchen workers had been assigned the job of delivering trays directly to the patients and there were consequences no one could have foreseen. Going from room to room with trays in hand, the workers saw the final destination of the hundreds of meals they had so routinely prepared. They began to see the patient who, before, was just a name on a piece of paper—the cancer victim who had no appetite, the child without a normal gut, whose only meal was liquid served through a tube. It had dawned on the workers that their service was just as vital to the patients as any medication could be. Trays began to go out of the kitchen designed with the needs and appetites of the patients in mind. Food was served hot and trays spotless and the meals themselves, still just hospital food, became celebrated instead of disparaged. The workers had come to care about the patients. They clamored for laboratory coats to wear while out of the kitchen and Julian quickly approved, wishing a little longingly that he had thought of it himself. It was a simple revolution that delivered far more than it cost and morale was soaring in the kitchen.

"It's a different place," Mrs. Fitzgerald said. "They are actually happy now. They even tell me what certain patients will eat and who needs special attention. I don't believe it, but we haven't lost an employee since day one. It's a miracle." She sighed heavily as though it were all was just another problem for her.

Julian found an isolated table by a window and while he ate he studied the welfare care that Betsy had given him. She had tucked the Review Board's notes on the case along with the welfare letter so that he would have a better sense of the case. Liberty Hill's board was composed of physicians who routinely reviewed troublesome cases and made recommendations. Their file on this case was thick. He began to read.

The reviews had begun in the third month of care and were, at first, sparse. A routine case, there was nothing other than the length of stay that the board commented upon. Emma Bond was, they agreed, tethered to a ventilator and unable to breathe on her own. Then the tone of the notes revealed a subtle change. Although the reviewing physician would not disagree with the management of the case, he was becoming impatient with it. His notes became terse and, if Julian read it correctly, indignant. Each one ended with the recommendation to transfer the patient. Yet nothing had been done. By the time he finished reading the complete file Julian could feel his blood throbbing. He folded the notes and leaned back.

Claude Peters, he thought, was a thorn in the hospital's side. And then he made the connection: this was the patient Leah had told him about! He had forgotten all about it.

With that realization he thumbed through the peer review sheets once more. This case had dragged on far too long and Emma Bond's list of diagnoses seemed endless. Pneumonia, abdominal distention leading to respiratory insufficiency, fever of unknown origin, and on and on. Month after month. What was Peters doing for this woman? Julian read on. A permanent tracheostomy. "Healing well," was the comment. Again pneumonia with appropriate antibiotic regime. There was even a note about Emma's impacted bowels, though what that had to do with her breathing Julian could not understand. Refusal to cooperate and depression was another diagnosis. Well, who wouldn't be? he thought. One final entry by the reviewing physician caught his attention: "Rehabilitation facility required as soon as possible." It was underlined in red.

Julian leaned back and stared through the window. Leah was right. This case was a nightmare that had been mismanaged right from the beginning. Although Peters hadn't actually done harm to the patient, he had simply neglected her benignly. As a result Emma Bond languished upstairs in a room costing eight hundred and seventy dollars a day.

That was it—money, plain and simple. Claude Peters was raking in a daily fee from welfare and sitting pretty. Although the state watched strictly over every case it supported, it was helpless to change Emma Bond's predicament. What did he get for his daily visit? Fifty bucks? That was peanuts to a physician, but over the period of eight months . . . Julian multiplied the figures in his head, then wondered how many other welfare patients Peters had.

He jumped to his feet and strode from the dining room, the file of letters clenched in his fist. In his office he marched passed Betsy's desk and barked at her, "Get Claude Peters on the phone." His door slammed behind him.

Betsy made a pleased little moue of her mouth and picked up the phone. "Certainly, Mr. Plumhouse," she said to the closed door.

Billy leaned against the wall and waited outside the office door. Earlier, he had tried the handle, but it was locked and there was a little sign on the door that said, "Dr. Russell will be in at one o'clock." It was one-thirty and he hadn't eaten lunch. His stomach was making loud noises. He glanced up each time the door to the dialysis room opened, but no one came across the hall to open the office. He didn't even know what Dr. Russell looked like. All he could do was wait.

The dialysis room looked okay, he thought, as he peeked in. The walls were done in soft pastels and the lounge chairs looked comfortable. Still, it was a strange room, like something he'd see in a spaceship with all those black boxes beside each chair, and the shining tubes of plastic which dangled over the patients. Figures, not quite human-looking, lay in their chairs. They looked the strangest, each one with an arm stretched out to the plastic tubes. No, it wasn't a spaceship, it reminded him somehow of a milk farm with long rows of cattle hooked to milking machines, only those animals at least moved and ate and looked around at themselves as if a little surprised. These people on the lounge chairs never moved. He knew, of course, that many of them were asleep. He wondered how Lily passed her hours in there. The door opened again and a tall man crossed the hall, took out a key, and opened the door.

"Dr. Russell?" Billy said.

"Yes?"

"Can I talk to you for a minute? Inside?"

The man glanced at him in a measuring way. Bright blue eyes studied his skin, looked into his eyes, and measured the tautness of his skin. It was all done in a fraction of a second. Then he nodded.

"Come in." He flicked on lights as he passed through the office and into an inner room. He shrugged out of a white cotton laboratory jacket and into a faded old woolen sweater. He had a kind face, unlined beneath a cap of white hair. "Okay," he said, "what can I do for you?"

Billy swallowed. "I want to donate my kidney."

"Yes?"

"Well, that's it. That's all." He shrugged.

"That's a wonderful thing to do. You just go to the Department of Motor Vehicles and they'll stamp your license for you."

"That ain't what I mean. I want to give a kidney right now."

The bright eyes that gazed at him never faltered. "I

see. Do you have one to give?"

The question startled him. "Yeah! I do. I mean, I pee okay."

"But you don't know for sure." Dr. Russell leaned back in his chair and put both hands behind his neck. "Maybe you had better tell me the whole story."

"Lily Webb needs a kidney and I'll give her one of mine."

"If you have one to spare," the correction came gently.

"Yeah. Will you do it?"

"I can't," Russell said. He made a motion towards the wooden chair beside his desk. "Take a seat, young man. By the way, what is your name?"

"William B. Fellows."

"Well, William, it's a mighty generous offer you're making, but the wheels don't turn quite the way you think they might. If you were a relative of the patient, then it would be considered. We'd do some tests to see if you were compatible, and since you're obviously a minor, it would have to be done with parental permission."

Dr. Russell's face brightened. "Say, you aren't related to Lily, are you?" When he saw Billy shake his head, he sighed. "Then we don't even know if there is tissue compatability." For a long moment there was silence in the tiny room. Then Russell looked up at him. "I'm afraid it's not—"

Billy burst out. "She's going to force you."

"What do you mean?"

"If you don't get her a transplant, she's going to do something to herself to force it. I don't know what exactly, but she'll hurt herself."

Dr. Russell was silent, his kind face troubled. Finally he looked up. "Listen to me, William, I'm very glad you have come to me. Maybe you can't help her physically.

And God knows I can't perform miracles. But at least knowing what's coming I can help her through this."

"That's why I want to—"

Russell shook his head. "It won't work. No doctor would touch you. I certainly wouldn't."

Billy blinked fast to keep his vision clear. Why didn't they understand? "Look, it's my kidney and if I want to do it, why are you standing in the way?"

"You are a minor, that's why. You can't make these decisions by yourself. Even if your parents agreed to it, I still wouldn't do it. I would want to see you grow into manhood first. Years from now, when we know you have good renal function or your children won't need a kidney from you, then it might be considered. Until then, you must hoard what you have. It's that simple." There was also the matter of lawsuits and informed consent, but Russell did not mention those.

Billy stood up. "Then I can't help her and I can't prevent her from harming herself, is that what you're telling me? That I have to just stand by and watch?"

Russell shook his head. "It isn't in your province, young man. You made a generous offer and I am sure you fully expected it would be accepted, Lily would get her kidney, and the whole problem would disappear. It doesn't work that way. I am sorry." He rose and as he walked to the door with Billy, he put an arm across his shoulders. Billy shrugged it off as if it were burning his skin. Russell's eyes filled with pity.

"Let me give you a piece of advice, William. Just go on being a good friend to Lily. Listen to her and let her talk to you. She probably can't do that with anyone else. On this end, I'll keep a close eye on her and at the first sign of trouble, I will step in. In the meantime, I'll keep this conversation just between us. Okay?" Billy started to walk away but Russell held him back. "Okay?"

"Yeah, yeah. Just remember, I warned you."

Billy shrugged off Dr. Russell's hand and left. When he was out of sight, he slumped against the wall and took a deep breath. He had wanted to be a hero in front of Lily. Now he was nothing more than a jerk all in the space of an hour. What would she think of him?

The corridor, its floor clear and shining, was empty. That was good because he could feel his insides quivering and he knew the hot burn of tears would follow. They were always there, it seemed. This time he let them fill his eyes and, leaning against the wall, he wept.

Chapter Ten

Katherine Weathers hadn't slept more than an hour or two, she was sure. It was her breathing. When she lay flat, the baby seemed to float up into her chest leaving no room for her lungs. For awhile, she propped herself up with pillows and managed to doze, but then her buttocks began to grow numb. She was just too heavy.

She tried lying on one side, but when Ben curled against her she felt as if her belly would pull her off the edge of the bed. It was a conspiracy between father and daughter, she thought a little resentfully. She ended up sitting on the edge of the bed feeling hopeless. Finally, she took her pillows and the afghan and settled into the chaise for the rest of the night.

When Ben awoke he saw her curled in the chaise asleep, her face tired and shadowed in the early light. He tiptoed from the room and went down the hall to shower. In the kitchen, he fed the cat, made himself some toast, and left the coffee pot on so that Katherine could have some when she awoke. He'd be damned if he would wake her.

". . . killing herself for that damned job of hers," he muttered to himself as he locked the door behind him and settled into a jog that carried him effortlessly up the hill to the hospital.

She slept until ten o'clock and then awoke with a start. The phone was jangling. She leapt up and then remembered that she'd better be a little more sedate; there was an ache in the small of her back that reminded her not too gently. She picked up the phone and propped it over her shoulder.

It was Evelyn Holden. "I wasn't going to bother you, Katherine, but something has come up and I felt you should know. There's a sick-out going on here. It started during the night. The phones have been ringing off the hook with suddenly sick nurses. I won't say what *I'd* call it, but it certainly sounds like something else, wouldn't you say?" Her voice was breathless with excitement.

"I'll be right there," Katherine replied. "It'll take me a few minutes—"

"No. I don't want you to hurry, I just wanted to let you know that there are a couple of ICU nurses that are out. By the way," Evelyn asked, "it isn't your time, is it?"

Katherine laughed. "Don't I wish it. No, I'm just not sleeping well lately. Baby's keeping me up nights. I thought that came later. I'll be up as soon as I can. Are they carrying on alright? What's the census?"

"You have seven patients and three nurses to staff the unit. They want to know if they can transfer two patients out. It's not their own shift they're worried about, it's the next two. And they say if there is a disaster, God forbid," Katherine knew the director was crossing herself, "they want plenty of empty beds. Tracy is out, of course, so I don't have much support around here this morning." Evelyn's voice took on the proper amount of self-pity. "It's the staffing on the floors. They are in deep trouble. I don't know whether to keep your patients in for their own sakes or . . ." Evelyn let her voice trail off.

"Call the unit and tell them to keep those patients until the floors can take them. If there's a question of safety, we will keep them."

It was so simple that she knew that wasn't why Evelyn called; she had probably already issued that order. It was polite curiosity as well as a plea for help. She murmured some reassuring words into the phone and heard the relief in Evelyn's voice. She had already half-peeled off her nightgown before she hung up.

It took forever to get the right temperature in the shower; she seemed to have grown enormous and could not reach her feet. Those poor neglected appendages. She regarded them sadly as water puddled around them. They'll have to soak as best they can. At least her hair would be clean, she thought as she rinsed it until it squeaked.

She gave up trying to pull on her pantyhose. The upper part of the nylons were supposed to stretch as she grew bigger, but the designers hadn't given a thought to how she could reach her toes to get them on. Disgusted, she tossed them back in the drawer. She pulled on a pair of white slacks, and over that she buttoned a blue smock. She scowled at herself in the mirror. There was just no way this process was attractive. She looked huge, that's all.

In the kitchen, she pulled the plug on the coffee pot and poured herself a generous mugful. Then she ate a bowl of bran flakes, so necessary but tasteless, wrinkling her nose at the blandness of her diet.

For Ben to have made the coffee at all was a miracle, she thought. He was becoming domestic after all. He could sew up a jagged laceration with the delicacy of a seamstress working on fine lace, but to measure spoonfuls of coffee against a known amount of water usually baffled him. She gave the quiet room a derisive snort, as if he were still there.

If they only knew the real Ben, the helpless Ben, those ER nurses would die laughing. He tried to help her make the bed one day when she'd grown too big to squeeze between it and the wall. But he stood there helpless, the sheets and blankets a total mystery in his hands until she released him with a sneering smile.

Reluctantly, she began to think of the problem now facing Liberty Hill. A sick-out was really a euphemism for a strike, but it lacked the official connotation and thus prevented the city from firing those who called in ill. It was a job action and Katherine knew it could be a very effective method of getting results but it would be difficult to maintain. Someone very clever was planning the scheduling of those "sick" and those reporting to duty. After all, no floor could go uncovered. It must be Tracy, she thought. No one else had such easy access to the employee telephone list but Tracy.

The coffee churned in her stomach suddenly and she pushed it away. Leaving the dishes on the table, she picked up her sweater and opened the door. At the foot of the stairs, the cat arched himself against her legs, purring loudly. She sat down on the bottom step and pulled him into her arms. Sun streaked the sidewalk with shadows of newly budded trees and the air was gentle on her skin.

For the first time in her pregnancy, Katherine wished she could simply sit there in the sun and wait for the baby to come, letting the trouble at Liberty Hill pass her by. There was no way she could know in advance how many of her staff would call in sick. There were usually five nurses on the day shift, four on evenings, and three at night. Legal or not, those were the numbers she had to work with. The thought suddenly came to her that she didn't know who was up there right now. What if the unit was in trouble?

She stretched, trying to ease the dull ache in her spine, and in response, the cat extended its claws and kneaded her thigh. She felt its needlelike claws pierce her slacks, drawing a speck of blood against the white fabric.

"Monster," she cried, pushing it away. "Oh damn, look what you've done!" The cat arched its back and glared at her, its ears flat against its skull. When she pulled herself up it gave her an angry hiss and scuttled away.

There was the usual parking ticket on the windshield, and as always, she tossed it on the seat beside her. Somehow Ben always managed to have them fixed. She drove up the hill, dreading the day before it had even begun.

She entered through the emergency room, hoping to catch a glimpse of Ben. It was quiet, too quiet, she thought. Somehow, she expected it to be a scene of chaos with one harried nurse to cover all the cubicles.

There was no one at the desk, not even Ben. She looked into the cubicles as she passed. Bed one held a tiny infant and over it bent the figure of a young woman. She glanced up as Katherine passed by. Her eyes were blank with fear. She cradled the baby's head with one hand, stroking its cheek with the other. There was a nasty gash on the child's leg.

Bed two was empty and three had signs of being just vacated. It was still rumpled and there was a faint smudge of blood on the pillow. Several empty syringes littered the stretcher. Katherine wondered if the patient had survived and was now in the unit. This was just what the staff feared—an emergency admission without the nurses to cover the unit. A curtain was drawn around bed four. She could hear someone weeping quietly behind it. Bed five was empty.

In the next cubicle, Ben leaned over the still form of an elderly man. Katherine hesitated, watching them. With an ophthalmoscope against the old man's eye, Ben leaned into the eyepiece. His head was so close that his nose and the old man's nose almost touched.

"How long have you had diabetes, Mr. Ruben?"

"Eighteen years, two months, and twenty days, sir." His hands, the nails neatly manicured, lay clasped as if in prayer upon his chest. They were very pale, so pale that Katherine thought she could see the nerves and bones beneath his skin.

"That long, eh? Well there are little hemorrhages in both retinas. That would account for the deterioration in vision." Ben straightened and placed his hand on the patient's shoulder. "I think that you had better get over to the Joslin Clinic. There's a doctor doing laser treatments on these cases."

"Laser!" The old man laughed. "Don't tell me about lasers. My grandson should hear you, Doctor. He thinks lasers are only for that crazy rocky music they play. I've seen them. Ooh, such lights. And the noise. I think Robby is going deaf because of it." The old man let Ben help him sit up. His frail body trembled. "He'll take me over there. I'll tell him there is a terrific laser show at the Joslin." He wheezed when he laughed and then he spotted Katherine standing by the door. His eyes grew soft.

"Hey Doctor, I think you'd better take a look at that patient. She needs you more than I. What do you want, little mother, a boy or a girl? Have a girl, they stick around when you're old." A middle-aged woman with silver hair stepped to his side. She shook her head apologetically at the old man's impudence. Katherine smiled at her.

She loved watching Ben. She loved the way his hand rested protectively on the patient's shoulder, the careful way he assisted the old man to a sitting position. Most physicians simply turned their backs or rushed off to the next patient, never caring that their words might frighten or anger a patient. Not Ben. He was the picture of contentment and there was an innocent glow in his eyes.

198

He had not yet grown weary from the pressing needs of his patients, the demands that could hollow his soul. With his sleeves rolled up untidily and stethoscope dangling from his neck, he was happily engrossed in his work. There was a dark red smear on the tail of his white coat. She knew it was blood . . . probably from the patient next door.

His smile grew sweet when he saw her and the world narrowed between them. She gestured toward the desk and he nodded. She was late but another few minutes would not make much difference now. Besides, it was such a beautiful day she hated the thought of burying herself in the unit. There was no way up there to get a sense of the day. The windows, what few there were, were all in the patient rooms, too far away from her desk. In here there were skylights which flooded the room with light. It was much nicer here, she decided.

She watched as the old man tottered off on the arm of the woman. Ben came up behind her and his hands slid around her waist caressing her belly. She leaned back.

"She says, 'Good morning, Dad.' And sends her love." Katherine squinted up at him. "Want to sneak away with me for the day? We can play hookey. Let's take a ride to Essex for fried clams and ice cream. What do you say?"

He shuddered. "What an appetite she has. We'll do it. We'll just run away." They laughed together, knowing it would never happen.

A shrill noise like an alarm clock grown large filled the room. They watched as Trish Curry hurried over to the ambulance radio.

A voice, badly transmitted with static, bellowed into the room. There was a distant sound of a siren behind it. "Liberty Hill, Liberty Hill. This is SeaMed One, SeaMed One. We are transporting a twelve-year-old male, auto accident victim."

Katherine's breath caught in her throat and she

glanced at Ben. His lips tightened.

The voice droned on, "Unconscious. Vital signs are as follows . . ." The sound of the siren filled the room, blocking out his voice for a moment. ". . . pressure: ninety over forty." Again the voice faded. Katherine could feel Ben's hand tighten on her shoulder. The voice returned. ". . . hundred and thready. Respirations are . . . negative. He just stopped breathing. I will . . ." The radio went dead.

"Where do you suppose they are?" Katherine asked.

"If they were across the river, they wouldn't be coming here, they'd go to City Hospital. They must be north of us, but how far, I don't know."

He clapped his hands together and shouted into the empty room. "Alright everyone, set up for a trauma victim. Get the team in here, and, Trish, try calling them back. Maybe the driver will hear you. Find out their ETA." He glanced at Katherine. "Stick around, honey, and man the desk."

She nodded. "What should I do?"

"Call X-ray. Tell them to set up for flat plates, lumbar, and cervical spines. Call the CT room and have them stand by for a brain scan. Get a lab technician and a respiratory therapist on standby. We'll need blood gases."

She had the phone in her hand before he finished. The radio static buzzed and she could hear the tinge of panic in Trish's voice as, again and again, she called the ambulance. Within one minute, what had been an eerily quiet emergency room was now a place swarming with nurses. Katherine saw them piling out of the lounge. It had been the coffee break, that's all. She should have known these nurses were just hiding out while the room was quiet.

A portable x-ray machine rolled on silent wheels through the doors, its driver obscured from sight. A technician followed, her arms full with black plates of film.

Stacy Price hurried by the desk, clasping intravenous bags and lines. She halted briefly, puzzled by Katherine's presence. "Are you staying? Good. Please call the supervisor and ask her to return my nurse. She took her to cover the floor. You've heard about the sick-out?" She didn't wait for Katherine's answer. "I want my nurse back. Stat!"

Katherine dialed the nursing office, wondering how she got caught up in all this. She didn't belong here. This was Stacy's job. Bev Britain identified herself over the phone. What was she doing there?

"Mrs. Webb is out sick," Bev said. "I'm filling in for the day, but I do not feel too good myself. I may be out tomorrow."

"Fine, whatever." Katherine cut her off. "I'm down in the ER and they need the nurse you pulled from here. They've got a trauma case coming in."

"What in the world are you doing there?"

Katherine bit her lip. "I just happened to get caught in the traffic. Can you send me the nurse?"

"Hah, there are thirty-two nurses out sick this morning and you want help. Go out in the street and flag down some warm bodies. That's all the help you're going to get this morning. Don't you realize what's going on here?"

Katherine cut her off and dialed the unit. "Leah? Can you free yourself and come down to the ER to help out? I'm stuck here."

She hesitated only a moment. "Be right down." The phone went dead.

There was absolute silence in the room as all eyes watched Trish at the radio. The forces needed for the coming minutes had been marshaled. Test tubes clinked as the phlebotomist swung the basket back and forth.

Danny Thomson, the respiratory technician with the face of a child, rolled up his sleeves and emptied his breast pocket. Katherine knew he was readying himself for the arduous minutes ahead. If there were to be the chest thrusts of CPR, he would be prepared. It could last for hours and he knew it. The only sign of his nervousness was the twitching muscle in his jaw. He stared off into space as if to gather himself.

When Leah pushed through the doors, Katherine felt her breath explode from her lips. "None too soon, I think," she whispered to Leah as the far off wail of a siren could be heard. Quickly she gave Leah the few facts she knew and prepared to leave the room. She could feel the thud of her heart against her ribs.

"Scram," Leah whispered back. "They need you upstairs."

Relieved, Katherine fled.

As Leah turned back to the desk, the loud voice from the radio blared out. "SeaMed One, SeaMed One to Liberty Hill. Estimated time of arrival one minute. Victim now intubated. We are bagging him." His voice sounded weary. Now Leah's heart rate accelerated.

She could see the picture clearly. The boy had stopped breathing; that was why they had lost radio contact. With the ambulance pulled over to the side of the road, and while cars streamed by it, the paramedics had inserted a breathing tube into the boy's lungs. Without light, with no x-ray to guide them, the men had begun the steps to preserve the child's life. The sound of the siren grew louder.

Ben poked his head out of the door. "Let's get the flat plate in place now." His eyes searched for the x-ray technician, who scurried by him, and caught sight of Leah. He gave her a little wave. "Are you taking Katherine's place?" She nodded, then they both looked at the glass doors that led to the ambulance driveway.

It was a dazzle of white sun. Light bounced upon the glass and sheeted through the corridor angling deep into the emergency room itself. It made Leah squint. Where was the ambulance? She could no longer hear the siren.

It must be close, she thought, they've shut it off. Then the vehicle was suddenly there, the bulky body slowly backing into the driveway. Yellow flashing lights on the roof rolled rhythmically, barely visible in the sun. An electronic eye set in the concrete wall of the ramp sensed the ambulance and sent the glass doors of the emergency room flying apart. Then the red and white doors of the van banged open.

It was dark inside, too dark to see clearly, but a woman emerged, lurched down the two steps to the ground, and stood waiting. The ambulance driver moved her aside as if she were a statue and began to muscle the stretcher out. It hit the ground rolling and Leah caught her breath at the sight of the tiny figure lying there.

It was all coming at her in slow motion. She watched as Trish Curry squeezed herself against the wall to make room for the advancing stretcher at the same time reaching toward the endotracheal tube that protruded from the child's mouth, to the black balloon suspended from its tip. It was over this bag that Trish and the attendant struggled briefly. He gave it a squeeze and glared at her as she tried to peel his fingers away from it. It only lasted for a second, but Leah thought he might hit her in another moment. Instead he seemed to realize where he was and relinquished and ambu bag with a sickly grin. His eyes looked hollow and weary and his face seemed glazed.

"Over here, over here," Stacy Price bellowed and the little group careened toward the sound of her voice. The emergency room exploded into action.

Danny Thomson followed the stretcher and behind him was his assistant, ready to rush to the computer with the child's arterial blood as soon as Danny obtained it. It was this report that would tell them whether the patient was being well-oxygenated by the hand-held ambu bag. The lab technician, his basket high over his head to avoid breaking the test tubes, squeezed in beside him. Somehow, the EKG technician managed to maneuver her bulky little machine into the cubicle. She had her paste ready, a fresh roll of EKG paper threaded into the cogs. Rubber straps, one for each limb, dangled over the edge of the machine. Soon it would reveal the state of the boy's heart.

Leah stood for a moment feeling the anxiety of not knowing what to do, only that she should be doing something, and then her eye fell upon the figure who had followed the stretcher along the corridor. It was like looking into the face of a sleepwalker, one so deeply locked in a nightmare that no amount of commotion could intrude. There was not a shred of hope nor a glimmer of life in that face. It made her look old, yet the hand that clutched at the door frame for support was young. Her fingernails were bitten down to the quick, a plain gold band encircling one of her fingers.

She hurried to her side. "Let me find you a chair," she whispered to the woman. It was like talking to the deaf. The woman's gaze was fastened on the scene before her, her pupils black with fright. Gently, Leah pried her hand from the door. "Follow me, please."

Without looking but praying that the woman would respond, she walked toward an alcove. It was a carefully claculated space reserved for just this purpose, away from chaos. It was there that emotion could erupt without imperiling the lifesaving action taking place around the corner.

The woman seemed to recognize its purpose. As soon as she sat down, she began to fall apart right before Leah's eyes. Her eyelids fluttered and her pupils constricted.

Color drained from her face.

"He's dead, isn't he?" Her fingertips trembled and she drew them over her face as if she were feeling for something that she could recognize. "Don't lie, tell me the truth," she whispered.

"Please, we are doing what we can. Tell me, what's your name?" Leah asked.

"Sharon Norman. Is he dead? I know he is." She began to gather herself, clutching at the arms of her chair.

"What happened, Sharon? Can you tell me?"

The words tumbled from her lips as though a dam had broken. "Oh God, it happened so fast. He was ahead of me on his bike. I saw the light turn red, but he kept going. The car hit him. No. That's not right. The car hit the bike and I saw Michael fly into the air. He flew so high that my first thought was that nothing could hurt him up there, that he'd be alright. I remember thinking to him, Stay up there, Mikey."

Her voice broke. "I couldn't make my legs move. I just stood there, you know how in a dream when you try to run away from something scary but your legs won't move?" Leah nodded. "That's the way I was. I wanted to reach him in time to catch him as he came down. But I couldn't. And when he came down, he looked like a little bundle of rags lying in the gutter. I kept thinking he'll get up any minute and come running to me, crying. But he didn't. He was so still."

She stood up suddenly and rushed toward the trauma room. It was a move of such speed and grace that Leah realized she was reliving that awful moment, not realizing that her legs had moved at the moment of the accident. She followed the fleeing figure around the corner.

"Let me by," Sharon shouted. The portable x-ray machine had been rolled to the door blocking it. She danced around it trying to see into the room and finally began a futile wrestle to move it. It gave Leah a chance to catch up with her.

"Sharon, please, you mustn't go in there. There's simply no room for you in there. Let them do their work. It's the only chance Michael has." At the mention of the child's name she could feel the resistance leave the woman's body. "You're going to have to be strong a little bit longer, can you do that? For him?" A cheap shot, she thought, but it worked.

As she whispered in the mother's ear, she evaluated the scene in the trauma room. Stacy and Ben were huddled over the strangely still figure of the boy. He was stripped of his clothing and his limbs sprawled loosely on the table. Leah could see dirt on his knees. As if that were all the damage done, she thought, dirty knees. Come on, kid, cry. Move around a little, for Christ's sake. But there was only silence. Long eyelashes brushed the child's cheek and a drop of dried blood streaked his cheek.

An intravenous line had been started in the boy's left arm and fluid poured through it in a steady stream. The endotracheal tube was now firmly taped in place, covering his mouth completely. A respirator was attached to it, pumping rapidly. They were hyperventilating the child so that his brain would not swell and his little chest reacted like a set of bellows. It was the only sign of life that Leah could see.

Danny was crouched over a limp right arm, his fingers steadying a large-bore needle that pierced the skin, and blood slowly filled his syringe.

Ben straightened briefly at the sound of Sharon's voice. He ignored her and looked at Leah. His eyes were flat, almost angry. "Get EEG in here for a brain-wave scan. Pupils are dilated."

It was shorthand for a prognosis of death. The boy's body was too quiet under those strong lights. Where there should be sobs of a hurt little boy and thrashing limbs of protest, there was nothing. Leah felt the sting of tears in the back of her eyes.

"Michael? Wake up," Sharon called out softly. "Mommy wants you to get up. Right now!" There was a touch of annoyance in the last words. She clung to the door, straining to see.

Just then a male voice boomed across the room. "Sharon?"

The woman jerked convulsively. "Dale? Oh Dale. He's so hurt!" She took a few steps toward him and then ran into his arms.

A utility belt hung from Dale Norman's waist, and the handle of his hammer swung against his thigh as his wife threw herself upon him. He had a red trimmed beard and deep blue eyes. They stared at Leah over Sharon's shoulder, puzzled. His hand patted her in an absent, comforting gesture. Leah turned and hurried to the desk. She swallowed back her tears and forced herself to dial the EEG room. The brain scan would reveal what she had seen in Ben's eyes.

Stacy was the first to emerge from the room. She threw her stethoscope down on the desk with such force that it bounced off and hit the floor. Neither made a move to pick it up. "I'll take over now," she said.

"Is he?"

"Oh no, he's pumping away in there for all the good it does. You'll be getting him upstairs." Her voice was thick and Leah had to turn away from the defeat in her eyes.

"I'll take him with me," she said.

Tracy swung the car into the drive at the front door of the hospital. "You don't mind walking around to the back, hon? I don't want anyone to see me here. I'm supposed to be sick, you know."

Lily cast a glance at her mother. Tracy was definitely excited. She looked like a kid playing hookey. She shook her head and sighed. "I can manage." It was just barely the truth. The few sets of stairs ahead loomed as tall as a mountain. But she was used to it.

"I'll pick you up when you're finished." Tracy's fingers tapped on the steering wheel. "In the meantime, I think I'll go to the beauty shop. What do you think, hon? Time for a perm?"

"Whatever, Mother." She closed the door to the car and watched as Tracy wheeled the car around the driveway. How long would this sick-out last, she wondered. The way her mother had worked it out, and from the length of time she'd been on the telephone, it sounded as if it would go on forever. She had to admit that it was a clever scheme. Tracy had it arranged so that every nurse took their sick time in sequence leaving the hospital adequately, though barely staffed. Having her home everyday, though, was going to be a challenge. She turned and began to trudge up the grand stairway leading to the oak doors. She did not look for Billy. He would be inside.

After she had been settled in her favorite station and the drum beside her began to whir, she dug into her notebook and drew out a sheet of paper.

"Would you like to read this?" she said to Steve Lambert. It was a poem. The swirl of her blood in the machine was soothing somehow.

"Love to," he replied, "but first I need another sample of your blood."

"What for? You already took some."

Steve shrugged. "Who knows? Dr. Russell just called, he needs some more."

"He's a vampire." Lily watched as her blood filled a small test tube. The poem was about Billy. It spoke of his eyes and the infinite kindness she saw in them. It told of the strange, shy rustlings inside, when she looked at him.

Steve read it and then smiled at her. "Who is this

lucky person?"

She could feel the heat in her face. "A boy, that's all."

Under the shade of the granite wall, their favorite niche now, she had leaned into Billy's arms and felt protected. His lips grew practiced and aroused her enough to set her insides quivering. She had even let him touch her breasts through the fabric of her blouse. His hands lingered as though touching crystal. He seemed to know without being told that it must remain only like this, that nothing could interrupt her routine. With a maturity that astonished her, he accepted what she could give and demanded nothing more. He knew there was no energy for more, that her schedule consumed it all. She loved him for that and her poem sang of it.

"I call him Bill."

"Yeah. Billy and Lily does sound a little too cute," Steve said.

"That's not why I call him Bill, stupid." She snatched the poem out of his hand. "How come we're all alone in here? Where are all the other patients?"

Steve's face sobered. "The sick-out, remember? We had to ship the patients to other units. You're lucky I'm here, otherwise you'd be out in east Oshkosh, too."

He capped the syringe and turned away, not seeing the thoughtful look on her face. This business was going to affect her, after all. She hadn't thought of that. Would Steve be here for her next treatment? If they sent her away for dialysis, then she wouldn't see Billy.

"Hey stupid!" she called out. "You gonna be here day after tomorrow?"

Steve nodded. "Be right back." She did not see the little smile on his face as he carried the vial of her blood in his hands.

In the lab he handed the vial to the technician. Dr. Russell straightened up when he saw Steve. He had been peering through a microscope and when he saw the question in Steve's eyes, he shrugged and turned back. He pulled the glass slide from under the lens of the scope.

"O negative." He said with a noncommittal smile. "Let's see what Lily is."

"Who's the donor?" Steve asked.

"We don't have a donor. Not yet, anyway. Don't get your hopes up. It's a twelve year old—trauma case. We're just window shopping right now. Whatever you do, don't tell Lily."

Steve gave the doctor a disgusted look. He wanted to wait to see if Lily matched the boy, but he couldn't leave her alone. Reluctantly, he left the lab and hurried back to the dialysis unit. For the first time, he regretted the sick-out that left him short-staffed.

Chapter Eleven

By noon, Julian Plumhouse knew the hospital was in real trouble. Thirty-two nurses had called in sick on the day shift and so far the personnel office had received sixteen calls for the evening. He knew that he might not be able to cover the house at all during the night. He began to call the temporary nursing services, calculating the enormous expense this job action would cost the city.

He leaned back in his leather chair and regarded the computer printouts littering his desk. Evelyn Holden leaned over them, staring at their contents as if she could divine a solution from them. On one sheet was a list of employees and their paid sick days still untaken. By his calculations, those nurses would be the ones remaining out. The others, the ones who had used up their allotted sick time, would be the working force during the coming days. It was a pitifully short list.

He knew the nurses tended to view sick days as a bonus to be used as they saw fit and for once Julian was grateful for their misconception. Had they hoarded those days en masse to be used now, then Liberty Hill would have to close its doors, probably forever. No hospital could carry itself that long and survive. Not a city-owned one, at least. That reminded him . . .

"George Tratten should have been here half an hour ago. Where the hell is he?" He flipped the intercom switch and spoke to Betsy Conte. "See if you can find the city attorney, please."

Evelyn Holden shook her head. "What good is it having him here? He'll go running back to City Hall and stir up a hornet's nest. Secretly, the Council is wondering how long it'll take to knock you off your feet, even though they want you to succeed. They're the ones who let the hospital run down and you're the hero who brought it back. It makes them look like incompetents."

"You said that not me," he smiled. "Tratten has to stop stalling. He just can't delay any longer. I want him to see this place under siege. Maybe he'll get it through his thick head that he must deal with these nurses."

"You said that not me," she replied with a little grin. "Listen, I want your authorization to offer overtime to those already here. That might ease the crunch on three to eleven."

"You've got it. Anything else?"

The director of nurses shook her head, her face soft with pity for this man. They had worked furiously this morning, closing wards and shifting patients to consolidate nursing care. She had seen the outrage on Dr. Sheen's face when Julian ordered the operating rooms closed. He had literally screamed into Julian's face until they were nose to nose. Julian had taken it without flinching.

She pictured the closed floors: three medical-surgical, pediatrics, operating suites, and obstetrics. There were five newborns in the nursery, but thanks to modern care the babies were now rooming with their delighted mothers. So far there was adequate staff to cover that department, but no more patients were to be admitted.

After she left Julian's office she took a quiet walk through the emptied floors. It was ghostly. The beds were stripped and the floors washed down. Drugs had been returned to the pharmacy and the medicine closets locked. She had seen this once before, this eery stillness. It was during the polio epidemic in the fifties. She had been at the General then. How furious the work was, consolidating the iron lung patients while the rest of the hospital emptied. Mostly it was fear that kept the sick at home. She remembered the long line of iron lungs, looking like the glass coffins they were. Except for the hum of their machine-driven breaths, the place had been eerily quiet.

It was the same now; she could feel the life draining out of Liberty Hill just as it had happened at the General. This time it might mean the loss of her job. The thought did not make her angry at the nurses. Attention should have been paid to them long ago. Why hadn't the city seen what was happening? God knows Julian tried to get a contract settlement. Thank God she was still a nurse, she could always get a job somewhere. And with that thought, she smiled, knowing that she was a nurse first and an administrator second.

She leaned against the window and watched a small procession of cars drive into the discharge area. Sunlight shimmered over their roofs and cast a surreal glow over the front of the hospital. Patients were leaving the hospital as fast as their discharges could be effected.

Suddenly she recognized the portly figure of George Tratten making his way through the crush of automobiles at the entrance. He had left his car at the bottom of the drive and was striding to the door in obvious annoyance at the inconvenience. He stood aside as a patient in a wheelchair swerved by him. She could see him almost stamp his feet with impatience. She felt sorry for Julian. It was going to be a long day for him.

She turned away and walked through the deserted corridors to the Intensive Care Unit. At the nurses' station she could see Barbara Haines sitting alone, and from the rigid way she held her head, Evelyn knew that the secretary was uneasy.

"Where is everybody?" she asked.

Barbara jumped. "Oh you scared me, Mrs. Holden. I've been out here staring at these monitors so long, I'm beginning to feel as though my own heart is going to stop. Those lines are hypnotizing."

"Do you . . . er . . . know what you're looking at?"

"Enough to yell if I think there's trouble." The secretary swiveled back to the monitors. "There's only a couple that have been worrisome. The others are in normal sinus rhythm."

"Where is Mrs. Weathers? Did she get here?"

"Yes. She's in room two. We just admitted a twelve-year-old boy with head trauma. It's pretty crowded in there." It was a polite way of telling Evelyn to wait, so she took a chair beside Barbara. Very soon, she found that her gaze was fixed on the cardiac monitors just like Barbara. It was making her nervous. She felt her heart take a roll in her chest.

They brought in two chairs, one for Sharon and the other for Dale Norman, and pushed them hard against the window. There was no other space available. The young parents sat together trying to get a glimpse of their son through the crush of machinery surrounding him. The bed, the respirator, and the column of instruments sitting next to it, took up most of the room. A bright light in the ceiling spotlighted the small still figure in the center of the bed.

His eyes were taped shut with oval bandages that made him look like a blinded baby owl. The endotracheal tube and the bite block that prevented him from crushing it held his mouth agape. Only his cheeks and chin were visible. Tubes hung over the bed leading to both arms. One was dark red with blood, the other clear and salty.

Another tube led from his penis and drained his bladder into a bag below the bed. It was pitifully scant with reddish urine. Wire leads from the cardiac monitor over the bed pockmarked his chest and sent messages to the green screen above him. Digital numbers flashed constantly. Although a blanket had been hastily pulled over his legs, his skin had puckered into goose flesh. He did not shiver. Under his body, a blue plastic pad pulsed with ice water that was thermostatically controlled by a probe sitting in the boy's rectum. His body temperature was being lowered in an effort to decrease his metabolic needs. All the equipment being employed on his behalf would not revive him. He had already been declared brain dead.

"Think of him strictly as a potential donor," Ben had whispered to Leah as he helped her slide the body into bed. "He's a set of eyes, a heart, kidneys. You can only protect those organs from deterioration while we try to get the parents' permission. If we don't, then it's cabbage patch nursing care. We'll get him started on Solu-Medrol and keep him on ice." And then he'd left them alone.

It took thirty minutes for Leah and Katherine to get the boy settled into bed with the wires and tubes properly sited. A chart had been assembled and now Leah made her first entry, trying to keep her face neutral against the anxious glances of the boy's parents. Surprisingly, the kid had a healthy set of vital signs, she noted. Blood pressure was normal. His slightly fast heart rate was beginning to slow in response to the ice blanket. The boy's breathing was being mechanically driven.

If only he'd go into a lethal arrhythmia, she thought, it would end quickly then, but she knew Michael's heart was too young and strong to quit. It was going to be a stubborn body. She looked him over carefully. There were very few overt signs that the boy had been hit by a car. No lacerations, no swollen abdomen, not even the usual cut lip. Other than his scraped and dirty knees, there wasn't a mark on him. She wondered how she was going to get out of this room without answering truthfully the inevitable battery of desperate questions.

She had been through this before. It shouldn't be difficult. But it always was. She saw herself in the roles that were being played out in this room. She was a parent and this could be Nikki. She was Michael himself with Maddy and Red hanging over the bed, just as the Normans were doing right now, their faces agonized. Why hadn't he died back there on the street?

Dale Norman looked at her. "When is the doctor coming back?"

"He will look in on Michael this afternoon," she said.

"That's all? Why isn't something being done?"

"He'll wake up," Sharon said before Leah could reply. "We'll wait for him to wake up."

Dale's arm slid around her waist and she leaned against him, staring down at the boy, the back of one hand pressed trembling against her mouth. The expression on the father's face was growing thunderous, easy for Leah to read. The truth was slowly revealing itself to him as if it were a book whose pages were growing shorter and shorter until there was only one line left to read. She swallowed hard.

As she hung the chart on the foot of the bed, her hand brushed the blue ice blanket beneath Michael's body. She'd forgotten how cold it got. If Norman knew the pad was one of the measures being taken to preserve organs, he'd go mad. Soon, he would be faced with three choices for his son, none of which would restore him. He could allow the taking of donor organs and it would all be over quickly. He could refuse that and decide to wait. That would be the worst, she thought, the body could exist for years. Or he might come to the decision to terminate all life support. Then it would become a legal matter with judgments coming from a bench. Though he could not realize it now, Dale and Sharon were at a crossroads and these few moments right now would be the most peaceful of their ordeal. She left the room.

Billy Fellows saw it all, saw the arrival of the boy and knew by the crowd of attendants around the bed that the child was gravely ill. He heard the whispers outside the door, the words *brain dead*.

He had lingered by Dorothy's bed longer than usual because she was finally awake and seemed to be her old self once again. She looked so young. Her hair had been washed and tied back with a red ribbon one of the nurses had brought in. They'd even propped her up in a chair and covered her from chin to toe in a pretty blue blanket. Someone had patted her cheeks with rouge.

As usual, she didn't seem disturbed when Billy told her that Frankie had left. She shrugged and said, "He'll be back one of these days. He always comes back with his tail between his legs, don't he? Got a cigarette, Billy-Boy?" She smiled at him, almost coyly, he thought.

"You know I don't, Ma."

"Can you get me some?"

He nodded. She'd never understand what he wanted.

They were moving her out of here and that meant that he had only a short time to convince her to talk to Dr. Russell. He'd never see Lily again if he didn't. Two-Gus said to give her the chance. He would, but he didn't think it would do any good. He took a deep breath.

"Ma, there's something I want to tell you. It's serious, so I want you to think about it before saying anything. Okay?" He wanted her not to smile at him anymore.

"I've never seen you so glum, Billy. I know you've been worried about me, but I am going to turn over a new leaf. Yup, you are looking at the new Mom. Other than that, nothing's going to change, darlin'." Her hand waved over the room as if it had a personality of its own.

"The nurses say there's a diabetic classroom right here in the hospital I can go to." Her voice faded uncertainly as he stared at her. "It ain't about me, is it?"

Patiently, he began to explain to her about Lily. She listened, her eyes growing wider. He could see the color leave her face and the two sweeps of rouge become like bruises on her cheekbones. His heart sank. He sat on the chair facing her, his hands hanging between his knees.

She was silent. No flippant word, no easy laughter to dash away the tension that was like a blade of steel between his shoulder blades. The only evidence of her dismay was the constant twining of her fingers in her lap. Billy stared at them as if they had life of their own. Finally, her hands came together as if in prayer and he looked up at her.

"Soon enough, you'll be leaving me, too," she said. "You're growing up too fast for your age." He opened his mouth to reply but her eyes stopped him. "From what you say, it all depends on whether you are a match for this Lily. Her blood and yours, am I right?"

He nodded, feeling excitement begin to course through him. She did understand after all!

"It's Dr. Russell. He says he wouldn't even consider it. That's why I need you to talk to him."

"We'll get him to test you," she said, 'we,' he thought, not 'her,' but 'we,' "as soon as I'm out of here, okay?"

"No, it's got to be done now. You can write him a letter, couldn't you?" He hadn't realized he'd leapt to his feet. "I . . . I'll get you some paper." She seemed so young somehow, so defenseless that he felt the back of his eyes stinging. He leaned over and kissed her on the cheek. He hadn't done that in a long time. "I'll be right back," he whispered and hurried from the room.

As he passed the room next door, he glanced in and saw the young couple standing over the boy's bed. He saw the way the mother's head was bent at the neck, exposing skin that was white and delicate. The line of her cheek and the color of her eyes were hidden by a swath of dark hair. For a moment, he felt as if he were looking at a statue. She could have been anyone.

At the nurse's station, he waited until Katherine looked up at him. "What is it, Billy?"

"My mother needs some paper and a pen. Can you give me some?"

"Sure." Katherine pulled open a drawer and fished some hospital stationery from it. She uncapped a new pen and held it out to him. "She's looking so much better this morning, isn't she?"

He was busy thinking and did not answer her. "I think she will need to have this witnessed. Could you do it?"

"Of course. I'll be in when she's ready." Katherine hesitated. "By the way, were you planning to visit Two-Gus?"

"Yes, how did you know?"

"He called here just a moment ago. You've made a few friends here, Bill. And he really needs one. I think he's lonely."

Leah stopped by Billy's side. "And say hello for me. Tell him I'll be up to see how he's settling in after I get through."

Katherine watched him walk away. "Someday, if I ever have a boy, I'd like him to be like that one. He's a neat kid now that his big brother had disappeared." Suddenly, a strange look passed over her face.

"What is it?" Leah asked. "What's the matter?"

"I can breathe!" Katherine said. "For the first time in six weeks, I can breathe." She looked down at herself. "I do believe she's dropped a foot and a half. It's as if I'm myself again. She's become separate."

"They used to call it lightening. Is that the way you feel?"

"Yes, I believe I've shed twenty pounds." There was a

219

self-searching dreaminess in her voice. "It happened so fast, I thought something was wrong. It's a strange feeling." She looked up at Leah. "As a matter of fact, I don't think I can stand up. It feels as if she'll plop right out if I do. Even the backache is gone."

"What backache?" Leah wrinkled her brow suspiciously.

"Oh, I've had it all night, but it's gone now, thank God. Here, help me up."

"If this baby decides to make her debut, I'll be here to catch her, but I warn you, I don't know nothing about—"

"Birthin' babies, I know." Katherine grunted as she stood erect. She had indeed dropped. The waistband of her slacks was loose around her middle. She gathered it into a bunch. "Look, I can see my boobs again. They're separate." She began to giggle.

"Are you alright?"

"My God, I feel wonderful! Can you imagine? Feeling good and looking so funny?"

They began to laugh together. All the tension of the past hour was gone.

Finally, Katherine gasped. "I'd better sit down or I'll burst."

Leah helped her into the chair. "Don't you think you ought to call Dr. Price? I mean, what if you've gone into labor?"

"Don't be silly. With my low pain threshold, I'd be writhing on the floor if I were." Her eyes were thoughtful. "I don't want Ben to know about this. I want to savor the moment for a little while. Don't you tell a soul, hear?"

"I swear, but I'm not going to let you out of my sight today." Leah suddenly clapped her hand to her mouth. "What if Maternity is closed? Oh lord, what a time to go into labor."

"Then I'll have my girl right in room ten. We've got an empty bed."

Leah gathered together her equipment. "In the meantime, Emma awaits my service. Call me if you need me." She left the station.

Katherine stared after her. Something was going on, and it wasn't just in her belly. It was in Emma's room. The woman looked positively radiant this morning. At report this morning, the nurse mentioned that Emma's night had been extra quiet. No ringing the bell, no calls for suctioning. "I think she's doing that by herself," the nurse mentioned casually. That was probably it. Emma was beginning to assert herself. She would mention it to Dr. Peters, if he ever got here.

In Emma's room, Leah reached in her pocket and pulled out Danny Thomson's blood gas report. "Here it is." Emma reached for it greedily. She stared at the numbers and finally looked up at Leah.

"Don't understand," she mouthed.

"I'll explain them. You won't need to know what all the numbers mean, just the last two. The oxygen and your carbon dioxide. If you had perfect lungs then the O_2 number would be close to one hundred and the CO_2 would be near sixty or fifty. That's the ideal. We know, though, that you probably never had those perfect numbers, not since you were a baby." She began to smile at the notion of Emma as a child, but at the patient's fierce glare she caught herself. This was deadly serious business to Emma.

She tossed her head at the card. "Get on with it," the gesture said.

Leah looked at the numbers. "Your oxygen level is seventy. That's not bad for you. The carbon dioxide is a little too high, though. It's sixty-five. I think you did remarkably well last night." She looked up from the card. "But you're tired. I can see that in your face." Emma shrugged. "If you get exhausted, you won't be helping yourself. The numbers won't improve. You've got to get some sleep, otherwise you won't be able to keep it up. Try to balance yourself a little throughout the night. Sleep as much as you can."

Emma pulled the inevitable plastic board from underneath her blanket. With the long fingernail she kept sharp for writing, she scribbled on the plastic sheet and held it out for Leah to read.

"I want more gases done during the day."

"Oh no. I can't do that. Danny's the only one to agree to this. I can't get another therapist to help us. Even he's reluctant. Listen, if we get enough of these morning readings and they are good ones, we can present them to Dr. Peters. He'll have to agree to wean you when he sees them. Don't push me, Emma. I could get fired for doing this, never mind more."

Emma threw the blackboard on the floor and turned away from Leah. For the next hour, as Leah bathed and readied her for the day, Emma kept her eyes closed and her face grim.

Two-Gus settled uneasily into the bed and studied his new room. At least there was a decent view of the harbor and the sun was streaming through the window. It had been days since he'd seen the daylight.

He was on the top floor, Leah told him as she wheeled him through the near-empty ward. "Bev Britain runs this unit," she whispered from behind. "She's very efficient." Somehow that had a warning note to it and an apology for the cold stare the head nurse had given him as Leah pushed him by the desk.

He was in a room across from the nurse's station and for the past half-hour, he tried to ignore the furtive glances of the staff as they went about their chores. He rolled on his bad side, trying to ignore the pain in his shoulder. Anything was better than seeing the curious eyes.

A maple tree, newly budded with swollen red and green pods, brushed against the glass. He watched it, imagining its growth throughout the next few months. Those fragile little cups would burst with windmill seeds and then with star-shaped green leaves. Later, they would turn from apple green to what? Scarlet? Yellow? The secret of those leaves would be revealed only when the cool winds of autumn enveloped the tree. He wondered if he'd see the promise of these lush and swollen pods.

How long did he have? His thoughts turned inward, to the spores of death that were inside somewhere, coursing through his body. Why didn't he feel it? Somehow, there should be some malevolent vapor that he could taste, some niggling evidence of it. He felt nothing. His hemophilia always announced itself long before a visible bleed. There would be an almost unbearable ache in his joints as they filled with his blood.

His thoughts turned to his newest drug, AZT. "There are no guarantees with this, Two-Gus," Milly said that morning. "It won't prevent the inevitable. But it will reduce symptoms and give us some time."

He had never seen her like this. Solemn (did he see a little fright in her eyes?), she studied the little brown vial in her hand. It was as if she were trying to see through its opaque surface to the very molecules inside. He did not like the look on her face. She was usually happily aggressive in her treatment of him.

He showed her the article he had torn out of the reading material Leah gave him. "Anything I can use?"

"So, you've been up to your usual tricks," Milly said. When she looked at him, the worry disappeared from her face. She was always happy that he studied his disease. "I will be starting you on this, too. As soon as we get some.

Monoclate has been approved for treatment of AIDS patients. I don't know how you found out so fast. You must have an ally around here somewhere and I think I know who it is."

Her face grew thoughtful. "The only trouble, Gus, is that we don't know everything to know about this newest drug. We think it will strengthen your T-cells against further invasion from the virus. We just don't know."

"So I'll be a hemophiliac guinea pig, I don't mind. If I get into trouble, I'll give you a buzz. Who knows, you might even write a paper on it. Think of it, Milly, you'll make headlines," he said playfully.

She ignored the jest. "I want you to keep a diary from now on. I want to know every little twinge that hits you, understand? Keep note of times, too, in relation to dosage."

So far today he'd felt nothing except a little ache where his heart was. That was because he had been moved. Against his better judgment he had let the ICU become a haven and Leah his champion. Arguing with and cajoling the other nurses in there, she had worn down their resistance until the unit was finally a safe place for him. He basked in their attention. He was their pet, their special patient. Even Sandy McCracken (he came to know all their names), who vowed never to step into his room, became responsive to his needs. Now it was over and the whole process had to begin again. What if there wasn't another Leah on this floor?

She promised to come each day. While she helped him with his physical therapy, he had tried to explain to her how it was. Perhaps it was because she was the symbol of what hospitals had become: his mother, his wife, his friend. Did she understand?

The hospital was central to his existence and had been since he was a child. How does one explain that a building and its politics were family? It was more than that, it was his meeting place, his social life, and his primary home. He knew how it worked; he'd even learned to accommodate its crazy routines, like never ring the bell at change of shift, for instance. He'd learned to pattern himself to its needs rather than his own. It was a strange society to which he'd adapted and emerged with a sense of superiority. There was one word for it, he concluded finally, *survivor*.

But there was more. There was a contract. Unwritten and unsigned, the hospital guaranteed a measure of safety for him in return for which he would be a "good" patient. Only now there was a catch. With AIDS, he could not live up to his side of the bargain. He could see it in their faces. If that was so then there was no reason to be "good" anymore.

He crossed his arms over his chest and then remembered the purplish stains on his skin. Unlike his blood, these were invaders. At least his red cells, as deformed as they were, were keeping him alive. These splotches on his chest, these were quiet killers sent by a malevolent virus. They were out to destroy him. He picked up his gown and studied the skin on his chest. The welts were raised at their violet borders and looked like sharp claws extended across his skin. Cancer was reaching deep inside his body. His stomach turned.

"Here's your supper tray." A young girl in blue stepped into the room and set his meal before him. "Do you know how to crank up your bed? It's electric, you know." She chewed gum with staccato snaps that sounded like little gunshots. Her black-fringed eyes barely fluttered over him. "I'll be back when you're done." She pulled his door shut behind her. At least she didn't mask herself, he thought.

He fingered the tray; it was made of stout cardboard and paper plates and plastic utensils sat on it. Unlike the unit, everything here was disposable. Evidently this head nurse wasn't taking any chances, he thought. His sandwich was wrapped in plastic and a pickle, nestled against the bread, had leaked through it, staining it yellow. The carton of milk was warm. He pushed the tray away.

When she made sure Two-Gus was settled in his new room, apprehensive but comfortable, Leah hurried to the desk and sat beside Bev Britain. The head nurse had already begun the task of admitting this new patient to her floor. Leah watched as she peeled a strip of red and white labeling from a roll. With a black felt-tipped marker Bev wrote in large letters, *suicide precaution*. Then she pasted it across the front of Two-Gus's chart. Leah winced.

Bev ran an efficient floor. Every slot above her desk was labeled so that appropriate lab slips would never stray. The drawers had alphabetical contents listed on their fronts. There were wire trays marked "in" and "out." Tiny flags coded the charts that needed attention. Nothing went unmarked on Bev's floor, even her staff.

They were a stable group, moving about their duties with the precision of automatons. It was one of the most effective wards in the hospital. The floor, however, was staffed only by new graduates. No experienced nurse ever transferred to Bev's floor, not after they learned what it was like.

Over the years, she had developed a system of management so complicated in scope, so intricate that no substitute nurse could divine its purpose. Even Bev was trapped within her own system; she never had time to see a patient.

She handed Leah the chart. "Slip it in the rack, will you? Third from the left, up four slots."

Bev reached for a set of lab slips and began stamping

them with Two-Gus's charge card. During Leah's report, Bev had not ceased activity. Buttons were flipped, charts repositioned, drawers tidied. Now she began to erase Two-Gus's nursing care plan and Leah groaned silently. She had spent an hour on this plan, she had labored over it, listing each problem Two-Gus faced. She should have known better.

She watched as Bev wrote in large red letters, "AIDS." Naturally, that was the most important diagnosis, but that was a medical one and had little relation to the nurse in Two-Gus's room. Beneath it, she wrote, "Hepatitis." Finally, the suicide note was inserted.

"This man might be in a dangerous state of mind," Leah said softly. Bev nodded, trimming the corners of the Kardex with a tiny pair of scissors that were tied to a drawer with shoelaces. "His door should remain open." She had seen the aide close Two-Gus's door.

"It makes the girls feel safer. Don't worry, Leah, we've had many precautions up here and haven't lost one." Bev flashed her a brilliant smile. "Besides, where can he go? I'm right here. Now is there anything else?" She was being detained and showed her impatience.

"Dr. Malcolm comes every other day—"

"Yes, and stays five minutes, right? They're so effective, those shrinks." She leaned closer to Leah. "He isn't queer, is he?"

"Who? Malcolm?"

"Our AIDS patient, who else? Come on, you can tell me."

"For God's sake, he's a hemophiliac. As for his sexual preference . . ."

Bev shrugged and stood up, dismissing Leah. "I know, it's none of my business. But if my staff knew he wasn't gay, they'd be a lot kinder to him."

"Then there's something wrong with your staff and it probably comes right from the top."

She left the desk before she exploded. Somehow, Two-Gus will have to be careful up here. He has to, she thought. Passing his door, she poked it open with her toe, enough so that she could see his feet and one corner of his tray. Then muttering to herself and casting fierce glances at the nurses around her, she walked to the elevator. When the doors opened she slipped inside, not seeing Claude Peters leaning against the back wall.

"If it isn't my favorite ICU nurse. What on earth are you doing up here in Nazi-land?"

For once she was not annoyed to see him. "I was trying to settle a patient in up here. It's not an easy task."

"What? You don't like Das Fourth-floor Führer?"

She began to smile. "Is that what you call her? I thought the doctors loved Bev."

"Only the dumb ones," Peters said. He stepped beside her. "Let's talk about you and me. How about a drink after work?"

She turned her back on him and crossed her arms. "When the sun sets in the east."

"Okay. That's tomorrow, I hear. Wanna meet at the Grog?"

The doors slid open and she escaped without replying. For a moment, Claude Peters stood staring after her and then turned and headed for the administration wing. Before Julian's office door, he straightened his tie and slicked back his blond hair. Then he pasted an artificial smile on his face and breezed into Betsy Conte's office.

"Hello, gorgeous. Is His Highness in?" He leaned over her desk and nuzzled her neck. He could see the bright red flush begin to stain her skin.

"Oh stop it, Dr. Peters. Come on, I won't be able to get my work done for the rest of the day. Ooh, you've got me all bothered."

Her eyes told him differently. She was sizing him up, testing him to see if he were ready to make a move.

Somehow, he felt as if he were up against someone far more experienced than he. He straightened.

Her eyebrow rose. "All talk and no action. I knew it. Someday, Doctor, I'm going to pin you up against the wall and unzip those legendary trousers of yours. Just to see if it's really there like they all say." She cocked her head toward Julian's door. "He's busy. Have a seat."

"Can't wait, my dear. If he can't see me now, he can find me on my rounds."

She sighed. "Just a minute. Let me see what he says."

Claude Peters turned his back on her while she clicked on the intercom. "You can go in, Dr. Peters," Betsy said, smiling sweetly at him.

Julian Plumhouse was stretched back in his chair with his feet up on the desk when Claude Peters entered. There was a man seated across from him and by the set of his shoulders, Peters could almost feel the tension in Julian's office.

"George Tratten, Dr. Peters. Mr. Tratten is the city attorney. He was just leaving." The heavy-set man reached out and took Peters's hand. It was clammy and cold.

He barely acknowledged Peters's presence. "I'll be back at seven o'clock, Julian. Let's hope these fool nurses will listen to reason. Otherwise the city is prepared to go to court to halt this so-called sick-out."

"Good for you," Peters murmured and Tratten's face brightened at the unexpected support. "It's about time we stop letting a bunch of union thugs lead us by the nose."

"Yeah, just my thoughts exactly," Tratten said, gathering his coat and briefcase.

"Remember, George, seven o'clock. Or you'll have my resignation on your desk." Julian let his feet drop from the desk with a thump.

Tratten and Peters said together, "What?"

"That's right. My resignation. If you think I'm going to stick around and watch this place close its doors after all my work to bring it back from the grave, you've got another think coming. This hospital will be shut down tight within two weeks if you don't give those nurses a contract." Julian rose to his feet as he spoke. His normally pale face was even whiter than usual and with his wiry gray hair, he looked like a wrathful ghost. "Now take that information back to City Hall and see what your politicians think of it." He turned to Claude Peters, who had not realized his mouth was open until Julian's eyes fastened on him. He snapped it shut.

"You and I have a problem, Doctor. Sit down."

For a moment George Tratten stood there frozen, then he realized he'd been dismissed. With his coat dragging on the floor, he opened the door and closed it behind him, leaving one corner of his coat snagged. Flushing he reopened the door and snatched up the offending cloth. Then he shot an angry glance at Julian and slammed the door behind him.

Curious, Claude Peters watched as Julian opened a desk drawer and slid out a manila folder. "What's this all about, Julian?"

There was no answer. Julian opened the folder and read the contents of it very slowly. In a moment, Peters could feel a sense of unease growing right between his shoulder blades. What had he done?

Julian looked up at him. He laid the folder down and closed it. "I've been doing some research on you, Doctor, something I ordinarily would never do with a member of the medical community. But it has been called to my attention that you might be abusing the hospital and furthermore defrauding our state welfare system." He leaned back in his chair and once more, his feet went up on the desk. Right on that folder. Claude's eyes followed the gesture.

"What are you talking about?"

"I'm talking about your welfare cases here at Liberty Hill, one in particular whom Medicare refuses to support any longer. How is it that you more than any other physician here at the Hill have managed to maintain the longest stays of your state-supported patients?"

"First of all, Plumhouse, I have a right to know who my accuser is. You say it's been called to your attention. Who was that? The little nurse in ICU?"

Julian's face remained composed but his fingers tightened on the arms of his chair. He said nothing.

"Well? Is that all it is? For Christ's sake, Emma Bond is on a respirator. She's dependent on the damned thing. She is, however, on the waiting list for Salem Rehabilitation and that's all I can do with her." He rose to his feet. "If it's any consolation, Mr. Plumhouse, Medicare is threatening to cut me off, too. Liberty Hill isn't the only entity with welfare's thumb on its neck. It's not my business to see that Liberty Hill collects its fees. I have enough trouble getting my own."

He walked to the door and just as his hand grasped the knob, Julian's voice hit him like a steel dart.

"You're headed for trouble, Claude, like losing a set of privileges here at Liberty Hill if you don't work on getting your Medicare patients, all of them, out of hospital. You've been warned."

Julian kept his voice calm but after the door closed upon Claude Peters, his breath came out in a rush. That was the first battle. There'd be more, if he knew Claude Peters. His gaze fell on the incriminating file on his desk. He had learned a lot about Peters from it, more than he wanted to know.

Inside that folder was a list of patients at Liberty Hill that was too lengthy to be merely coincidental. Peters's welfare caseload outweighed any other physician's at the Hill. He was nothing more than a merchant and it had all escaped notice because the numbers were scattered throughout the year. No one had thought to collate his caseload; it was never done. If Medicare hadn't protested the fee abuse, this list would never have been made. To make it worse, there was, incredibly, another file, this one separate from Liberty Hill's. It was developed with the cooperation of the welfare board. Peters didn't know about this one. It dealt with his nursing home caseload. The local geriatric facilities were bulging with his patients and Medicare charges against them were staggering. The man was making over one hundred thousand dollars a year on his poverty-stricken patients alone.

If Peters did not heed his warning, Julian would have to call in the Medical Board and present them with the facts of the case. It would be an embarrassment not only to Peters but to Liberty Hill as well. He swerved his chair around so that he could face the window. Far out on the blue of the harbor, he could see the triangle of a sail tilting against the wind. It made him think of Leah. She had promised to take him out there, and right now it seemed the only peaceful place to be.

It was near the end of shift in the ICU and although it had been a frantic day without full staffing, the quiet now was in direct contrast to the rest of the day. Katherine watched as Leah and Carol Rafferty made their last minute notes to end the shift. She had helped with patient care today due to the shortage, and she could feel it in the small of her back and her aching feet. Let me never forget, she thought, just how physical nursing is. Yet, though she drooped with fatigue and waited for the shift to end, there was a small knot of pleasure in knowing she remembered how to make a patient comfortable, how to measure micrograms of drugs in relation to kilograms of patient weight (she was sure she'd forgotten that), even how to suction a patient. She laughed to herself remembering Emma Bond's scowl and the question on her blackboard, "You know what you're doing?"

It was easy to take for granted the staff's skills in here. There was an awesome amount of mechanical equipment in the unit yet none of it daunted them. How convenient it would be to forget the human being lying in the bed and concentrate on the machinery surrounding him. Yet they never did. She loved them for that.

As she stretched and rubbed the back of her neck, she could hear the comforting sounds around her. The buzz of the respirators, the small clucks of the drop-measuring intravenous machines, even the faint hum of the cardiac monitors. White noise. It was the peaceful time of the day. She could almost forget the tragedy in Michael Norman's room. Almost, but not quite, she thought. That would be a pleasure to leave behind. The young parents had been in there since morning. Without food, without comfort, and, she knew, finally without hope. If it weren't for that case, the unit would be serene. If anything happens, let it happen after three, she prayed to herself.

The doors to the unit slid open and Claude Peters walked in. I knew it, she thought with a groan. He would have to come now. She heard Barbara Haines mutter, "Oh shit." It meant paperwork for her and she wanted to get out on the dot of three.

"How many patients do I have?" Peters said as he brushed by Katherine.

"Just one, Doctor. Just good old Emma," she said.

He made an exasperated noise with his lips. "So what's new with her? Any change?"

Katherine saw Leah's head come up from her chart. Don't say a word, my girl, she thought to herself.

"No change," Leah said, handing him Emma's chart. "Just the usual." She hesitated, then added. "There is one. Emma wants to learn to suction herself. She thinks she can do it better because she knows when she needs it."

"That's alright," Peters said, standing beside Leah and

rummaging through Emma's lab work. "Everything looks normal. I'll write the order to teach her." He smiled at Leah. "Is she your patient today? Good. Let's go see her together."

Leah's eyebrows rose. "I . . . I have these other charts."

"Only take you a moment, Miss Swift." He did not wait for her to reply, but strode toward Emma's room. Leah followed, casting a shrug at Katherine.

Once inside Emma's room he turned on her. "What have you been telling Julian Plumhouse? I know you and he have a thing going. Have you been crying on his shoulder?"

Emma rattled her bedrail to get his attention. He ignored her and glared at Leah. "Well?"

"I don't know what you are talking about," Leah said. She turned to leave the room, but Peters caught her arm. As she tried to pull away his fingers dug into her skin. "Let me go," she whispered.

Behind them the bedrail shook even louder. Peters leaned closer. "I know all about it. You've been running to him with this case. I can have you fired for this, you know. I won't, but you've been warned. Keep out of medicine." He released her.

"And I can have you arrested for assault," Leah said. "I won't, but if you lay another hand on me, I will. Now pay attention to your patient."

She glanced over his shoulder at Emma. The woman's mouth hung open and when she caught Leah's eye, she gave her a thumbs-up sign. "Good for you," she mouthed. Leah felt a smile begin to come over her face. She turned away and left the room.

"What's the matter?" Katherine asked when she saw the expression on Leah's face.

"He's a bastard, that's all." Leah grabbed up another chart and sat down with a thump.

Chapter Twelve

By seven o'clock Two-Gus knew they had skipped his medication time and he suspected that it wasn't an oversight. He was supposed to get Keflex at four and the new one, AZT, every six hours. That would have put that dosage at six o'clock. His supper tray sat on the table just as it had been brought in three hours ago. Now he needed to use the bathroom. He pushed the button and peered at the nurses' station where he could see his light flashing over his room number, but no one was there.

Holding his injured left shoulder steady, he threw back the blankets and swung his legs over the side of the bed. There were no slippers in place; no one had unpacked his bag. The floor was cold against his feet and a little gritty. Holding his arm against his waist, he got to his feet, feeling his heart fluttering against his ribs. He cursed his lack of strength. How many steps was it? Four, five?

He made his way to the bathroom, sweat breaking out across his brow. When he was finished he was too shaky to reach the flush handle. The bandage on his shoulder was dry and it pricked his skin like sandpaper. It should have been changed earlier, but, like his medication, that procedure had been skipped as well. He lay on the bed, the covers too far to reach. Out in the corridor, he could hear someone laughing. He closed his eyes tiredly.

"Mr. Ragust?"

There was someone standing just outside his door. She was pulling on a gown, mask, and gloves. How long he had been asleep he didn't know, but his legs were chilled.

"Is there anything you need before I come in, so I won't have to change again?" the nurse said.

He shook his head. "The toilet, I couldn't flush it."

"Ooh, naughty, naughty," she said. "You're supposed to be able to do that yourself. Didn't they tell you that? This is a self-help floor. And the chlorine, did you forget that? You are supposed to flush with chlorine." She disappeared into the bathroom and in a moment, he heard the rush of water.

"I have your medication," she said, reentering the room and pulling a little cart after her. "And I'll change the dressing while I'm here." She pushed a little plastic cup toward him.

"I need water."

"That's what I mean." With an exasperated sigh the nurse leaned out the door and called, "Norma? Bring me a pitcher of water, please. I'm all done up. What a pain in the neck precautions are."

Two-Gus decided to ignore her. He peered into the medicine cup. The Keflex was blue and white, the other, a strange color of mauve, must be the AZT. The nurse poured water into a cup and pushed that toward him. So far, she had managed to avoid contact with him. He wondered how long she could keep it up.

"I have to change your dressing and settle you down for the night," the nurse said. He could feel the coolness in her gaze as he swallowed the pills. Finally, she turned away and began to fuss over the equipment cart. Snapping a brown paper bag open and folding its edges back, she propped it open by his thigh. Then she peeled open a sterile sleeve of gloves along with several packs of dressings. At last she turned her attention to the dried mess on his shoulder.

It was going to hurt. "Wet it with saline first," he said.

"I know, I know. Please don't tell me what to do." Her eyes flashed at him over the mask.

But she did as he said and poured fluid over the old bandage. When it loosened, he glanced down at himself. The incision looked clean and the suture line was pink. Where the rubber drain had entered his shoulder was healing circle of skin. It looked like a gunshot wound. She squeezed an antiseptic ointment over the site and there was no sensation, neither cold nor warmth. He knew the nerves there had been severed. He looked up as she layered the incision with four-by-fours. She had good technique. He read her name pin: Edna Cote.

"Are you a Miss Cote or Misses?"

She did not answer. While he watched, she gathered up the soiled dressings and dumped them in the brown paper bag. If she hadn't been wearing a mask, he knew her mouth would be a thin disapproving line. She left the room tugging the dressing cart behind her.

"Hey, you forgot to unpack my things. I need a urinal and my slippers."

"Later," she replied from the safety of the hallway. "I've already degowned." Her final words seemed particularly malicious. "You should have asked before."

The room grew dark but he did not bother to switch on the light. From the corridor, he could hear the sounds of a ward settling itself for the night: laughter, loud and boisterous; pain that came in a quiet gasp; aimless conversation. The silence in his room was deafening.

"Hello." It was Billy; sudden and unexpected joy flooded him.

"God, I'm glad to see you. Mask up and come on in, old sport."

Billy gestured at the pile of gowns by the door. "Do I

need these?"

"Not unless you plan to operate on me."

The boy smiled uncertainly. With a glance over his shoulder, he entered Two-Gus's room.

"I brought you this." It was the usual Coke.

"Thanks. Here, pull up a chair." Two-Gus opened the can, ignoring the ache in his shoulder. "How's your ma?"

"Good. She's your neighbor again. They put her on this floor, too. Would you like to meet her sometime?"

"Yes, I'd like that. When she's feeling better, of course." He took a swallow of the syrupy sweet drink. "And the diabetes? She is getting straightened out?"

"Jeez yeah. That nurse, Leah, gave her an armload of books on diabetes, enough to fill a library. Ma's been reading them ever since."

"Good ol' Leah," Two-Gus said. "She did that for me, too."

Billy shrugged. "It ain't gonna do no good, though. Once she gets home, she'll forget again. It's too complicated for her and besides, she hates the needles. All it means is that I will have to give her the shots myself. I don't mind, but I know damned well she won't let me. To her, I'm just a kid."

The nurse, Edna Cote, stuck her head in the room and glared at Billy. "Can't you read? This patient is on precautions. You're supposed to check with the nurse before entering."

Billy jumped to his feet as she spoke, an embarrassed flush climbing into his face.

"Oh, leave the boy alone," Two-Gus said softly.

"You stay out of this," she said.

"I said, leave the boy alone, or I'll come over there and cough all over you."

She gasped. "That's nasty."

He began to make the motion to get out of bed and her

238

eyes widened in alarm. Billy stood caught between them, his face puzzled. Finally, he sat back down.

The nurse turned on him. "You're taking a chance with your health, young man, just being with him. But I guess you've been doing that right along, eh?"

Two-Gus caught the implication. He began to hack and cough, throwing back the covers. The woman hurriedly backed away and disappeared.

"What'd she mean by that?"

"Pay no attention to the voice behind the screen," Two-Gus intoned, mimicking the Wizard of Oz. Billy grinned.

"She's just trying to throw her weight around," Two-Gus said. "Nothing better to do with herself. It sure isn't like the ICU."

He lay back in bed. "Now where were we? Oh yes. What to do about your ma. I am not a preacher, but I think you've come to a fork in the road with her. The first choice might be the most difficult, but the most rewarding.

"You can take charge of her." At the scorn that came over Billy's face, Two-Gus cocked his head. "No good, huh? She'll fight it tooth and nail. I can understand that. She's been making the decisions for you all your life. Maybe she'll give in if you're persistent. After all, she's been mighty sick. Maybe she's ready for a steady shoulder to lean on. At least the two of you will be together and she'll be cared for in some fashion. She might like that." He hated to think of Billy's life with that in his future.

"That other option is the one Frankie takes. Disappear when it gets tough. He has every right to do what he does, and in a little while, so will you, though I don't think much of it. No matter which choice you make, ultimately you have to get on with your own life."

"That's swell," Billy muttered.

"Look at me," Two-Gus commanded softly. "Now tell me about the girl. . . . What's her name?"

"Lily. That ain't looking so good neither," Billy said. "I met her doctor. He isn't one bit interested in using my kidney."

Thank God for him, Two-Gus thought.

"But Ma wrote him a letter giving her permission. Maybe it might change his mind."

This kid was damned heroic, but his mother left a lot to be desired. Two-Gus decided that tomorrow he would get out of this room and talk to the woman.

The hallway lights dimmed twice and then a voice over the intercom announced the end of visiting hours. Billy stood up.

"Will you be back tomorrow?" Two-Gus asked. As always the intensity of his feelings toward this kid astonished him.

The usual reply came back. "Don't I always?" Billy grinned at him.

When he was alone, Two-Gus lowered the head of his bed and stared at the ceiling. Why did he care so much about the kid? There was so much he had to think about without getting involved in someone else's life. The answer was simple—it was the dilemma the kid was in. What was his future? Growing up on Hancock Point was a poor enough beginning. He could end up on the street. There were drugs out there. Hookers. And poverty. He could see Billy's innocence turning to cynicism within a year, especially with a mother who could not even manage herself. It came to him that perhaps in this neutral place, the hospital, Billy had a chance to learn about options. Right now he was facing choices no kid should have to decide.

There was also something more. Billy had chosen him. Why, he could not begin to guess. The kid accepted him completely, no questions asked. Could he turn his back?

Undecided, troubled, Two-Gus stared at the ceiling until his eyelids grew heavy. Soon, he slept. His ten o'clock medication time went by.

The fever hit him in the darkness of night. He was awakened by the sheets burning against his skin and the familiar pervading chill arising from his bones. With a sense of foreboding, he understood that this was AIDS. It was uncompromising. It struck in the night, and his dreams of refuge were mockeries. There was no time off for good behavior or sweet dreams.

Outside his room there was a dim light at the desk. The nurses had gathered under it as if sheltered from a storm. He could hear them. They talked quietly and it soon came to him that they were talking about him. He listened sadly.

". . . quarantine them all until they die and the disease dies with them. It would end it once and for all. This isn't just TB. This kills. If they could isolate tuberculosis patients who were not a life threat, why not these? Most of them are queers or junkies anyway."

He pulled the blanket tight around his neck, but it didn't help. He was freezing. His fingers sought and found the call bell. There was break in the conversation. Someone sighed, "My turn."

She stood at his door. "Yes, Mr. Ragust?"

"I need another blanket, I have a chill." He fought to keep his teeth from rattling.

"Anything else?"

He shook his head watching, half afraid that she would disappear. Suddenly the chill left him as swiftly as it had hit. It was replaced by a burning along his ribs, like a hot knife suddenly flaying him open. He gasped with it.

The nurse, masked and gloved, spread a cotton blanket over his and he shriveled under its weight. It was burning! He managed to wait until she left the room and then he pulled it off, hoping she would not return and think him ungrateful.

The rest of the night he alternated between chills and fever and the strange burning in his ribs. By morning he was exhausted.

Below him in the ICU, Pat Connor, draped in her usual blanket and poised on the stool before the cardiac monitor, looking as she always did, like a squaw before the campfire, saw Emma Bond's cardiac line begin to slow. She yawned, waiting for the respirator alarm to signal. There was nothing. The digital readout began to drop more rapidly from eighty, to sixty, to fifty. The blanket flew to the floor as Pat dashed into Emma's room.

Emma's face was peaceful and the room dreadfully quiet. The respirator had been shut off. How had she missed it? That accounted for the slowed heart rate. Asleep, Emma had forgotten to breathe. She leaned over the bed and switched on the machine and its alarm shrilled, waking Emma. For a moment she stared puzzled at Pat and then took a deep shuddering breath. Instantly, the monitor recorded an increase. She gave Pat a sheepish grin.

"I'll pretend this didn't happen, Emma, but if you are going to sleep, damn it, put yourself back on the vent, understand?"

Emma raised a middle finger at her and rolled over. The vent groaned under pressure and as Pat watched, Emma's heart rate once more floated up to eighty. She had her suspicions before, now she was sure. Emma was weaning herself.

At Michael Norman's room, she peeked in. The kid should be turned and suctioned, but the parents were asleep. She'd be damned if she'd wake them up just to watch their brain-dead child get tossed around. They were exhausted. She picked up the blanket once more and settled on her stool. Beside her, the aide they'd sent to help her during the sick-out was fast asleep, her head cushioned on her arms.

It wasn't until Milly Gold's visit the next morning that anyone became aware of Two-Gus's condition. No one had bothered to take his morning set of vital signs. He'd finally slept, too deeply to wake for breakfast. His tray sat untouched on his bedside table beside a basin of bath water.

Milly stared at the red streak along his ribs. "Shingles," she said. "You've got herpes zoster."

"*Moi?*" he managed to gasp. "I thought that was a little old lady's disease."

"It's an opportunistic infection. Little old ladies have decreased immune systems. So do AIDS patients. We start you on Cortisone and something for the pain."

"You might as well stop the alphabet drug. It didn't do a thing. What about that Monoclate?"

"That should arrive today, but we'll keep you on AZT as well. Those shingles have been brewing long before this, Two-Gus. I want to see if it clears up."

As she talked, her gaze swept over the room, not missing the untouched tray, the dry new soap bar. Her eyebrows came down tight until they formed a straight line. She turned on her heels, leaving him to stare after her.

At the nurses' desk, she leaned over and hissed at the head nurse, "Get that man something to eat and give him a bath. Where are his morning vital signs? Why aren't they on his chart? Are you ignoring this patient? Because if you are, I'll have you on report. This patient developed complications during the night and no one knew it, did they?"

The substitute nurse for Bev Britain rose to the challenge. She smiled. "Look around you, Doctor. How many nurses do you see? None, right? I'm all alone on this floor. Me, twenty-six patients, and two aides. We are in the midst of a sick-out here. If your patient can't feed himself, and I know he can, that's too bad. Let me remind you that this is a self-help floor. I will get you his vitals as soon as I'm finished."

Milly's eyes were hard as marbles. "Now, nurse. Do it now, not later. I am going to stand right here and stare at you until you get up."

The nurse pursed her lips and reached for a stethoscope, then she leisurely walked to Two-Gus's room and began pulling on a paper gown. Milly's eyes rolled in exasperation. She opened her mouth to reprimand the woman, then snapped it shut. No sense in antagonizing her, she thought. The woman would probably take it out on Two-Gus. She grabbed his chart and sat down in the chair just vacated by the nurse.

Within an hour the fever was gone, thanks to two aspirins. Two-Gus smiled to himself. Milly was getting forgetful in the face of his new disease. Aspirin was forbidden to him. It could make him bleed. Things are different now, he thought. Nothing seemed to matter to her as long as she could make him comfortable. This is the life of a dying man for sure, he thought. They give you the world.

He sat up and struggled into a fresh johnny that she had laid across the foot of his bed. Thank God she had come along when she did. She had washed his back as tenderly as a mother with a child. She had even helped him into the bathroom and then swabbed the toilet with chlorine. All the time, she muttered to herself, "Self-help floor they call it. I call it no help, that's what I call it. A good floor for lazy workers. They ought to string up these people." She pronounced it "peepuls" which sent him into gales of laughter, sending her away with a satisfied gleam in her eye.

He wandered to the door of his room and waited until

244

he caught the attention of a young girl dressed in blue.

"Will you please bring me a telephone? They seemed to have lost mine."

She hurried away, but soon reappeared and thrust a pale green phone into his hands. Pain sheeted across his ribs as he held it.

"You shouldn't be out of the room," the girl hissed at him.

"And you shouldn't be talking to me without a mask." It was a nasty remark, but he liked the fright in her eyes. The power of AIDS, it had some advantage at least. He turned away and sat on the edge of his bed.

He wouldn't have thought he could remember the telephone number, but the bright voice on the other end of the line told him he had.

"White, White, and Cohen," it said.

"Mr. Ragust for Mr. Cohen," Two-Gus replied.

In a moment, the booming voice of his attorney came over the wire. "Is this Lazarus? From whence do you arise, old man?"

Two-Gus smiled to himself. If this gentle man knew the truth, he'd be horrified at the gaffe.

"Hi Pete," he said. "How goes the world of wonders? Set any precedents lately?"

"Every day, my boy, every day. The law and I are one, you know that. What can I do for you?"

The abrupt question told him that Peter Cohen was interrupting something important for his call.

"I am ready to talk wills."

There was a little gasp on the other end of the line. "Did my ears hear right? Did you sire an offspring?"

He smiled to himself. "Can you make a house call? I'm in the joint again. Over at Liberty Hill this time."

There was a pause and Two-Gus knew Peter was looking through his calendar. "Why can't you stay at a real hospital, like right here in town? Why do you go out in the hinterlands? Tomorrow at ten o'clock," Peter said.

"It's only over the bridge, Pete. Don't be so melodramatic. I'll be waiting." He disconnected without waiting for an answer.

Though his chest felt like it had a red-hot zipper sewn into it, and he knew the fever could erupt again at any moment, he felt strangely satisfied. Something had been decided last night. When or how, for he had slept throughout the long hours when the wrenching pain eased, he did not know. All he knew was that the moment he'd awakened, all the pieces were in place. He knew what he had to do. And he could hardly wait for tomorrow.

The shades in the family waiting room had been drawn against the fierce spring sun. A small room, it was used to isolate the Intensive Care Unit visitors from all others. The room made Leah nervous; the air was stagnant in here, it smelled of old cigarettes. It made it hard to breathe. Her knees almost bumped against Sharon and Dale Norman. She wanted to be yards away from the Normans, away from what was about to happen in here, but Michael Norman was her patient.

She glanced at Dale Norman and though she knew he'd slept only in naps throughout the night, there was a freshness in his face, a naked hope as he waited for Ben Weathers to speak. Sharon, on the other hand, had nothing but despair etching her face. She seemed like a sleepwalker. She knows, Leah thought.

Ben took a deep breath. He looked down at Michael's chart in his hands. Without thinking, he flipped it open while the others watched, as though there was something hidden in there. Somewhere in the figures, the laboratory had missed something: the x-ray or the CT scan had been misread.

He coughed and Leah could see the faint tremor in the

hand he used to cover his mouth.

"The news is not good," he said. "I wish I could tell you something else, anything other than what I have to say." The papers rustled in his hands. "Michael's injury is so great that his body cannot support life."

What followed, the silence, was thunderous. There was no reaction. The Normans stared at him, waiting expectantly, as if he had not spoken at all. If they heard him, they had already dismissed the words that damned their son's life.

To Leah, the room became filled with electricity darting back and forth, seeking receptacles, and finding none. She reached over and took Sharon's hand in her own. It was lifeless.

Finally Dale spoke. "You mean that he is going to die?"

"I mean that he already has," Ben said.

"How can you say that? He's in there." His hand waved in the direction of the unit. "His heart is beating. I . . . I saw it. It's still beating." He glanced at Leah for comfirmation.

Ben's eyes were focused on the floor. Without looking up, he muttered, "He has suffered brain death, Dale. The only thing keeping the heart going is a primal reflex. That and the respirator."

Then Dale caved in. His face became deathly white and his fists, clenched before, now curved open upon his knees. Leah half-rose to her feet to go to him, but Ben shook his head at her. Tears began to well up in Dale's eyes and he drew a great stuttering breath.

Now Sharon spoke up. "I can't believe that with so little attention paid to him, you could come up with such a diagnosis. How do you know he's dead? You saw him only for a moment." Ben did not reply.

Sharon turned to Dale. "We'll take him to Childrens Hospital. They'll know what to do. We can do that, right?" She glanced at Ben and saw his nod.

"I know that you want better answers, Sharon. I'd want to do everything possible too, if Michael were my child. The problem is, we have. If it were a broken bone, if a lung was punctured, we could fix that. It's this piece of paper that tells us." He tapped the EEG report. "There is no brain activity. We will, of course, do another test, but I'm afraid it will only confirm—"

"Get another opinion." Her voice was flat.

"Yes," Dale said, wiping his eyes with the back of his hand. "Get another doctor in here to look at him."

"I will," Ben said. "There is a fine neurological pediatrician at Childrens, Dr. Ned Chimes. I'll ask him to take a look at the boy." He stood up. "I just want you to understand where we are right now so that you'll be prepared to take what comes."

"If he's dead, then what else is there?" The words shot across the room at him. Sharon wiped her mouth with an ugly, brutal gesture. "What else is there?"

"I simply meant that you might not want his opinion, either." He motioned to Leah. "We will leave you alone for awhile, but we'll be in the unit if you need us."

Outside the door, he leaned against the wall and exhaled. "I will never get used to that. But it's only the first step. The next is even more terrible. Wait until they meet Chimes."

Leah wiped her eyes with a tissue. "What do you mean?"

They walked into the unit and the sound of the respirator in Michael's room seemed to float out to meet them.

"When Dr. Ned Chimes finishes his examination of the boy, he will jump all over those parents to donate the body. It's going to get emotionally brutal and he won't let up. They'll come to hate him more than they hate me."

He went to the desk and Katherine looked up at him,

sorrow in her eyes. "In the meantime," he said, "we get a respite while we wait."

"Do you think they will give in?"

"I couldn't begin to guess how they'll react. Right now, they are having a hard time accepting what I've told them. They are denying it. And they're angry. They're angry at me, not you people here. That might be a help."

"What do you mean?"

"As long as they can direct that anger at me, then it leaves you as the friendly party. You are the ones they'll turn to in order to get comfort. At the same time, you're going to have to try to make them accept reality. You'll be walking a fine line for the next day or so."

"What if the boy's heart stops beating?" Leah asked. "I mean while we wait?"

"Do you think it will?" he shot back. She shook her head. "I don't either."

He began to dial.

Chapter Thirteen

"Are you allergic to fish, Mr. Fellows?"

Billy shook his head, he was too numb to answer. Things were happening so fast. With his mother's letter clenched in his hand he had once again waited outside Dr. Russell's office, determined to make the man listen to him.

But this time Dr. Russell seemed almost jovial. He read Dorothy's letter, noted the witnessed signature and then looked up from his desk.

"You really mean business, Mr. Fellows. This doesn't automatically override my feelings on the matter, but it does give you a little credence. I will go upstairs and meet your mother, to talk with her a little bit."

Billy's heart leapt.

"We still don't know, though, whether or not you have a kidney to donate, do we?"

Dr. Russell pulled out a manila folder and slipped Dorothy's letter into it. With a large felt-tipped pen he lettered Billy's name across the edge of the file. With that gesture, Billy knew it was official. He had begun. He wanted to run to the dialysis unit and tell Lily. He wanted to shout it to the rooftops.

"There is no way to find out unless you have a kidney

test. Let's do that and then go from there." Dr. Russell picked up the telephone.

They had ushered him from the lab, where seemingly endless vials of his blood had been drawn, to the x-ray department. They wrapped his arms around a cold photographic plate and took a picture of his chest. Then he climbed upon a table, his bones knocking against the hard surface, and stared at the big machine poised over his head.

"Make a fist, Mr. Fellows," the technician said. "We are going to start an intravenous in your arm in order to give you the dye. You might feel warm all over and even have a funny, metallic taste in your mouth, but that's normal."

He barely felt the needle entering his arm, and soon he was alone with the faintly humming machine hanging over him. There hadn't even been time to find Lily. For all he knew, she had already left dialysis and gone home. If he didn't tell someone soon, he thought he would explode.

It did not occur to him that he was also about to find out if he were healthy. The machine whirred to life and he thought, this is it. Somehow he knew this machine would be his accomplice.

It had begun to drizzle when Lily opened the door and looked for Tracy's car. The weather matched the way she felt. They had sucked her blood extra hard today. She felt it in the weary tremble of her legs, the faint tinge of nausea left over from the treatment. Even the headache, normally wiped out by the machine, was still there. It was a consequence of two days of revolution.

She had eaten all the forbidden foods. She had even tasted a beer, but didn't like the taste of it. She should have had an eggnog instead. What made her angry was that she had been too afraid to skip her treatment. The frightened look in Billy's face, the careful way he hovered over her defeated the whole idea, and she had gone to dialysis, disgusted with herself and him, knowing it was going to be tough. Steve Lambert chided her. Her creatinine was out of sight. And she had gained five pounds. What was she thinking of? She told him to stuff it.

It was the worst four hours she'd ever had. Besides the nausea and vomiting which after awhile made her stomach muscles ache, Steve had to tilt her chair almost upside down in order to keep her from fainting. The room swam before her eyes and she kept swallowing back the bile that rose in her throat. At one point, she cried out that the machine was draining away her life. Even Steve, who had told her once that he had no sympathy for incompliant patients, hovered over her, coaxing her to the end. When, at last, he screwed down the plastic clamp over her fistula and pulled the hated tubes, she crouched in the plastic chair and wept.

Tracy's car swept into the drive, the windshield wipers sending little mists of spray into the air. The sidewalk seemed to shimmer under her feet as she walked down the broad granite steps. Tracy leaned over and opened the door for her and she flopped into the seat, leaning her head back.

"You look dreadful," Tracy said, barely glancing at her. "I've got your bed turned down and the radio on." She braked at the entrance to the hospital, looking left and right.

"Are you going out?" She felt the back of her eyes stinging.

"Mr. Plumhouse wants to talk turkey. I think we've got a contract."

The car began its dipping ride down the hill and Lily could feel every bump. Circle Street, to Half-Circle Street, the car bounced. Her stomach swooped over the crossings.

"Take it easy, will you? I feel sick to my stomach."

"Sorry, I guess I was excited," Tracy said touching her toe to the brake. "I just can't believe it. Our sick-out must have really worked! I mean, why else would he call me in?"

At home, Lily allowed her mother to help her into a clean pair of pajamas. With the covers drawn tight to her chin, she lay in a stupor. Tracy fussed around the room. She knew her mother wanted only one word and she'd be gone.

"If you feel up to it, we can go to Quincy Market tomorrow. There's some wonderful little shops I want to see. How does that sound?" Tracy hung her bloodstained shirt in the closet, not seeing the mark.

"Do you know that I was the only patient in Dialysis today?"

Tracy shrugged. "It's to be expected. We all have to make sacrifices. Look how many sick days I've given up." She lit a cigarette and inhaled deeply.

Lily's stomach heaved. She turned on her side, away from the smoke and the meaningless chatter. Could she do this again? The next time would be worse, if there was a next time. How long would it take before they moved her to the top of the transplant list? She knew Steve Lambert's nursing notes reflected today's misery. Did that help the cause?

Actually, when her creatinine was too high it was rather a pleasant state for her. It sent her into a listless torpor from which she did not want to stir. Awake, she would dream and they became gentle little confusions that sometimes made her giggle. It alarmed everyone else. They would not let her stay that way. She'd die that way, happy and disoriented.

While her mother chatted, Lily closed her eyes and let her tears soak into the pillow. Then she felt Tracy's hand upon her forehead.

"I didn't know . . ."Tracy whispered. "You are really bad, aren't you?" For a moment there was silence. Then she added, "I'll stay with you, babe."

For a moment Lily held her breath then she released it with a sob. More tears soaked into the pillow and ran into her ear. She began to hiccup. She felt so young, such a baby.

Tracy sat on the bed and the weight of her body made Lily slide against her hip. She gathered Lily into her arms and held her, staring out the window. Lily fell asleep listening to the sounds of her mother's breathing and the soft hiss of the rain on the roof.

Julian Plumhouse leaned back in his chair and regarded George Tratten. The city attorney sat across from his desk. He had taken a fresh linen handkerchief from his breast pocket and wiped it nervously across his mouth. The computer printouts lay before him like an indictment. Then he reached in his briefcase and pulled out a single sheet of paper.

"This is the best I can do." He handed it across the desk and then stared over Julian's shoulder at the window. It had begun to rain heavily and the wind rattled the glass.

Julian gave the City Council directive a cursory glance and his heart gave a little thump. It was better than he expected. But he would not let this political hack know it.

He laid the paper on his desk and sighed. "I don't know if this will end the sick-out. Do you know that as of four o'clock our emergency room will stop admitting patients? That the operating room closed this morning? There are empty floors out there, George."

The lawyer's face took on an anguished expression.

"Listen to me, Plumhouse. Those damned fool nurses must come to their senses. This is a bona fide genuine offer."

Julian managed to keep his face straight. The man sounded like a circus barker. "It's about time, I might say."

Tratten shrugged. "This is the way we handle city contracts, Julian. We treat the city contractors, the rubbish collectors, the street cleaners, everyone who works for us as though nothing is negotiable. At the last moment, when they're about to walk, we make 'em an offer and they jump at it. Like, you know, a drowning man? It works every time."

"At the expense of hundreds of thousands of dollars a day? Is that what you call efficient city government?" Julian snorted with derision.

"I admit this got a little bit out of hand. But we're on track now. Your job is to get those fucking nurses back in here."

Julian sighed. He would love to sink his fist into the man's fleshy paunch. The light flashed on the intercom.

Betsy's voice came over the wire. "I have Mrs. Webb on the line. She says it's urgent."

Julian did not reply, but picked up the phone. "Yes, Tracy? What can I do for you?"

Tracy's voice was cold. "You'll have to get someone else to negotiate. I can't leave my daughter alone. She's sick."

"Sorry to hear that. Is there anything I can do to help?"

"I handle my own troubles just fine, Mr. Plumhouse. You can help by settling the mess up there. Now, I don't know who is available. Anyone will do, actually. If you call around, you'll find someone and I can confer with her from here. I don't care."

Her voice sounded tired.

"Of course. Please do not worry. We all want an amicable settlement here. I'll do the very best I can." He hung up and turned toward Tratten.

"Seven o'clock, George. Our union rep can't make it, so I'll call around for a substitute."

"Are you talking about the Webb woman? Thank God. She scares the hell outta me." Tratten stood up and gathered his briefcase and raincoat. "Keep that contract offer under lock and key until I get here. I do the talking, not you."

But Julian was not listening, he was on the intercom to Betsy. "Notify the kitchen that we want sandwiches and coffee sent to my office at seven o'clock. Enough for, say, six people."

He flipped off the switch and rose to stretch, leaning with extended arms against the window frame. He saw George Tratten emerge from the front door and scuttle to his car, his head bent against the wind. Traffic to the hospital had diminished greatly since the patient exodus. That meant that Liberty Hill was down to a level that it could manage. How long it would survive without full population, he had no idea. One week, he guessed.

He opened a door adjacent to Betsy's office and slipped into the little bathroom. The light over his head made sharp angles of his face. He stared at himself for a moment and then leaned down and began to splash cold water over his face. The clock in his office showed quarter to three.

The evening shift began to straggle in and Katherine held her breath waiting to see how many showed up. All afternoon she had waited for the sick calls, but none came. They were here, quiet and a little withdrawn, but here. They gathered around her desk for report. Behind her, Leah sat with the last chart. She was writing furiously.

It was a relief to know that the emergency room would not be admitting patients tonight. Now if there was a crisis out on the floors, the unit could handle it. They'd have an empty bed. She flipped open the Kardex and began the process of handing over the unit.

It was only when she began to review Michael Norman's case that she sensed an awakened interest. The nurses leaned forward to catch her quiet voice. It was a dry review of his systems. After all, the only damage was to his brain and that was invisible. His heart was strong, his kidneys were functioning, and although his breathing was absent, the respirator was handling that function on its own. She recited the statistics in a low voice so that Dale and Sharon could not hear.

Though the case was strictly coma care and therefore easy, she could tell that no one wanted to be assigned to it. It was rare to have a child in here, much less a brain dead one, and the problem was complicated by the presence of the boy's parents. Michael, himself, was a perfect patient. He made no demands, he didn't cry, he was compliance itself. It could drive a nurse crazy.

"Respiratory is managing his gases," she said hopefully, as if that were a selling point in Michael's favor. "The only meds he gets are Solu-Medrol and aspirin." God, she sounded as if she were selling a product. The feeling made her all the more guilty, but she could not help herself. "He's had two units of packed cells and that's finished now. His intravenous is at one hundred c.c.'s an hour. And his output is fine."

She looked up into the ring of faces around her. They had turned to stone. She looked at Mark Berlin and whispered, "You'll have to make the decision for them."

He nodded. "I'll take him. I don't have kids."

Relieved, she closed the Kardex and prepared to stand up. Just then, the phone rang and the group of nurses groaned. It was expected. Since the sick-out began, the evening supervisor had been pulling a nurse to cover a poorly staffed floor. It was a minor exasperation to the nurses who had prepared themselves for the harrowing eight hours in the ICU, only to be pulled for floor duty. They hated it.

But it wasn't the supervisor tonight. It was Julian Plumhouse.

"I need a favor, Katherine. We've had an unexpected development that might lead to a settlement tonight. The only problem is that Mrs. Webb can't be here to handle negotiations. Is there anyone up there willing to stand in for her?"

"Just a minute, I'll see." Katherine held the phone to her chest and signaled to the nurses. When she relayed the message, no one volunteered.

"No way. I'm not taking Tracy's place. I wouldn't know how." Everyone's response was the same.

Katherine sighed, "Then I suppose I'll have to go."

"You can't," Leah exclaimed. "You should be at home with your feet up. I'll go. Only on one condition. Tell Mr. Plumhouse that I'm going to bring Nikki with me. I won't be separated from him for that. If that's okay with him, I'll do it."

Relieved, Katherine repeated the message to Julian only to hear him burst out laughing. Over the phone, she nodded her head to Leah. "I'll tell her. Good night, Julian. And good luck."

When she hung up the phone, she smiled. "He's thrilled, he says. Seven o'clock. Why is he thrilled, Leah?"

Two nurses chimed in together, giggling, "Yes, why,

Leah? Do tell us!"

Leah made a face at them, but her eyes were bright.

As she made rounds with Mark Berlin, Katherine filled him in on Michael's case. "The parents are holding up, though I don't know how. They know it's going to be a wait until Dr. Chimes comes in. I'd let them stay all night if they want." It was a suggestion, not an order, for Mark was now in charge.

He smiled at her. "They can stay as long as they want. I'll even encourage them to help with his care. It will help them get through it."

She found that her bottom lip had begun to quiver. "Thanks," she whispered, turning away so that he would not see the sudden emotion. If all went according to plan, by tomorrow the child in there would be just an empty shell.

When she reached the corridor outside the unit, she began to walk as fast as her feet would carry her and by the time she reached the emergency room, she was almost running.

"Take me for a long ride," she said to Ben.

He nodded, his long face compassionate. He threw his jacket over her shoulders and together they walked out into a gray and drizzling afternoon.

For the second time Two-Gus's supper tray went untouched and he slept through the change of shift. It was only when he moved and the ripping pain shot across his ribs that he roused, wincing. He saw that it had begun to rain heavily, that the maple tree outside his window was burdened with water. Its dark red buds began to break against the glass and fall to the ground. They never had a chance. When he awoke again, it was to see Billy Fellows, garbed in a mask, pulling his supper tray over the bed.

"You gotta eat," he said a little self-consciously.

"No appetite, my boy. You eat it." His mouth was as dry as a crust of bread, but his heart swelled at the sight of the boy.

Billy unrolled the utensils and shook out a napkin. "Look, you eat and I'll show you my secret."

"What are you talking about?"

Billy pulled up his sleeve and held his forearm so that Two-Gus could see a little black mark in the crease of his elbow. "See? They gave me a dye and took a look at my kidneys. It's done."

"You work fast," Two-Gus said. "When will you have the results?"

"Tomorrow." He leaned across the bed and pushed the "up" button. As the bed rose, Two-Gus could feel his arm brushing against Billy's chest. He resisted the impulse to gather the boy in his arms.

"Come on, Mr. Ragust, I can't have you starving yourself to death. I need you." Billy pulled a chair close to the bed and began to spoon some creamed soup into Two-Gus's mouth.

"Here, give me that." He grabbed it, spilling a little onto his gown. "No one feeds me. I'm no kid."

Billy sat back grinning. "Ma is up and puttering around in her room. I told her to come down later and meet you. Is . . . Is that alright with you?"

Two-Gus shrugged. "As long as she doesn't think I'll marry her. It'll be just friendship, that's all." Billy giggled. "Now that she's better, how long do you think she'll be in here?" He saw the smile fade from Billy's face.

"I don't know, Mr. Ragust. That's why I want her to meet you. Maybe you could explain things to her. She doesn't really understand that it's an operation we're talking about. If I told her, she'd probably drag me out by my heels."

"I'll talk to her, Bill, but I can't guarantee she'll agree. I don't know if I agree. It is her decision, after all."

Now a worried look came into Billy's face. "That's the problem, she's never been too good about making decisions."

"Everyone needs help sometimes," Two-Gus said. He laid down the spoon and automatically Billy reached over and pushed it to one side so that he could reach the inevitable pickle-soaked sandwich. Without thinking, Billy took half and began to munch at it.

"There's a fine for stealing patient food." Leah said, grinning from the doorway. The two of them looked startled. "Well, what do you have to say for yourselves?" She reached for a mask.

"Before you get all garbed, tell the nurse out there to give me my medication. She's late," Two-Gus said.

She turned and disappeared. Within a minute she was back with the little plastic cup in her hand. "It's because of the sick-out," she said. "They are down to bones in staff tonight."

"How long will this buisness last?" Two-Gus asked.

"Maybe the end is in sight. I'm going to a meeting tonight. But I wanted to pop in and say good night." She looked at Billy. "I heard that you went through with the kidney test. How did it come out?"

"I'll know tomorrow," he replied. "And Miss Swift? I never got a chance to thank you for taking care of my mother so good. I know she's better because of you."

To herself she thought that this little family of two did not have much chance at success. Teaching Dorothy about diabetes was like trying to teach a kid calculus. It wasn't because she wasn't bright. She was. It was her mortal fear of needles. Her body had become an enemy. She was certain that injections would destroy the tenuous hold she had on the world. With the insulin needle poised over her thigh, she whispered to Leah that she felt as if the real Dorothy was caged deep inside her body, and in there she had to hold herself still so as not to touch her electrified skin. It was a bizarre picture but one so vivid that Leah understood her fright, and sadly she realized that there would be more incidences of coma or shock in the Jelly Bean Lady's life.

Billy was going to be burdened with her care. How he handled it was something no one could tell. He was so tender with Two-Gus. . . . She watched him pour the last few drops of milk into his paper cup. His face was serene. Then she realized what she was staring at. A paper cup! And a cardboard tray. She felt a helpless rage begin to build.

Bev Britain had deliberately ordered disposable utensils, ignoring hospital policy and her own careful nursing plan. It was a careful orchestration of terror, calculated to instill fear in her staff and insult the patient. It was well known that she had a way of forcing the sick to adapt to her way of running the floor. They became model patients up here, a pleasure to nurse, Bev always said. How cruel, she thought.

Luckily, Two-Gus did not seem to notice, either that or he was too engrossed in Billy's company. He did appear almost happy tonight. And he'd eaten every morsel on his tray. It was the boy. Billy had given him a reason to live.

"I'll see you two tomorrow. Good night."

"Give 'em hell, old girl," Two-Gus said, glancing over at her. There was something in his eyes. What it was she could not tell, but it seemed like resolution.

Mark Berlin stretched and rose to his feet. It was time to turn the boy and suction him. He gathered up the tiny intravenous bag labeled in red that he had prepared earlier. It was Solu-Medrol, powerful cortisone that nature had devised to reduce inflammation. It would help diminish the trauma to Michael's body, but it would not revive him.

He glanced at the two figures by the window. Dale Norman's steady gaze met his. Sharon was asleep, but only lightly, he could see. Her mouth twitched as she dreamed. Probably a parody of the nightmare she saw when she was awake, he thought.

A soft light spilled over the power column next to the bed. It guided Mark's hands. He hung the medication bag on the pole next to the other liter-sized one and plugged it into the rubber port. The clear drops of fluid began their silvery flow into Michael's vein. He bent down to inspect the child's needle site. There was no puffiness of the skin, no discoloration that would mean an infiltrate. A small blessing. He did not want to stick needles into the kid, not with that gaze boring into his back.

While Dale watched, Mark fastened his stethoscope to his ears and placed the bell against the boy's chest. With the respirator heaving just beside the bed, he could not hear the air exchange at first. He closed his eyes and concentrated until the bubbly rushes of air came to him. Unable to cough, Michael was accumulating secretions in his lungs.

Everything he needed to suction was right there, taped to the power column—a bag of sterile gloves, a liter of saline, and the catheters, still sheathed in sterile packets. He tore open a set of gloves, hoping the noise would not arouse Sharon. Next he uncapped the sterile saline and poured a few ounces of it into a paper cup. With one glove on his right hand and isolated from the left, he pulled the sterile catheter from its envelope. From this moment on, until the procedure was over, his two hands would not touch. He was good at it. His technique, perfected over time, would give Michael's lungs an aseptic cleansing. There were no shortcuts to this procedure. Mark forgot the parents.

With his left hand pulling on the outside of the paper sheath, his gloved hand caught the catheter and held it free from contamination. Again the left hand reached out and disconnected the respirator from the tube that protruded from the child's mouth. Quickly, he slipped the catheter deep into Michael's throat. When it would go no farther, he lifted his thumb and the hiss of the suction line began to reach into the tube. Thick, clear secretions floated up into the catheter. There was no cough, no gag reflex. If he were to leave off the respirator tube, Michael would not breathe. It would be over in seconds. Mark's hand hesitated. He could end it now. Instead, he grabbed the tube and reattached it to the endotracheal line. The child's chest rose.

He waited for a few breaths and then repeated the whole procedure once more. When it was over he wound the catheter around his fingers and pulled off the glove over it. It was then that he noticed that Dale had come to stand beside him. His face was deathly white in the faint light.

"Did that hurt him?" he whispered.

Mark shook his head. He would not tell him that usually there was great protest over the procedure, that patients often fought it, that it could stifle a breath and produce violent coughs. With Michael there was no need.

"I have to rub his back and turn him on his side," Mark said. "Would you like to help?"

Dale nodded. The nurse showed him how to hold the boy on his side, the upper leg crossing over the lower, the shoulder positioned so that there would be no nerve damage. Though Michael would not notice it, if he were badly positioned, the great plexus of nerves in his shoulder, the ones that supported his arm and made his fingers move, could be permanently impaired.

Mark showed Dale how to silence the respirator alarm when the tube kinked. Then he began to rub the boy's back with long slow strokes. His fingers found the reddened ridges that had already begun to develop. If left alone, the skin would begin to break down. While Mark worked, Dale watched, his hands cradling the boy's body. When each pressure point had been rubbed with oil, Mark tightened the sheets underneath the body. Then he propped a pillow against the boy's back and another between his legs so that one would not rest upon another. When he was finished, Michael lay suspended in a cocoon of pillows. The process had taken fifteen minutes and through it all, he had not stirred.

He motioned to Dale with his head and Dale brought up the covers and tucked them in. It was only then that tears began to flow from his eyes, dropping onto the sheet over Michael's shoulder.

"He's really gone, isn't he?" Dale said, his shoulders shaking.

"Yes, he is."

"Then what's the use of all this?" His hand waved over the respirator and the intravenous line. "Why are they keeping him like this?"

"There was no reason not to. Not at the beginning. They couldn't know at the time that Michael was . . ." He stopped himself and searched for the right word. "That it was pointless. Their first concern was to help Michael to breathe. After that, they could not stop. Not legally, anyway."

"So what are we supposed to do?" Dale asked, looking at Sharon. She had stirred and mumbled beneath her breath. "She won't be able to handle this. I don't think I can. How do we stop this?"

Mark shifted uncomfortably. It always came in the

middle of the night, the final acceptance, the truth that hid itself in the complexities of daylight. And it never came when the doctor was there.

"There are ways," he said. "Legal ways, court orders, and all that." It was coming, and for all his might, he wished he were anywhere other than in this room. "Other ways."

"What other ways?"

Dale looked up at him.

"You ... uh ... might consider that Michael could help someone else to live, someone who would die without ... say ... a new heart." He knew he was screwing it up. He could tell by Dale's expression. It was as if his words had clawed across Dale's face. Mark felt a little sick. The young father turned away and stumbled to his chair.

The notion was planted and, though it was painful now, Mark knew it was better than what was coming tomorrow. Still, he hated night duty.

He handed Dale a blanket. "For your wife. They turn down the heat at night."

Dale spread it over Sharon, letting it flutter over her legs. Before he left the room Mark switched off the overhead light, leaving only the soft glow coming from the power column and the red eye of the respirator. It blinked in the darkness like a concealed animal.

When he returned to the room two hours later, the scene was unchanged. Sharon had curled into the chair, her head cushioned by her arm. In sleep her face looked pained. Dale was still awake. He leaned forward, his arms on his knees, staring at the still figure on the bed.

Once again Mark suctioned and turned the boy. And though Dale went through the motions, it was as if he'd already absented himself in some way.

This time he asked, "Why do you do all this? What's

the use?"

"It's what I do," Mark replied. "I couldn't *not* do it."

Dale had, by now, lost his fear of the tubing, the respirator, and the intravenous lines. He handled them with skill. He had even helped in the suctioning, holding the paper cup of saline with which Mark flushed the catheter. Something had happened. Though his face was agonizingly tired, there was something new. Mark could not tell if it was resignation.

The shift wore on in two-hour segments, and though Mark longed to avoid that room, he matched the vigil that Dale had begun hours before. When, finally, the clock crept close to eleven, he felt as if he'd returned once more to Vietnam, to some hidden battle he could hear but not see, to the wounded crawling out of the jungle. Dale's eyes were the same as those soldiers—night-hollowed by something hidden in the bush.

Chapter Fourteen

By six o'clock, Nikki was fed and bundled into a yellow two-piece fleece set. It had a large pink duck sewn across the front in cotton and on his rear, two ducklings in the same color. Red frowned when he saw his grandson dressed thusly. "It's for a wimp baby," he muttered.

While he played with Nikki, Leah showered and dressed in a heavy oiled sailing sweater and canvas pants. Around her neck, she tied a blue and red scarf. Her hair, curling damply against her back was tied with a tortoise-shell clamp. Eating a quick bowl of chowder and crackers, she then snugged Nikki into his backpack.

"I'll give you a ride," Red said, helping her adjust the baby's weight against her back. "No sense in hiking up the hill in the rain. He'll catch cold."

Instead, she smiled at him and said, "Take your wife to the movies. You need a break away from us." It was true.

Since her return, Maddy and Red had not left the marina and with spring launching soon to come, they would be tied down by the store and the pressing needs of their customers until the end of fall. Summer for them, as she well remembered, was a season of hard work and it made her feel a little guilty for saddling them with Nikki's care. Then she would remember the way Red's face lit up with joy every morning when Nikki toddled into the kitchen, the way Maddy's fingers riffled through his silky hair. She knew they had accepted her and Nikki without condition, and she loved them both for it. Soon, though, she would have to get on with her own life. She needed to find a place for her and her son.

Lights along First Street had flamed on, a steady blue gaslight that did little for illumination. With Nikki chattering at her in his deep voice, surprising in one so small, she bent her head and began a steady march that would carry her to the top of the hill. By the time she reached Circle Street, she was panting and her toes squished inside her deck shoes. Nikki seemed to have grown by ten pounds. As she climbed the hill he had grown silent, listening to her labored breath. He clung to her neck and tried to lift himself away so that she would not be burdened with his weight.

Inside the great front hall, she knelt and slipped the backpack from her shoulders and the sudden release of weight threw her off balance. She landed flat on her back with Nikki squealing in delight beneath her. He reached up and pummeled her cheeks in mock battle.

"Not now, you little monster," she exclaimed. "It's not playtime, this is big business."

And she remembered why she was here. Negotiations. With no idea of what was in store, she began to regret her decision to help with it. Tracy's phone call had come just as she had entered the apartment hours earlier.

"I understand that you are my stand-in for tonight's session. Do you have any questions about it?" Her voice was cool. "I thought I'd give you some hints as to how to conduct negotiations."

With Nikki clamoring for attention, Leah listened to Tracy's litany of advice. Don't accept their first offer. Listen to what they have to say and assess just how far they're prepared to go. "Then call me," she had said with a tinge of desperation in her voice. Don't make a move without me, her voice pleaded. The phone call did more to frighten than reassure Leah.

She rested in the hall for a moment and then turned and began to free Nikki from the harness. "Oh, you heavy little monster. It won't be long, young man, before you will be carrying your own weight."

Nikki reached out and patted her on the cheek. Did he understand her? In some way, she thought he knew everything there was to know about love. Had he forgotten Tony? That his young voice came from his father? Somehow she thought that he must remember everything from the moment of his birth and on, that he had stored it away in some primal corner of his mind to resurrect at a later time. Someday, he'd say with surprising accuracy, "Why did we leave the Southern sky?" She didn't know what she would say to him.

He held her hand and waddled down the hall toward Julian's office. The door was open and she pushed it so that Nikki could enter before her. Julian was there and so was Evelyn Holden. Neither of them looked refreshed. If anything, they were wilting under the long day's seige.

"Twenty-one sick calls on the evening shift," Evelyn said by way of introduction and not noticing Nikki. "We've managed to cover the floors, but it's going to be scary tonight."

By then, Julian had knelt on the carpeted floor and held out his arms to Nikki, but the baby, struck with sudden shyness, hid behind his mother's legs. A fat thumb sneaked into his mouth. Julian looked up at her with a broad smile on his face.

"Give him a minute and he'll be all over you," she said.
"I can wait."

Evelyn looked nonplussed at the sudden warmth in the office.

There was a table of food set up in his office.

Sandwiches, salad, coffee. Three big pots of it. Did that signal a long night? Leah hoped not. She shouldn't have brought Nikki if it did.

Julian nodded toward the table. "You'd better eat now. Later your stomach won't tolerate a thing."

"Are you trying to scare me?"

"I think he is," Evelyn said. By now, Nikki's hand was firmly locked into hers and together they walked to the table of food. "Tuna, little man?" She tore off a corner of a sandwich and handed it to him. Then she pulled him into her lap and he settled there as naturally as he would sit with his grandmother.

Over a filled plate, Julian said, "While we wait for George to appear, I've been doing some planning of my own. I thought it would be a good way to start the night off by saying that from now on the nurses will not be serving trays. It was an archaic custom anyway."

"Hooray," Leah exclaimed softly. "One small step for nursing." It pleased her that a simple one-hour demonstration had accomplished so much. Though it sounded like a miniscule concession, it had, in fact, advanced the nurses' standing within the hospital community. They were no longer waitresses. It also freed them to get on with their own tasks, that of helping their patients. If it meant feeding a patient, that was nursing; the lugging of trays was not.

"On the other hand," he went on, looking directly at Evelyn Holden. "I want documentation on the troublemakers here. They have been getting away with it for years. For starters, put Mrs. Britain at the top of the list. Any more insubordination from her and I'll have cause to dismiss."

"Agreed," Evelyn said briskly, her finger wrapped into Nikki's. She looked at the child. "He's a darling baby, Leah." Nikki wriggled from her lap and began to head for the table of food, both hands extended before him. "Ooh, the little devil looks like he's going after the whole deal. No half sandwiches for him."

Leah headed him off. She offered him a carrot stick and, contented with that, he deposited himself in the middle of the floor and began to gnaw on it.

Just then the door opened and George Tratten bustled in, coat flying, leather briefcase under his arm. The others hissed in alarm; he barely missed stepping on the baby beneath his feet.

"For God's sake. What's a kid doing here?" he said, annoyed.

"He's part of the negotiation team, George," Julian said. "Don't step on him."

Tratten's eyes rolled in exasperation. He plunked the briefcase on Julian's desk and pulled a yellow legal pad from it. He had yet to acknowledge Leah.

"Lemme eat and then I'll talk, alright?" Without waiting for an answer, he filled a plate with food and began to wolf it down. Finally his gaze rested on Leah. "You fillin' in for Webb?" He spoke with his mouth full, spitting crumbs of bread over the front of his suit. Nikki watched in fascination.

Tratten's eyes told her that he more than liked the idea of her presence. He studied her breasts and her hips, and then gazed fixedly at her crotch. His leer was so blatantly obscene that it was almost funny. He looked like a porno king. The only thing missing was a big gold chain around his neck. All the same, she felt her face redden. At her feet, Nikki stared up at her and she swore he winked at her. A dribble of carrot juice trickled over his chin. She plastered a charming smile on her face and turned toward the attorney.

"Do sit down, Mr. Tratten. It's so nice to meet you at last. I've heard a lot about you." She heard a quiet snicker behind her. "Here, let me take your coat. My, such a rainy night, isn't it? I don't think spring will ever

273

come. Seems such a shame to tempt us with one good day and then make us pay for it with a northeaster, doesn't it?" She heard herself chattering as she handed him a coffee cup, full and steaming. "Now do be seated, you must be famished."

She knew she sounded like a grand duchess, but it was working. Tratten slid docilely into a chair and held the coffee cup as if it were made of fine china.

"I understand you have something to tell us?"

"Er . . . yes. The mayor has authorized the following figures." The cup threatened to tip over as he struggled to reach his legal pad. "Three years, two percent increase each year."

"Oh, my goodness," she said, "two percent? You can't be serious. The cost of living is three." Tracy had coached her well. She flashed a glance at Julian. He was staring in open admiration at her.

"Don't give me that, Miss Swift, you've been over that for the past three years. Two percent." He sat back, beginning to enjoy himself.

"Three." It was like an auction. It was fun. She gathered Nikki into her arms and walked over to Julian and deposited the baby on his lap. Over her shoulder she repeated it. "Three percent."

"Three, two, two." Tratten shot back.

"Three, three, two." Now it was too fast! She glanced at Evelyn Holden. The director's mouth was agape and her eyes were going back and forth between them.

A little smile began to show at the corner of Tratten's mouth. He sat back and picked up a sandwich. With his mouth full he said playfully, "Be reasonable, Miss Swift." Again breadcrumbs sprayed his shirt. "Call your mentor and confer with her."

"Good idea," she said faintly.

"I'll watch Nikki," Julian said, looking at the baby in his lap. His hand was enormous against Nikki's leg and wonderment filled his eyes. He barely glanced up at her. "Use Betsy's phone."

In the outer office, she sat down and dialed Tracy's number. With one ring, Tracy's voice came over the wire. She must have been waiting by the telephone. "Well?" she demanded.

"They offered two, two, two. I've got him up to three, two, two."

She heard the soft explosion of breath over the phone. "Not bad," Tracy said. "Any concessions?"

"Not from him, but from Julian . . . er . . . Mr. Plumhouse. The dietary tray business. That's going to be handed to the kitchen."

"I knew that. He's been doing that for days. Don't forget," her voice failing to cover the excitement of the moment, "we must have that differential for night duty. Settle for fifty cents an hour, but ask for a dollar." She hung up.

They were close! Seven percent over a three-year period. The trays concession. That would carry a lot of weight with the nurses. For too long they'd been saddled with additional chores that did not belong to them: transportation, errands to Lab and Pharmacy, running for records. The list was endless and they were damned sick of being used. If she could get the night differential she would have a decent contract for them to accept, she was sure of it.

When she returned she saw that Nikki had positioned himself between Julian's legs. Using his two thighs as parallel beams, he swung his feet back and forth while Julian looked down at him, an expression of amusement and wonder on his face.

She made herself walk slowly into the room and all faces turned her way. Even Nikki fell still.

"Well?" Tratten burst out.

"Now, about night differential," she said. "We want

one dollar per hour." She sat down suddenly, not trusting her knees.

"One dollar? Are you crazy? Seventy-five cents!"

"Done!" Oh my God, she thought to herself.

Julian broke the silence that followed while George Tratten and Leah stared at each other. "That's it, then? We have a proposal?" Tratten nodded without taking his eyes off her. "Congratulations," Julian said. "A job well done."

"What about my sick-time proposal?" Evelyn said timidly.

"Forget it!"

"Not this year," Tratten and Leah said in unison and then began to laugh. He held out his hand, and, grinning like a fool, she took it. Almost immediately, his demeanor changed.

"This calls for a drink. Let's all head for the hearest bar." There was no answer. "No? Well then I'm off." He shook hands with Evelyn and then Julian.

"She's not a bad negotiator for a mere girl, is she?" Tratten said under his breath.

"Almost as good as you, George, maybe better," Julian replied.

Tratten leaned over and whispered in his ear. "I'd bet she could screw your brains out, too."

Julian's hand tightened briefly until a look of anguish came over Tratten's face. When he was released, he scurried from the office leaving the others to celebrate by tossing Nikki from one to the other, much to his delight.

With the office in darkness behind them, Julian, his arms full with a squirming baby, marched Leah to the door. She did not protest his offer of a ride home. It was much too wet to walk. At the door, he handed the baby to her with the command to wait for him. Rain sheeted the plaza, as she stood there, whipping horizontally through a curtain of light from a lamppost. Soon the headlights of the blue Cadillac swept over the drive and she hurried into the car.

On the swooping drive down the hill, she felt Nikki slumping against her in sleep. The car heater smoked the window and she felt as if she were on the inside of a great blue egg.

"I don't believe I did that tonight," she said to him. "It seemed so easy that maybe I made a mistake."

"Listen to me. You just negotiated the best contract the nurses ever had. Don't you worry about mistakes, you handled yourself like a pro back there, and none too soon, I might add. Now we have to go about reopening the hospital."

"What do you mean?"

"You don't think the nurses can simply walk back in, do you? There aren't many patients left."

She hadn't even thought of that. The nurses would have to choose whether they were going to take more sick time or suffer unpaid days while they waited to be called back to work. So there was a price to be paid for the sick-out after all. She wondered if they realized it.

"We'll let Tracy handle it," Julian said. "She knows the routine and she has all the names on a list. She started the whole thing, she can finish it."

The chain-link fence rose up into the light as Julian nosed the Cadillac into the parking lot. He hurried her through it, Nikki fast asleep in her arms, and guided her down the gangplank.

"Don't slip," he muttered, trying to maneuver himself and her down the steeply swaying bridge.

"I won't. Don't you," she replied, clutching at him as his leather shoes slid out from under him. She managed to hold him up until he regained his footing, trying not to laugh. She was glad it was dark and she could not see his face.

In the store, Red had left a tiny light on over the

staircase. So they had gone out after all. She was glad; she wanted to show him the place, especially her favorite place, alone.

After she laid the sleeping baby in his crib, she took Julian's hand and once more they crept down the stairs to the marina shop. A faint clean odor of tar, polishes, and paints filled her nostrils with sweet familiarity. She breathed it in. There was a serenity here that was born of the very place it served: the sea. For some reason it was very important that she show it to him as if there were an imaginary test here that he must pass.

There on the left were little jars of deck wax. Beyond was a wall fitted with hundreds of tiny drawers that Red had built. They were filled with screws of every size and shape a ship would need, made of metals, bronze, and brass, that lay gleaming in her hand. Some of them had delicate crosses etched in their tops, others had wings like butterflies. They had once been her toys, her dolls, her patients, whichever the game of the moment had been.

There were turnbuckles in burnished woods, over which Julian exclaimed. They had been fashioned from exotic trees, like ebony. She had once threaded yarns of wild colors through them and strung them throughout the store. A sultan's tent she declared, much to Maddy's amusement.

But her favorite spot of all was hidden behind the staircase, where great rolls of lines stretched to the farthest corner of the store. It was in this place that she tried to make him see the world in which she had grown up, for it was all gone now and existed only in her memories.

When she was little the lines were made of hemp which had a special smell of the hot and distant Orient. To her it was a place of great mystery and she could almost see the islands from which they came. This corner of the store became her own private island. There had been tarred hemp, coiled in great loose circles that left sticky black spots on her fingers. There was dry clean hemp that she would pick into a thousand blond pieces and fashion into a wig. Then, as Maddy watched, she would make her majestic procession around the store, a castaway princess with a train of palm fronds trailing behind.

The great loose coils were gone now and in their place were dacron and nylon rolls that were covered in plastic. They made the wall against which they were stacked look like a giant clock of endless wheels. She tried to imagine it for him—the scent of palm and coconut oils and hot sand beneath bare feet—but it did not work for him and it wasn't fair to expect that it would. Her magic world was over.

She could lay her hand on the most remote piece of equipment in the store in a matter of minutes if Maddy needed it. She had been doing it since she was six years old and for some reason it was important for Julian to know that. He would then know her. She leaned against the glass counter and watched as he wandered through the aisles. She saw him pick up a jar of oil and sniff at it. He rubbed a brass chain length against his jacket until it had a sheen of gold. She began to smile at the contented look on his face.

Finally, when he had circled the store and returned to where she waited, there was wonderment on his face. He had seen the magic of this place and been given a glimpse into her memories. She knew he had passed her mythical test. There was no need for words; the silence between them was full of sound. It roared in her ears and drummed out the beating of her heart.

He gathered her in his arms and kissed the corner of her mouth, the hollow of her neck, and finally the curve of her breast. She led him up the stairs and into the little room that hung over the water. The bed protested their weight and a window, beaten with rain, shook as he unbuttoned her shirt.

The next morning, when Danny Thomson showed her Emma Bond's newest blood gas figures, Leah knew at last that she had been right. But she didn't say a word as Danny studied the figures.

"I wouldn't have believed it," he said. "They're one hundred percent improved. Look, her O2 is up to eighty-five. The old lady did it."

Leah stifled a laugh. Emma wasn't old; she was only forty-two. "What about her carbon dioxide? Isn't that too high?"

"Yeah. But don't forget she's a chronic lunger. She's probably had a high CO2 all her life. I don't think she could get that down." Danny grinned at her. "What are you going to do with these gases? You *are* going to show 'em to Peters the Great, aren't you?"

"Oh no, we just did these for the exercise—of *course* I am. Why do you think Emma went through all this? She's been working on her own, without anyone's help, just to prove she can do it. I don't dare wait much longer either, she's wearing herself out. She could collapse from exhaustion and lose all the ground she's gained."

"You are right. I've looked at her, you know, every morning. She is getting tired." Danny hesitated and then said something that made her feel good all over. "Listen, why not let me do it. After all, I'm leaving and Peters can't do anything to hurt me. Let me present these gases to him."

"Oh Danny, you are a gentleman. When are you leaving?"

"Twelve more days. I handed in my resignation last week."

Leah thought for a moment. "Let's say I let you

present an argument to Peters. What are you going to say to him?"

"I thought about that. I'll say that I think he's an asshole and should have done these months ago." At Leah's shocked gasp, Danny laughed. "It's true, but I will say it in a nice way. What I will stress is that I have a lot of people rooting for Emma and if he doesn't carry on with her weaning in a way that she can get some sleep during the night, they will not think too highly of him. I'll let him think that those people are physicians, not just us peons. That should motivate him, don't you think?"

Leah reached around him and gave him a hug. "Go for it, Danny. I'm relieved that someone else is willing to take on Emma's battle for me. Thanks." Then she kissed his cheek and swore that she saw a red blush begin to climb up his neck.

She had been the hit of the crowd around the time clock that morning. Somehow, between the night before and seven o'clock that morning, the grapevine had circulated the news of her triumph at negotiations. And though the crowd was small, it was a noisy and happy one. Even Tracy had given her a hug.

"Well done, Leah," she had whispered into her ear. "I couldn't have done a better job. But if you tell anyone I said that, I'll call you a liar."

The unit was fully staffed as though the sick-out had never taken place. It created a problem for Katherine, one she'd never had to deal with before. She had too many nurses and too few patients. It was a happy place to be, each nurse assigned to only one patient. Even Sandy McCracken went peaceably about her chores.

Upstairs, though, the scene was different. On Bev's floor the staff was, as usual, rushing through their assignments. No extra nurses had been called in to work and Bev grumbled about it all morning. She was sure that she, alone, was being penalized for the sick-out. She snapped out orders this morning as if she were a drill sergeant.

They'd given Two-Gus a rotary electric shaver and it did not work well. He dismantled it to see why. It was filthy with dried hair and some fuzzy material he did not care to think about.

"Here are some alcohol pads. Please clean the razor after you use it," his nurse said. She disappeared without another word.

He had to use all the pads to clean the little wheels. Bits of dust he knew to be dead skin cells and stubble clogged the blades. It was a wonder it turned at all, he thought. Still, it was a pleasure to clean himself. He hadn't cared before. He dipped his comb into a cup of water and dragged it through his hair. It was too long again. He wondered if a barber would touch him now.

He was examining his gums in the little stainless steel mirror they'd given him when he felt the presence of someone standing in the doorway. He knew instantly that it was Billy's mother. She wore a hospital robe, blue-striped, and shapeless. Unisex, they called it.

So this was the Jelly Bean Lady. She was incredibly thin, like a starved bird. Other than a gentle curiosity in her eyes, there was no resemblance to Billy that he could see.

"Hello, Mr. Ragust." She glanced around the room. "Guess we've been neighbors all along and didn't know it, huh? First downstairs and now up here. Billy . . . he's my son. He told me about you." She remained by the door, gazing at the stack of gowns and masks piled outside. "Can I come in? I mean, you ain't catchy, are you?"

"Please do, but you might want to put on a mask." He laughed at himself for hating those things as vehemently as he did. "I wouldn't want to cause you any more trouble than you've already had. You are better, aren't you? I'm so glad."

"They tell me you've become Billy's best friend here. Is that right?" She tied the mask over her face.

There was, of course, no answer to the question, but it pleased him mightily to think it was true. He watched as she shuffled in, paper slippers on her feet making dry rustling sounds. She pushed the chair against the wall and flopped into it with a sigh. "Whew. Hey, I thought I was getting stronger but that walk down the hall knocked me for a loop." She did look pale and sweaty above the mask, he thought.

He waited.

"If you got a minute, I wanna talk about Billy to you."

"I thought you might," he replied.

"He's gotten some fool notion that he's going to be a hero and give away his kidney. Don't that beat all? What do you know about it?"

Two-Gus shrugged. "Just about that, no more, Mrs. Fellows. He seems determined to go through with it, though. How do you feel about it?" He knew he sounded like a shrink.

"How can I feel anything if I don't know anything? Jesus H. Christ, I wake up in a strange place and there's my baby telling me he's going to shuck himself of a kidney. Talk about coma! I thought he was in one."

They had tied back her hair with an elastic band, but as she talked her thin fingers picked at the strands until there was a wild-looking fringe about her face. For some reason, Two-Gus thought of Olive Oyl.

"Can you tell me what the hell's going on?"

"Let me see if I can. He met a girl who is in kidney failure. If I have it right, he's fallen in love with her and now he's doing the only thing a young man in love can do." She looked puzzled. "He's laying his coat in the puddle."

"Huh?"

"Gallantry, Mrs. Fellows. It still lives, if only in the hearts of the young. Your son wants to do a very brave thing. The only trouble is, there are many hurdles he has to overcome."

"Yeah," she said. "And I'm one of them. I have to get outta here and back to work. Otherwise lover boy won't eat too good, if you catch my meaning." He didn't, exactly.

"You know how young love is. It doesn't think of practical matters." He liked her. "But there are considerations he has to be helped with. For instance, he has many years ahead of him to live with only one kidney. If something were to happen to him, an accident, God forbid, or an illness . . . I think that he is too young to take that kind of gamble. On the other hand, if the doctors think it is safe, then who am I to argue?"

"Speaking of doctors," she said, "how come none of them has talked to me? I am the friggin' breadwinner around here, you know. Jesus H.—"

She was about to launch into another tirade when Peter Cohen stuck his head in the door.

"Am I interrupting something?"

Dorothy stood up immediately. "I better be going," she said to Two-Gus. "But I'll be back if that's okay with you. It's been good talking to you, Mr. Ragust." She nodded shyly at Peter Cohen and slipped by him.

"Come back after lunch," Two-Gus called out, but she had disappeared.

Peter's eyebrows rose. "She isn't quite your type, old boy, but then I never know what kinky goings-on you're up to." He did not ask how Two-Gus felt, or even what was wrong. Peter knew about hemophilia; he was used to the connection between hospitals and his friend.

"Put on a mask, Cohen. I wouldn't want you to catch my bug. It would ruin your love life." He smiled happily at the young attorney. Peter did as he was told but his eyes were puzzled.

"Here," Two-Gus cleared the bedside table, dumping the soapy water into his urinal and piling the shaving gear beside him on the bed. He pushed the table toward Peter. "Get out your notepaper and start working. I haven't got all day. First of all, I have to ask you about the legal right of a minor. Can they donate an organ?"

He knew that Peter's mouth had dropped open behind the mask.

"And second, how do I go about leaving some money to that minor. I mean, so that no one can get their hands on it." It was a cruel thought, having just met Dorothy Fellows, but there were considerations. Like a no-good brother that might like some of it.

Peter coughed gently. "How old is this minor?"

"Fourteen."

"Will wonders never cease," Peter said. "All these years I've been your friend and you never told me you had a kid. You miserable Dago."

"Kike." The word shot back. "Come on, Pete, do I look like a dear old dad? This is a kid I just met. And that was his mother. I want to do something for the boy."

He sat back happily and began to relate the circumstances that led to this visit and for a few minutes, Peter Cohen listened. Then, at Two-Gus's command, he took out his pen and began to take notes. Underneath the mask, Peter's mouth tightened in disgust, but he said nothing.

At the end of thirty minutes, he cried out, "Enough. I've got writer's cramp." He slapped the notebook closed. Then he stood up and stretched and walked to the window, leaned against it and stared through the glass.

"You've asked me about minors' rights," he said, not looking at Two-Gus. "I'll be honest with you, Guinea man, I don't know the answer to that. It's easy enough to find out, though, and I'll get back to you on it.

"This business of your will, though. This concerns me and I wouldn't be a friend or a good lawyer if I didn't question your motives. I've been telling you for years to make a will, otherwise the Washington sharks will gobble up all your money. But I'm not happy with this. I know it's your money and you can do with it what you wish, but damn it, you stupid Wop, you must be under the influence of drugs. You can't be serious about this." His voice had risen so loudly that an aide poked her head in the door.

"Anything wrong?"

Two-Gus flapped a hand at her and she disappeared.

"I'm dead serious," Two-Gus said to Peter Cohen.

"Ragust, listen. Wills aren't written in granite. You can change this at any time. So you want to leave the kid something out of gratitude, that's great. Leave him a little trust fund that will grow and, in time, give him a nest egg. But this . . ." He shook his head. "You've gone too far, Guinea man."

Two-Gus looked at his friend. If he didn't know better, he swore Peter was about to cry. It was true that Pete had worked hard over the years to maintain his income. He'd even made a sizable increase in the mother lode, Two-Gus thought. It must kill him to have to hand it over to a stranger.

"Please," Peter whispered. "Tell me what's going on? Does it have to do with this particular hospitalization? Is this different?"

"Later, Peter, later. As soon as they discharge me, I'll come over and we'll break open a bottle together. In the meantime, you get cracking on this business. Time is of the essence, my good Jew friend."

Peter shook his head, but gathered his notebook and briefcase. He held out his hand but Two-Gus suddenly drew back. For the first time an unreasonable fear of his own disease came over him. There would be no time for breaking open a bottle. He avoided the hurt look in Peter's eyes.

"Scram," he whispered to him. "And don't overcharge as usual."

Peter looked at Two-Gus. There was something different this time. He pulled the mask off his face and walked from the room. Passing through the lounge, he spotted the woman he'd seen in Two-Gus's room.

She glanced up from her magazine. "Have you got a cigarette?"

He shook his head. "Sorry. Oh, you can go back in now. He's alone."

"Nah, you probably wore him out. Billy says he gets awful tired easy. That kind does, I guess. Christ, what I wouldn't give for a butt." She turned away and began flipping the pages.

It was strange not having Emma Bond for a patient this morning. She belonged to Sandy McCracken instead, and from the noises coming from the room, Leah suspected the two women were not getting along. Just as well, she thought, that'll keep Emma going until Peters the Great makes his entrance. She is sharpening her claws on Sandy.

She dawdled at the desk beside Katherine, not yet willing to face the sad little group in Michael Norman's room. From report that carried over from the evening shift through the night shift, it was plain that Sharon and Dale were going to stick it out without respite until something happened. Other than going to the cafeteria for their meals, they never left Michael's side.

She gazed at the door and sighed. Katherine looked at her.

"Do it. Just go in there, do what you have to do, and get out. While they are at breakfast. Then you won't have to feel like you're on the head of a pin."

"They've been so quiet all morning," Leah said. "No questions, nothing. In fact, I think they've resigned themselves, either that or they're plain worn out. They are just waiting."

Katherine glanced at her watch. Pretty soon Dr. Chimes would come through those doors and she was dreading it. She had met him once before in a case like this. As she remembered it, she called him a beast right to his face. Of course, she was much younger in those days and had been filled with horror at the doctor's method. The way he handled that case had made her shudder. Yet she supposed there was no other way. If he were gentle then the family could wear him down with unreasonable demands. That's why he was rough on them. And just maybe there was a human side to him as well that needed shielding from the reality of his work. She wondered if he slept well at night.

She watched Leah enter Michael Norman's room. It had been the right decision to assign her to the boy. She returned to the page of orders she had been transcribing.

Katherine's belly was in the way forcing her to extend her arms just to reach the paper on the desk. She knew that in another couple of hours, she'd ache with the strain.

Last night she was convinced she was going into labor. She spent the evening timing contractions and glancing quickly at Ben, hoping he would not notice. He didn't. Whatever they were, they were awfully damned vague for labor pains. She couldn't even tell when one began. Wasn't she supposed to time them? She always thought labor announced itself with an undeniable pain that would make her howl. These were so fleeting that she felt foolish and ignorant. She lost track of their comings and goings. Was the last one six minutes ago? Ten? Was this another one coming? After awhile, she forgot to count. Some nurse she was. She thought of her mother's warning about the water breaking. What if it happened right here on the sofa? She should have padded it. Instead she got up with a start and headed for the bedroom. Better pad the mattress. That would never dry if her water broke. Was it a lot of water? Or was it a gentle trickle? Leaving Ben to watch the news, she climbed the stairs and began to cry. With tears pouring from her eyes, she lined the bed with three thicknesses of towels and then crawled into it feeling like a hopeless mess. She was asleep before Ben came up.

So much for last night's labor, she thought as she stamped a lab slip and handed it to Barbara.

"What's this?" Barbara asked.

"Mrs. Greenough's routine lab work, why?"

Barbara cast her a disgusted look. "She isn't a cardiac case, remember? She's the G.I. bleeder." She tore up the slip. "I'd better keep an eye on you today."

They looked up at the door together as Sharon and Dale Norman came in.

"They look awful," Barbara said. "They should have gone home last night."

"Would you?"

"No."

Dale stopped at the desk. "Do you know when the doctor from Childrens will be coming?"

"No, but it's usually in the afternoon." Katherine hesitated. "Mr. Norman, why don't you go home and get a little rest? You and your wife look ready to cave in."

He turned away. "There's plenty of time for that." And he followed Sharon into Michael's room.

"The sooner this is over, the better all round," Barbara said. "The tension in here is awful. The whole thing gives me the willies. In the old days, dead was dead and you couldn't do a thing about it. There weren't respirators around to keep a body warm. Today, you gotta have the Supreme Court's decision to pronounce death.

It's giving me a headache. I should transfer out of here."

"Oh God," Katherine breathed. "He's here. I thought it would be later." She was peering through the windows of the unit doors. Barbara glanced quickly to the entrance and watched as Ned Chimes entered the unit.

He did not enter, he charged. The unit doors banged behind him against the wall and his high-heeled boots hit the floor with staccato clicks. He had on tight blue jeans and a checkered shirt. All he needed, Katherine thought, was a ten-gallon hat. Trotting on his heels was his nurse. Katherine had forgotten her. Chimes arrived as a team, though why he needed a nurse was beyond her.

Chimes marched to the desk, swiveled an extra chair beside Katherine and flopped into it. His nurse leaned against the counter, one hip resting against his shoulder. She was chewing gum with the snap of a machine gun. On her white lab coat was pinned a plastic identification badge. She was Trixie Cavaletts: Transplant Team.

They sleep together, Katherine said to herself.

"Alright, where's the donor?" Chimes said, and Barbara gasped. "Come on, I don't have all day. Chart? Chart?" He snapped his fingers and glanced around as if the patient's record would rise up instantly and settle in his grasp. Katherine placed it gently on the upraised hand.

"The patient is in there, Dr. Chimes," Katherine said, pointing at Michael's room. "But I must warn you that the parents have not reached a decision. In fact, I don't think they've even thought of donating. They are waiting for you."

"That's the trouble with you nurses out here in dreamland." His voice was high. "You had all night to coach these people. Instead you sit around wringing your hands and dripping tears. We need organs. Why don't you people realize that?"

The nurse, Trixie, nodded malevolently. She snapped

her gum and Katherine thought of a pair of nesting rattlesnakes.

Chimes sighed. "Okay, tell me what we've got. Good kidneys? Heart? Corneas intact? Well?"

Katherine swallowed. The nurse, Trixie, spoke up for the first time. "Come on, Ned. Let's go take a look-see, huh?" She had a deep Texan accent. "I've got an eye case waiting. And they'll hog tie me if I don't get back by noon. Let's roll it."

"You're right, darlin'. Ain't she the cutest thing?" he said to Katherine, and she nodded dumbly. "She keeps me on the straight and narrow, old Trixie does. Best damned technician in the OR."

Trixie rolled her eyes, bored.

Chimes opened Michael Norman's chart and went through the laboratory reports. Then he perused the other tests that had been done and looked up at Katherine. "Where's the second EEG?" His eyes narrowed.

Katherine swallowed. "It's booked." And knew she'd made an error.

"Booked? What does 'booked' mean? Why isn't it done?" Chimes turned toward Trixie. "See? This is what I have to put up with. They've had all night to get these tests done so that I wouldn't have to wait and what do they do? *Booked.*" He slapped his forehead in exasperation.

Trixie slid a glance at Katherine and then looked away as if embarrassed. Chimes jumped to his feet and hitched his jeans up, cupping his genitals and adjusting them as if he were wearing a jock strap. It gave Katherine a chance to slow the beating of her heart.

Over his shoulder, he said, "Get 'em up here. That should have been done hours ago. Come on, babe," he said to Trixie. They disappeared into Michael Norman's room while Katherine shakily dialed the phone. He was right, of course, the EEG should have been done last night.

"I'd donate something to that bastard," Barbara said, when Chimes was gone. "I'd donate a fist in his nose, the arrogant little creep."

"He hasn't changed since I saw him last," Katherine said. "I don't know how he gets a hangnail donated with his disposition."

"I pity those people in there," Barbara said, gazing toward the room.

Ned Chimes strode into Michael's room with his hand stretched out to the air. When he reached Dale, he grabbed the father's hand and pumped it up and down. Then he glanced at Sharon and nodded. The smile on her face faded. He turned and looked at Leah and his face broadened into a lewd smile. He had yet to look at the child on the bed.

"I'm Ned Chimes and this is my assistant, Miss Cavaletts." He turned to Trixie and muttered out of the corner of his mouth. "Take off the badge, sweetie."

Leah watched as Trixie whipped off the offending title and stuffed it into her pocket.

"I am going to examine your son and have another brain wave test done. I can't answer any questions until that is done. It wouldn't be fair. Do you understand?"

Sharon's face brightened. "Yes, of course, Doctor. Whatever you say. But he's ever so much better this morning. I swear he almost opened his eyes and looked at me."

Behind her Trixie rolled her eyes and snapped her gum.

Chimes went on as if Sharon had not spoken. "You'll have to leave the room while I do my examination. It will take about thirty minutes and then another half-hour for the EEG to run. When I am finished I will come out to talk to you. Not here. Out there." He pointed in the general direction of the waiting room. "Is that clear?"

"Or what?" Dale asked. His eyes were flinty.

Sharon gasped, her hand flying up to cover her own mouth as if it would stop her husband's menacing voice.

Chimes held up a surrendering hand. "Hey, nothing meant there, Mr. Norman. It's better my way, really."

Dale's face had grown thunderous. "Come on," he said to Sharon, not waiting for her but stalking from the room. Sharon hurried after him.

"*You* can stay," Chimes said to Leah. "We can always use another pretty face."

Behind him, Trixie cleared her throat loudly. Then Ned Chimes began to examine Michael Norman. It was the most thorough neurological study Leah had ever seen.

He began his examination at Michael's head, starting on his eyes. With a wisp of cotton he drew a delicate line across the boy's open eyes. There was no flicker of response. He rotated Michael's head rapidly with Trixie holding the child's eyes open. His blue eyes rolled away from the turns. It was the doll's eye sign and it was ominously present. With the room darkened, Chimes flicked a bright beam of light into both eyes, and then repeated the gesture twice more.

"Blown," he whispered to himself.

"His pupils have been dilated from the beginning," Leah said, and wished immediately that she had not spoken. Chimes appeared not to have heard. He studied the retina of each eye, ophthalmoscope pinned to his own eye. He took a very long time.

"No bleeding. The retina appears intact."

Trixie took notes as he spoke. Then she looked at Leah. "Wanna get some ice water, honey? A few c.c.'s and a twenty c.c. syringe." It was apparent that she had gone through this procedure many times.

"It's ready," Leah replied.

"Hey Ned! We got ourselves a live one."

"Yeah, yeah, where's the ice water?"

Without looking up, Chimes held out his hand and Leah found herself fighting an impulse to squirt it into his ear. Instead, she handed over the loaded syringe.

Chime injected a small amount of ice water into Michael's ears and watched to see if he would gag. There was no response. Then he straightened and abruptly disconnected the respirator. The machine's alarm squealed. Leah reached behind Chimes and switched if off.

She took a deep breath and held it. Come on, she prayed to the child, one deep breath. When she began to fight the urge to open her mouth and gulp air, Chimes reconnected the respirator letting his own breath explode from his lips. It was the first hint of his concern for the child since he'd come into the room. From Michael there was no effort to breathe. If Chimes had left him off the vent, the only sign of life would have come from the cardiac monitor and even that, in a few seconds, would begin to show a dying heartbeat.

Why did she feel the sting of tears in the back of her throat? Somehow she wanted to prove Chimes wrong, that's all. One effort to breathe on Michael's part and this offensive little man and his over-made up girlfriend would depart. It was then that she noticed Trixie had turned her face to the window. Her chewing gum had disappeared.

"Looking good," Chimes said to himself. The rest of the examination went more quickly. Now that he knew the cranial nerves were dead, the skeletal muscles would most certainly have ceased to function. He tested each limb, hammering delicately for a reflex, then letting an arm or leg drop back, observing how the limbs fell to the bed, looking for any defensive muscle action no matter how discreet. There was none; Michael's legs flopped to the bed and never stirred. Finally, he drew a small pin across the boy's soles. Not even the splay foot response of brain damage could be seen.

He nodded to the EEG technician and then slumped into a chair, watching as she prepared Michael's scalp for a second EEG test.

"Output?"

"Excuse me?"

"Urinary output."

"Oh. Fifty c.c.'s an hour." Leah replied.

"Color?"

"Clear yellow."

"Good, let's up his IV to five hundred c.c.'s over the next thirty minutes while our little friend here probes for brain waves. I want to challenge the heart and kidneys. Got any coffee?"

"What for?"

"Gotcha!" he exclaimed and began to laugh. He sounded as if he were a wheezing donkey. "To drink, for God's sakes. What'd you think? I'm going to give him an enema with it?"

Trixie snickered at her. "He always does that. Don't pay him no never mind." She turned to Ned. "You're just a big kid, Ned. A big kid."

"Yeah, I know, but I got her good, didn't I, Trix? Huh?"

As she opened up Michael's intravenous line so that the fluid seemed to pour in, Leah said over her shoulder, "Help yourself. It's in the kitchen. There's a box there for your quarter."

He grinned at her. "Cheap. No freebies for a visiting fellow? I've traveled a long—"

"Make it fifty cents. Each," Leah said, knowing she was a damned good negotiator. Tension quickly evaporated in the room and they all trooped out to Katherine's desk.

When the EEG was finished, Chimes studied it while Trixie excused herself and went to the bathroom. "Look at that," he said. "Nothing but artifact from the respirator. That brain's as flat as a pancake. It's a wonder he still has a heartbeat. By tomorrow, he won't."

He looked at Katherine and Leah. "That's it, ladies. We have a donor. Now I'll go work my magic. Wanna take bets while I'm gone? Five bucks. I'll give two to one odds that I get him." He missed Barbara Haines's shudder.

As he passed by Katherine's desk, he handed her the EEG study. "Here, you can paper your living room with it."

"Oh, what an awful man," Barbara exclaimed when he had left the unit. "My husband won't believe it when I tell him about this."

Katherine stared at the closing doors. "I almost took him up on the bet, but I didn't dare. They wouldn't send him on these missions if he didn't have some success."

"I'll bet you five dollars he fails. I know Dale Norman pretty well by now," Leah said.

"You're on," Katherine replied absently.

Leah went into Michael's room and stared down at him.

"One breath, kid, that's all you needed. Why didn't you breathe just once?" She wanted to reach down and shake the boy.

Chapter Fifteen

Ben's office was just a cubicle added on to the back section of the emergency room. There was barely enough room for the three men gathered there: Ben, Ned Chimes, and Dr. Russell. In fact, Ned was perched on one corner of Ben's desk. One high-heeled cowboy boot swung back and forth.

"You gotta strike now while the iron's hot. I want that kid. I've got a twelve year old waiting for a liver, a dialysis list a mile long, and umpteen eyes looking for corneas. The heart, well, that'll be used, it's a matter of finding the right recipient."

"I have a kidney patient right here at Liberty Hill," Russell said softly. "I want her to have one."

"Now, now, Doctor," Chimes said playfully, "play the game according to the rules. No favorites. Is she up on the list?"

"Of course she is," Russell said, nettled. "And I've already matched them here in our lab. There's no reason why—"

"That don't mean beans, Doctor, you should know that. It's our lab that counts, not yours. And furthermore it's *our* decision. Don't be greedy."

Russell stood up abruptly. "Now listen, you little—"

Ben Weathers looked from Chimes to Russell. "Gentlemen, calm down. God, we're wrangling over this patient like a bunch of coyotes."

Chimes nodded happily, his eyes lighting up at the reference. It was obvious by his dress that he was from the West. Either that, Ben thought, or he was acting the part. Russell settled back in his chair grumpily.

"What can we do to help?" Ben asked Chimes. "Have you prepared the parents?"

"Of course." Chimes smirked at Ben. "I play the bad guy in this scenario. They hate my guts, but they understand the facts that the patient is dead. I also plant the seed of thought in their minds and when I'm certain that they are about to wring my scrawny neck, I bow out. That's when you men step in. You're the white hats, okay? The heroes to the rescue. It's your job to get their consent. Most of them won't give in, but the few who do make this project worthwhile."

Russell stood up. "You don't need me for this. The parents don't even know me. I'll bow out now, if that is alright with you."

"Aha!" Chimes exclaimed. "It's one thing to want something, it's another to work for it, huh?"

Russell's face went white. "Now listen, you little creep. If I step in now, the parents would be up against the wall with their throats bared. I'm supposed to walk in there and demand my kidney? No way. I couldn't do that and I couldn't go down on my knees for it either." He walked to the door.

"Not even for your little kidney patient?" Chimes's face was deadly. Russell hesitated and the silence in the little room was heavy. Chimes looked down at his boots. "That's why I have this job and not you, Russell. I would get down on my knees if it would help. The trouble with you people out here, is that you don't see the lists of names, the recipients from all over the country who are waiting for organs. They die waiting.

"You don't get the phone calls from desperate parents whose kid is turning bright yellow with jaundice right before their eyes. You never hear from heart recipients but we do, every day. They are near death and they know it. They live for the sound of a ringing telephone.

"Oh, yeah, you might have one or two patients, but you get them off your hands as fast as you can. You call us up and add their names to the list and then sit back and wait for a call. In the meantime, you dialyze them and pat them on the head. You tell them that they must be patient and wait for their kidney. That's very neat and clean for you. But not for us in the real world."

Ben listened to the man, his mouth hanging open in surprise. Gone was the flippant cowboy and in his place was a young and desperate physician.

"I'm the one who has to scrounge up the organs for you. That's my job and I don't mind doing it." He shrugged into a denim jacket and snapped it shut. "I just get sick of having to plead before men of medicine. I shouldn't have to."

Russell turned back and stared down at Chimes. His silver hair clung in tight curls to his head. He had grown pale as Chimes spoke. His lips quivered as he said, "I apologize, Chimes. I don't know what I was thinking of. You are right, of course. I will go down on my knees with those parents. Right now, in fact. Just . . . just tell me. Is there a chance that my patient will get her kidney?"

"I can't promise anything," Chimes replied, "but I'll look her up. What's her name?"

There was triumph shining in Dr. Russell's eyes. "Lily Webb," he said, and squeezed past the little physician, disappearing in the direction of the Intensive Care Unit.

Trixie looked in the door. "Ned." Her tone was warning. "Come on, Ned. I gotta get back or I'll get killed."

Chimes looked at Ben and his face dissolved into happiness. The change was astonishing.

"Ain't she something? Best little technician in the operating room. And she loves me."

Ben shook his head in wonder as the little doctor swung an arm across Trixie's shoulder and cuddled her. She had absolute power over Chimes.

He held out a hand and Chimes grasped it. "I'll do what I can, Ned. And then I'll give you a call by the end of the afternoon. Is that alright with you?"

"Yeah, Ben, thanks." Ned gave Trixie a sloppy wet kiss on the cheek. "Only don't wait too long, the donor won't last through the night. And even now there might be deterioration of the organs. Keep his blood pressure up, huh?"

He pivoted Trixie around and left Ben's office. As he walked away, Ben could see one hand drop down and cup Trixie's bottom.

Katherine stared at Dr. Russell. She had seen him frequently, but for the life of her, she could not remember who he was.

"Yes, Doctor?"

"The Norman family? Are they in there?"

Katherine nodded her head warily, and then it came to her. He was the head of Dialysis. That was why she rarely saw him. Instantly she thought of Lily Webb.

"They are in there," she said faintly.

"Thank you." Dr. Russell turned away and walked to Michael Norman's room. At the doorway, he hesitated.

Leah finished suctioning the boy. She pulled her glove off, covering the suction catheter in it. As she looked up to throw it in the wastebasket, she saw Dr. Russell standing there.

"Hello, Doctor. Are you here . . . ?" She stopped. He

was staring at the boy and his face was drawn.

Dale Norman turned at the sound of her voice. He had helped Leah, just as he had done with Mark Berlin. By now, he was an expert at the procedure. He knew how to shut off the respirator's alarm. He had the little cup of saline ready to flush the catheter. He no longer blanched as the plastic tube was sent deep into his son's throat.

The physician cleared his throat. "Mr. Norman? Mrs. Norman? I am Dr. Russell. Can I have a word with you?"

Dale nodded. The hope he had carried inside all night was gone and at the sight of yet another physician he was wary. He walked to Sharon and sat beside her and waited. Dr. Russell pulled a straight chair into the room and brought it close to the young couple. He kept his eyes resolutely away from the figure on the bed.

"I am terribly sorry for what has happened to your son. He looks like such a fine boy." He cleared his throat as his voice cracked. "If there was only something we could do, we'd do it. I'm sure you know that."

"What do you want?" Sharon asked. Dale reached over and covered her hand tightly.

"Perhaps if I tell you who I am, you'll understand. I am a nephrologist. A kidney specialist." He did not fail to see the stiffening in Dale's back. "I . . . I cannot do anything for your son. There is, however, something you can do, and in a way it might help you through this ordeal. Michael can give a gift of life to someone. To others whose lives are living hell. Wouldn't it help to ease your pain if you know he could do that?" He did not wait for them to reply but rushed on.

"I have a young patient, a girl who needs a kidney so that she can live a long, full life. Please think of it, a gift of a kidney, and a little part of Michael will still be with us, with you."

Sharon's head began to shake. "Go away."

"I beg you to consider it," Russell said, his face white.

"She is only fourteen. With Michael's help, she could live a normal life. She could have children and grandchildren. Through her, Michael's spirit would live forever."

"I can't," Sharon began to moan. "Don't ask me. I can't."

Dale had said nothing until now. "Jesus, man. We can't let him go. I know you realize what we are going through, you probably see it all the time." His voice grew thick. "He's our son. If we say yes, we're condemning him. Don't you see that?"

Dr. Russell nodded. There was a shine of tears in his eyes. "I certainly do. Asking you to take steps that are so final is the most painful thing I've ever had to do. If it weren't for my patient, I'd never ask, believe me. But I must. She desperately needs a kidney. I beg you to say yes. As God is my witness, I know the decision will ease your suffering later."

By now Sharon was sobbing openly. She curled over herself, her hands covering her face. She swayed back and forth in the blue plastic chair. Dale pulled her into his arms and cupped her head into the crook of his shoulder. He began to rock with her, making whispering sounds in her ear. His shoulders began to shudder.

Russell got to his feet, his actions slow as if he'd suddenly grown old. His gaze met Leah's and she could see the tears in his eyes. Her own vision grew blurry and she swallowed hard as she watched him leave. Once outside the room, his body crumbled. He leaned against the wall, one hand covering his face. For a long while he was motionless.

Leah turned back to the bed and through her tears, she drew a blanket over the boy's shoulder and pulled up the side rails. It was an automatic gesture that was, if she'd thought about it, pointless.

* * *

"There it is. Faneuil Hall," Lily said. The tiny building looked freshly scrubbed in the morning light.

"That little thing? That's what you were bragging about? Some cradle of liberty, that is." He scuffed the toe of his shoe into a frail shrub that had been set into a circle of brick.

"It's dainty, dummy." She leaned over and read a bronze plaque set into the wall. "It says here that it was designed by Bulfinch."

"Whoever that is."

He was sulking, that she knew, she just didn't know why. She'd never seen him like this before.

"Come on, let's go inside. They still use it for meetings. Civil rights stuff and all."

She pretended not to hear "Big deal" delivered in a dark voice behind her. They walked across the brick-paved arcade and entered the old building. The noise from the busy marketplace faded. In the upstairs meeting room, gold-framed portraits of stern men in starched collars peered down at her. She stopped and studied them, waiting for his mood to change.

He had flopped onto a bench as she wandered about the room. Finally she came full circle and sat down beside him, grateful for the rest.

"What's the matter with you? You are sulky today."

"Nothing," he said.

"Did I do something wrong? Are you mad 'cause I made you came all this way?"

"It ain't . . . isn't you. It's this place. You know, I've lived here all my life and never gave a shit about it. I feel stupid."

"So? I've never seen Bunker Hill. Big deal."

He went on as if he'd not heard her. "All these places the tourists come to see, I don't know. They think it's a special thing and I never gave two farts about it. It's dumb. I'm dumb."

She sensed that he was beginning to put pieces of a

puzzle together, and though they never mattered to her, these historical places, it seemed to mean a great deal to him.

To go to Faneuil Hall was, for her, to explore the exotic world of forbidden foods in the stalls outside. The tiny cafés that lined the marketplace. She could study the great red and yellow rinds of cheeses from Norway; the fish and fruits and cartons of leafy greens; the chunks of fried dough with sugar sprinkled over them. All these things had the same significance—they were not permitted. They teased her and she always left the area in anger that she could never taste anything. That was what he felt, too, she thought.

"Look up there," she said, "see that chandelier?"

"Yeah, so what?"

"It lighted the room for John Quincy Adams and now it's lighting for us." He looked up at the delicate arches of brass.

On the stairway, she whispered to him, "Put your hand on the rail. Feel how smooth it is? You can almost feel where they touched it. I can almost hear their voices."

He smiled at her at last. "I love you," he whispered. He took her hand and together they wandered outside into brilliant sunlight. They passed the Magic Pan, the Bagel and Lox Shop, the Café Stella with its exotic Italian ice creams. She managed to ignore them all.

At the waterfront, she had to sit down and rest. While he waited, he ran his hands over the great iron bollards that lined the waterfront. She thought they looked like giant mushrooms and asked a wrinkled old man what they were.

"To tie up the great sailing vessels that used to come from the Old World, young lady," the old man said.

In the Aquarium they followed the crowd around the curving walkway that circled the cylindrical fishtank towering through three floors of the building. On the second-floor landing, she grew breathless and he quickly found a concrete bench beside the wall. They sat there peering into the watery world before them, trying to ignore the throngs of children racing by them.

There was a constant circling of great and small fish swimming gill to gill. He wondered why the sharks ignored prey just beside them. Instead there was only a majestic and mindless circling of silvery bodies in water so clear that it appeared to be air.

It was then that Lily revealed her plan to him. Her voice was muffled and hollow in the great room. It seemed to float to the raftered ceiling far above. He listened with a growing sense of alarm. When she finished, she could see the fright on his face.

"When did you think all this up?" He watched as a sea turtle bumped into the glass wall and slowly recoiled from it, confusing the progression of fish behind it.

"For awhile," she replied. She didn't think he should know that it scared her. "I have no other way to make them give me a transplant. If you help me, I can pull it off. Listen."

A sea bass fastened its wide rubbery lips against the glass and hung there. Billy wondered if it was the only way it had of freeing itself from the maddening circle for a little while.

As she stopped talking, he felt suddenly old. He wanted to run away. Instead, he sat there and watched the fish and felt miserable. What if it failed and she died?

He stood up, leaving her behind in the semidarkness of the hall, the only light coming at him from the tank. He rubbed his hand against the glass where the fish were suspended. There was no flicker of fin and then he knew the swimmers inside had no knowledge of him or of their predicament.

She came and stood beside him, ignoring the fanged

mouth that was just inches from her face. Her eyes had the same intense blaze that he saw in the water.

"Well? Will you help me?"

For a moment, he was tempted to tell her about the blood test, the kidney test, just to let her know he was trying to help. But he couldn't, not yet, not without knowing what the doctor would say.

"I'll think about it."

She linked her arm through his and kissed him on the lips but he jerked away. "Not in front of all these people," he hissed.

"I don't see people, I just see a lot of dumb fish," she said.

There was a tidewater pool where children could touch and move the tiny shelled creatures on display. They watched as a toddler solemnly plucked a snail from its wet rock and put it on his arm. A tiny crab darted across a water beach and scuttled under a rock. Another child rolled the stone aside and laughed as the crab hurried to another. Over and over the child dismantled each hiding place until the crab finally sat exposed, its feelers quivering.

Doing nothing, Billy thought, is sometimes the only thing to do.

In a small tank set into the wall, an electric eel slithered from its cave and crossed an electric line. A blue light blazed suddenly through the water. It was a small cataclysm. Lily shuddered and pulled him away. "This place is giving me the creeps," she said.

They made their way into the sunshine once more and headed for the train. Above the commerce of the marketplace the train gained speed and then dove beneath the harbor. When it emerged into Atwater the scenery was changed. The town was in severe depression and it showed. Here the street was shrouded by overhead tracks. There were no tiny shops with clever wares in the windows. Half the storefronts were boarded up and across the street the navy yard seemed to menace the town from behind its gates. It blocked all view of the open water. There was a fatigue to the town and it seemed to settle over Lily like a gray cloud. She wilted slowly.

By the time they reached her street, she was leaning heavily on Billy's arm and though, by now, he was accustomed to the final hours of her good day as it wound down, he could see that her body was accumulating poisons. It frightened him. She seemed to age with each passing hour.

He waited while she wrote her letter, folded it, and put it into an envelope.

"Are you sure you want to go through with this?" He hoped she'd changed her mind, but instead she handed him the envelope.

"Mail it." Then she leaned into him and rested her cheek on his shoulder. His hands came up automatically and he felt the delicate bones of her spine, the curve of her waist. He fastened his thoughts on the building at the top of the hill. It held all the answers. He left her then and hurried there, the letter in his pocket weighing far more than it should.

Two-Gus had trouble holding the pen in his hand. He peered at the document that Peter Cohen laid before him. Finally Peter leaned over and put his finger on the line, marking it for him. He wrote his name with a wavering hand and then lay back exhausted and watched Pete's secretary notarize each sheet of paper with her stamp. When she was finished, she stuffed the papers into a slim leather case and left the room. Peter turned to Two-Gus.

"You'd better tell me what's going on. Am I going to execute this will sooner than I think? For Christ's sake, tell me."

Before Two-Gus could reply, Milly Gold walked briskly into the room. "He hasn't told you?" She stood beside the bed and began to probe at Two-Gus's abdomen. Then she studied the purplish welts on his chest.

"There are two people in the world," she said, "only two, to whom your words are sacred. Your doctor and your lawyer. No, I take it back. There's three—your mother. But yours is dead. I know the truth and that leaves Peter out in the cold. You should tell him."

Peter looked from her to him. For the first time in Two-Gus's memory there was no quirky smile on Pete's face. He seemed at a loss for words and that was out of character, too.

"You can tell him, Milly. I give permission."

Milly nodded. "Are you having any shortness of breath? Pain?"

"There's pain everywhere. I feel as if I have the flu. Even my bones ache."

"The nurses tell me you don't eat anything. I can see it; the pounds are dropping off. You must eat."

"Why?"

She did not skip a beat. "So that if a cure is found you'll be around to get it."

"What does that mean?" Peter Cohen said. Until now, he'd respectfully stood to one side while Milly completed her examination. Now he came to the bed and looked from Two-Gus to Milly. "What do you mean if a cure is found? What's he got? AIDS?" He started to laugh but caught himself, his face paling suddenly.

Milly's eyebrow raised. "The shyster is smart. That's the diagnosis, Peter Cohen."

Two-Gus watched the change come over Cohen until he could not bear to watch anymore. He closed his eyes and turned his head to the wall.

"Why didn't you tell me?" Peter said, his voice

cracking. "Why did you hide it? I had a right, for chrissakes..."

Two-Gus heard the sounds as Peter gathered together his briefcase. He heard the soft swish of cloth as Pete swung his coat over his shoulders, then the pad of shoes going to the door.

Pete hesitated. "I . . . I'm late for a conference. But I'll be back when I have more time. Take it easy, Gus."

Two-Gus did not see Pete tear off his mask and throw it away as if it were contaminated.

Milly made a clicking sound with her tongue. "It's a shock. I'm sure he'll come back when he has time to adjust."

"Peter isn't very good around sick people," Two-Gus said, looking toward the empty doorway.

Milly took out her stethoscope. "Bend over, sonny, and take a deep breath." She listened to the heavy sounds in his chest as his lungs expanded seeking air. When she finished examining him, she settled into the chair Peter had left. Two-Gus watched while she wrote her notes. She was a staunch friend as well as his doctor. His heart broke a little when he thought of Peter Cohen.

"It sounds as if you're developing another spot of pneumonia. I am going to order a chest x-ray and restart your antibiotics. I think we've caught it early."

"Milly."

She chattered on, not listening until he shouted, "Milly for God's sakes, why don't you listen to yourself! This disease is killing me. It's not like hemophilia. Why are you doing all this? Can't you let it go?"

"Never! Not as long as there is breath in my body. What's the matter with you? This isn't the first time we've been stuck, Gus. There were times that I despaired of pulling you through a bad bleed. Maybe we don't know everything about this farcockten AIDS." She spat the word as though its very newness to her made it an affront to her art. "But knowledge is coming in fast and furious. I intend to keep you in the best possible shape for it. Understand, Sonny?"

"So far there is no cure and it's running the show."

"I know that, Two-Gus Ragust, I'm the doctor, remember? But if you give up, then nothing helps. Not the best nursing care, the sophisticated meds, surgery, nothing."

She turned away, lapsing into a mumble of Yiddish while she fussed over her papers, stuffing them into her scarred black bag. No sleek calf-leather briefcase for Milly. There was a run in one of her stockings. Somehow it made her seem vulnerable.

"Alright," he said. "You win. I'll eat, I'll take the medicines, whatever you say."

He began to cough and his chest constricted as if bands of steel were being riveted to his ribs. There was not enough air suddenly and he retched with the effort to breathe. Milly leaned over and pounded on his back until he felt a hot metallic ball forcing its way up to his throat. He grabbed a tissue and spat into it. They both looked at the stain. It was bright red.

"Give me that," she said. Her eyes were angry.

"Uh-uh, it's catching, remember?" He balled it up and threw it into the little paper bag fastened to his bedrail.

For the first time, he heard alarm bells going off in his head and a sense of dread growing in his belly, as if there was a mushroom inside him. It was the blood, the first visible evidence that something foreign was deep within and it was AIDS. From the bright red immutable fact of it, he grew frightened.

"Will you be back?" he asked, hating himself for the question.

Her eyebrows rose like black wings. "Of course, Two-Gus. We'll work together on this thing. Sometimes you lead the way, sometimes I will. No more adversaries, eh?"

He did not know whether to believe her, but he clung to her words as if he were drowning.

Billy sat on the wooden bench outside Dr. Russell's office. The clock at the far end of the corridor clicked. It was too quiet in here. At least there were lights on inside the office. He swallowed the knot in his throat.

The door opened and Dr. Russell looked down at him. Billy leapt to his feet.

"There's no need for you to come in," Dr. Russell said, holding out a brown manila envelope to him. "Your kidney test is in here, as well as your chest x-ray. Keep them. You are a healthy specimen, but I'm afraid not compatible with Lily Webb." In his eyes was compassion. "Take the tests. They are yours. And, young man, I appreciate what you tried to do. Lily will get a kidney, believe me."

"She doesn't." He was so sure! He knew they fit together. It seemed like such a right thing to happen. Shit!

"Why did you lead me on? Why did I go through those tests?"

Dr. Russell's face lengthened. "I'm sorry. That was my fault. We're human, too, Billy. Somehow, I thought if all the pieces fit together, something might come of it. I was wrong and it wasn't fair to you." He backed into the office and shut the door, leaving Billy standing there.

He wanted to pound on the door, but instead walked blindly down the hall. Now there was no choice, he'd promised. It was a short walk to the front entrance, but he wished it were longer. Just outside the door, there was a blue mailbox. He stood before it, his hand on Lily's letter. Once gone it would be irretrievable. When the blue lid clamped down over the letter, he turned away and stumbled to the granite wall. There, while the sun dropped behind the Boston towers, he sat there stunned.

Sharon let Dale lead her out to the front steps. It was the first time she'd been outdoors since the accident and, though the sunlight was fading, she squinted. Together they wandered to the parapet that curved against the hospital and leaned against the wall. Neither spoke. She seemed smaller somehow. He felt numb.

It was quiet on the hill. The noises from the streets below became muted as they floated up to the wall. The scent of lilacs hovered over them. A lone seagull swept in from the harbor and circled the hill and then dived to the flat calm water below. They both watched it.

"What will we do?" Sharon asked.

"Let's walk."

"Not too far. I want to go back."

"I know," he said. "Let's get a little fresh air. We can talk out here."

But they did not speak. There was a wall between them just as thick as the granite against which they leaned. He couldn't tell what she was thinking, which way she'd chosen to go, or even if she'd already chosen at all. And he needed something from her. He couldn't do this by himself.

It was then that he heard the sounds. They were coming from somewhere on the other side of the parapet. At first he thought it was the involuntary groans of a man making love and he began to lead Sharon away, but then he leaned over and peered at the plaza below. It was a boy, huddled over himself, and he was crying.

"What is that?" Sharon whispered.

"It's a kid crying," he said.

"Come on, let's go back."

"Maybe we can help. We should go see what's wrong."

"Oh Dale. We've got what's wrong. He's just a boy. Come on." She fell silent when she saw the tight look on his face.

"Michael's just a boy, don't forget. I'm going down there. He shouldn't be crying alone." He walked down the few steps to the next landing and then he was standing before Billy.

"Want to talk about it? I'm a good listener."

Billy looked up quickly and wiped his eyes on the back of his sleeve, while Dale sat down beside him. He knew this man. And his wife standing over there. They were the ones with the kid in ICU.

"Want to tell me what's wrong?" Dale asked. He signaled to Sharon and reluctantly, she moved to the bench and sat down. She slumped against the wall and closed her eyes.

"Is it someone in the hospital? Are you in trouble?"

Billy nodded and the bitter words tumbled out. All his life he'd listened to people, to Dorothy and Frankie, to teachers and doctors, and he waited for their words to make sense, not because he had none for himself, but because they had so much power and he had none. So he believed them, and while he waited, other things that they didn't tell him about, bad things, happened. And they always caught him by surprise. He knew how it felt to be a punch-drunk boxer—look to the right, and the blow came from the left. Believe and the unbelievable occurred. Feeling pulled and pushed until the world tilted beneath your feet and became a dangerous place to be. All while you waited. He told Dale about Lily.

"She's sick and now she wants to get herself so much sicker that she might die. All so that they'll pay attention to her. She wants me to help, but you know, I'll just be sitting there and watching her die."

If Frankie hadn't left this might not have happened. Or

if Dorothy had done what she was supposed to do; taken care of her own damned disease, he wouldn't be in this mess. He began to cry again, and Sharon sat up suddenly.

"I've got to get out of here," she whispered to Dale. But his hand bit into her arm and held her there. He could hear her breath, ragged in her throat.

"What's the girl's name, Billy?"

"Why? So you can stop the thing? She'll never speak to me again."

"It's better than the alternative, isn't it?"

After Billy had whispered the name to him, Dale put an arm around his shoulders. "Promise me you won't go through with this scheme."

"What difference does it make. She could do it without me. At least I could look after her."

"You're right, Bill, I hadn't thought of that," Dale said and Billy flashed him a grateful smile. "You could act as a go-between. But you must keep her doctor informed. If she gets too sick, you'll have to bring her in. Will you do that?"

They stared at each other and Billy was the first to look away. He did not reply. Dale sighed and then took Sharon's hand.

"Come on, honey, let's go back." He led her up the stairs.

In the unit, Claude Peters leaned over Katherine's desk and bellowed at her. "Where is Leah Swift?"

"Upstairs, why?"

"Get her down here. She and I are going to have a serious talk. Do you know what's been going on behind my back?"

Katherine shook her head, her mouth parted. "What?"

"She's been weaning Emma Bond, that's what she's been doing. Against my express orders." His eyes narrowed suddenly. "You did post those orders, didn't you? You haven't conspired with—"

"Now just a minute, Claude, hold your fire. This is the first I've heard about it. What's going on?"

"These." Claude dragged a fistful of ABG's from Emma's chart. "Someone stuck these in here so that I would see them. Whoever it was didn't have the courage to tell me what they've been up to. It must be Leah. She's the one who started the whole business."

Katherine picked up the slips and studied them. There was one blood gas for each morning. She noted the times. Seven a.m. That meant Danny Thomson drew the blood. It also meant that Emma was weaning throughout the night. Immediately she thought of Pat Connor. Was Pat responsible for this? Then she saw the figures, saw the increasing oxygen levels, point by point. Whoever the culprit, the fact remained that Emma had improved. She looked up at Claude.

"Are you ignoring these values?"

"What do you mean?"

"You *are* going to do a proper weaning now, aren't you? You can't ignore these."

"Naturally, Katherine," he said. "What I'm pissed about is the fact that my orders were ignored. That means I can't trust you nurses, and that someday it may harm a patient." His manner changed. "Did you know that someone from here ran to Julian Plumhouse about Emma?"

Katherine burst out laughing. "Now you're paranoid, Claude. I don't believe that for one minute." But she wondered about Leah. "Look, I don't know who's responsible for this, but I'll find out and have a talk with them. It was wrong."

"Let me know who it is. I want to deal with her, too." Peters scribbled on the prescription sheet. "These weanings are to run exactly as I've written. Please note that Emma is not, I repeat, not to wean during the night.

We'll proceed in the daytime only."

Katherine nodded. It was his usual method of weaning and, though she did not agree with it, at least it was a beginning. As far as she could see, putting the patient back on the vent for the whole night simply slowed up the process, for much of what was gained during the day was lost at night. She admitted to herself that Claude did have success this way and she was glad for Emma's sake that he'd begun the process. But it wasn't just these blood gas slips that prompted him. It had to be something else. Julian Plumhouse, probably. He must have said something to Peters.

DO NOT RESUSCITATE

The no-code label on Two-Gus's chart jumped out at her as she pulled his chart from the rack. Bev had plastered the warning label across the front of it. Quickly Leah thumbed through the chart until she came to the order sheet. With a sinking heart, she read Milly's final words, the words that would allow Two-Gus to die without a fight.

She went into his room. He was asleep, his mouth open and his lips fluttering with every breath. He looked a little more gaunt than yesterday, if that were possible. He was changing so quickly!

Gently, so that he would not awake, she took his wrist in her fingers and counted his pulse. One hundred and thirty. The beats were like moth wings fluttering against her fingertips and his skin was hot and dry. There was the smell of damp ashes in her nostrils. She tiptoed from the room, struck by the speed of this disease. She leaned over Bev's shoulder.

"I want to be notified if Mr. Ragust expires. Will you do that?"

"Why? Are you a relative?" Bev smiled. "Just kidding. I'll mark his chart." She prepared another red strip to be pasted under the no-code. "Hey. Congratulations on the contract. That'll pass the vote like a breeze. It's a nice little raise. I just wish they'd send me more nurses."

"They will, as soon as more patients are admitted. It takes time to reopen floors, I'm told."

"Yeah," she rolled her eyes, "I hear you're rubbing elbows with the top brass lately. Is Plumhouse as good as they say?"

"Better, Bev." She gritted her teeth into a smile. "Tell me about Mr. Ragust. What happened to him overnight?"

"Oh God, he's a mess. He broke out with shingles, another pneumonia, and hemoptysis."

No wonder he was losing ground so fast. He'd begun to cough up blood from his lungs.

"He's sure fading fast," Bev went on. "I wish I could say that I was sorry for him, but I can't. He's a danger to all of us. One accidental needle stick and it's good-bye world. I think we ought to get special hazard pay to care for these people. From the looks of it, we're going to be getting a lot more AIDS in here." She looked up at Leah. "Do you suppose the new contract—?"

But Leah had left the desk and in the elevator, grateful that it was empty, she sniffed back her tears. Not to fight, that's what hurts. It is what he wanted, she was sure. He had the right to decide that. Somehow, though, it didn't quite jibe with his personality. He'd been a fighter all his life.

The minute she entered the unit, she saw that something had happened. It was written all over Katherine's face. She beckoned to her.

"Let's go in the lounge for a moment. I want to talk to you."

In silence they walked back to the little room that was

cluttered with empty coffee cups and ashtrays filled with old cigarettes. Automatically, Katherine began to clean up the mess.

"What's the story on Emma?"

"Uh-oh. Claude found out, huh? Danny said he'd tell him."

"Danny? What's he got to do with this?"

"It's his parting shot. He agreed to do the gases."

"Well, he didn't tell Claude a thing, he merely pasted the gases in Emma's chart and left them for Claude to find."

Leah smiled. So Danny had lost his courage after all. "I confess. I asked Danny to draw the bloods. But I didn't instigate the weaning. Emma did that by herself."

"I know. I could tell that she was doing it at night. Did Pat know?"

Leah shrugged. "I don't know, you'll have to ask her. Listen, I'm the one who started this whole business. Emma wouldn't have done it on her own. She did, however, conduct her own weaning without anyone's help. The important thing is that it worked. Now if Claude Peters wants to string me up, he can do it. I'm not sorry. If Emma Bond gets to walk out of here then it's been worth it."

Katherine rubbed the small of her back as she straightened up. "Okay, Joan of Arc, you've said your piece, now I'm going to say mine. I'm not going to be around to protect you much longer. The fact of Emma Bond's improvement is not a justification for what you did. You took on the practice of medicine and that's something no nurse can do. Do you think I like watching Peters the Great practicing bad medicine day after day? I don't, by God. But I'm a nurse and that's what I do. What I do is protect the patient with good nursing care. If I observe anything blatantly wrong with the physician's handling of the case, I go to the supervisor. From there it goes to the director of nurses and from her to the administrator. You went over everyone's head, didn't you? You went straight to Mr. Plumhouse."

Leah gulped. "Not officially. I just was talking to him and it was one of many things we talked about."

"Peters has been called in, and he's blaming you for it. Leah, you've just slit your own throat. Going to the administrator and bypassing normal channels is to make enemies from the ground up. Frankly, I'm angry that you took that route."

"Now just a minute. What I told Julian was in confidence. It wasn't official and I had no intention of going over your head. It just happened." She couldn't believe it. Julian wouldn't have acted on her words. Would he?

For a moment there was silence in the room, then Katherine sighed. "I wanted to use you as my substitute while I'm on maternity leave. Now I don't think it's a good idea. I don't think you could handle it, not with Claude Peters coming in every day. He would make your life miserable and I can't risk the stability of the unit." Leah nodded. "Now I've said my piece and you can consider yourself counseled officially. Now go out there and take care of your patient. I'm going to stay here and steal one of these cigarettes."

"Don't do it. Think of the baby," Leah said timidly. She walked to the door.

"There you go again," Katherine said with an annoyed voice. But she stuffed the cigarette back into the pack. It crushed and she ended up throwing it in the rubbish. The door closed behind Leah.

She went directly to Michael Norman's room and grabbed the child's intake and output chart. It took two tries before she was able to add up the figures for the past eight hours. Fifteen hundred c.c.'s in, four hundred out. Another fifteen minutes and she'd be out of here. Let me get through the next quarter-hour, she prayed, hanging the clipboard on the foot of the bed. Her fingers trembled.

Then she knelt and emptied the urine bag. There wasn't very much in it. The little boy was finally failing. At the sink in the corner of the room, she scrubbed her hands with a little bristle brush, scrubbing so fiercely that at first she did not hear Dale Norman's voice behind her.

"You're going off duty?"

"Oh, I didn't hear you come in. Yes, it's near three o'clock."

"Yes. We'll be going also."

"That's a good idea, you need some rest."

"That isn't what I mean. We won't be coming back."

Sharon was leaning over the bed, stroking at the pale, damp hair across the boy's forehead. She appeared to be far away.

"Oh," Leah said. "Is there anything I can do?"

"Yes. Will you get some paper and an envelope? I'll leave permission for organ donation."

Behind him Sharon choked back a sob as the respirator delivered an automatic sigh and the boy's chest rose and fell. They watched it. When she felt the water drying cold and numb on her fingers, Leah started.

"I'll . . . I'll get the paper." She brushed by Dale, squeezing herself against the wall so that she would not touch him. He seemed breakable.

When Katherine saw her face, she paled. "What is it?" Her gaze darted to the cardiac monitor to reassure herself that Michael's heart was still beating.

"They are going to donate! They must have decided while they were outside. You'd better call someone."

She opened a drawer and began to rummage through the forms that were there. She couldn't seem to see anything.

Barbara Haines put her hand over Leah's. "I'll find it," she said, her kind face solemn. "Whatever it is."

Now that the decision was made, a strange urgency came over them. It was as if time were running out and things must be done quickly before something happened.

Katherine picked up the phone and dialed the emergency room. Ben was the child's primary physician. He'd know how to manage this.

Barbara Haines handed Leah the blank stationery. Then she thought for a moment and pulled out an authorization form.

"Maybe you'll need this, too, I don't know," she said, grimacing. "Ooh. Just let me outta here. It's ten minutes to three. I could have been out of here and home free."

Leah looked at the form. It was a standard permission slip with blank spaces for the procedure. They used it for everything, from the removal of a hangnail to permission for major surgery. Now this.

With her hand cupping the phone, Katherine whispered to her, "Get them both to sign." She waited for Ben to answer his page as Leah walked into the room.

Dale took the papers from her and turned away. Leaning against the bedside table, he began to write. Except for the rhythm of the respirator, the room was silent. Sharon had dragged a chair to the edge of the bed and lowered the bedside rail. With one hand, she stroked the boy's arm. Leah watched her, jamming her hands deep into her pockets. Her fingers were trembling.

When he finished, Dale handed the paper to her. "You'd better check it to make sure it's clear."

Leah looked at the paper with its clear, strong handwriting which simply said: I give permission for the donation of the organs of our son, Michael Norman. His kidneys are to be given to Miss Lily Webb.

"I think it's alright," Leah said, "but Sharon has to sign it as well."

"I can't." Her voice was muffled.

"Sharon, you must," Dale said. "Come on, honey, it's just a piece of paper. It isn't going to change anything for us."

"It's like signing his death warrant."

"But you know it isn't." He knelt by her side. "It's too late for that. Mikey died out there, on the street."

At the diminutive of the child's name, Sharon lifted her head. "It's easy for you, isn't it? Why is that, Dale? It's because you never spent much time with him. He was a mouth to feed, a body to clothe, and a nuisance when he cried."

Dale groaned and turned away.

"I'll leave it here," Leah whispered. "Take your time."

"No, Goddamn it!" Dale pulled Sharon to her feet and began to shake her. "Sign the fuckin' thing. He's dead! Don't you realize that? There's nothing you can do about it, you dumb—" He broke then and began to sob, a strange dry husking sound that came from somewhere deep inside.

Behind them the respirator shrieked suddenly. It broke the tableau of figures around the bed and halted Dale's sobs. Leah leaned over the bed and straightened the kinked tube. Immediately the machine resumed its relentless work.

"I hate that thing," Sharon muttered. "Oh Jesus, give me the pen."

She signed the letter and held it out to Leah. The paper fluttered in her hand. "Take it, before I change my mind."

At the desk, Leah leaned against the counter, breathing heavily as though she'd run a gauntlet. Katherine was on the phone.

Ben's voice was gentle. "I'll be right up," he said. "Can you call Childrens and locate Dr. Chimes?"

"Yes," Katherine said as she read Dale's note. "Oh, just a minute. There's a stipulation here."

"What do you mean?"

"You'd better come up here." She pressed the button that disconnected the line and immediately began to dial again.

When the operator at Childrens Hospital came on the line, she asked for Dr. Chimes.

A female voice answered, "Pedi-Neuro," making a song of the two words.

"Dr. Chimes, please, this is the ICU at Liberty Hill Hospital."

"I don't know if he's around. I'll take a look." Katherine heard the phone drop. She waited. Over the wire she could hear background noises coming from the hospital across the river. A child was crying. Someone laughed and it sounded like a donkey braying. "Come on," she muttered. Two voices, arguing heatedly, went across the wire and then diminished. The child cried on, a thin monotonous wail. The back of Katherine's neck began to prickle.

"Chimes here." Immediately she could see him. The cowboy boots, red checked shirt, and Trixie hanging on his arm.

"Dr. Chimes, this is Liberty Hill ICU. You examined a Michael—"

"I won, didn't I?"

"I beg your pardon?"

"That's five bucks you owe me. Didn't I tell you I'd get him?" He began to chortle, and then shouted, "We got one. We've got a donor."

Katherine shuddered and clamped the phone to her breast. She looked at Leah. "He's positively drooling."

"Hello? HELLO!"

"Yes, Dr. Chimes, I'm here. I was just gagging at your glee."

"Yah, yah, just have the five bucks ready. I'll get the team ready to roll. You still got a blood pressure?"

"What's his pressure?" Katherine asked Leah.

"One-twenty over eighty."

Katherine repeated the figures to Chimes.

"Nice work," he said. "I want the kid to get a continuous drip of five milligrams of Solu-Cortef an hour. Pour in the artificial tears and keep the corneas covered."

Katherine sniffed. "I can't take orders from you, you should know that."

"Oh well, you can't blame me for trying. Tell Dr. Weathers what I said, he'll write 'em." He disconnected the phone.

It was three o'clock. Neither nurse made a move to leave. The next shift had come in and were gathered around the desk. No one spoke. They waited.

Finally, Leah broke the silence. "I'll stay on."

"You don't have to," Mark Berlin said. In his eyes there was compassion.

"I'll stay." She turned away to call home.

The doors opened and Ben walked in. "Where's the permission?"

Katherine handed it to him without a word. He read the short note and then sat there, tapping it against the counter.

Twice in the ten years that Katherine had been head nurse there had been two cases similar to this. In each it had been a simple procedure. The care of the patient was transferred to the transplant team as soon as it arrived. In the operating room the kidneys, heart, liver, and eyes were removed, the patient disconnected from the respirator and pronounced. It was all very precise. The center of attention, those lumpy and bleached pieces of tissue, were packed in gay red picnic hampers and rushed away.

This time it was different. With the simple statement that Dale had written, a new consideration was involved. Now instead of one operating room and one set of technicians, two would be needed: one for the donor and one for the recipient. Two rooms, two teams, and coordination between them so that no organ would be without perfusion longer than necessary. It was going to be tricky.

"We'd better get Chimes again before he leaves Boston."

Again, Katherine dialed Childrens Hopsital. While they waited, Leah returned to the desk.

"Don't we give the parents a chance to back out?" she asked. "What if they change their minds?"

Ben did not reply. Instead he gave her a gentle smile.

The answer came to her as he knew it would. Of course it could happen. There was always the chance right up until the moment of harvest. A change of heart was a fact that the transplant team lived with. It was one of the constraints of transplantation, unspoken yet always present in each case. She imagined that it must have occurred at some time over the years.

When he saw that she understood, he said gently, "See if you can find Dr. Russell. He'll have to stand by." She picked up the other phone.

Katherine finally located Ned Chimes in the emergency room. They had found him climbing into the ambulance that had been standing ready. She handed the phone to Ben and then turned to the waiting staff.

"Come on, let's begin report. We do have other patients here."

When she came to Michael's Kardex, her voice dropped so that the parents would not hear.

It was remarkable, Mark thought as he listened, that she could review the case with the same attention to detail as she had the other unit patients. Her tension was belied, though, by the tapping of her pencil on the desk.

"Any questions?" she asked.

"Do we accompany Michael to the operating room?" Mark asked.

"No, just give the team assistance if they need it. They usually won't ask. They are very professional about the whole process. Oh yes, the chart stays here."

That was the final note. The fact that his medical records would not accompany him to the OR was the keynote. Michael had ceased to be a patient.

Sandy McCracken stretched her thick legs out before her. "I shoulda stayed home sick one more night. What a lousy thing to come in to." She stared at her scuffed white shoes.

Leave it to her to think of something like that, Katherine thought. Tracy must have spent the night on the phone making sure the nurses would begin to return to work. She had forgotten all about the sick-out.

Ben's voice cut across the unit. "I don't care about your sacred list, Doctor. You've gotten everything else you wanted, now don't screw up."

Katherine winced, casting a glance toward Michael's room. She put a finger across her lips but Ben did not notice.

When he finished with the call, Leah held out the other telephone to him. "Dr. Russell is on the line."

"Dick? Can you get going on your patient's transplant? Yes, Lily Webb. You'd better call her in."

He stood up and walked into Michael's room. Leah followed.

"I wouldn't want to be in her shoes," Sandy said.

"Or Ben's," Katherine answered.

Chapter Sixteen

Hancock Point jutted into the east bay of Boston Harbor. It was the first point of land to receive the sun's light and it was the first to lose it. By the time Billy stepped off the bus and made his way to the apartment building, he was shrouded in the soft gray dusk. Stark red brick buildings around him made the shadows even deeper. The playground was empty. It stretched without weed or grass, trampled by the feet of many children living in the project. Over the courtyard the odors of cooking food drifted into his nostrils. When the steel-clad door clanged shut behind him, he was in darkness. The superintendant had forgotten to replace the caged light bulb that lit the dim interior. He raced up the stairs, familiar with the passage in the dark.

There was a light shining through the crack under the door. She was there. Somehow, he hoped she would change her mind. He'd even tried to frighten her out of coming to the Point. Muggers, druggies, they were all there, he'd warned her.

He began to worry. Was she already in there getting sick? He did not know what he would do if she did. The horrible events of his mother's sickness, the way he and Frankie had botched up her care had frightened him badly. What if Lily died on him? The thought of the next hours and the long night ahead was enough to make him turn tail and run.

He pushed open the door and the earthy smell of beef and vegetables and onions was as surprising as if there had been smoke or flames greeting him. Dorothy was the one to produce those wonderful scents. The rich brothy air made him realize how much he'd missed her. He swallowed back a lump of sadness in his throat. Lily was there, standing at the tiny stove in the alcove of the apartment. It wasn't a kitchen really, it was just a wall lined with dented appliances that made up part of the living room. There wasn't even a window to gaze from and the faucet dripped continuously into a rusty stain on the white sink. It wasn't the first time he wished they had a better place to live. He just wished it a little more fervently when he saw her there. It shamed him.

She had changed from the skirt and blouse of their ride to Faneuil Hall to faded jeans and a loose navy wool sweater. Her hair was tied back with a beaded band. She looked rested and freshly bathed. With the sleeves of her sweater pushed up over reed-thin arms, and one of Dorothy's stolen white aprons tied around her waist, she was happily laying the plates and silver on the table. She looked up and smiled at him.

"I made dinner."

"You didn't have to. I was going back to the hospital. I could have eaten there."

He saw the hurt in her eyes and the way the smile faded to a thin line. "Suit yourself. I'll shut it off."

"Uh . . . no. It's good. I mean it smells good." He wanted to punch himself in the head.

It was all gone, the easy familiarity and the joy he felt when he was with her. He could see that she was as nervous as he. Above the shy color of her cheeks there were tight little lines between her eyes and then around the corners of her lips. Her fingers trembled. He couldn't tell whether the effort to make the meal had sapped her strength or that she was as scared as he.

The scratched and lopsided table had been set with candles. She must have bought them; Dorothy never thought of things like candles. A long crusty loaf of bread cut on the diagonal lay across the table like an exclamation point. She had wrapped it in paper towels. He settled himself at the table and struck a match to the candles.

"Let's eat." He avoided looking at her.

"Oh shit, we don't have to do this, if it bothers you this much," she said, sitting down opposite him. "The hell with it. I don't need your neuroses screwing me up."

If there was anything he wanted more than to forget all this, he couldn't think of it. "Let's eat." If only he could have told her that Dr. Russell was going to use him for a transplant.

She rose and ladeled stew into his bowl. Big thick chunks of beef steamed up to him. His stomach rumbled and he hoped she hadn't heard it.

"Listen." The lie came so easily. "I talked to Dr. Russell about donating my kidney. He's going to think it over." A piece of beef settled in his stomach like a rock. But her face lit up.

"He did?"

"Yeah. So if I chicken out on this we'll still have that to fall back on."

"Yeah, okay. Oh Billy, I think you are so wonderful. No one else would do this for me." She tore off an end of the bread and then another and held it out to him. "Did he seem like he'd do it? I mean, he didn't laugh or anything, did he?"

"No. He was . . . serious." The food was definitely growing into a lump of clay in his stomach.

"I don't see why he would laugh. I mean, if you were

my brother he'd jump at the chance to take your kidney. You talked to your mother, right?" Billy nodded, keeping his head down. "She must love you very much." He didn't know whether to swallow or spit. One wrong answer and he'd be caught in the web of lies.

"She can stay with my mother during the operation. They'd be good company for each other." She looked up at him. "I'll agree."

"Huh?"

"If it scares you too much, then I'll go to dialysis. Let's just go tonight and see how I do, alright?"

He felt a sweat break out on his forehead. He jumped up and left the room. In the tiny bathroom, with the overhead light bulb swinging back and forth shooting planes of light over his face, he stared at himself in the mirror. He was such a liar. A stupid liar. Once she found out, she'd never speak to him again.

After a moment, he ran the water, waiting for it to turn cold. Then he splashed it over his face and felt for a towel.

When he returned, she had switched on Dorothy's pink plastic radio. BCN came in playing Steely Dan. The candlelight flickered in her eyes.

"How soon will it happen?" Dale Norman asked Ben.

"Hours, a few hours," Ben replied. "Arrangements are already underway."

Dale nodded. "Then we should probably leave now?"

Ben managed to look at him. "Yes. That's probably the best thing. You must have someone you should call."

The two men looked down at Michael and then at Sharon. She was kneeling by the bed. They could not tell if she was listening. Leah walked around them and stooped by her side.

"Let me help you up," she whispered. "Come now, Sharon. This is the hardest part, I know. I'll help you through it."

Sharon gazed up at her. Although she was pale and trembling, there was something new in her face. Leah recognized it; Sharon was letting go. Leah swallowed the burning lump in her throat.

"Yes, I know," Sharon said. "But there's something I want to do first. Will you take those eye pads off him?"

"Yes, of course."

When she had finished and Michael's face was clear and pale beneath the spotlight, she stepped back. The two men watched. Sharon reached up and unfastened a tiny gold cross from around her neck and placed it around Michael, adjusting it so that it nestled in the hollow of his throat. For a moment she stood there, her head bent, her lips moving soundlessly. Then she leaned over and gently brushed his closed eyelids with her lips.

"I'll leave now," she whispered.

It was too easy, it was like moving a life-sized doll. Leah guided her to the door. Just outside she felt a tremor go through Sharon's body and the pressure of her weight against her arm.

"No. Oh no, I can't leave him all alone!" she moaned.

"She's falling!" Leah cried as she felt Sharon's full weight sagging to the floor. Ben caught her in his arms and between them they managed to keep Sharon from hitting the floor. Her hair had swept across her face. Ben half-knelt and lifted her into his arms.

"Let's get her in the lounge and bring smelling salts. Is Dale with us?"

"I'm right behind you, Doctor," Dale said, his voice hoarse.

As he passed the foot of the bed, he let his hand come down over the boy's foot and for a moment he held it. The sound of the respirator filled the room. He turned away.

* * *

When the telephone rang, Dr. Russell had snapped off the light in his office. He had one hand on the doorknob. He gave it a twist and the phone shrilled again. Sighing, he recrossed the room and picked it up. Later he would think back that if he had avoided Ben Weathers's call, Lily would have lost her chance, not only for this operation, but perhaps forever.

After speaking with Ben, he dialed Dialysis. Steve Lambert picked it up on the first ring.

"Is Lily Webb on schedule for today?" Russell did not bother to identify himself.

"No, Doctor. She's on M-W-F's." Steve hesitated for only a moment. "Is she going to get that boy's kidney?"

"Yes, give me her home phone number."

Russell flicked the phone switch and when the dial tone came back, he dialed the number Steve had so jubilantly given him. Russell began to smile to himself.

"Oh damn!" Tracy's fingernails were wet with fresh pink polish when the phone rang. She peeled the cigarette from her mouth, careful not to smudge her nails and dropped it into an ashtray. Passing the television set, she turned down the sound, but kept her eyes fastened to the screen. She loved everything about Vanna White: her glamorous hair, the slinky gowns, the job she had. Especially that. She was America's dream girl.

On the sixth ring, she muttered, "Alright, alright." She blew on her nails one last time and picked up the phone.

"Mrs. Webb? Dr. Russell here. Can you get Lily right up to the Hill? We have a kidney for her."

She gasped as if she'd been shot. They'd waited so long for this call that she had forgotten that it could ever come. "Ah . . . she's not here."

"Get her in as fast as you can."

"But I don't know where she is!" she cried, trying to make him understand. "We didn't know . . ." She was going to Boston for the day with some boy. Damn that boy. She glanced at her watch. "How much time do I have?"

"I think we'll have about four hours. Don't feed her and let me know the minute she's on her way." Russell hung up and once more began to dial.

Tracy turned back to the television set; Vanna had just spun the wheel. There was a vacuous smile on her face and all of a sudden she did not look real.

The operating rooms were clean and dark. All the cases had been done and only Olive Meecham was left to close up. She slung off her soiled blue warm-up jacket and threw it in the hamper. Far off, down at the nurses' desk, the phone shrilled. Olive sighed and muttered, "Shit."

She hurried to the front of the suite. "Operating room, Olive Meecham speaking."

"This is Dr. Russell, Miss Meecham. We're going to need two operating rooms in the next hour. Will you get set up, please?"

"I'll have to call them in. It *is* after three, you know, Doctor." Automatically her eyes went to the on-call sheet. "What's the case?"

"There are two." He heard the hiss of dismay, but continued on, "A nephrectomy in one and a transplant in the other."

"Is that Tracy Webb's kid?"

"Yes." He paused for a moment. "But, of course, that's confidential, Miss Meecham. And we're going to need a steady group. No tears, remember."

"Right. I'll get right on it." Without waiting, she pressed the disconnect button and called the evening supervisor. "Guess what?"

*   *   *

Richard Russell sat in the darkness of his office. In his mind, he ran over the two cases as they would progress. He would need only one anesthesiologist for Lily; the donor was already intubated. The transplant team was fully staffed for the nephrectomy, but he needed an assistant for the implant. He redialed the phone.

Katherine picked it up with a sigh. She'd never get out of here. "ICU." She forgot to announce her name.

"Dr. Russell here. Is Dr. Weathers still there?"

"Yes, he's with the Norman family."

"When he comes out, will you ask him to assist on the case?"

Katherine made a face. She had hoped Ben could drive her home tonight. Now when he did get home, which would be late, he'd be exhausted and depressed. It wasn't fair. She rubbed at the small of her back. It had been achy all day.

It was fully ten minutes before Sharon revived enough to get to her feet. When she opened her eyes and realized that she was lying on the battered couch of the lounge and that several pairs of anxious eyes were watching her, she struggled to sit up.

"I'm sorry," she said. "I thought I'd be alright. It just came over me."

"It's okay, honey," Dale said. "Don't apologize. Are you alright now?" He sat down and put his arms around her, wiping a rough palm against her tear-streaked cheek.

She nodded, wrapping her arms around her chest and shivering. "We've got to go home, Dale. My parents are waiting for our call."

Ben spoke up. "If you think you'll be alright, I'll leave now."

Dale nodded and signaled with his head toward the door. "You can leave us alone now. We'll find our way out."

Ben left them there and hurried back to the unit. Leah

caught his arm as he passed Michael's room. "Are they alright?"

He shook his head. "They'll never be alright. But they're doing the best they can."

"Another minute with them and I'd have passed out, too."

He patted her on the shoulder.

Katherine watched as he approached the desk. She was alone, finally, the evening shift dispersed to their patients. "Ben."

His eyes grew wary. "What?"

"Dr. Russell needs you to assist. He says it's for the implant on Lily, but I think he means the nephrectomy. Which case would that awful Dr. Chimes do?"

"He'll do the implant. We'll do the harvest." He turned away and left the unit. She pitied him. It was over for the parents and for the nurses who cared for Michael, but not for Ben. It would go on for him until the operation was over. I hate this, she thought.

By four o'clock, Dr. Russell had not heard from Lily's mother. A faint unease stirred inside. She should have kept track of the girl at all times, he thought. Abruptly, he donned his white coat, locked the office, and headed for his unit. There were patients there, lined up in their chairs and hooked to their kidneys. They were waiting, too. He'd study their charts and decide which of his patients would be the best candidate for the transplant. One of them would be compatible with the donor. And it would have to be someone fairly small. The donor weighed only . . . He entered the unit, forcing his mind off Lily Webb.

By now, Tracy was getting frantic waiting. There was a train every thirty minutes from Boston. Surely, Lily would have been on one of them. She did not know whether to go down to the subway stop and wait there, or stay at home in case Lily arrived by cab. She looked down at her fingernails and realized she had systematically scraped off the fresh polish so carefully brushed on only thirty minutes ago. She sat by the window where she had the best view of the street and, in earnest, applied her thumbnail to the rest of the pink paint.

In the operating room, Fat Marge Desormer waddled toward the back table, her dripping arms held high before her. Olive Meecham smiled at her over her mask. Fat Marge was her favorite scrub nurse. She loved the way Fat Marge worked, the easy flow from table to stand, the economy of her movements. In here, Fat Marge was the slim ballerina.

Olive stood ready to help her into her sterile gown. It was a time they both loved, no matter what the hour. They talked with their eyes, almost like a gaze between lovers. The measured dance of the procedure to come was still ahead of them. The great lamp was still dark and they had the room to themselves. It was a time of quiet anticipation and order. No matter what came later, they had these moments of peace. They savored it.

With Fat Marge now shrouded in greens and her hands encased in gloves, the two nurses turned their attention to the great bundles of linens, the trays of instruments. Their movements became intricate and precise. Scalpels were laid precisely along the edge of the Mayo stand. Clamps were lined up at the back of the stand, a gleaming row of steel, stacked against a rolled green towel. Long Mayo clamps and rib retractors snugged into a fold along the short edge of the stand. As fast as Olive tossed the sterile packets of catgut onto her stand, Fat Marge gently straightened and pinned them beneath a towel. Black silk with fine steel needles already attached were left in their tinfoil packets. She would rip them open as she needed them when it came time to sew skin. Together they counted sponges and refolded them for easy handling. When the fully laden tray was packed and ready, Fat

Marge draped it with a sterile piece of linen. Then she turned her attention to the back table.

Across the scrub room, another green-gowned nurse was following the same ritual and when both rooms were finally ready, the stands and table were covered with sterile sheets and scrub was broken. They left the dark rooms behind and went to the cafeteria for supper. Fat Marge was the first in line, her tray was the heaviest, and at the cash register, her meal the most expensive. Fat Marge believed in being fully sated before a case.

Mark Berlin steadied a syringe and then plunged it into a sterile bottle of saline. He looked up as Leah passed the medication room, her arms laden with linens.

"What are you doing?" he asked, flipping the saline bottle upside down.

"I'm going to give him a bath." She marched past the door.

In Michael's room, she filled a basin with hot water and with a soft cloth she began to bathe the child. She peeled away the eye pads she had replaced just minutes ago and gently washed the crust from his eyelids, then she dropped two doses of artificial tears over the dark blue eyes. She decided to leave off the new pads until she was finished; he looked more whole that way. Carefully, so as not to disturb the endotracheal tube, she moistened his lips with a little cream and even swabbed his teeth with hydrogen peroxide.

"Can't have you going anywhere with bad breath," she whispered.

Then she soaped and rinsed the boy, taking her time, drying each limb as she finished it. She tried to ignore the ominous swelling of his feet and hands. She had noticed it this morning and knew that nature was now running its course with Michael Norman. It had begun to sacrifice his extremities in order to conserve vital organs. If left much longer, the feet and hands would become cyanotic and the skin would begin to blister. She covered him with a fresh johnny, not bothering to tie it at the back, but instead, draping it over his body like a blanket. The gold cross at his throat gleamed.

When she knelt to pull a fresh sheet beneath his hips, tugging them tightly into place, one swollen hand came down and touched her lightly on the head. She froze, feeling her throat close down. But it was only the way she had balanced the hand on Michael's hip as she worked over him. Now it hung motionless over the side of the bed.

Oh stop it, she said to herself, it's only a body now. A donor. She placed a fresh set of eye pads over the long curly eyelashes. They helped mask his face.

Then she settled by his bed and began to complete her chart. As she worked, it came to her that these notes would be the last official words about Michael as a patient. The next would be at his funeral. Think of Lily, she said to herself sternly. No more dialysis, no more blood transfusion. The simple act of voiding her own waste would give her a freedom she had never had. She could get on with the business of growing up. Over the chart, she glanced over at the still form on the bed. He couldn't have come, this little donor, at a better time. She closed the chart and walked from the room.

"Are you all done?" Mark asked. She nodded. "Then go home."

"There's something I have to do first," she said. "But I'm leaving the unit now. His chart is up to the minute and I've signed off." Mark watched as she gathered up her jacket and purse.

"See you tomorrow. Oh, by the way . . ." Leah halted. "You did a nice job with Emma. Congratulations. Too bad you couldn't change her personality, too."

She shrugged and said. "At least we'll have a chance to see her out the door."

She pushed through the double doors. The halls were quiet as a church and she rode the elevator down to the first floor listening only to the rush of air above her. With a heavy heart, she turned right and headed for the administrative offices.

Betsy's Conte's office was dark, but underneath Julian's door a faint slash of light told her he was still there. She knocked on the door and waited.

When he saw her a broad smile came over his face. "Leah! I'm so glad to see you . . ." The words died and a puzzled look came over his features. "What's the matter?"

"You ratted on me, Julian. You told Claude Peters what I asked you not to. I thought I could trust you." She crossed her arms and planted herself in the doorway, her hands on her hips.

"You are talking about the Emma Bond case," he said. "But I didn't rat on you, my dear. I had my own case against Peters that had nothing to do with you." He took her arm, urging her to come inside. "I want to show you something before you explode." A little smile flickered at the corner of his mouth.

She pulled away from him. "No, I won't step foot in here. This office is a trap. I just wanted to tell you what I think of you. I think you are a first-class bastard whose only interest in life is the running of this lousy hospital!

"The other day was a date, just an ordinary everyday date, and what we talked about was supposed to be just between us. If I had known you for the heartless bastard that you are, I'd have kicked you out rather than spill my guts. I thought I could trust you. I even thought there was something special between us. I made love to you." She slammed her hand against the door. "Oh, what a fool I was. It's always Liberty Hill first, isn't it? And it wasn't love we made, it was just sexual release, wasn't it?"

A pained look came over his face, but he turned away and opened the gray file drawer. Rummaging through it, he drew out a manila folder and thrust it at her. His eyes were dark.

"Here. Take a look at this. Maybe it will convince you. I know Peters is blaming you for our confrontation. He almost got a black eye for some of the things he said about you. But you are wrong if you think I betrayed you. I would never do that. Leah, I love you. I've fallen in love with you, damn it!"

The folder slid open and spilled at her feet. They knelt to pick up the pieces of paper and their knees bumped together.

Then their heads banged and she fell onto her hip. She sat on the floor looking up at him. "You what?"

"I love you." He knelt by her side and gathered her into his arms. "It's too soon, I know. I mean, we've only just found each other, but damn it, I knew the minute I laid eyes on you that there could be no one else for me. You must believe that."

"I do." She rubbed the spot on her head. "So what is all this?" She pulled a sheet of paper out from under her bottom.

"It's nothing. I mean, it's just a bunch of documents from the Board of Welfare. They have been building a case against Peters for months. I only just found out about it. That's how come I got in on the whole thing. He's stabbing in the dark accusing you. But that's not important. Forget Peters. It's us I want to talk about."

It was then that the tears that she had been holding back all day suddenly erupted. She sobbed against his chest and he held her, bewildered, patting her shoulders. When she quieted after a few moments, she told him about Michael Norman.

"Oh, Julian, sometimes I hate what I do, it's so damned painful. Why did I go into this? Why couldn't I be a singer. A writer?"

"I don't know. Can you sing?"

"No."

"Good. The world needs poets, but it also needs you and me, though it may not appreciate that little fact. I wouldn't have met you if you were a famous writer, either. Think of the loss."

She managed to smile at him and said, "I keep hoping God will step in with a miracle and bring this kid back to life. I want it so bad, that I can't leave for fear of missing it. It would confirm His being, wouldn't it? Think of how wonderful it would be to witness a miracle. Nothing else would ever be important."

"Maybe that's why He doesn't."

"This is such a final step," she went on as if she hadn't heard him. "Even if God were to step in, He might be too late. Of course I know that sounds silly, but that's what seems wrong about taking matters in your own hands. Maybe we've gone too far. We've taken God's job away from Him, so there's no chance of a miracle. We've become cynical, we don't care about life anymore." She looked up at him. "I know I sound crazy. I've become emotionally involved in a case and nurses aren't supposed to do that."

"I am sure his mother would rather have that than some uncaring, cold-hearted nurse taking care of her son. It's okay to cry, darling. I love you for crying."

He leaned over awkwardly and covered her mouth with his lips. For a second, she almost pushed him away; it seemed a little indecent at a time like this, but through the blur of her tears, she could see the deep-etched kindness in his face and his hands around her back were bands of strength. He was comforting her in the way men did, offering shelter with his body, and warmth from his heart. There was a crazy mixture of love and sorrow in the kiss.

Tracy propped the note against the lamp by the door where Lily would see it the minute she came in. Then she threw a tan raincoat over her shoulders and slammed the door behind her. It had begun to rain and when she reached the sidewalk, she looked up, but the hospital was shrouded from sight. She bent her head against the rain, not caring that her makeup, always so carefully applied, would be streaked. They had to wait for Lily. As she hurried up the hill, she pictured in her mind the set of circumstances taking place on Lily's behalf. It would take the transplant team at least a half-hour to reach Atwater. Rush hour had begun. And the OR was closed. That meant time, too, to round up the scrub nurses, get them to the Hill, and then set up for the case. That was another half-hour. Time. The donor had plenty of that; he had lasted through the night and his heart and blood pressure were still strong. All would be ready for Lily. All we need, she thought, was time to find her. God, why didn't we remember the rule! If only she had kept track of where Lily had gone. Waiting for a donor had become a distant dream. We'd forgotten it, Tracy thought with a moan.

Water splashed against her legs as she stepped off the curb and dashed across the street. Her breath was becoming a roar in her ears. She glanced up and caught sight of the hospital in the rain. It looked like a fat, ugly toad squatting at the top of the street. A seagull swooped silently overhead and let loose a splash of feces. It splashed just before her feet. She stepped over it and began to cry.

* * *

"I ain't seen him all day," Dorothy said to Two-Gus. "Here I am all discharged and waiting for that boy to come and bail me out of here and I don't even know where the hell he is." She lit a cigarette, pulling Two-Gus's empty cup toward her for an ashtray.

Two-Gus inhaled the smoke gratefully. It cut into the fever and soothed away the nightmares that swooped over him every time he closed his eyes. He let Dorothy ramble on. If she only knew how glad he was to hear her complaints.

"Everyday he's here like clockwork. Now when I need him, he ain't. He's getting more like Frankie everyday.

"The nurses are giving me dirty looks now that I'm supposed to be outta here. Like now that I'm all of a sudden cured, they don't want me hanging around. Don't sit on the bed, they say, you might mess it up. Do you know they even made me lug my tray out to the sunroom? I had to eat all alone out there. They said if I was going to smoke I'll have to do it there." She sniffed at him. "It'll be your turn when you feel better. They make you think you're wasting their time."

"That's not likely to happen to me."

"Huh?"

"It looks like I won't be getting better."

"Oh Christ, I'm sorry to hear that."

The look on her face was genuine, maybe pity, but that was alright. It was the same ingenuous face as Billy's. He struggled to sit upright and quickly Dorothy helped plump the pillow behind his back.

"Thanks," he gasped. "Listen, I've got to tell you something."

"Yeah? What?" She lit another cigarette from the burning stub of the old one.

Though she was dressed in street clothing, the pallor and the thin, strained look on her face made her still a patient to him. Like most, he knew she would accept what he had to say without restraint. It was a peculiarity of hospital life. There was too little time and sickness always precluded outside influence.

"Billy has become a special person to me." She nodded her head as though she heard that all the time. "I don't have a son. For that matter, I don't have much family left. But if I did, I'd want my boy to be just like him. He has a gentleness that defies all convention."

There was genuine confusion on her face at that. He started over.

"Look," he said. "I love your kid. It's that simple. And I figure I'd like to see him have some chance at a good life. So I've left him a little something in my will."

Now her eyes grew huge and he laughed.

"Don't get me wrong, Mrs. Fellows. It isn't a fortune."

"Dot," she corrected him.

"Dot. There'll be enough to put him through college and give him a good start." He reached over and pulled open his bedside drawer. He handed her a card. "This is the name of my attorney. If anything happens to me, you get in touch with him."

"Jesus H. Christ on a crutch!" She peered at Peter Cohen's card. "Why? I mean what about your family?"

"There's only a sister and she's well cared for, believe me. If you count a board of directors who send my quarterly account in the mail, that's all the family I have. No, Billy is the closest I'll ever come to having a child. I hope you don't mind sharing him with me for a little while."

"He's a good kid," she agreed, "if he ever shows up." She tucked the card into the pocket of her skirt and stood up.

"Well, Mr. Ragust, I thank you for what you are doing and I will keep in touch with this lawyer fellow. But I don't plan to change anything else."

Her easy familiarity was gone and there was a watchful

look on her face. She walked to the door. He felt a little sad that their easy relationship had been strained by his gesture. He could see that she was thinking about strings and how committed she would have to be. Or was she wondering how to get control of Billy's windfall? With that thought he realized that she might be regarding him as a foe. He wished that he could tell her that with the gift he wanted only one thing in exchange: Billy's presence for just a little while. He wanted to tell her that but there was a stiffness in her back as she walked to the door. It showed in the way she pulled off the mask and threw it in the basket. Maybe she couldn't be anything else, he thought. In her shoes, he'd probably do the same thing, take the money and run.

The room smelled of stale cigarettes. The air was hard to breathe. He wanted to cry.

Chapter Seventeen

"But I don't know where she is," Tracy cried. She leaned over Dr. Russell's desk and said to him, "Can't you wait a while longer? You told me we had four hours. It's been only half that. Listen, Doctor, she would never forgive us, you or me, if she missed out. God knows what she'd do to herself to pay us back. She's only fourteen years old. You know at that age, she's apt to hurt herself just to get revenge."

Dr. Russell's face was kind but his words were like hammer blows to her. "My hands are tied. Those organs are going to be harvested whether or not Lily is here. I must say," he looked away, "that you both were warned to be available at a moment's notice."

"We've waited for a year," Tracy said, willing the fury inside to die down. How dare he chastise her! "One year waiting for that telephone to ring. Now you listen to me, Dr. Russell. This hospital owes me. It's taken twenty years of my life and given very little back. If the truth were known, it's treated the Webb family badly. It let my husband die like a dog out in the hallway. It's made me pay every penny over and above my allotment from the government for Lily's dialysis. Twenty years and it wouldn't even pay for that. Liberty Hill has sucked the

Webb family dry. Well, now it can do something. It owes me something if only out of consideration for a long-term employee. Give me two hours."

He nodded. There was something in his face. Was it shame?

"I'll hold off surgery. I don't know how, but I will," he said. "But what are you going to do?"

"Find her," Tracy said.

She left his office and headed for the front desk. By the time she reached the hall, she was panting. The clerk on duty looked up indifferently. Out of uniform, Tracy was just another visitor to her. "Yes?"

"Give me Mrs. Fellows's room number." She stood there tapping her fingernails on the counter impatiently.

"She has been discharged."

"What? When?"

"I don't know. All I know is that room is empty. In fact, it's booked for another patient."

"Which room was it?"

"Four-twelve."

Tracy reached over the counter and snatched up the telephone. The clerk looked incredulous. "Hey, you can't do that." She reached for the phone but Tracy pushed away her hand.

"This is Mrs. Webb. Has Mrs. Fellows left the hospital?"

The voice came over the line. "No, but I wish she would. She's waiting for someone to pick her up. She's making a nuisance out of herself up here."

"Hold her there."

Tracy cut her off and replaced the telephone. She looked at the desk clerk. "Next time I ask you a question, young woman, you get the answer and get it right, understand?" The woman nodded, her mouth open.

On the fourth floor, Tracy glanced into the room. Though it was officially empty, it still held the air of being occupied. The bed was rumpled and there was a tray on the table. At the desk, she said to the evening charge nurse. "Where is she?"

The woman shrugged. "Probably out in the sunroom. She's a smoker."

Willing herself not to run, Tracy turned and retraced her steps, passing the empty room once more. The sunroom was at the far end of the corridor. At the doorway, she scanned the room and settled her gaze on a thin woman thumbing restlessly through a magazine.

"Mrs. Fellows?" The woman looked up at her. "Where is your son, Billy?"

"Who wants to know?" The answer shot back.

Tracy exhaled and walked to the couch. "I'm sorry. I should have introduced myself. I'm Lily Webb's mother."

Dorothy's face brightened. "Billy's little kidney friend. Hi."

"Hello. Look I'm trying to find Lily and I've exhausted all other possibilities. I think she may be with your son."

"What's he done?" A wary look came over Dorothy's face. "He's a good boy."

"I'm sure that he is. I must find Lily or she'll miss out on a transplant. There is a kidney for her. She's waited a year for this and I can't find her." The last words came out in a half-sob. "Do you know where he is?"

"I'm waiting for him, too. I was supposed to be out of here hours ago and I don't know where the hell he's got to. I tried calling the apartment, but there's no answer."

Tracy looked up sharply. "Where is that?"

"Now wait a minute. He wouldn't take a girl there. He's too young, if you know what I mean." Dorothy grinned at her.

Tracy's lips thinned. The woman was simply too coarse for words. "You have no idea where your son is. Fourteen years old and you don't know where he is?

What kind of mother are you?"

Dorothy's reply shot back without hesitation. "And who appointed you God? Get lost, lady." She turned her back to Tracy and opened her magazine, the only evidence of her anger the slap of pages.

Tracy stood there, her knees trembling. "I'm sorry," she said. "I'm so upset that I don't know what I'm saying. Please. Can you help me?" Inside, she was cringing at her own words. She'd like nothing better than to simply dismiss this woman as a simpleton. "If Lily doesn't get this kidney I don't know what she'll do. She could make herself sick, very sick, just to get back at us."

"Like I said, I don't know where Billy is," Dorothy said without looking up. "If I see him, I'll ask. Now I ain't gonna talk to you again. I hope things work out for your daughter, but you don't impress me none. You come in here, Mrs. High And Mighty, looking down your nose at me and criticizing me. You don't know where the hell your own kid is. How come you don't keep track of her?"

For a moment, Tracy was silent. "You're right, Mrs. Fellows," she said in a low voice. "I've been a fool. I . . . I'm begging you. If you know anything at all . . . please." To her shame, she felt tears flowing down her cheeks.

Dorothy did not look up. She flicked a few pages of her magazine.

Finally she looked up. "The guy in four-fourteen might know something. He's friendly with Billy." She stubbed out her cigarette and rose with a sigh. "Come on, I'll introduce you."

"Who is he?"

"I don't know. His name is Two-Gus."

Tracy groaned. That was all she needed, the AIDS patient. She followed Dorothy down the corridor.

"You shouldn't be in his room. He's contagious."

This time Dorothy stopped in her tracks. She leaned

against the doorjamb, one arm high over her head and a foot crossed over the other.

"You really are a fool," she said. "Do you want help or not?" Tracy nodded. "Then you go in and talk to the guy. And don't look down your nose at him, like you did me. Is that understood?"

Tracy nodded again. Inside her nerves had begun to scream.

"Hey, Two-Gus? It's Dot Fellows again. Are you awake?"

Leah stepped into view. "He's awake, just barely." When she saw Tracy, confusion came over her face. "What are you doing here?"

Dorothy spoke up for her. "We trying to find Billy. We think her daughter might be with him. They've got a kidney for her."

"I know that," Leah said. "She's supposed to be in the OR right now. I had no idea she wasn't ready."

Tracy found her voice. "They are giving me some time to find her. Does he know where they might be? Can you ask him?" She nodded at Two-Gus.

Dorothy made a disgusted "tch" sound with her tongue. "Jeez, lady. Ask him yourself." She looked at Leah. "She's something else, this lady."

Now Two-Gus spoke up. He had feigned sleep while the three women at his door whispered. So they had a kidney for the girl. Thank God. "They are at Billy's house."

Tracy whirled around. "What? What did you say?"

"I said they are at Billy's house. They're in hiding." He felt exhausted.

Tracy exhaled in relief. "Thank God." She flew out to the desk. Over her shoulder, she called out. "What's the address?"

Dorothy told her and asked, "What are you going to do?"

"Call the police, what else? They'll be the ones to get

her here the fastest."

Two-Gus closed his eyes. The police. Billy would be frightened.

Leah spoke up. "Tracy, police cars, sirens. That'll scare those kids to death. Why don't we ride along and take some of the fright out of this for them." The two women disappeared.

Dorothy Fellows lit a cigarette and watched them hurry away. Then she turned to Two-Gus. "Want a little company, Mr. Ragust?"

"Certainly, Mrs. Fellows, make yourself at home." She seemed to have forgotten her earlier distrust of him. Another blessing indeed, he thought.

"I have a suspicion that it's going to be a very long night." Dorothy inhaled deeply and blew out a haze of blue smoke.

Once again his room filled with her smoke and chatter and he could close his eyes and pretend that his life would always go on.

There was no great wrenching pain when Katherine's water broke. In fact, there was nothing but the surprisingly comfortable feeling of warmth on her legs. She looked down at the widening puddle at her feet. "Oh my. Oh, oh. What do I do now?"

She seemed incapable of deciding her next move. Should she leave the puddle on the floor and drive up to the Hill? Or should she mop it up? Could she even drive? The practicality of her questions baffled her and she simply stood there looking at the life fluid darkening her shoes and spreading in a pool on the kitchen floor.

Then the thought struck her: the baby was coming. She was really coming! And with that pronouncement, she was swept by a sense of exhilaration so keen that she mistook it for fear. Her heart thudded heavily in her chest. Then her practical side took over.

Gingerly, she stepped out of her shoes and left them in the center of the pool and on tiptoes she went into the little back hall bathroom where she snatched up a towel. Making a rolled pad of it, she placed it between her legs and pulled her wet slacks over it to hold it in place. Then she eyed the toilet. Should she sit there? Would the water finally stop? Somehow, it did not seem the smart thing to do. Maybe the baby would fall in.

She could feel the towel becoming sodden. She took another and hung it over her shoulder for a replacement. Then another. She grew pleased with herself. Now if the baby came, she could wrap it up in this towel. Good thinking, old girl.

She'd forgotten that there was supposed to be some labor pain. There wasn't a hint of it, strange. She looked down at herself.

She could feel her feet making tracks in the floor. They slapped against the tiles. In the back hall closet was an old pair of Ben's sailing mocs. She slipped her feet into them, thinking that he wouldn't mind them getting wet. Besides they were supposed to be deck shoes, antiskid. She giggled a little hysterically to herself. The lump of towel between her legs made it difficult for her to walk. She was glad he wasn't here to see it. She was almost sure he'd laugh.

As she passed the offending puddle, she pulled off the pretty dusty rose tablecloth she had bought only last week and tossed it over the mess. Instantly it darkened. Probably ruined, she thought. She did not dare stoop to mop it up. She'd never get up again.

It was then that she felt the first grinding cramp in her belly. Definitely it was nothing like the fleeting ones she had felt before. This meant business. This was growing into a vise of steel that screwed down her girth until she thought for a moment that she might burst. She grew scared. For a fraction of time it jolted the world from its ordinary spin and she was left with one hand on the back of a chair holding on for dear life. She wondered if she should pant. But no sooner did she remember to pant, then the problem arose as to remember which kind, the puffing one or the puppy pant? Lips out or in? Oh, which one? The pain began to ease and she guessed she'd skip it this time. But when it was over, she took a deep cleansing breath just as her instructor taught—in through the nose, out through the mouth. She tried to keep her lips from trembling but she couldn't and her breath came out in a whistle. Feeling foolish, and dreading the next time, she waddled to the kitchen telephone, the towel between her legs growing soggy. Her eyes began to water as she dialed.

It was picked up after the first ring, almost as if she had known the call was coming. "Hello, Mother?" Katherine said. Now the tears began in earnest. "Can you come and get me?" She felt like a baby.

"Are you asleep?" Billy asked.

"Not yet," Lily replied. "It's raining so hard, I almost think it's going to burst through the roof."

"It's the metal roof. It always sounds like that. I used to think I lived in a tin can when it rained."

She had curled into a ball in the middle of the double bed. There was a single wall lamp lit and it cast a pale shaft of light across her face. He leaned against the doorway, hesitant to sit on the edge of the bed. So far, he could see no evidence that she was getting sick.

She had helped him stretch the fitted sheet across the mattress, laughing as the mattress popped it off when she fitted the opposite corner in place. She insisted on using her own sheets, her own pillow. She had even brought a stuffed bear. "Hero Teddy," she called it. Now she held it cradled in her arms.

After he helped her wash the stew dishes, they had played cribbage and the little ivory pegs marched twice around the board. He'd won the game. She declined a rematch. The evening hours seemed to stretch before them and he began to reach for words.

He showed her the little bathroom and gave her a fresh bar of Dorothy's special soap. It smelled of violets. He could hear the water running and imagined that her face was soapy fresh.

He turned the dial on the pink plastic radio, but there was nothing that held his interest. He glanced at the clock. What was she doing in there? After awhile, he swore to himself that the clock had stopped and he wondered how he was going to get through the night.

When she emerged from the bathroom, she seemed to have become even younger. She had wrapped herself in a matching flannel gown and bathrobe. The robe buttoned to her neck and then zipped closed to the tips of her feet. She had pulled back her hair with an elastic band and it stretched the skin over her cheekbones bleaching them of color. He looked at her and thought to himself, oh God, this is a mistake. From the look in her eyes, he could tell that she was feeling the same.

"We can call it off you know," he said softly.

"But then I'd never know if it would have worked."

She sat down across from him, in the little built-in table overlooking the rain-washed courtyard. Below them, lights from the other apartments gleamed like yellow beacons in the night. Their knees touched.

"It's weird here," she said, gazing through the window.

"It's a project, courtesy of the town of Atwater."

"Welfare?"

"So what?"

"So nothing, stupid, don't be so touchy."

They were headed for a quarrel and he knew that if it happened, it would be all over.

"I'm not touchy. I don't like people thinking we can't take care of ourselves. This place is just temporary. As soon as Frankie sends money, and Ma gets her job back, we don't need no help. Besides, she's paid taxes all her life, why shouldn't she get some of the benefits when she needs them?"

Lily shook her fingers as if she'd been burned. "Pardon me. How come you think you're the only ones in the world with troubles?"

"You think we're down on our luck, don't you? We're low class living in a project, huh?"

"I never said that, you did." Her face was rigid with anger.

He slid out from the table and walked to the closet. Inside was a rain slicker. Beside it was Frankie's old yellow jacket. He wished Frankie were here now. She watched as he pulled on the poncho and fastened the hood over his head.

"Where are you going?" He did not reply. "You won't tell anyone, will you?"

If he looked at her now, he'd cave in. He heard the desperation in her voice; it would be there in her eyes. He opened the door and rain, hanging in drops on the flimsy aluminum door, spattered the floor. There was something he should say, but he hurt too much. He stepped out into the night and pulled the door shut behind him.

His footsteps grated on the iron stairway. Below him an animal, a cat, he thought, scuttled through a path of light and disappeared soundlessly. Maybe it was a rat, it was a night for rats. He stepped off the steel stairs and onto the asphalt. Feeling his way, for the courtyard lights were out as usual, he made his way to the street. Far off, he could hear the wail of a siren. Drug bust going down, he thought. He stood there, feeling miserable. Rain drummed on the hood of his slicker.

Headlights bounced across the slick streets and he watched them grow larger. Blue lights flashed over them. Cops. He shrank back into the darkness of the building, not knowing why he was suddenly alarmed.

The car screeched to a halt. Behind it, another swerved to avoid hitting it and angled toward the sidewalk, its lights catching him. He was engulfed by piercing blue flashes and automatically, he shaded his eyes against the glare. Two figures emerged from the back seat of one of the cruisers. For a moment he thought it was his mother and a swell of gratitude rose up. But then he realized, of course, that it couldn't be Dorothy. His hope faded.

"Billy!" Leah cried out. "Thank God we've found you! Is Lily with you?"

Now he thought he'd faint. How did they know? The woman behind her brushed past her and strode up to him. With two fists planted on her hips, the woman leaned into the light and stared at him. Her eyes were hollow. Two bright circles of rouge stood out against the white of her skin. She looked like a mad clown.

"Where is my daughter? Where is Lily Webb?"

The rain stung his face. He looked from her to Leah.

"She's here," he said, relief flooding through him like hot oil, soothing. "Upstairs. Top floor."

Without a word, Tracy turned and began to dash across the yard. In the darkness they heard her stumble and fall. Her cry was muffled. Billy turned to Leah.

"It's wonderful, Billy. They've got a kidney for her. That is if we can get her there in time," she said. There was no anger in her face.

His relief came in the form of a dampened sob. "When? Where?"

"Right now. At Liberty Hill."

While he answered the policeman's questions, his thoughts were on the boy in the ICU. They were giving

Lily his kidney. He'd cried in front of his parents like a damned baby. And now he was on the verge of crying again. It was happening. It didn't matter that Lily was mad at him. All that mattered was the fact that he was no longer responsible for her.

Out of the corner of his eye, he saw the door open. The blue lights circled endlessly. He could see people leaning from their windows, peering down at them. A minute later, a small figure appeared, sheltered from the rain by Tracy's coat. Lily peered out from the folds of the coat, her face white and dazed.

Leah held the door for them and the blue lights circled. Once more he had to shade his eyes to see her. He took a step forward, then he did not know what to do.

"Come on, Billy, hurry up." It was Lily calling. She sounded impatient. With relief, he crept into the backseat of the police car beside her.

Chapter Eighteen

When the double doors of the ICU swung open with a thud, Mark Berlin did not look up. He recognized the sound. It was the stretcher from the OR. He arose and went to meet it. Olive Meecham, her scrub suit covered by an open green gown and her hair covered in a flowered paper cap, pushed the stretcher ahead.

Mark nodded at her and helped maneuver the gurney inside Michael Norman's room. Behind Olive, not bothering to help, was an anesthetist, tall, bored. A mask hung from his neck. In his ear was a small device much like a hearing aid from which dangled a long cord.

When the stretcher was alongside the bed, the anesthetist produced a black rubber ambu bag. He disconnected the respirator and attached the bag. He gave it a lazy squeeze and Michael's chest rose. Then he nodded, steadying the boy's head between his hands. At Olive's quiet count, Mark and she slid the boy over onto the stretcher. Another squeeze, another breath. The room was still, more still, Mark thought, than it should be even with the vent shut down. He reached across the gurney and unhooked the intravenous bag, handing it to the anesthetist. Then he took the clean blanket that had spread over Michael earlier and tucked it tightly over the boy. There were goosebumps on his skin. He tried not to think about that.

"Do you need me?" he asked. They were the first words any one had spoke.

"No. We'll manage." Olive said, tugging on the foot of the stretcher. It bumped the doorframe and her face looked pained.

"I can help." Mark said.

"She said we didn't need you. We don't," the tall man said.

He gave the stretcher a little push with his hips and squeezed the bag once more. Mark gave Michael a final glance. If only there was some little sign, a grimace, a clenched fist, anything. But there was nothing except the gaping tube, now held slightly sideways by the anesthetist. It made Michael look like a baby bird, reaching for some morsel held over his mouth. Mark leaned against the wall and watched the quiet procession leave the unit.

The ceiling lights in operating room three were ablaze. Fat Marge was scrubbed once more, gowned and gloved and sitting on a stool waiting. The temperature in the room was a chilly sixty degrees. When the great lamp went on, it would heat up the five-foot area on which it would be focused. Sometimes, if a case went on too long, they would sweat beneath their masks and gowns. As she pushed the gurney into the room, Olive stripped off the johnny and blanket and dropped them into a basket outside the door. Naked, Michael Norman entered the operating room.

It took several minutes of adjusting the table so that the lumbar area was exposed. It had to be just right. The table looked broken, a shallow inverted V, with the boy's body stretched over it. Straps across the chest and braces at the shoulders held him in place. One arm was stretched upon a board and taped. The anesthetist sat down and attached the cord dangling from his ear to a disk he had taped to Michael's inner arm. Hooked together in this way, he could hear Michael's blood pressure as it beat with every contraction of his heart. The endotracheal tube was connected to an identical respirator that had breathed for him in the ICU. It began to rumble. Settled on his stool, the anesthetist pulled his clipboard onto his lap and began to write. Time, date, hour, minute.

A light flashed on in the adjoining room drawing Fat Marge's attention. Dr. Russell stood at the sink gazing in at them. Then he hit the faucet button with his knee and proceeded to scrub. Idly, Fat Marge took up a hand towel and unfolded it. As she waited, she eyed her stand, mentally assessing the instruments for any that might be absent. She felt the beginnings of heartburn, only in her it moved rapidly to her bowels. It always did at the beginning of a case. She hoped she could pass the gas quietly. She stood up as Dr. Russell entered the room, his arms held high and wet before him. They did not speak.

She handed off the towel to him, careful that his skin did not touch her glove. Their gestures from now on would be exact, precise. It was all to preserve the sterility of the room, the instruments, and drapes. Nothing would be allowed to threaten the patient on the table.

She lifted a gown from her back table and shook it down, holding it so that her own hands were enfolded within its outer side. Dr. Russell slid his arms into it and Olive stood behind him, pulling it over his shoulders and tying it. The gloves came next. Fat Marge felt a rumble of gas in her belly. Grimacing and clenching her buttocks together, she held out first one and then the other glove. As soon as he was gowned, Russell turned to the patient. Relieved, Fat Marge allowed the gas to rumble quietly from her.

"How is his pressure?"

"Good." The anesthetist did not look up.

"What *is* his pressure?"

This time he did. "Oh, sorry. One hundred over sixty. Heart rate is ninety."

Olive now began to scrub the surgical incision area. Painted with orange, the boy's skin took on the look of unpeeled fruit. One swollen hand flopped as she scrubbed. Russell watched.

In the next room, lights came on and the second set of instruments were uncovered. The sound of water running and loud voices intruded in the quiet room. Dr. Russell peered over his mask at the figures in the scrub room.

"Get me a stool and a towel," he said quietly when Olive Meecham had finished her scrub. With his gloved hands wrapped in a green towel, Russell sat primly erect, the towel cuddled against his chest. It was not an affectation, but a necessity: the front of his gown and arms were considered sterile.

"Well, we meet again, Dr. Russell," Ned Chimes said as he entered the room, his dripping arms held high. "I must say you've had a bit of luck for your patient." He cocked his head at the empty room next door. "Where is she?"

"On her way, I understand." Russell watched as Fat Marge handed Chimes a towel. The younger surgeon wiped vigorously, his short arms turning pink. When he was finished he lobbed the soiled towel into a corner. Olive scowled and hurried to pick it up.

"This is the scenario. What we do in Boston is harvest the first organ to be used and close that incision. After the transplant is completed, we come back in and take the other organs. Being out here in the boondocks makes it a little tricky."

"Why?"

"Well, we need a liver for a four year old with biliary atresia. Ordinarily we'd go after that organ first, because the need is the greatest. But since the kidney recipient is here, we'll have to take that and then transport the donor to Boston for the liver. It's the best way to preserve it. The eyes we'll take last. They freeze."

Fat Marge closed her eyes briefly.

"Then," Chimes went on. "We'll deliver the body to the mortuary of your choice. How's that for service?"

Dr. Russell did not reply.

"You can come in and observe the implant if you wish," Chimes said.

"Thank you, Dr. Chimes. That's most kind of you."

Chimes did not miss the sarcasm. His bright eyes flicked over the surgeon. Then he turned away and stared at Michael Norman.

"You do a lumbar approach, eh? That's good. Just leave me long veins and arteries to work with, okay?" When there was no answer behind him, he spoke to the anesthetist. "Keep up a good pressure on this kid. He's got to last another few hours." The anesthetist stared passively at him.

It was all happening so fast. Lily could feel her heart drumming in her ears. Her knees were hitting each other beneath the sheet. It was cold in here. The intravenous bottle hung over her head. There was a red label stuck to it, but she could not read it.

"What's in that?" Her teeth chattered.

Tracy leaned over and stroked her head. Her eyes glistened with tears. "I . . . I think it's something to prevent rejection, honey." Her hair was wet and it shone like a black bathing cap on her head.

They'd put a ridiculous white paper hat over her hair. It kept sliding down over her eyes everytime she moved. She reached up and pushed it back.

"Where did Billy go?"

"He's waiting somewhere, I don't know," Tracy replied.

"I want to see him when it's over, okay?"

"Okay." Tracy's hand was cold on her cheek.

"Can I have a blanket?" Tracy disappeared. In a moment, she returned with a white blanket and unfolded it over Lily's body.

"Um. It's warm."

"They keep them heated."

"How much longer?"

Tracy disappeared again. Behind her was a short man with a paper cap on his head. "This is Dr. Chimes, Lily. He's going to do the operation."

"How do you do?" She closed her eyes suddenly. It was too much to bear. She just wanted it over.

"Hiya, Lily. Now listen to me, kid. We're going to take you inside now. Everything we do in there might look scary but it's all for you. We're all covered up, the drapes and towels and everything in there is only to protect you. You're the important star in this act. Do you understand that?"

Lily opened her eyes and looked at him. "How do I know this'll work?"

His eyes crinkled over the mask. "Smart cookie you got there, Mrs. Webb." Tracy sniffed. Chimes leaned against the stretcher rail and covered Lily's hand. It was cold like her own.

"We know that you and the donor are compatible. And you are getting medicine to prevent rejection. We have a ninety percent success rate in this business, so I'm assuming you are going to be in that percentile. If it works as it's supposed to work, you'll be peeing beautiful yellow urine within the next hour or so. That'll be the first question you have when you wake up. Remember just ask, 'Any pee?' They'll tell you."

Lily looked at him. There wasn't much to see except his eyes. They were deep brown and fringed with light lashes that made him look like a sleepy puppy.

"I trust you," she whispered. Tracy leaned forward to hear but Chimes swiveled his ample bottom to block her.

"And I love you, babe," he whispered back. He disappeared and all that was left to stare at was the white tiled ceiling.

When she could not stand the quiet in the waiting room one minute longer, Leah slipped away, leaving Billy to stare at the walls. On the second floor, she raced past the ICU doors and turned the corner to the operating room suite. The blank doors stood closed. She pushed but they remained shut and instantly she remembered that they were electrically controlled. There was a round brass disk set into the wall. She hit it and the doors flew open, almost slamming against her hand.

She ran into the suite and then stopped abruptly at a fat black line drawn across the floor, reminding her of where she was. This was forbidden territory to anyone in street clothes. The suite was in darkness except for the farthest set of rooms. There, the lamps pooled through the window onto the polished floor. They were so far away and she could go no further.

It had been a long time since she'd worked in an operating room, but she'd be damned if she'd forgotten the protocol. She pushed through a little side door, marked "lounge." Sure enough it was the nurses' changing room and stacks of greens lay on a shalf. Quickly, she shed her clothes, leaving them on a battered plastic sofa. She pulled a scrub suit from the pile knowing in advance that it would be too big. It was. She pulled the drawstrings of the pajama bottom and the material bunched around her hips. The cool starched fabric stood by itself. It made her feel naked. On the wall was a dispensing machine from which she pulled a flowered paper cap and a mask. She tucked her hair carefully into the cap and tied it tightly at the back of her neck. Holding the mask over her face, she reentered the suite and hurried toward the blaze of lights at the far end of the hallway.

The two rooms were side by side separated only by the scrub sinks and the huge autoclaves. In here, there were banks of windows that overlooked each room. She entered the scrub area timidly now, her courage fleeing. Which room was Lily's? She did not want to look in the other, but when she peered into the room on the left there was nothing to see, nothing familiar. A drape of green over which masked and gowned figures huddled. On the right, the scene was similar. Which was Lily's?

She sagged against a sink. And it was then that she heard music, Elton John singing quietly in the room on the left. That had to be Chimes in there. He would have music in his room. She leaned over the sink and looked. Now that her mind was steady again, she could see the heightened activity in this room, different from the other. There was an anesthetist huddled at the head of the table. Bottles of intravenous fluids swayed overhead almost in rhythm to the music. A circulating nurse sat upon a high stool writing on a clipboard. Every once in a while, she would come to the back table and survey it, a maternal gesture, to replenish a supply of sponges, pour a fluid into a shining steel basin. Leah watched her, remembering the routine. But she did not recognize the nurse. She stared at her, willing her to look up.

Instead the anesthetist rose from his stool and headed for the door. He passed Leah as if she were not there and hurried into the other room. He bent over the head of the table, listening through his little earpiece. Apparently he was satisfied with what he heard. Leah realized then what little attention Michael required—an adjustment of the vent settings, a blood pressure reading, a pupil check.

The anesthetist was managing both cases.

As he left that room, heading back to Lily's, Leah spoke to him. "Excuse me. Will you tell the circulator that I'd like to speak to her when she has a chance?"

"I've got enough to do. Come in and talk to her yourself. What do you think this is, a coffee klatsch?" He hurried to the head of the table. Leah followed, hesitating just inside the door.

All eyes around the operating table lifted and stared at her. She could feel a heat spread up over her cheeks. She felt as if she were on the head of a pin.

"Aha! Another delightful pair of eyes to gaze upon. Come on in, sweetheart." Chimes's gaze lingered for a moment and then dropped to the green draped figure once again. "Mayo." He held out his hand and the scrub nurse slapped it with a pair of fragile-looking scissors.

Olive Meecham hurried over to Leah, a puzzled glance in her eyes. It was then that Leah remembered the ritual of eye-talking. A raised eyebrow, a frown, a wink. They all had special meaning in here for the nurses who worked in surgery.

"I'm Leah Swift from ICU," she whispered. "Is it okay if I watch for awhile?"

"Sure. Just stay away from the field." Olive walked away.

Leah found a quiet spot at the foot of the table, crossed her arms over her chest and gripped her scrub shirt with both hands. It was an old habit. It kept her hands from accidentally contaminating the sterile field before her.

There was nothing to see. No indication that it was Lily beneath those drapes. Not even the wound was visible from here. All Leah could see were the flashing hands of the scrub nurse, constant, fluid movement from table to stand to the waiting hand encased in rubber. The slap of instruments punctuated the music behind them. Sponges were unfolded meticulously and placed at hand so that they would offer quick staunching of blood. Needles locked into forceps and were readied, thread was tucked under a towel so that its end would not accidentally fall beneath the sterile field.

For awhile, Leah was lost in the remembrance of the clean, precise actions in here. From the measured pace, she could tell that the case was going smoothly. There were no shouts, no sudden movements hand to hand, and no hurried conversations with the man at the head of the table. Only the music carried across the room.

She wished she could say something. How the patient was doing? Where was the donated kidney? Was it in place? Had they begun the careful suturing of vein to vein, artery to artery? But it was forbidden. Only the surgeons spoke in here. The nurses communicated with their eyes.

Instead she began to study the progression of instrument use. It might tell her where they were in the case. As soon as sutures were taken up, then it might mean that the kidney, Michael's kidney, was here. It took her awhile to familiarize herself. Knife, clamp, ties, scissors. There was nothing in that except the hint that they were still approaching the site or readying it.

Finally, Chimes said something. It was a moment before she realized that he was speaking to her. "You're from the ICU, aren't you? Come on up here, you can't see anything there. Get the girl a stool to stand on." The last he directed at Olive.

The circulator pushed a foot stool behind Chimes.

"No, no," he said impatiently, "Not there. Put her up here between me and the head of the table." All this he said not looking up. His hand came up, waiting, and the answering slap of scissors came. He plunged it into the incision.

Olive beckoned with her eyes and Leah meekly stepped around the table. Her fists had become locked onto the fiber of her suit. She stepped up on the stool and instantly the scene was clarified for her. They had fashioned a deep pocket in Lily's side. It was built on stout layers of black silk thread, a nest, a cobweb. Though she was unfamiliar with the anatomy before her, she could understand the tedious process of readying a bed for the donation.

"You wanna know where the kidney's going, don't you?"

"Yes, Doctor."

"You thought we'd put it right where the old one is, huh?"

"Thought you might."

"Nope. Not enough room up there. This is more accessible and in the event that it has to be removed, we can snip it out real easy."

She did not reply. She peeped over the frame at the head of the table. It was Lily, though unrecognizable. Her hair was wrapped in white paper. Her eyes were sealed shut by pads. And the endotracheal tube distorted her mouth. Only the nose, straight and narrowed above the tube was familiar. And the cheekbones. Tonight they seemed to pull at the skin of her face. There was not a drop of color in it. The skin was translucent.

She shouldn't have looked. This was Lily, Nikki's friend—a child she'd known all her life. This figure beneath the sheets had now become significant. Now when she looked into the deep cavity of pink tissue and saw the stain of blood on the green towels, it was Lily's blood she saw. She swallowed. Her belly began to ache in sympathy with the pink flesh beneath the drape. She swallowed again. And began to wobble on the stool.

Olive caught her just in time. Pulling her away from the field, she hissed through her mask. "Take a breath! A deep breath."

"Okay. I'm okay." But it was a lie. She allowed herself

to be helped from the room. In the scrub area Olive left her alone, hurrying back into the room, muttering curses under her breath.

There, clinging to the scrub sink, she waited for the roaring in her ears to vanish. Without looking in the other room, knowing that if she took only a brief gaze, she might be swallowed up by the blackness that rimmed her vision, she waited for strength to come back into her legs. Finally, she wobbled away from the lights and allowed the darkness of the corridor to swallow her up.

Tonight someone had fed him, coaxing him to taste something that resembled oatmeal. It was baby food. Two-Gus swallowed it, humiliated. The pureed fruit stung at the sores in his mouth and he protested. They took the tray away. Later, someone else had given him a backrub with hands firm, stroking a warm lather across his back. He wondered why the sudden attention. He lay against taut sheets, wondering what came next. They had told him that Milly would be in tonight. That was unusual in itself; she rarely made rounds at night. He must be getting worse. If he were, it wasn't so bad. There was no pain and, better, no awful chills.

He listened to the sounds coming from the nurses' station. Someone needed an enema. A voice complained. Something about doing that on days, not evenings. It wasn't fair, an enema took up the whole shift. He wondered to whom it was not fair. Mr. Whately in bed three was crying again. Could someone call his wife? He wondered about Mr. Whately. He was accustomed to the talk now, and noticed that he was no longer the focus of attention. He dozed peacefully only to awaken to the pressure of fingertips on his wrist.

"Hello, Two-Gus."

"Milly. How nice to see you again." But he wasn't

fooled. There was some reason for the visit. She pulled a chair up to his bed, scraping it like a fingernail across a slate. His skin crawled. "This is totally out of character for you, old girl. It sends up the red flag, you know."

"We've got a problem, Mr. Smart Man. Your level of red blood cells had dropped. It's a side effect of the AZT." She sounded dejected. "I'm trying to plan the next attack."

"I'm anemic? So? There will be less to bleed." His little joke fell flat between them. "Discontinue the drug." It was as gentle a command as he could muster.

"But that would leave us . . ."

"I understand that. It doesn't matter, Milly. I'm tired, you know. Maybe I'm tired of fighting. I'd like to rest and see what happens." She usually interrupted him at this point in his argument but tonight she only sighed. "I have no energy left to fight on, Milly. Do you understand?"

"No."

"Flat out then . . . I don't want any heroic measures taken on my behalf if the breathing stops or the heart flutters. I guess I have to say that nowadays or I'd be put through the wringer otherwise."

"I wouldn't put you through that, Gus. Not you."

That was a departure. Milly, the fighter, admitting defeat? Or was someone else directing this show? Suddenly, it was as clear as day. There was no one directing any show. To resuscitate an AIDS patient was to beat a dead horse. A waste of time and money. AIDS folk died, that's all. How lucky we are, he thought, to avoid those tubes and machines that keep a body warm and wet and pulsing with fruitless life. Then the thought came to him: if she'd given up then she would not be coming here anymore. He decided to take the initiative.

"Dr. Weathers can manage the scenario from now on. I've already retained him." The lie came easily. "I'll have a letter drawn up in the morning."

"You're not getting away with this, Two-Gus. I refuse to be fired." He thought he heard a catch in her throat. He waited and then heard the snap of leather. She was fumbling in her case. Then he heard her blow her nose. Ah, she was so predictable.

"You are fired, Milly. Now scram, I'm sleepy."

"I'll see you in the morning. You'll change your mind."

"Please." For a moment he thought he would lose control. "Don't make a big fuss. I don't have the strength to fight with you. Just believe that it's better this way. Let someone else take over for you. If you want to visit, fine. But hands off the case."

For once she was speechless. He heard the chair scrape the floor. Heard the snap of her bag. He even smelled the sweet womanly odor of her body as her skirt swirled about her hips. He wondered if she knew how wonderful that earthy smell was to him. Then he knew, by the silence that followed, that she was gone.

He concentrated on the strange numbness in his legs. It had begun earlier and he hadn't told anyone. He had lifted the sheet to peer at his toes just to make sure they were still there. They were blue and swollen. That was hours ago, now the coldness had reached his thighs. This is how it is, he thought, to die by inches.

"How far apart are the pains?"

"Four minutes, no three, I think." Katherine lay upon the stretcher in cubicle one.

Mary Ann MacGregor, her mother, lingered by the door. Her eyes were as sharp as a hawk on the nest. "They are three minutes," she spoke up. She was almost disapproving as she answered the nurse.

Trish Curry grinned down at Katherine. "You have

plenty of time. Dr. Price said to move you up to Obstetrics as soon as you came in. Can you sit up?"

Katherine nodded, but there was another pain approaching. She could feel it gather strength somewhere in her spine. It began to circle around. She held up her hand to Trish and began the little panting breaths she learned at Lamaze class. Somehow, it was wrong, though. She'd always thought the breaths cancelled the pain, but they didn't. It grew bigger. Her belly felt clenched in upon itself, a vise that should never come from her own body. How could the baby stand that kind of pressure? She felt the first hint of panic. But Trish's face was calm. She laid her hand on Katherine's abdomen, watching the clock. The pain focused deep inside.

Finally, Katherine cried out, "Ben should be here. Can you page him?" Then she went back into self-absorbed concentration on her belly. It was now rock hard. Mary Ann MacGregor disappeared.

"That was a good one, Katherine," Trish said, when it was over. "One full minute long. Take a nice deep breath."

Their roles had reversed. It was Trish who was now supervising. Her young face was serene. She was wonderful, Katherine thought, so kind and knowing. She opened her mouth obediently and drew in air.

They had unceremoniously pulled off her slacks and the sodden towel with it. Now she lay naked beneath the sheet and knew that the paper pads lining the stretcher were soaked again. She had never known that childbirth was unremitting wetness. Trish reached under her hips and pulled away the pads. For a moment she lay dry. It was a luxury.

Mary Ann reappeared. "Ben is in surgery, Katherine. They say he'll be tied up for awhile longer, but they'll give him the message that you're here. I'll stay with you until he comes."

"No, Mother, you go home now. It's apt to be a long night and there's no reason for you to wait. We'll call as soon as the baby comes."

She began to take control of herself again. Besides, the relief in Mary Ann's face was almost comic. If it hadn't been for the whiteness in her face and terror in her eyes, Katherine would have smiled. My mother, the mother of three—she's scared out of her wits.

Mary Ann nodded, gathering up her raincoat. "I will run along then," she said, as if she were going to a tea. "Be sure to tell him to call us." It was always "him" as if it were all Ben's fault.

Katherine remembered then why she was here. The baby was coming! And so was another pain. She took a deep breath, reaching out for Trish's hand.

"Ready?" she asked. Trish nodded, placing her hand on Katherine's belly once more.

This one was bigger than all the others. It was too big. It was frightening. She kept muttering to herself to hold on, it won't last much longer. It can't. She almost lost her breath. She tried to speak, but there was no voice in her. She squeezed Trish's hand, frightened.

"It's okay," Trish whispered. "Hang on, is it easing?"

"Oh yes, at last. You're wonderful, Trish, don't leave me, please." It was Trish who knew everything. She'd even made the contraction end. Katherine forgot the cleansing breath. She had forgotten everything they taught her. It was simply shocking that a labor pain could be that intense. They didn't tell her that. Lies, that's what they told in those classes.

"Now listen, Katherine, I want you to pant like a pup on the next contraction. Remember? Get that diaphragm moving like a little bellows."

"You're right. I forgot all about it. That's why Ben should be here." But she knew he'd never remember that business. He'd stand back and purse his lips and watch her. He'd be very clinical. The rat! She almost wept with self-pity. "Another's coming."

"Remember the breathing, Katherine."

Then Trish's voice receded and a movement like thunderclaps hitting eardrums drowned out all thought. She opened her mouth to cry. Instead a great urge to push came over her and she groaned under it.

"Oh my God," Trish murmured. She unlatched the stretcher and began to push it out of the room.

All the while, Katherine's stomach clenched and a sweat broke out on her forehead. Unaware, she pushed harder.

"She's crowning," Trish called out.

"Oh, I'm going to be sick!" Katherine cried.

"It's okay, be sick all you want."

The stretcher began to fly down the hall, and the ceiling tiles blurred above her, making her dizzy. Oh hurry, Katherine said to herself. If we get there, this will be over. This is awful! No, stupid. The baby's coming. Think of her. Think only of her.

"Am I going to lose it?" The stretcher halted. She heard the clang of the elevator bell.

"Lose what?" Trish sounded annoyed.

"The baby." She almost wept then.

"No way. You're *delivering* a baby. All is well." The stretcher rolled into the elevator and the walls seemed to close in. There was no air in here. "Hang on, Katherine. We're almost there." For a moment there was blessed peace and then once again the urge came over her. It was all encompassing, blocking out the rest of the world.

"Oh." She knew she was saying something but she could not hear her voice. She felt her head rise off the pillow as if lifted by a giant hand and then she was up on her elbows pushing hard. Trish said something but she could not hear. There was something down there, underneath the sheet. Suddenly her belly seemed to sink in upon itself.

"The baby's coming!"

"Yes, yes. I know." The elevator doors slid open and, feet first, Katherine entered the maternity floor.

"No, no, it's here." She thrust away the sheet and stared down at the tiny wet face between her legs. There was a fringe of absurdly black hair plastered to its head. She watched as the dark blue eyes opened and stared solemnly at her. There was a breath and finally a plaintive sob, then the baby resumed its study of her face.

"Oh my God!" Trish breathed. "Help, somebody! It's here."

"Relax, Trish, it's over." Tears blurred her vision and hastily so that she would not miss one moment of this child's arrival, she wiped her eyes on one corner of the sheet.

With the stretcher now flying down the corridor and Katherine holding onto the rail for dear life, the baby lifted its fist to its mouth and began to chew it.

"Hello, little girl," Katherine cried out as they flew into the delivery room.

They had propped him into this absurd-looking chair with a tray that locked him in and a platform for his feet. A geri-chair, they'd called it, for your own protection. He felt foolish and betrayed. It wasn't a wheelchair that he could propel along the hall, although it did have little wheels beneath the foot rest. This chair was a patient restraint and they could plant it wherever they liked. It had taken two aides ten minutes to get him properly locked into it and it was only after they walked away that he realized just how trapped he was. He could not stand up and walk away, he could not unlock the tray table that held him upright.

What was worse, was that they had left him in a

conspicuous place. "So we can keep an eye on you," they'd said, not quite in the hall but just inside his doorway. Though he could not see clearly, he knew he was the object of curious glances as visiting hour began. They had placed him just beside the red warning sign posted on his door, as if he were a beacon, as effective as a skull and crossbones label on a jar of poison. He sat there too weak to voice rage, too humiliated to call out.

"Hi Two-Gus." As always it was Billy who showed up just as he was in his deepest despair.

"Get me out of here, Bill." His voice came out as a croak past the lump in his throat. "Push me to the sunroom, will you? If I get any more stares I'll go mad."

"Sure, sure."

He felt the chair begin to move, to cross the threshold and turn.

"Hey. Where do you think you're going?" a nurse called out. "You can't take him outta his room."

"The hell I can't," Billy said. He put a face mask in Two-Gus's hand. "Here, tie this on and away we'll go." Two-Gus missed the stony stare Billy gave the nurse. He slipped the mask over his mouth and nose.

The sunroom was little more than a widening of the corridor with glass doors leading to the sun deck. There was a television set, its screen dark, a few battered chairs and ashtray stands filled to overflowing. The smell was stale and thick with cigarette smoke. Billy flung open the French doors and the odor of tidal shifts and damp spring rain on asphalt filtered into the room. Then he pushed the geri-chair next to the door and pulled up a rose-colored plastic chair. He sat down and curved his arms around his knees, staring out into the night.

"It's over, Mr. Ragust. Lily had her surgery and they say she's doing fine."

"So why do I hear infinite sadness in your voice? You should be kicking up your heels. Think of all you went through hours ago—the worries, the secrets. They're over now."

"Oh, I'm glad alright. I mean now she has a chance to do everything any other person would do."

"And maybe forget her friend Billy, too? You think she will?"

"She might. She probably will. After all, I'm part of a scene that she can put behind her if she wants. I almost don't blame her. I would remind her of bad things."

"Why don't you wait a bit to decide that. It's a little early, isn't it? Now that you don't have the transplant business between you, you might have a better chance to establish a normal relationship. Give it a chance."

The boy sighed as if he didn't believe him. "Ma's waiting for me. She's chewing nails, she's so mad at me. I've got to get a taxi for us. She wants out of here so bad, she could spit."

"It is late. She's probably tired. Are . . . are you coming back in the morning? To see Lily?"

"Nah. I'll wait until she calls me."

Two-Gus felt torn inside. "That's probably for the best. When she's up to it, bring her a dozen red roses, you hear?"

Billy stood up and then reached over and squeezed Two-Gus's shoulder. "I'll be back in a couple of days to see you, Mr. Ragust. I'll bring you a Coke, okay?"

"Yeah, sure kid. Listen, before you go, unlatch this infernal tray, will you? They've got me locked in here like a damned baby." He could smell Billy's young skin as the boy stood before him and pulled the tray off. He reached out and ran the back of his hand down his cheek.

"Listen, Kid. You've been a good friend to me and I thank you for it. I'm sure Lily will think so once she's on her feet. Be patient, old man. If she doesn't, well she can't be too bright. She'll be missing out on the best man to come down the pike. Now run along." For a moment, he thought Billy was going to embrace him but he flapped his hand to wave him off. "Go on. Your mother's waiting."

When he was sure Billy was gone, Two-Gus bent his head into his hands and wept quietly.

They found him at ten o'clock when his medicine nurse searched the halls for him, his pills in the little plastic cup. The geri-chair was tipped over, lying just beside the low ledge of the sunroof. It was not a long fall—two flights to the roof of the emergency-room wing. But it was enough.

Chapter Nineteen

"Take a deep breath, Lily, and open your eyes."

The voice seemed to come from somewhere above her head. It must be God, she thought. Obedient to the command, she inhaled. It hurt and she decided to sleep a little longer. Maybe the pain would be gone next time she awoke.

"Hey, sleeping beauty! Don't you want to wake up? It's over. The operation is all over."

At that, she looked up into the dopey eyes of Dr. Chimes. Though his face was covered by a mask, she could tell he was grinning.

"Is there any urine?"

"You better believe it! Sixty c.c.'s an hour, Lily."

"That's nice." The long dark tunnel she'd been in before closed over her once more. She missed the tears in Tracy's eyes, the grin on Billy's face. She slept.

Hours later, she awoke with a start, her heart suddenly hammering in her throat. The room was lit only by a night-light over the sink in the corner of the room. Her side was hurting. Her tongue felt thick as if it were layered with cotton. She wondered why. She wanted to hear the clink of ice cubes against a glass and feel the icy slide of water in her throat. Then she remembered.

She reached down between her legs. There was a tube there and her fingers traced it over the edge of the bed. One of those catheter bags. She grasped it and pulled. It was heavy and as it came into view, she saw, reflected in the dim light behind it, her own urine. Lots of clear yellow urine. She let the bag descend gently through her fingers until at last, she could feel its weight across her legs.

No more dialysis machine, no more long hours hooked by the rope of flesh in her arm. She ran her fingertips over it. The ugly cord was nicked and hard. No rivers of poison there any more. Her veins and arteries were pure at last. They'd get rid of that cord and it would all be just a memory.

It's in there, she thought, picturing the pool-shaped little organ. It doesn't belong to me, but it's in there and it's working. She thought of it as newborn. It was hers now. It was getting stronger on her own rich blood, and it was pulsing with life, and filtering the very fluid that bathed it. Her lips began to move. "Dear God," she whispered, staring in wonder at the ceiling.

Then she thought of food, wonderful food: hamburgers, eggs, orange juice, steak. She reached over and pushed the call bell. French fries, Coke. She pushed the bell again.

"What is it, Lily?"

"I am hungry," she said and began to cry.

Across from the abandoned navy yard the neon sign of the Rusty Scupper flashed on and off sending shafts of red across the rain-washed street and onto the padlocked steel gates. By twelve o'clock, Leah and Julian were the only customers in the place. The bartender seemed to have forgotten them. He sat on a stool, absorbed in a television documentary about bushmen in the Kalahari

Desert. Leah stared at the scene as if trying to make some sense of it. Her eyelids fluttered. On her third drink, she was more than a little drunk.

"Come on, princess, I'd better get you home," Julian said with a little smile on his face.

"It's too late," she said. "I missed Nikki's bedtime."

"You can see him in the morning, that is, if you don't have a monstrous hangover. Your folks will think I'm a bad influence on you. Besides, this isn't the celebration I had in mind. Come on, let's get you home."

She looked stricken. "Oh, Julian, I am sorry. I shouldn't drink, it depresses me." She pushed away the glass and called over to the bartender. "Hank? Could I have—"

"Nothing more, Leah, your father would kill me," the man called over his shoulder, not bothering to turn away from the television set. Julian laughed.

"Damn bunch of nursemaids around here," Leah muttered. "I just wanted some coffee, Hank. Daddy wouldn't object to that." To Julian she said, "That's what I get for growing up on the waterfront. They all treat me as if I'm still a kid."

"I know," he said comfortingly. "It's not fair, is it?" She stared at him suspiciously and then burst out laughing.

The bartender, Hank, came over and began to clear the table, staring fixedly at Julian's hand covering hers. He waited until Julian removed it, and then he proceeded with agonizing slowness to clear the table. "Getting late, Leah," he said. He moved Julian's glass several inches away and wiped the ring of wetness it left on the varnished wood. Almost casually, he swept up Leah's glass from her fingers.

Leah pointed a finger at him. "Next time, we'll take our business elsewhere." The bartender shrugged, casting an accusing glance at Julian.

"I think we'd better go," Julian said when Hank had retreated to his perch behind the bar. "He thinks I am corrupting you." He pulled Leah to her feet and she wobbled against him. Unprotesting, she allowed him to cover her shoulders with her slicker.

Hanging onto Julian's arm, she managed to sweep past the bartender without stumbling. Outside, the wind snatched away her hood. She stood still while Julian retied it.

"Alright, my girl, one brisk walk around the block and then in you go." He swung an arm around her waist and together, they set off along the glistening black street. When, at last, they stood at the wrought-iron gate to the marina, he was shivering and she was cold sober.

He wrapped his arms around her, pulling her into his body. They kissed, oblivious to the wind, their faces cold and wet. Once again, she felt the sweet lift as his lips explored hers.

"I hate to leave you," he murmured.

She could feel his hands holding her against his body and his thighs seemed like hardened steel against hers. A gust of wind rattled the gate behind them. It sounded like a ship's bell and the effect was immediate. She pulled away, shivering.

Over Julian's shoulder, she could see the sprawling shape of Liberty Hill. It seemed etched against the clean night air, its massive lines somehow comforting. Stolid and unchanging, it was always there. She pressed her cheek to Julian's and whispered, "Tomorrow and forever."